Praise for Brynn Kelly's *Deception Island*

"Nonstop action and romantic tension sizzle…."

—Publishers Weekly

"*Deception Island* is a brilliant thriller that will have you begging for more. The plot is a maze of surprising and harrowing twists and turns that lead to a dynamic conclusion."

—Fresh Fiction

"What. A. Ride. *Deception Island* held me in its clutches from the very start. From the ambitious storyline to the well-crafted characters, this debut novel speaks of a promising future in fiction for author Brynn Kelly."

—Harlequin Junkie

"It was rough, raw and real, with a storyline that hypnotized me and some of the best character development I've had the fortune of reading."

—The Romance Reviews

"Kelly's debut is an impressive, emotionally intense, pulse-pounding page-turner."

—The Reading Frenzy

"This pulse-pounding romance will leave you breathless and aching for more."

—Joyfully Reviewed

"Surprising twists and turns coupled with strong, dynamic characters make this one a pleasure to devour."

—StuckInBooks.com

"It's nonstop suspense and desire on the beaches and in the jungles of remote Indian Ocean islands."

—Romance Reviews Today

DECEPTION ISLAND

BRYNN KELLY

HQN™

Recycling programs
for this product may
not exist in your area.

ISBN-13: 978-0-373-78964-1

Deception Island

www.HQNBooks.com

Printed in U.S.A.

CHAPTER

1

Time to get this over with.

Rafe Angelito signaled his two crewmen. They pushed the RIB off the beach and leaped in, the scrape of the hull on pebbles the only sound in the moonlit bay. As he'd predicted, the American had brought her yacht closer to shore than usual for the night, to shelter from the trade winds belting through the Indian Ocean.

Michael pulled in the bowline while his brother Uriel lowered the outboard motor and gunned it. Rafe tested a thin rope, coiled it and stuffed it in his pocket. A pampered heiress wasn't likely to give them trouble, but with his son's future at stake he wasn't taking chances. A kidnap for a kidnap.

He cricked his neck. Time for action, at last. Since dawn they'd followed the yacht through the archipelago, awaiting the right moment to strike. A lightning operation—grab the woman, leave the yacht. Even if she got out a mayday call they'd be gone before anyone responded.

"Faster," he ordered, the language of his childhood awkward on his tongue.

"Yes, Capitaine."

Rafe's jaw tightened at Uriel's facetious comment. "Call me that again and I'll rip out your throat." This week he wasn't a French Foreign Legionnaire. He was a Lost Boy again, whether he liked it or not.

Michael handed him a phone, nodding at the screen. A text.

Rafe clenched his teeth. Gabriel again. *What is happening, my brother?*

He yanked off his glove, gripped the railing and replied one-handed in his native language. A few minutes and we'll have her.

And I'm not your brother, you son of a bitch.

A reply came in seconds. Don't mess this up, Raphael, or your boy is mine for good.

Rafe's gut twisted. His son was sheltered, innocent—everything Rafe never had a chance to be. Right now, Theo was supposed to be home with his grandmother on Corsica, going to school, learning to fish, playing football. But the Lost Boys had come in the night, just as they'd come for Rafe as he'd lain sleeping in the dust of a refugee camp nearly thirty years ago.

Another buzz. He likes his uncle Gabriel. He'll make a good lieutenant, when I've finished with him.

Theo's face filled the phone's screen, terror lacing his dark eyes. Rafe's heart kicked. Next to his son, with an arm slung over the boy's shoulder, a man grinned. Gabriel. Two decades older, but no mistaking the machete scar splitting his nose. Rafe tightened his grip on the phone. What kind of "uncle" would snatch a nine-year-old to blackmail his father into committing a gutless crime?

Gabriel, that was who. But why kidnap the daughter of an American senator? The Lost Boys' usual trafficking victims were lost themselves—unwanted girls and women sold into prostitution, or orphaned boys forced to become child soldiers, like Rafe. This heiress was the closest America had to a princess. A stupid risk, but at least Rafe could ensure no harm came to the woman—or his son. Best-case scenario? Within the week her father paid the twenty million, she went home and Rafe got Theo back. Worst-case?

Crack. A cobweb of splinters spread across the screen, fracturing the image of Theo's face. Rafe loosened his grip and shoved the piece-of-crap phone in his pocket. The worst-case scenario would not happen. He pulled on his glove. He was an *imbécile* for thinking a past like his could remain buried.

His gaze swept the yacht, which was silvery and skeletal with its sails stowed. No movement. With luck she'd be asleep. On signal, Uriel swung the boat around to the northwest, setting up for an approach from the yacht's leeward side. Rafe yanked down his balaclava and signaled his crew to do the same. Wouldn't do to have their faces broadcast on the American's live webcam.

"No mistakes," he growled. "Anyone hurts the girl, I hurt him."

The halyard clinked against the mast as the yacht rocked in the swell. Holly Ryan closed her eyes and stretched out on the deck, soaking up the pleasure of dozing to the current's ebb and flow.

She inhaled the velvety air and sighed. The sound rolled out into the night, joined by the slap of water against the hull and the strain of a distant motor. Tropical heat seeped into her skin. If only life could stay this way forever—waking at dawn and anchoring at dusk, sun-bleached hair clumped from swimming, freckled skin rough with salt.

She linked her hands behind her head. The boat wasn't a hell of a lot bigger than her prison cell and only marginally more comfortable, but it was intoxicating just knowing the horizon wasn't blocked by a concrete wall. Hallelujah. So what if the real Laura Hyland sipped champagne on her father's superyacht somewhere off Bali while Holly did the hard sailing? Holly could get drunk on the smell of freedom—out here it came salty, with notes of seaweed.

Four more months of sailing and Holly would have fulfilled her end of this screwed-up bargain and earned enough money to wipe clean the disaster that had been her life so far. In the meantime, she'd damn well enjoy it. She'd done worse things for lesser reward.

Closer now, the motor whined as it was pushed faster. Bit late for a fisherman, and no villages lay along this stretch of rain forest. Precisely why she'd chosen the spot for an anchorage—the fewer people she faced as Laura, the better. Even in Indonesia, people had heard of the New York socialite and her solo circumnavigation. Though she did resemble Laura after a hurried makeover, Holly couldn't risk anyone figuring out the truth.

The motor's pitch dropped—it was slowing, the water swishing around it. On approach. She bolted upright, the back of her neck prickling. Moonlight glinted off an inflatable with three large figures on it. No lights, closing in. Her breath shuddered. Not one of the local fishing boats. A journalist looking for a scoop—but out here, at this time of night? Hardly. A shark-finning boat? Dozens of large sharks had glided past the yacht in the last few days.

Whoever they were, she had no escape. By the time she weighed anchor they'd be on her. A mayday call or flare wouldn't do shit, out here in the middle of nowhere.

She skidded into the cabin, snatched up her pocketknife and stuffed it in her shorts pocket. What else could she use for a weapon? Damn the senator for refusing to let her carry a gun. She eyed the radio, biting her lip. No time for a call—if these guys cornered her down here, there'd be no escape. She sprang back up the ladder. The inflatable drew up to starboard, the men silent. Balaclavas. They wore balaclavas. Shit. She spun around. *Come on, come on.* Her gaze landed on the winch handle. She wrenched it out of its socket, tested its solid weight. Good old-fashioned heavy metal.

As one man tied up and pulled the boats alongside, another stepped onto the yacht's stern, wobbling as if he straddled a tightrope. He was burly but perhaps not a sailor. That could work in her favor. She moved the winch handle behind her, out of sight.

"What do you want?" she asked, sounding more confident than she felt.

"We don't want to hurt you." The deep voice came from the bow of the inflatable, in thickly accented but precise English.

Her cheeks iced over. In her experience, people who said that usually did the opposite. The burly man advanced, feeling for his balance. Was that seriously an Angry Birds T-shirt?

"Who are you?"

"We are taking you with us." The guy on the inflatable again. He said something to his crew in a language she couldn't place. His voice was authoritative but at ease. She chanced a look. He leaned against the console, arms crossed. Confident, but casual with it—like he'd done this a hundred times. He was even bigger than the guy coming for her, but more athletic. Not good.

"You won't be harmed if you cooperate," he continued.

Her blood chilled. "You're pirates? You've got to be kidding me." She was almost halfway through this job, halfway to her new law-abiding life. Not even Blackbeard was going to ruin that.

He laughed, deep and calm. "I wish I was joking, Laura."

Laura. This was no random heist. What was his accent—Russian? Eastern European? Not one of the notorious Indonesian *lanun* pirates who patrolled the Strait of Malacca. This archipelago was far enough south of the main shipping lanes that thieves weren't supposed to consider it profitable. So much for sticking to safer waters.

It was a long time since she'd had to fight a man. She had one advantage—they thought she was a helpless socialite. They weren't expecting trouble, and if they were kidnapping her for a ransom, they wouldn't want to kill her—yet. She swallowed. She could play the frightened girl, give them false confidence and try to escape. In what—her tender? That thing wouldn't win a race with a jellyfish.

She could tell them the truth, but why the hell would they believe her? Even if they did, what then—they'd apologize gracefully and be on their way? Fat chance.

"No, please, you can't do this to me." She let her nerves show in her voice. The Angry Birds guy was five feet away. Another few steps… "I'll scream, I'll… I'll… My daddy's a United States senator, a retired marine. A webcam is broadcasting your every move. He'll track you down in minutes." She cringed, inwardly. Too much?

"Nothing to be worried about," said the man on the inflatable. "We'll take you somewhere comfortable for a few days, your father will pay a ransom, you will be freed."

"No. Please…"

Angry Birds jumped down onto the deck. Holly sprang backward, onto the bow. She slid her legs apart for stability, her bare feet compensating for the yacht's movement. The man on the boat growled something. Angry Birds shouted back. One word was clear: *Capitaine.* He approached gingerly, his palms up, placating her. She cowered, as if bracing for the moment of contact, her pulse pummeling in her ears.

He inched closer. *Patience.* She tightened her grip on the winch handle. Her days of being someone's punching bag were long dead. She waited until he was within a yard of her, then pivoted her torso, letting her hand whip with the momentum, and bashed the handle into his face with a dull, meaty crack. He wobbled, forced to prioritize regaining his balance over capturing her. Yelling from deep in her chest, she drove her heel into the side of his knee, buckling it. As he collapsed, she shoved him backward. The boat tilted with his weight and he slid into the water, one hand clutching the grab line. Her leg muscles clenched, finding equilibrium, her soles clinging to the deck like limpets. Gasping for breath, she cracked the handle onto his fingers. He splashed into the inky water with a howl.

The boat rocked, and she jumped backward to avoid following him in. Hands grabbed her biceps, from behind. Damn. When had a second man come aboard? She bent her knee and rammed a heel into his groin. Awkward, but effective—he grunted and eased his grip, just enough for her to swivel out of it. It wasn't the *capitaine*, just the other goon, now bent double and panting. Before he could straighten, she clutched his head and rammed her knee into his face. Bones crackled, he yelped. She sprang back.

Instinctively, he brought both hands up to his face. Holy crap, she'd broken his nose? She wasn't as out of practice as she'd thought. She launched a flying kick into his stomach, but it glanced off. Damn. He flailed but regained his balance, shook himself and fixed his hooded eyes on her. She retreated, panting. What now—the knife? She didn't want to risk getting close enough to use it—and bloodshed wasn't her thing. Angry Birds splashed about below, no doubt fighting the pull of his heavy boots.

Stern instructions came from the boat. The *capitaine* sounded frustrated with his men but bored, like he knew capturing her was just a matter of time.

Not if she could help it. She sprang behind the boom, her free hand fumbling to loosen the mainsheet. The pirate inched forward, a dark stain spreading across his gray balaclava. She swept the boom toward him. He stumbled and shot out his hands to catch it. Before he could recover she hurled the handle. It clocked his broken nose. Bingo. He roared and reeled back, but righted himself. He spat indecipherable words, blood and saliva dripping from his mask, his arms spread out for balance, hands clawed.

Damn. She should have thrown the knife—who knew her aim would be that good? She didn't trust her chances now. She zipped her pocket, spun and plunged into the sea. Once the cool water swallowed her, she jackknifed and propelled herself under the yacht, kicking and pulling against the tug of the swell, feeling her way around the keel's smooth curve. Her chest ached for air. She surfaced silently on the port side, in the moon's shadow, and devoured oxygen as quietly as she could.

Urgent voices sounded above her. How long could she tread water and wait for rescue? Could she fool them into thinking she'd drowned? Laura's website must be getting a million hits with this on the live stream. The woman's craziest fans watched 24/7, keeping up a constant social media commentary. When Holly had sunbathed on the deck in Laura's bikini she'd nearly broken the internet, even though the images were kept low-res to cover for the body switch. Help could already be on its way.

"Laura, you can't stay down there forever. We will find you." The *capitaine* switched languages and spoke sharply to the other men, his voice ringing out from the deck of the yacht. Two men on the yacht and one in the water equaled none in the inflatable. What were her chances of slipping away in it? Better than her other options.

She filled her lungs, pulled herself underwater and followed the hull out in the direction of the men's boat, coming up for air in the shelter of the yacht, blinking her stinging eyes clear. The inflatable's bowline stretched above her head, tied alongside. She retrieved her knife and popped the blade.

Clinging to the yacht's grab line, she hauled herself up as far as she dared. The yacht shifted with her weight. She froze. Deep voices murmured as the men searched. They'd find her in seconds. She stretched up. Moonlight winked off the blade. The line was inches out of her reach. Shit. Footsteps approached.

She dived and felt her way under the inflatable. The hull was metal and shaped into a deep V—no ordinary rubber boat. If she could steal it, she could get to the other end of the archipelago, at least. She'd passed a couple of inhabited islands that morning.

She popped up on the far side and clutched a cleat, forcing herself to suck in air as if through a straw. Could she sneak aboard and release the bowline before they got to her? She'd have to get in from the stern—the sides of the hull were too steep, and heaving herself up would draw attention.

Something brushed her bare calf. She gasped, drawing up her legs. Had Angry Birds found her? Nobody surfaced. Her heart thundered. If it wasn't the man, what was—?

A nudge, then something rough skimmed her leg. Not human. A white-tipped dorsal fin sliced through the black water. Holy crap, a shark. One of the oceanic whitetips she'd seen earlier? It'd be testing her, trying to figure out if she was prey. Oh, God. She gripped the knife with one hand and the cleat with the other, forcing her legs to still. It'd expect prey to thrash, to swim away. Stillness would confuse it, right? She fought the urge to hyperventilate. From the port side of the yacht came splashing. Angry Birds. Doubly bad—he was closing in on her *and* baiting the shark. Her arm shook with the strain of holding herself steady.

A panicked shout burst from the yacht. Had they spotted the shark, or her? She caught movement to her left. Angry Birds slogged through the water with clumsy strokes. Blood trailed from his nose, where she'd clocked him with the winch. He flinched, and his gaze darted below. Was the whitetip scouting him out, too? Or were there more than one? She fought an urge to order him to be still.

He yelled, suddenly thrashing. Holy shit. Fast footfalls and shouts responded from the yacht. Didn't they have a gun? The man's body lurched downwards, his scream splitting the air. Her hand spasmed, her muscles burning. Ah, crap, she couldn't just watch.

"Get a life preserver," she shouted. "If he can grab it you can pull him up."

"Where is it?" The *capitaine's* tone was urgent, but not panicked, like a shark attack was a minor distraction.

"The stern, starboard side."

She didn't stay to watch. With shark and men occupied, she swam as smoothly as she could to the stern of the inflatable, fear clawing her stomach. She pocketed the knife and reached for the ladder, her arm still shaking. The boat swung away. Her fingers slipped off the rung, and she splattered into the water. Crap. Sandpapery skin brushed her sole. Her blood froze. A wave rocked the boat, smashing the outboard into her fore-head. She swallowed the flare of pain. Ten yards away, the water churned. A feeding frenzy? The man had stopped screaming. A cry rang out, followed by a splash—too big to be the life pre-server. Jesus, had another of the men gone in? Shouts echoed from everywhere—in the water, on the deck.

Another nudge on her leg, harder. She flailed for the ladder, forcing her eyes open against the water slapping her face. How many sharks were there—a whole school? Did they even travel in schools? Did it freaking matter?

A wave dunked her, sweeping her from the boat. She fought her way back, her lungs ready to burst. Her hand hit the rung and she caught it with one finger, lurched forward and clamped the palm over it. Roaring with effort, she anchored her thumb underneath and held on, the bitter burn of salt water in her throat. With the current dragging her away, she had no chance of hauling herself up. Her forearm strained near to snapping. The water swished with the force of something big shooting up underneath her. Her every muscle clenched. She hadn't survived twenty-nine years of crap to die like this.

CHAPTER

2

Something tugged on Holly's hand, then clamped under her arms. She thrashed, a scream ripping through her. No give. No pain, either. Maybe she'd die before it set in.

She flew into the air, weightless. What the hell? Below her an oval of ragged teeth crested the water and fell away into blackness. Still she soared. Her stomach dropped. *Boof.* Breath smacked from her lungs, pain shot through her nose. She'd landed, on something hard. A man's chest—the *capitaine*, his arms wrapped tight around her, lying under her on the floor of the inflatable. The boat tilted to starboard. He threw them toward port, then to the center. The vessel wobbled and righted. Silence cloaked them. Holy crap. The shark hadn't caught her. He had.

Something bumped the hull. She held her breath. A few dozen teeth on a few tubes and they'd be dessert. But everything stilled except the man's heaving chest and his quick panting rustling her hair. She wheezed in relief, gulping in air. Her nose throbbed.

"Are you hurt?" he said.

Her jellied muscles begged for reprieve. *No! You're not giving up this fight.* She took a steadying breath, raised a fist and slammed it into his stomach. Her arm bounced off, pain ripping up to her shoulder. He barely flinched. His arms tightened around her, jamming her nose into his chest. He hooked his legs around hers, pinning her with solid weight. She couldn't even wriggle.

"I'll take that as a no," he said, huskily.

"Let me go."

"Sure. We can't lie here all night. But know that you can't overpower me. Run and I'll catch you, fight and I'll win. You are coming with me tonight."

"Why are you doing this?"

He paused. "Money. What else?" His tone was flat with bitterness. "Cooperate, and no harm will come to you. You have no choice but to trust me."

Trust him? She'd never met a man she could trust and wasn't about to start with a pirate. He released his grip, though his muscles remained tense. She coasted down his body and sat up. He sprang to his feet, towering over her. Just what was she up against? The balaclava shaded dark eyes. A tight black T-shirt outlined the taut chest she'd landed on. No wonder his stomach was impenetrable—even in the moonlight she could count the ridges of his six-pack. His sleeves cut across biceps that looked sculpted from granite. How the hell would she escape that?

"What happened to your friends?" she said.

"Gone to a better place than the shit hole they came from."

"I'm sorry." What a way to die.

"I doubt that." He grabbed her wrists and yanked them behind her.

"Ow!"

"I do not trust you to cooperate." He deftly tied a rope around her wrists, tighter than handcuffs and just as unyielding.

"I can see trust is going to be an issue between us."

The odds were better now, one-on-one, but he was right—if it came down to a battle of force, he'd steamroller her. He was iron strong, icy calm. Military, probably—and proper military, not some amateur militia. Wasn't *capitaine* French for captain? A battle of wits might be a more even fight.

He moved swiftly to her feet and bound them, then secured her to a railing, disturbingly practiced at restraining a human being. Could some foreign military be behind this? Was it a declaration of war, a political statement? Instinct told her he was lying about doing it for the money. He moved to the bow, surprisingly catlike for a man of his build. Definitely military.

"You have a satellite phone on the yacht? A laptop? GPS? Weapons?"

"If I had weapons would I be sitting here like this? But, yeah, sat phone, laptop, GPS. Knock yourself out."

"Where are they? Tell me everything I need to grab so we can take them."

We? A tense edge had crept into his voice. Should she answer? Her options numbered roughly zero. Besides, when she escaped she'd need the sat phone to make a rescue call. She gave him a rundown.

"What else should I pack for you?"

"Sorry?"

"What else do you want to take? You know I'm kidnapping you, yes?"

"I'd figured."

"You'll need some dry clothes. Ah, I'll grab everything."

"ChapStick," she said, automatically. *Two men just got eaten by sharks and you're asking for ChapStick?*

He paused. "This is some kind of lipstick?"

"Yeah, because that's the first thing I'd think about when I'm getting kidnapped." She jammed her salt-scoured lips together. *Shut up.* He'd expect her to be hysterical, not snarky. "Forget it. Get clothes, whatever. Why am I giving packing orders to a pirate? Or are you technically a terrorist?"

The inch of brown skin visible beside his eyes crinkled. Was he smiling? This had to be the most surreal night of her life. "Go with pirate."

"Where are you taking me?"

"You'll see. There'll be no escape for either of us until your father pays."

Either of us?

He checked her bindings, jumped from the bow onto the

yacht's stern and disappeared from her limited view. Agile as well as strong—a formidable opponent. His calmness chilled her as much as his strength. A sharp mind was more dangerous than a muscular body, and he evidently had both.

She shifted. Something pressed into her thigh. The knife.

This wasn't over.

Rafe crept over the deck and dropped into the cabin. Feigning imbalance, he smashed his shoulder into the interior webcam, knocking it to the floor and stomping on the debris. Gabriel would be watching the heiress's webcast. No need to let on that Rafe was taking all the equipment he could prize off the boat, now he was no longer guarded. Let him believe that once Rafe and the woman were stranded on the honeymoon island, they had no way to communicate with the world.

He snatched up a large backpack and tipped out the contents. He had a couple of hours at most before rescuers arrived, and he'd already lost a good half hour securing her.

He shoved in an armful of clothes, with more force than necessary. Two more Lost Boys gone tonight, their blood on his hands as much as Gabriel's. He exhaled heavily. He'd seen too many of their kind meet death too early. Boys who grew up with no one to give a damn about them and died with no one to mourn them.

But Gabriel had survived, somehow. The aid workers must have lied about him dying in the firefight at Odeskia, to prevent Rafe running back in to find his only friend. Rafe narrowed his eyes. No use blaming them. They'd given him a chance to claw his humanity back after five years as a killing machine. Given the same mercy, Gabriel might also have become a different man.

He pulled a network of cords from the walls and shoved them in the bag. The woman had been more effort than he'd bargained for. Where did a society princess learn to scrap like that? That was dirty street fighting, not some rich girl's martial arts hobby. And she was far prettier than the photos and videos he'd studied—a raw, strong natural beauty, not some delicate doll.

He scoffed. What had he expected? Only a fool underestimated his quarry. She'd survived three months alone at sea. And even someone as vain as Laura Hyland wouldn't wear lipstick and stilettos on a solo sailing trip.

But she had said something about some lip thing. He swept a bunch of bottles and tubes into the bag. His heart twisted. The last time he'd packed up a woman's things was a year after Simone's death, when he'd finally forced himself to clear her belongings out of their villa on Corsica. The coconut scent of her shampoo still haunted him. Later, he'd found Theo sitting by the garbage bin. The kid had unpacked every bottle and tube and lined them up along the tiled floor, like miniature tombstones.

He zipped up the bag. Thinking about his wife wouldn't help his son. Phase one was complete. Phase two was to get the heiress to the plane, then to the island. Phase three was a week guarding her—alone, now. Going by tonight's events, that was likely to be more bruising than he'd anticipated.

The thought of phase four made his hands move faster—return the heiress unharmed and get his son back. Would Gabriel keep his end of the bargain? Rafe's jaw tightened. He'd better. For all his vices, the Gabriel whom Rafe had known had an unshakeable sense of honor toward the brotherhood of the Lost Boys. Hopefully he still did—and still considered Rafe a part of it.

A clicking noise filtered into the cabin. He tensed. *Merde.* The RIB's motor was about to start.

Come on, you piece of crap. Holly turned the key over. Nothing. Surely it didn't need the choke—it was still warm. She couldn't risk flooding the motor.

The *capitaine* bolted up onto the deck of the yacht, her backpack in hand. With the bowline untethered, the swell pulled the drifting inflatable away. He'd have to swim for it. As long as she got the damn motor started they'd be swapping boats tonight. He crouched, swinging the bag onto his back. Weird. Was he giving up that easily?

She flinched, as a thought struck. The kill switch—she hadn't checked for one. She fumbled around and found a coiled lanyard at her feet. She must have knocked it out, in the darkness. Her hand trembled as she felt around the console. *Calm down. You can do this.* There. She clipped the cord onto the switch and flicked it on. The *capitaine* sprang up and sprinted down the yacht toward her, arms pumping like a bionic man's. Dang, was he going to jump for it? Her heartbeat quickened. She turned the key. The motor chugged to life. Relief surged through her veins.

She reversed the throttle, just as he leaped from the yacht. *Adieu, Capitaine.* His large shadow flew toward her. *Clonk.* His skull smacked into her forehead, hurling her backward. No way. She thumped onto the deck, pain radiating out from her spine and consuming her head. Her vision fuzzed out. What was he— Superman? He had her pinned, again, his face an inch away.

He rolled off her, panting, and touched a palm to his balaclava-clad forehead. Her eyes came back into focus, zeroing in on the knife as it rolled away. She dove for it. As her hand closed, he caught her arm and spun her. In a microsecond, he was astride her, clamping her torso between his thighs. He calmly plucked the weapon from her fingers.

"What did I tell you about running, princess?" He pulled off the balaclava and sucked in a breath. "And fighting?"

Holy crap. The moonlight bounced off sharp cheekbones, tanned skin that plunged into a strong jaw shaded by stubble, and a black buzz cut glistening with sweat. His dark eyes glittered with adrenaline and his huge chest heaved. As pirates went, Johnny Depp had nothing on the *capitaine*.

She shook her head—the only body part she could move. *He's kidnapping you, you moron.* It was far too soon to get Oslo

Syndrome, or Stockholm Syndrome, or whatever was the name for loopy people who fell for their captors. She'd evidently gone too long without a good-looking man in her life. Or not long enough.

His gaze strayed to the frayed remains of the rope he'd bound her with. *"Merde,"* he whispered, his full lips twisting into an impressed smile. *That* good-looking, *and* he spoke French?

Focus. How long until he figured out she was an imposter? And then what? Feed her to the sharks? He'd be better off taking the yacht—fat chance the senator would pay to save *her* neck, with his precious daughter lying low in luxury.

"I see we need to set ground rules, princess."

"You can get off me, for a start."

His knees tightened against her waist. "When I say *we* need to set ground rules, I mean *I* need to set ground rules. I gather this is how a kidnapping works—the kidnapper gives the instructions, the hostage follows them or suffers the consequences."

He flicked open the knife and made a show of running his finger along the steel. The skin on the back of her neck crawled. She'd sharpened that blade just hours ago.

"You need me alive."

"For now, yes." He rested the blade against her ear, just lightly enough to avoid piercing the skin. "My job is to keep you alive until your father pays, but no one said anything about keeping you in one piece. That is your choice."

Her mouth flooded with saliva, but she didn't dare swallow. "Where are you taking me?"

"You'll know when we're there." He ran his free hand around her waist and patted down her pockets. "Get up."

He removed the blade and loosened the grip of his legs, giving her just enough leeway to wriggle away. He leaped to his feet, like the world's largest gymnast. "You're driving, princess."

She pushed up to standing. She barely reached his bowling ball of a shoulder. Short of praying for a tsunami to tip him out of the boat, her options were limited. Forget coming clean. Then there'd be no reason to keep her in one piece. She had to play this out. Maybe on dry land she'd have more chance. "Aye, aye, Capitaine."

His jaw tightened. So the title meant something to him? "We head northwest."

To the next island? Could she escape and find a village, maybe track down an NGO? She needed to find a chink in this pirate's well-muscled armor, and quickly.

Twenty minutes later, Holly counted two dark figures waiting on a beach ahead of the inflatable. Dense beech forest soared into a charcoal sky pinpricked with stars. No lights, buildings or vehicles, but plenty of cover. Could she grab the backpack and run, get out a message via the sat phone before they caught up?

One of the figures waded knee-deep into the water. One yank of the wheel and she could take him out.

"Keep it straight, princess."

The *capitaine* slid up beside her, his voice a warning rumble, his right hand coasting down her arm to enclose her hand as she steered. Her fingers twitched, his grip tightened. She willed her breath to settle—he wouldn't always be watching her, guessing her next move. There would be a chance for escape.

"Put it in neutral and leave it running," he said. "The sand drops off steeply."

They eased into shore. The man held the bow while the *capitaine* hauled Holly's backpack over his shoulder. Her forehead throbbed where he'd smacked into it. He stepped into the water and held out a hand. She ignored it and jumped, splashing into warm water up to her knees, her feet sinking into fine, sloping sand.

The *capitaine* spoke in clipped, urgent raps. Holly picked up a word: *Michael*. A couple of the prison inmates had spoken a language like that. Where had they been from? Ukraine?

She fought to keep upright without the rocking of the boat underfoot. She took a step, her sea legs heavy and graceless, as if gravity had doubled its force and was coming in sideways. No way would she be able to run. Her heart thunked. There went plan A. Three months ago she'd been seasick from the ocean's incessant movement after so many years run aground in prison, now her body was freaked out by the absence of it. Great.

The *capitaine* pushed the inflatable off the sand as the man jumped in and shoved it into Reverse. One down. As the engine faded, the air filled with the screech of a zillion insects and God knew what else. Would she be kept here? Surely not. The island was only a few miles from her mooring—a long stretch of land, but narrow, as far as she could remember from the GPS. Rescuers wouldn't have to look far. The tension under her ribs unwound a notch. Maybe this wasn't such a professional operation, despite the *capitaine*'s commanding presence.

His hand closed around her upper arm, urging her forward. She shook him off, but the sand rose and fell under her like a tide, and she stumbled sideways. He caught her waist, swept his other arm under her legs and lifted her as if she were a child.

"Put me down."

"It'll be quicker this way—and I can keep an eye on you."

The world swayed. She gripped his shoulder, beating down a surge of nausea. What choice did she have? The disorientation hadn't been this bad after even the longest sailing trips she'd done as a teenager. But after six years of walking on concrete and baked dirt in a Californian prison, maybe her mind wasn't as quick to adjust. And this was the first time she'd set foot on land since she'd been dropped onto the boat off the coast of San Francisco.

When the heiress had taken the helm to sail into Samoa, then Cairns, Darwin and Bali, Holly had been secretly stashed in Laura's stateroom in one of the senator's superyachts, surviving on military ration packs and banned from showing her face.

There she'd waited for long days while the heiress flounced off on her one-woman environmental crusades—endangered Sumatran orangutans, rising sea levels, dying coral reefs… How long until Holly got her land legs back? Hours? Days?

The *capitaine* adjusted his grip and pulled her into him, one hand pressing into her thigh, the other firm around her waist. His warm, earthy scent coasted around her, like rain pounding dusty ground.

At least she was doing a good job of appearing to be a help-less society-page diva, however unintentional. She might as well save her strength, while sapping the *capitaine*'s. Even in darkness, the air was too hot and damp for sweat to evaporate.

A short, wiry man waited on the dry sand above the waterline, his head wrapped in a red bandanna. She might be able to take him down on a good day, even if she had no hope against the Spartan. But today wasn't a good day. And he carried an assault rifle that was almost half his size. The *capitaine* spoke to him in the same language as before. The man dropped his beady black gaze to her wet T-shirt, smirking, and muttered something. The *capitaine* snapped out a sharp answer, tilting her slightly to turn her chest into his. Protecting her honor, or staking his claim? Either way, it worked—the man lifted his gaze and sneered at her captor instead.

They plunged down a sandy path winding through rain forest, the *capitaine*'s stride long and sure as he followed the man's bobbing flashlight. Insects screamed like the world's biggest electric drill, in surround sound. After half a mile the guy's breath hadn't even wavered with the effort of carrying her. Lines etched between his eyes hinted at inner tension, but outwardly he was as fit as he looked. She'd kept up her fitness in prison with endless, pointless jogging around the yard, but sailing had required a different strength. It had left her with toned arms and legs, but she hadn't stretched them into a sustained sprint for years. Running from him—even when she got her land legs back—was looking like less of an option. She'd find another way to get quality time alone with the sat phone. Even Superman slept, occasionally.

Or did he?

The thick canopy gave way to a long narrow clearing. Moonlight reflected off a small plane. In the shadows, a dark figure waited. She pressed her lips together, tasting salt. How far could they fly in that—to Sumatra, Timor, Borneo, Australia? Right up to Singapore or Malaysia? Tens of thousands of islands, a gazillion square miles of jungle—even if a search was launched, rescuers had no chance of tracking them. Damn.

CHAPTER

3

The *capitaine* lowered Holly to her feet, next to a heap of bags. The ground tilted, and she tipped onto hands and knees. *Whoa.* Their escort laughed. The *capitaine* barked orders, and he stuttered something and jogged off toward the plane.

"You'll be okay in a few hours, princess."

She rolled onto her back, gripping the rocking earth, swallowing bile. "You know I'm not royalty, right?"

He strode to the bags and hauled something out. "The daughter of the future American president? Closest I'll get to a princess, princess."

Correction: the furthest. He was Captain Calm again—the hint of tension erased from his face. She should have tried to chuck him out of the boat when she had the chance.

"You want to change out of those wet clothes?"

She shook her head. The dampness shielded her against the pulsing heat. And she wasn't about to strip for him.

He held up a long-sleeved jumpsuit. "Time to suit up."

"What do I need that for?"

He threw it to her, pulled her running shoes out of her backpack and dropped them on the ground. "Warmth, mostly. It's cold up at 15,000 feet. And tie your shoelaces tight." Why did his mouth twitch, as if he was hiding something? "Can you get it on by yourself, or do you need help?"

"I'll be fine." She snatched the jumpsuit. "As long as I don't have to stand up."

The suit was big enough for a gorilla. She wriggled it on while sitting on the ground as he pulled one on himself, followed by a harness. Were they going to clip themselves to the plane? He shouted something to his crew, then knelt beside her. "Don't zip up your jumpsuit yet," he hissed.

He hauled her backpack toward them, and pulled a rope and harness from his shoulder.

"No need to tie me up," she said, lying back down. "I won't be running anywhere." *Yet.*

"It's not for that." He glanced at the plane and swallowed, his Adam's apple bobbing. Nerves? "Sit up. Stay still and be quiet."

She pushed herself up to sitting, her breath shallow. He knelt and slipped his hands down each side of her neck and along her shoulders, pushing the jumpsuit off again. Her face chilled. What the hell did he intend to do?

He fiddled around inside the backpack and pulled something out—her sweater, with the rectangular outline of her laptop and sat phone inside it. "I need you to carry this." Placing it firmly on her chest, he looped a strap in a figure eight around her shoulders, holster-style, and tied it tight. He pulled the jump-suit back up her shoulders and zipped it to her neck. Hands a blur, he jammed and zipped other bits of electronic equipment in her pockets, his gaze darting over her shoulder to the spot the men's voices drifted from.

He didn't want them to know what he was doing. Why? *I need you to carry this,* he'd said. Like he was asking a favor, like they were in this together. He pushed the harness under her legs. Lifting her hips, she let him slide it under her bottom and up over her back and waist, her body fizzing with awareness of his touch. Ridiculous. She sure had a talent for being attracted to the wrong man. Evidently her mind and body hadn't learned a thing since Jasper had sucked her in when she was nineteen and spat her out four years later, right into the eager hands of the Feds. *You're sworn off men, remember?*

She allowed the *capitaine* to pull her to her feet. The sat phone was hers—now she just needed a few minutes to fire it up and get out a message. He leaned in to adjust the harness and check the clips.

"I don't get it. What's the harness for?"

"Safety." His forehead was etched with concentration as he yanked tight the straps on her shoulders.

The man who'd been waiting in the shadows sauntered up and spoke. He was nearly as big as the *capitaine* and wore a grubby pilot's cap. The *capitaine*'s gaze flicked up to catch hers for a second, eyes hooded in warning, then he calmly turned, picked up her backpack and threaded it onto his chest. The man grabbed it and yabbered something, sharply. The *capitaine* shrugged and muttered a reply, pulling off the bag and unzipping it. He held it out in offering. The man reached in and pulled out a bottle of shampoo, then dug around thoroughly, emerging with a bra. He held it up and grinned a gap-toothed smile.

"Give that back, you pervert." Holly stepped forward. The *capitaine* shot out an arm and she tumbled into it, forced to grab his shoulder to keep from falling.

"Easy, princess." He yanked the bra from the man's hands, stuffed it into the bag, zipped it and pulled it back onto his chest. He strode a few yards to a larger bag she hadn't noticed—not the one he'd pulled the jumpsuits from—and lifted it onto his back, fiddling with clips and straps.

The pervert strolled toward Holly, thumbs tucked in his belt loops, buggy eyes checking her out like she was dessert. She shuffled backward, not trusting herself to take large steps. He pulled up inches from her, his breath stinking like fish oil, and reached for her hair. "Miss America," he whispered, in a murky accent.

She ducked away, fighting to keep her balance. If he made a play for her, what could she do? She could hardly stand up straight, let alone defend herself.

Suddenly, he lurched sideways and sprawled onto the ground. He snapped out several words, anger flashing in his eyes. The *capitaine* stood over him, drawn up to full height, chest massive, jaw set, arm still outstretched from shoving him. Playing good cop, bad cop?

No—she'd been caught in that game enough times to know this was for real. He was protecting her, all right. Just what was the dynamic here?

The *capitaine* spoke, quiet and dangerous. The pervert's eyes narrowed. He scrambled to his feet and spat on the ground, an inch from her foot, but maintained his distance. She exhaled. Thank God *that* wasn't about to happen, at least.

The man unleashed a series of bitter words and held out his hand to the *capitaine*, palm up. The *capitaine* slapped a mobile phone into it. So that was why he was so keen on her equipment—he wasn't allowed his own. Someone else had to be pulling the strings, leaving him to do the dirty work. Was he a hired gun? His bearing and commanding tone weren't those of a lowly henchman. This was a man accustomed to leading, a man who didn't trust whomever he was taking orders from. That conflict could work to her advantage, as could his evident protective instinct, if she played it right. And if she was good at anything, it was playing people.

The pervert fiddled with the phone and held it up. The flash seared her eyes. Taking photographic evidence she was alive? How long did they plan to keep her that way?

Half an hour later she sat cross-legged on the cold metal floor at the back of the plane, g-forces churning her stomach and spinning her head. If her balance had been warped before, it was tied in knots now. The seawater soaking her clothes felt like it was snapping into ice in the chill of the altitude. Fat lot of use the jumpsuit was.

And what was with the transparent plastic roller door on one side of the plane? What kind of scrap-heap plane had a door like that, and no seats? The wiry man sat beside it, gun slung over his shoulder, beady eyes staring at her. Only a finger-width of metal and a pervert pilot at the controls separated her from a couple of vertical miles of nothing, with a sudden stop at the bottom. At least the roar of the engine was muffled by the helmet the *capitaine* had eased over her head. But why the goggles and harness? He hadn't clipped her to the plane, so what was the point? Or had the whole getup been an excuse to find hiding places for the electronics?

She struggled for breath, the thinness of the air escalating the growing panic of watching her window of escape close. She swallowed, hard, to equalize her ears. Her body might have given in—for now—but her mind certainly hadn't. The electronics equipment digging into her ribs was as good as an escape pod.

The *capitaine* eased up behind her. She flinched. He cradled his legs around hers, his knees splayed either side of her waist. "Time to strap up," he shouted. "We're approaching the dro..." The thundering engine engulfed his words.

"The what?"

He fastened a series of clips at her shoulders and waist and pulled on the straps, yanking her spine hard up against the backpack strapped to his chest. They were clipped together? He stretched out his legs so they rested, hot and solid, either side of her thighs. Her heart sped up. Okay, this was getting weird.

"When we open the door, wrap your legs around the undercarriage of the plane."

"When we what? Are we landing?" She hadn't noticed a drop in altitude.

"When we jump, I need your chest out, legs curled back and head up. You know this, yes? Like a banana. A banana with its arms out."

"Jump? Are you shitting me?"

"Hold tight. The plane will turn."

She swayed in time with the *capitaine* as the plane banked, then corrected. The thin man gave the thumbs-up and rolled up the plastic door. Wind whistled into the plane, flapping the guy's bandanna. Holly clutched for a handhold on something, anything. All she found was the *capitaine*'s thighs. His quads clenched into rock under her gloves. Her belly lurched. They were parachuting? He pushed forward. She resisted, but he had all the power. She tried to twist away. He grabbed her arms and straightened her.

"If you want to live, do what I say," he shouted into her ear. "If you fight this, if you grab for me, I might not be able to pull the cord and we'll both die. Best thing you can do right now is relax."

Relax? What kind of a psycho was he? He slid forward, shoving her ahead of him. Her stomach churned like a washing machine.

"Don't be so tense, princess. I've done this a thousand times."

"Pushing your luck then, aren't you?"

Another shove and her legs dangled out the door. Nothing but thin air lay between her shoes and the ocean. A whole lot of thin air. The water shone silver in the moonlight, interrupted by patches of darkness, like black holes. She retched, and clamped her mouth shut. Vomit would only spray right back into her face.

"Best not to look down."

No kidding. She snapped her focus straight ahead. Death was not in her game plan. As the man said, she had no choice but to trust him, for the next few minutes, at least. Just as well he was a 250-pound slab of muscle.

No. That made no sense, right? Wouldn't his weight just mean they'd hit the ground with a bigger smack? Would she hit first, or would he? Physics had never been her thing.

"Don't forget, wrap your legs backward," he shouted. "Rest your head back on my shoulder and look up. When we're in

the air, keep your arms extended and curl your legs back. Banana, remember?"

Holy Moses. She was really going to do this. Wind buffeted
her jumpsuit, flattening the fabric against her. She didn't need
encouragement to wrap herself into him. If she could nail their
bodies together, she would. He'd obviously done this before,
and right now the more immediate threat was the deep blue
sea—or worse, the land. She closed her eyes, tried to block her
thoughts. Banana, banana, banana.

Her stomach plummeted. Air rushed at her exposed cheeks.
Her eyes flicked open. A shadow loomed overhead, retreating.
The plane. Oh man, they were falling. Her sinuses pinched. Her
nerves pelted panicked messages into her brain. Even through
the goggles, she struggled to keep her eyes open. A piece of fabric flapped against her cheek like a jackhammer. What was she
supposed to do again? Arms back, legs extended? No, the other
way around. They righted and stretched out parallel to the earth
as wind buffeted her jumpsuit. The pull of the harness suggested
the *capitaine* was still attached, at least.

The pain behind her eyes intensified, as if someone was shoving needles into her skull. Was something about to pop? This
couldn't be healthy. An hour or so ago she was being rocked to
sleep by a gentle ocean swell, and now this?

She squeezed her eyes shut, forcing her mind to imagine herself skimming over the water in a yacht, as she had every endless
night in prison, returning her to the happiest time of her life:
the three years she'd spent working at the sailing school in Los
Angeles, trading honest labor for a place to crash and a chance
to sail. But then she'd fallen for the wrong man and got suck-
ered into running cons for him by her desperation for love and
money and survival. Yada yada yada.

Pressure thumped into her chest, and something yanked them
upwards. Oh, God. What had gone wrong? She opened her
eyes. A red parachute stretched above them. The rush of the

wind had silenced, leaving her panting the only sound. They'd stopped dead, as if suspended.

"Holy crap," she said. People did that for fun?

"How was that?" He sounded as if he was grinning.

"Terrifying, you jerk. You could have warned me."

"Anticipation only makes it worse. Do you trust me now?"

"Even less."

"An hour ago you probably thought that wasn't possible."

Was it only an hour since they'd left the inflatable? How far could a small plane fly in half of that? In the hull, in the darkness, she'd had no grasp of their direction. "Where are we?"

"I can't tell you that."

"Because you don't know?"

"Oh, I know just what I'm doing."

If he did, he sure didn't sound happy about it. Islands were scattered beneath her feet—dark patches among the silver, with not a light in view. Uninhabited? Dang. What body of water could it be—Andaman Sea, Indian Ocean, Strait of Malacca? The land forms didn't look familiar from any maps she'd studied. She heaved in a breath. At the movement, something poked into her ribs. The GPS unit. It could pinpoint her location. She could get a message away on the sat phone with her coordinates and threaten to go to the media if the senator didn't rescue her. She gritted her teeth. For now, she'd play the helpless victim. If the *capitaine* wanted a princess, he'd get one. But the second he let his guard down, she'd be gone.

Rafe steadied his breath to clear the adrenaline of the 200-kilometer-per-hour free fall, and pulled the toggle to ride the wind to the northeast. Once they'd dropped another three hundred feet, the air currents would take them northwest. His coordinates had been smack on, but Penipuan Island was only twelve square kilometers, and the biggest clearing was smaller than a football field. If he didn't read the conditions right, they'd wind up snared on a tree—or worse, bobbing in the ocean. At least there wasn't some insurgent with an AK-47 taking potshots, like the last time he'd fallen from the sky. Tonight he was in far better company.

The heiress raised her gloved hand to her ribs for the third time in as many minutes.

"Has the comms gear slipped?" he said.

"The way you strapped it on? I hardly think so."

He raised his eyebrows. She was coping surprisingly well. He'd been prepared to knock her unconscious if she'd freaked out about a parachute drop in these conditions, but she was far tougher than he'd expected—and she had a sense of humor. She might need one, to spend a week with him.

And he might need to watch his back. She wouldn't be the pushover he'd counted on—and with Michael and Uriel gone she was all his responsibility. She turned her head, and the skin of her cheek caught the moonlight, smooth as satin. Tough *and* beautiful. He grimaced. *Tu agis sans passion et sans haine. You act without passion and without hatred.* He'd recited the line every day of his nineteen years in the Legion, but it'd never resonated as strongly as it did now. He must put aside his anger toward Gabriel and even his fear for Theo, and treat the heiress honorably. She was a prisoner of war, not a woman to covet. The objective of his mission must remain clear: save his son.

He frowned. The Legionnaire's Code of Honor hardly applied. If his *commandant* got wind of this he'd be out of a job and in a French prison quicker than he could say *Honneur et Fidélité.* Outcast from an outcast's army. The *commandant* was already suspicious about Rafe's claim to be on bereavement leave. Who would a widower, an orphan and a loner mourn? But Rafe had been tied to the Code of Honor so long—after too many years without one—that he couldn't shrug it off, whatever the circumstances.

Instinctively, he calculated the distance and time to ground.

"When we come in to land, raise your legs straight out ahead of you, knees slightly bent, and let me do the work. For you, it'll be like easing into an armchair."

"Is that where we're going?"

He followed the direction of her finger to the dark oval of land beneath them. The breeze warmed with every foot they descended. The coolness at altitude had been a relief after days of gagging humidity. "That's it."

"There are no lights. Is no one meeting you?"

"It's uninhabited."

"So it's just you and me?"

Her tone carried a note of hope. "You and me and thousands of miles of ocean. No boat, no helicopter, no airstrip. We're a hundred kilometers from the nearest inhabited island, nowhere near a shipping lane, and pleasure boats don't come this way." Gabriel had chosen well. They were imprisoned by water. But now, he had comms. He just had to figure out what to do with them.

"They stay away because of pirates?"

"Currents and reefs, mostly. But yes, pirates, too. Don't worry, *ma chérie*, I will protect you."

"Before or after you cut off my ear?"

He flinched, and the chute lunged, forcing him to make a hasty correction. He'd forgotten his empty threat, but it wouldn't hurt for her to believe he was capable of it. "Do exactly as I say and you won't be harmed. We'll be on the ground in two minutes."

"And who will protect you from me?"

He eased the parachute into line for the final approach. He was beginning to wonder that, too. "I don't need protection."

Outside the Legion, the only person on Rafe Angelito's side was Rafe Angelito. Same as it had always been. Same as it would always be.

CHAPTER

4

They skidded across a clearing, sea grass scraping the seat of Holly's jumpsuit. A gentle landing, as promised. How did someone get that practiced at parachuting? You'd have to be in adventure tourism or the military, and the *capitaine* was no chirpy tour guide. So she was dealing with a paratrooper? Weren't they the elite soldiers—dropped behind enemy lines on secret missions?

Her stomach knotted. He became more formidable by the minute. He unclipped them, pulled her to her feet and let go warily, hands splayed in the air either side of her, ready to catch. The earth remained steady. Gravity had begun to take her side, at least. He busied himself with unhooking clips and gathering the parachute, with the deft movements of a man drilled in the routine.

Beside the clearing, a long stretch of ocean beach thundered rhythmically. Otherwise they were surrounded by rain forest, screeching with insects. Was there a building, or would they sleep outdoors? A palm tree rustled overhead. She flinched.

"Bats," he said, following her gaze upward, to where ragged black shapes glided. She shivered. Concrete jungles were more her thing.

"Don't worry, they're vegetarians. It's the mosquitoes you must watch for." He stripped off his jumpsuit, his dark, sleek clothing emphasizing his tall, taut body. More Batman than Superman, perhaps. Give her a brooding mystery man over a clean-cut farm boy any day.

Except today. And only ever hypothetically.

She fumbled with her gloves. "What do I call you?"

His dark eyes fixed on hers, unguarded for a second, as if it wasn't something he'd considered. "John," he said, his mouth curling at one corner.

"Short for Long John Silver? Or long for Captain Jack Sparrow?"

"I have no idea what you're talking about."

"I prefer Jack."

He shrugged. "Suit yourself."

She exhaled away the tension. If he was reluctant to tell her his real name, he must be planning to let her go. But what if the ransom wasn't paid?

She jammed her fingernails into her palms. Even if the senator didn't intend to pay, he'd have to at least go through the motions of searching for his daughter, after the publicity of the live webcast. He wouldn't want the bad PR of admitting Laura had misled the public, with the primaries looming. Would the US military become involved? Did this count as a diplomatic incident? Terrorism? Jack might seem like the real deal, but one man couldn't hold his own against a whole unit or platoon, or whatever pack American soldiers ran in.

Could he?

"Stop thinking so hard," he said, crossing the gap between them in three strides. He laid a fingertip on her forehead. She froze. Some kind of threat? He stroked down to the bridge of her nose. Holy cow, he was smoothing out her worry lines. "You have nothing to be concerned about. You'll be back in your rich woman's world soon enough."

He stilled, and stared at her, his forehead creasing. She gulped. Was he noticing the differences between her and Laura? He flinched, removed his finger and shook his head slightly, as if banishing an unwelcome thought. Had touching her been an instinctive reaction, a mistake?

His focus dropped to her shoulders as he began to unclip her harness, muttering some kind of chant in French. His gravelly scent washed over her. Her body heated up, as if it'd just realized it was back in the tropics after their high-altitude reprieve. She shivered, which made no sense at all. He reached down to slide the contraption over her hips, his fingers grazing her stomach. She lurched away. "I can handle that." This was not a man to get worked up about, no matter how fine a specimen.

She wriggled out of the harness. Beyond the white tips of the breakers, the full moon lit a silver path to the horizon. Even if she could mobilize rescuers, how long until they arrived?

"You'll have plenty of time to admire the scenery." Jack's deep voice made her jump. "Now, we find shelter." He nodded to the sky above the jungle, where heavy clouds were rapidly snuffing out the stars.

At least the horizon was still out there. This might be a prison, but it wasn't a cell, with no stars visible beyond the floodlights, no hope of hearing the sea, no hope of anything. At least here there was still a chance of rescue or escape, however small. She was alive, for starters. And not as helpless as he might believe.

"I need to go to the bathroom," she said. "Like, right now."

He started, as if suddenly awkward. Awkward was good. She could play on awkward. She hopped from one foot to the other—as much as she dared without risking falling on her face.

"I'll just find a tree to go behind," she said, eyeing the fringe of darkness beyond the clearing. "Seriously, dude, I'm about to burst my bladder all over this suit."

He grimaced. Oh yeah, he was picturing it. Job done.

"Go down to the beach," he said, quickly. "Less chance of snakes and spiders. But watch for scorpions—keep away from driftwood and rocks."

Ugh. She was only used to dealing with human predators. The beach could work, though. She could scoot around the sand dunes and up into the jungle. "Flashlight?"

He pulled one out of a bag. "If you're not back in three minutes, I'll come after you."

"What do you think I'll do—swim home?"

A smile tugged at his lips. "Three minutes, princess."

That's all I need.

Rafe began repacking the chute and harnesses. A large piece of fabric and a bunch of clips and straps could have a dozen uses on a deserted island. He looked up, lining up the Orion Nebula with the star Alnilam to confirm where north lay. The villa was on the northeast of the island, beside a lagoon.

Phase two was complete. Gabriel's men had come through this far, at least. They hadn't dropped him in the ocean, they hadn't harmed the heiress, they hadn't shot them both dead. Maybe this fool mission might actually succeed. Maybe Gabriel would keep his word. While Rafe held the trump card—the woman—he was in a position of power. As long as he kept her alive and in sight, phase three had every chance of succeeding.

In sight. His gaze snapped toward the beach. Three minutes was up. Light spilled from behind a sand dune. The jumpsuit wasn't the easiest thing to get out of, if you weren't used to it, if your hands were still shaking from the buzz of the free fall. He'd give her another minute.

Merde—he should have taken the sat phone. Too busy trying not to think about her bladder, or any other body part. He couldn't afford to lose the equipment before he figured out how the hell to get them out of this, without triggering Gabriel's suspicions.

He stuffed the last of the chute into the bag and zipped it, then shrugged both packs onto his back. The light on the beach hadn't moved. The air grew hotter and wetter by the minute. Better get the princess to shelter before the storm hit.

He jogged to the beach. "Laura?"

No answer. The swell had increased, the waves smashing onto

the sand. He yelled louder. Nothing. His chest tightened. He
closed in on the beam, sinking to his ankles in sand. The flashlight was propped on a rock. No Laura. *Merde.*

He switched it off and gave his eyes a few seconds to readjust.
She'd run off down the sand. He followed, stepping in her footprints to save energy. The trail ran out at the edge of the rain
forest. He scanned the foliage, found a recent disturbance in a
stand of bamboo, and stepped noiselessly through the gap. Tracking someone in jungle this thick was easy, and he was trained
to operate in darkness. She'd have to push through the foliage
blind, leaving tracks, making noise, burning energy. She only
had a four-minute head start. He smiled. Cat and mouse. His
favorite game.

Why was the damn thing not working? In pitch darkness,
Holly felt for the buttons on the sat phone and punched them for
the tenth time. The screen stayed resolutely black. It'd been fully
charged that afternoon, so it couldn't be the batteries. Could
it have been damaged when the *capitaine*—Jack—jumped from
her boat? Or when they'd plummeted at God knew how many
miles per hour? She was screwed. What now?

A fern rustled next to her. She pulled her feet onto the rock
she was sitting on. Snake, scorpion or spider? After a minute
the noise stopped. She eased to her feet and backed away—into
something solid. She gasped, swiveling. A tree. *Get a grip, princess.* Could she creep back out to the beach and make a bonfire
to attract a ship or plane before Jack found her? And how the
hell would she light it—rubbing sticks? Put her in a city alley-
way and she'd know just how to survive. In the wild she couldn't
tell a turtle from a stone.

"Thought I told you not to run."

She yelped. Where the hell had he come from? A click, and
light filled the forest. That, at least, was an improvement. She
blinked rapidly. "I walked."

"You ran." He rested the flashlight's beam on the sat phone. "Hard to get that working without the battery."

"Ugh. You took the battery." Of course.

He tapped a pocket on his thigh. "As you said, trust is going to be an issue between us."

White light flashed through the forest. A second later the sky rumbled. "We go this way. You take this." He passed her the flashlight. "Give me the equipment. Stay close behind me and step where I step. Stomping should scare away snakes and scorpions—and watch for spiderwebs. You're no use to me dead."

Dude, I'm no use to you alive, either.

She followed him, stamping until her feet throbbed. The roar of the ocean receded. Something touched her bare neck. She gasped and froze.

He turned. "What is it?" Concern flecked his tone.

She slapped at her skin. It was wet. She exhaled. "Nothing." Spooked by a drop of rain. More drops rattled on the broad leaves around them.

He grabbed her shoulder and coaxed her around. "Give me the light."

He eased his fingers under the collar of her jumpsuit, brushing her nape, then scooped his palm around her upper back. She shivered. Light spilled over her shoulder as he searched. He circled his hand to her upper chest, brushing the tops of her breasts, and released her. She stumbled to reclaim her balance.

"All clear."

"What should I be scared of? What's the most dangerous thing out here?"

"Humans." He returned the flashlight and turned back to the jungle. "Me, in particular."

"That's a given." Humans she could deal with. "I mean, what animals, what insects?"

"Snakes, mostly," he shouted, walking again. "Only half a dozen species will kill you, most of them in the water—cobras, kraits, sea snakes, coral snakes, vipers… If a krait gets you, you have about a fifty-fifty chance—but by the time you get the first symptoms you're dead. And there's scorpion fish and stone fish. The sharks you've already met. In these jungles a bunch of spiders will give you a painful bite but probably won't kill you. Same with the scorpions—the sting hurts, but you'll live." He looked up into the canopy. "And the slow loris can give you a poisonous nip."

"The what?" She followed his gaze. "You're making that one up."

"Looks like a sloth, but smaller. It probably won't kill you, unless the bite gets infected."

"Good to know."

"The biggest killer's the mosquito. They kill more people than the others combined." He held out a hand to help her navigate a boggy patch. She ignored it. "Malaria, dengue fever, Japanese Encephalitis… Don't worry, princess, we have spray."

Lightning strobed. Thunder snapped through the sky and shook the ground. Rain pelted her through the thinning canopy. Jack moved faster, crashing through the undergrowth like an elephant, ducking under branches, stopping occasionally to hold them back for her. A large hulk loomed ahead—a rusty tin shed, rain shelling its roof. Their accommodation? Jack charged into a thicket of scrub, and she tumbled through behind him, into air. A path. That was an improvement.

"Nearly there, princess."

After another hundred feet the path widened into a grassy clearing. Lightning illuminated a wooden cabin with a thatched roof. Jack crossed the lawn and took the steps to the veranda in a single stride. A lizard the size of her arm scampered out of his path and disappeared into the darkness. She shuddered.

"Stay here," he said as she reached the veranda. He dropped the bags on the doorstep and jogged out into the rain.

She wiped her face with her sleeve, though it was just as wet. They were beside the sea again, but the waves on this side of the island lapped rather than crashed. Two arms of dark land circled a patch of still blackness. A lagoon. She inhaled the fresh, fertile scent of jungle and sea. Rain splattered all around. She'd been in worse prisons, and this one had a guard who was a step up from the correctional officers she was used to—in so many ways.

A motor shuddered to life, a hundred feet away or more. An outboard engine? But he said there'd be no escape until the ransom was paid. A light flickered on above her head, and a yellow glow spilled from a window. A generator. Not a boat. Her shoulders slumped.

Jack returned, walking as calmly as if it were a sunny day. Rain slicked his buzz cut and flowed down his face. He opened an insect screen, unlocked the door and held it open. "Your suite, your highness."

Low lamps lit a bed scattered with pink frangipani petals and draped in a mosquito net. A window seat was stacked with red and turquoise cushions. On a glass coffee table, a bottle of champagne nested in a bucket. "Good grief."

"Did I mention we're on honeymoon?"

She froze. One bed. Her gaze darted to meet his, her stomach flip-flopping.

"Bed's yours," he said, quickly, lowering the bags to the floor. "I'll take the hammock outside."

She exhaled, switching off the flashlight and dropping it on the window seat. She wouldn't put it past him to carry out his threat to relieve her of a finger or two—he was evidently a professional—but there was honor in him, too. He wouldn't take advantage of the situation in *that* way.

So he'd booked a honeymoon suite—a honeymoon island. Good cover for a woman in her late twenties and a good-looking man not much older. Would someone come to service the suite, replenish their supplies? Could she get a message away—or steal their boat?

He crossed the glossy floorboards, leaving a trail of water, and unlocked another door. "Bathroom is out here."

A covered deck held a vanity and mirror, but otherwise the "bathroom" was a tropical garden enclosed by a brushwood fence. In the center, a miniature thatched roof covered a shower. Garden lights lit spears of falling rain.

"Check for snakes and bugs before you use the toilet," he said, indicating a door off the deck. "Hungry?" He brushed past her on his way back inside. She inhaled sharply, to make herself concave.

"Starving." All that flipping and clenching in her belly must have burned her calories since dinner. Her meal of fish and rice seemed a lifetime ago.

She grabbed a white towel so thick it could have been a quilt, and blotted her hair.

Inside, the *capitaine* opened a cooler chest on a bench in a tiny kitchen. A rectangular scar nearly the size of a dollar bill dominated his right forearm, a patch of rough, paler skin gouged out of the brown. Hell of a burn.

"Pastrami, blue cheese, gruyere, olives, mussels, lobster…" He stacked several plastic boxes on the bench and carried them to the coffee table, balancing a baguette on top.

Her mouth watered. She didn't even remember what half those things tasted like. She sat on the window seat, opened the nearest box and stuffed a strip of prosciutto in her mouth. They wouldn't go to all this effort only to poison her, so what the hell. "This is not what I'd expected," she mumbled, her mouth lighting up at the salty hit.

"I imagine it's not. Look, I have nothing against you, this is not personal, so we might as well just…" He frowned.

"You were going to say, 'Enjoy it.'"

"…eat up. And get drunk, if you like." He waved a hand over the champagne. "All yours. The ice has melted, I'm afraid."

"Where did all this stuff come from?"

"It's part of the deal when you book this island. They supply everything, drop you off and leave you alone. No one will be coming to check on us, if that's what you're hoping. All we can do is sit tight."

Dang. "You'd better pour me a glass, then."

He swiftly uncorked the champagne, filled a flute and returned the bottle to the bucket.

"You're not joining me? Are you Muslim?"

"No, just sensible."

She sipped, and her mouth buzzed with apple and vanilla. She tabled the glass with a clatter. Last time she'd drunk champagne she'd been arrested. Jasper had bought it, to celebrate their biggest con yet. She'd been half-cut on the stuff when the door had fallen in. He'd arranged the whole thing, the alcohol ensuring she wasn't at her sharpest in the interrogation. While she was in one room naively sticking to their agreed line that they were both innocent, he was in the next, turning federal witness against her in exchange for immunity. Which left her here, drinking expensive champagne with her pirate captor, while Jasper was no doubt screwing waitresses on some Caribbean island and wallowing in the millions of big-bank and fat-corporate money the Feds believed Holly had stashed. If only.

She scratched the spot on her lower back where Laura's people had lasered off the tattoo of the jerk's name. Well worth the pain. Hard to believe she'd once been so sucked in by the novelty of someone giving a damn about her—or pretending to. That wouldn't happen again. Being alone trumped being betrayed.

"*Santé,*" the *capitaine* said, raising a bottle of water.

"You're not what I expected in a pirate."

He laughed, curtly. "You're not what I expected in a princess."

Fair point. "You can't believe everything you read in the tabloids."

"Obviously not. I thought you'd parachuted before, for starters."

Her cheeks chilled. Laura probably had. She popped an olive into her mouth. "Like I say, you can't believe everything you read."

He tilted his head, frowning. "There was a video of you doing it, on YouTube."

Crap. "I've never done it with a pirate before. Parachuted, that is."

He sat opposite, his large frame barely contained by the wicker chair. "I find it strange that you didn't have protection, going through these waters. Like you were just waiting for some bastard to turn up. You were a kidnapping waiting to happen—you're lucky it was me."

"Luckiest day of my life."

"If you were my daughter, I wouldn't have allowed it. Or I would have had a contingency plan, at least."

I am the contingency plan. This was exactly why she'd been hired. Unlike the precious Laura, Holly was expendable. She pretended to chase the olive stone around her mouth, to buy time. No one in the world would notice if she disappeared—not even the parole officer she'd bought off with the senator's money—and no one would ever believe Laura was connected to such a lowlife. Everything had been clandestine, from the way the senator's private investigator had sniffed around to find a suitable candidate, to the way he'd tracked her down upon her release, and pounced. *We need someone who can melt into the woodwork afterward, who can keep her mouth shut,* he'd said. Oh, she'd heard the subtext, as clear as if he'd shouted it: they needed someone who wouldn't be missed if she drowned, or worse.

"My father is...easily persuaded. He leaves me to do my thing, I leave him to do his. I very rarely see him— I was raised by nannies while he spent most of his time in Washington. He outsourced me." She grinned, hoping it sounded like the kind of joke a bitter rich girl might make. Of course Laura would have parachuted—and of course she'd have put it on YouTube. What else did Jack know about Laura that Holly didn't? She'd have to be more careful.

He studied her, his head cocked.

"What?" she said, hovering a piece of pastrami in front of her mouth. Her stomach twisted. She hadn't slipped up again, had she? She'd read enough about Laura in gossip blogs and social pages to know the heiress rarely saw her father.

He gripped his quads and dropped his gaze to the floor, like something had occurred to him. What had she said? Her gaze rested on his thighs. She could still feel how those muscles had bunched when she'd clutched them on the plane. At the time, she'd been too terrified to process the information. But that… that was a very human reaction. A very *male* reaction. And smoothing her worry lines—what was that about? Maybe he wasn't as bulletproof as he appeared.

He shook his head and pushed to his feet, weariness weighing down his eyes. "I'll check for wildlife and leave you to enjoy your castle, princess. Put this food in the fridge when you're finished—I'll switch it on now. And tuck in your mosquito net before you go to sleep. We don't want them getting a taste for blue blood."

Minutes later, he shut the door on her, taking the electronics with him. A key turned and scraped as it was removed. Despair clanged in her chest, the way it had every time she'd been locked in her cell for the night. She sipped the champagne and let her head fall back on a cushion, fatigue enveloping her. She closed her eyes. The room swayed like a boat.

How stupid was she to think that getting this job meant her fight was over? Her entire life had been a fight for survival. Ever since she was a kid, knocked around daily by her father, she'd set herself small goals—survive the beating, survive the day, don't let him see her fear. As long as she kept waking up every morning, she was still winning. Tomorrow she'd figure out a way to survive another day, and then another, then another.

And the quads? The worry lines? There might be a way in under Jack's armor, after all. She smoothed a finger down the curve of the glass. Maybe it wasn't time to say goodbye to the old Holly just yet.

CHAPTER

5

The hammock on the veranda creaked as Rafe settled into it, the sat phone and laptop on his chest. When he was confident the princess wouldn't try to escape, he'd make his call.

His body ached after days of tension, but tonight sleep would evade him. Until now he hadn't stopped moving—and hadn't spent a minute alone. He'd flown to Indonesia under guard, prepared for the mission, tracked the yacht, grabbed the girl. Now he could do nothing but hope—and he wasn't the hopeful type. While Theo was locked in hell, he was trapped in paradise with a beautiful woman. He'd better not have made a mistake in going quietly.

And then there was the woman. Two innocent lives at stake, because of him. He doubted he needed to worry about her emotional state, at least. She was as tough as any soldier in his company—and as beautiful as Simone. He exhaled, raggedly. So maybe it *was* possible for him to react to a woman like a normal man did.

Just as long as he didn't act on it.

Focus. What time was it in Corsica—early evening? His commando team would have just finished eating. Perfect. Michael and Uriel, God rest their broken souls, had at least given him the space to quietly mobilize a backup plan.

He drummed his fingers on the laptop, hearing Laura move around inside the villa. So her father had *outsourced* her. Like Rafe had done to Theo, after Simone's death. He could have given up the Legion, become a fisherman on Corsica like Simone's brothers, or taken over her water sports school. But he carried a darkness inside him and battled it every minute. What if it spilled out one day, when he was alone with Theo?

Instead, he'd sold their home, closed her business, left Theo with his mother-in-law and embarked on ever more dangerous missions, on communication blackouts for months at a time—Côte d'Ivoire, Mali, Guiana, Somalia, Cambodia… Hiding. Hiding from the guilt, hiding from a vulnerable little boy he cared about so much that it hurt, smack in the chest. Telling himself Theo was better off with a grandmother who knew how to show him love than a messed-up father who didn't know what the hell to do with him.

It'd been the same with Simone—he might have loved her, whatever that meant to someone who'd been trained to hate. But if so, he'd been too damn scared to let down his guard. He didn't understand normal human behavior. Why the hell she'd been attracted to him in the first place, he'd never know. They'd only married because she got pregnant. A few years later she'd had a brain aneurysm. By the time word reached him, in a desert in East Africa, the funeral had been and gone. He never got a chance to redeem himself. He rolled in his fingers the twin gray-green amulets that hung from his neck, each on a leather cord. His, and Simone's. A warning not to break any more women's and children's hearts.

A mosquito whined in his ear. He slapped his face, and the squeal muted. He hadn't been there for Theo then, and he hadn't been there when Gabriel's men had come in the night. He'd been en route back to Corsica after wrapping up a mission in Mali as they were sneaking his boy out of the country.

Rafe had walked into Theo's *grand-maman*'s house, expecting his son to run and greet him, and found instead the terrified woman bound and gagged and three soldiers waiting to escort him away. How long had Gabriel been watching them? Rafe clutched the phone. Gabriel's instructions were clear—if Rafe involved anyone else, he'd never see his son again.

He'd have to construct his contingency plan carefully. If Gabriel had contacts in the Legion—which seemed likely, given his intelligence on Rafe—they'd notice if several legionnaires suddenly took leave. But one? It was a gamble, but not as big a risk as doing this without backup.

Water poured off the roof, drops ricocheting up into the hammock. It was hot enough for him not to care about being wet, though that in itself was a danger. He peered out at the rain. He couldn't risk calling from here—the less she knew the better. He dashed to the shed they'd passed earlier and shoved the door open. Something scuttled into a corner. It was a storage bunker and guardhouse, with gardening equipment, basic aquatic gear, a set of bunks. He inspected a roll of thick plastic—it'd do for a waterproof laptop case, later. Rain drilled on the tin roof. He laid out the comms gear and reinstated the batteries. Laura had been updating a blog regularly, with photos, so she had to have a strong satellite connection. After a few minutes, he figured out how to hook up the laptop to the internet connection via the sat phone, after first checking it wasn't sending a GPS signal. It'd be suicide to make the call directly from the sat phone— whoever was paying the bills would see the number he dialed. He drummed his fingers on the laptop casing. A Skype call to a landline, using his personal account? Yes. All they'd be able to discern was that the sat phone was used in the Indonesian region.

He laid the sat phone outside the hut, where it could catch the signal, and dragged the USB cable just inside the shed door. After firing up Skype and disabling the video, he dialed his base. He asked for Flynn in English, in his best attempt at an Australian accent, shouting over the rain while muffling his voice. Not that his lieutenant ever got calls from home. After a few reconnects and holds, a gruff voice came on the line.

"Allard."

Merde. Of all the guys to answer the phone. "Can I speak to Lieutenant Flynn?"

"*Non.*"

"Caporal Armstrong?"

"*Non.*"

"Capitaine Angelito?" For good measure.

"*Non.*"

Rafe pressed his lips together. He couldn't go right through his commando team. Maybe they were all out training—or drinking, more likely. One more. "Sergent Levanne?"

"*Non.*"

"Where are they?"

"Who is this?"

"Flynn's brother. It's an emergency." Rafe knew his lieutenant didn't have family, but Allard probably wouldn't. He wasn't a guy anyone took into his confidence.

The line went quiet. Finally, Allard spoke. "Guiana—South America. Deployment. Can't be contacted."

Putain. "Camopi?"

"*Oui*...yes."

Rafe winced. Of all the Legion outposts the team could be in, they picked Camopi, a hundred clicks upriver from nowhere? Even if Rafe got a message through, and Flynn could extract himself, it'd take forty-eight hours at least for him to get to Asia. "When will he return?"

A pause. Rafe pictured Allard's I-don't-give-a-shit eye roll. "Weeks. Months."

"Thanks, mate."

Rafe ended the call and leaned against the tin wall of the hut, clutching his temples. He could send a coded message to Flynn, over the internet, but it might not be picked up for weeks.

He was on his own.

Rafe woke to sun on his face. The insect calls had given way to birdsong. Had to be late. He sat up in the hammock, planting his feet on the floor to stop the world swinging, and pushed away the mosquito net. His mouth was as dry as the white sand on the beach a few meters away.

He pushed himself up, cricked his back and knocked on the villa door. "You awake, princess?"

No answer. A tingle of suspicion crept up his neck.

Another knock. "Princess?"

He pulled the key from his shorts pocket and unlocked the door. The bed was empty, the shutters open. A gauzy curtain sailed up before an open window, an insect screen tapping on the frame. The door to the bathroom was ajar. No one there.

Damn, he usually didn't sleep that solidly. Years of commando training had him bolting out of bed at any suspicious noise, his instinct honed to recognize risk even as he slept. How could he have missed her leaving the villa? He hadn't had a chance to do a proper scout of the island—what if a boat had managed to get through the infamous network of reefs and currents, and she was right now waving it down?

He jogged out onto the veranda and spotted movement in the lagoon, beyond the jetty that jutted into the azure water. She was swimming for it? No, her long, languid strokes were parallel to shore. She was...doing laps. His muscles unwound. He stepped inside, yanked a bottle of water out of the fridge and chugged it until his throat relaxed. Probably trying to keep in shape for her next photo shoot. He ripped off a handful of baguette and wandered back outside. She'd turned, heading to shore, the low sun lighting up lean, lightly tanned arms as they circled through the water.

When she reached the shallows she stood, her body glistening as she rose, barely covered by a bikini. Breasts, legs, curves.

"Mon Dieu."

She looked up, straight into his eyes. Damn, he'd said that aloud. As she walked—sashayed—to the villa she combed her hands through her short hair.

"Not scared of sharks, then?" He deserved the *Légion d'honneur* for sounding that nonchalant.

She shrugged smooth, freckled shoulders. "What are the chances of getting attacked twice in twenty-four hours?"

"High, around here. I'd rather not have my treasure stolen from me when I've only just secured it."

"Who says you've secured me? I could have slit your throat while you slept."

He leaned against a pole and took another swig from the bottle. "With a bread knife? Might have taken a while."

"I'm persistent."

"You would have got lonely here."

"I'd have coped."

Up close, her body looked strong, toned—not as delicate as she appeared in her perfume commercials. The body of a woman who'd never worked a day in her life, who had all day to spend in a gym. And what couldn't be fixed by a life of leisure could be fixed by a surgeon. There'd been speculation of a nose job, lip implants. The surgeon must have been good. She looked wholly natural. Her nose was straight and her lips were full and pink and...*and not something you should be looking at.* She strolled past, close enough that he could smell the salty freshness of her.

He allowed himself a glance at her back. Strong shoulders curved down to a narrow waist. The bikini rode low on her hips, revealing the tiny V that only belonged to a woman with a good *derrière.* A ragged scar was carved into her lower back, in a looping formation. He narrowed his eyes. Not a scar.

"Who is Jasper?"

Her head snapped around, her eyes wide. "What?"

"Your tattoo. Former tattoo."

She twisted, straining to look, as if it was the first she'd heard of it. "Someone I'd rather forget."

"The scar's still pink. Someone you decided to forget recently?"

"Uh, yeah. I'd been meaning to get rid of it for a while."

"Your boyfriend's name was Logan, not Jasper. I read about the breakup. You'd been with him nearly ten years."

"Don't remind me."

"If my girlfriend had a tattoo of her former lover on her body, I wouldn't want her leaving it there for a decade."

"Maybe that was why he dumped me. Bit slow on the up-take, Logan was."

"Story was that you dumped him."

"Like I say, you can't believe everything you read in the media. I'm going to try out this shower."

She walked inside, the screen door snapping shut after her. He watched until she faded into the dark interior. Jasper. He'd read everything about her he could find on the internet while preparing for the mission—and there was a lot—and not once had a Jasper been mentioned. Rafe would have remembered the name—there was a Jasper in his company, a shifty guy he'd long ago learned to keep an eye on.

Laura and Logan had been America's golden couple. They'd been together since she was a teenager, so Jasper had to have come before him. A first crush, a childhood sweetheart? But why wait so long to erase a youthful mistake, when she had all the time and money in the world, and a widely reported fixation on her body image? He crushed the empty water bottle. Parachuting, Jasper. It didn't add up.

Holly shut the bathroom door and rushed to the mirror to inspect her back. Hell. The scar had sunburned and the skin around it had tanned, so the letters stood out in sharp relief, pink on brown. They hadn't looked so obvious a month ago—the scar had been fading into her pale skin. No wonder the damn thing had started itching. She should never have nicked Laura's bikini—she should have stuck with her own cheap one-piece. Jack wouldn't have known it was from the Walmart bargain bin.

Had he bought her explanation? She walked to the shower and turned it on. A hiss spat out, by the cabin wall. She yelped and sprang back. A gas cylinder firing up, not a snake. Sheesh, she was jumpy.

"Everything okay in there?" Jack shouted, over the fence.

"Fine."

Scanning for peepholes, she stripped off the bikini and stepped under the stream of water. Or would voyeurism be a good sign? Not that Jack seemed the pervert type. A guy like that would have women lining up to strip for him, though he'd sure taken a good look at her body just now.

She closed her eyes and dropped her head under the water. The sickly sweet scent of jasmine wafted around. Bliss. Her first shower in weeks. Expensive-looking toiletries were lined up on a stand. Might as well use them—someone was paying good money for this place, someone who wouldn't be happy if the ransom wasn't paid. And neither would Jack.

What was his deal? He seemed so confident, yet occasionally desperation crept into his voice, or his expressions. Reading people was her strength—borne of necessity—but she couldn't get a fix on him. His tense conversations with the men at the plane, hiding the comms equipment, the things he'd said—*no escape for either of us…* He obviously wasn't the ringleader here. His bearing, the way he'd protected her from the pilot and treated her with respect…that suggested a man with principles. She didn't buy that he was doing this for the money, so what else would drive a seemingly decent man to kidnap?

One thing she'd confirmed she read right—he was physically attracted to her. His eyes had sparked when she'd walked back from the beach. He'd studied her head to toe. She might have been in prison for most of her twenties, but she hadn't forgotten that look in a man's eyes. She'd exploited it in many a bank employee and rich asshole, under Jasper's instructions. If the FBI investigator who'd interrogated her had been a man rather than a sixty-year-old woman, she might have had a better chance. Jack might not be an easy target either, but if she could get him to fall for her, he'd be less likely to kill her when things went to hell.

And just how was she going to do that? The man was made of granite.

She smoothed conditioner on her hair—that alone was more of a luxury than she'd allowed herself in years. She'd been so disgusted with herself for the cons she'd pulled with Jasper, trading on her looks and her youth and her red lips, that until her Laura makeover she'd renounced every vanity except ChapStick. Some of the jobs she'd done for him had required more than flirting. And though she'd never crossed the line from the kind of physical intimacy Jasper called "innocent" and "harmless" to sleeping with the marks—thank God—each time she'd be left feeling nauseous and dirty. She'd take a long shower—just like this—and scrub raw every part of her body, wishing she could scour her soul. But then Jasper would act so grateful and pump up her confidence, and before she knew it she'd be doing his dirty work again. *My brains, and your body, babe—unbeatable.* She shuddered. Just the thought of that smooth voice... The femme fatale, they'd called her at trial, the scarlet woman who'd lured and corrupted poor, defenseless Jasper. If only.

This time she'd be using her body to save her butt, not to earn acceptance. She closed her eyes and let the conditioner run off. One last con and *then* she'd become an honest woman. She could be that girl again—she had to.

CHAPTER

6

As the day heated up, the birdsong subsided to the odd call or squawk and even the insects muted. By late morning Rafe was sitting on the veranda, leaning against a pole, his eyes going screwy as he stared at the brilliant water of the lagoon. Staying still was eating him up from the inside. Somewhere out there his son was being subjected to God knew what and all Rafe could do was wait for the sign the ransom was paid, wait for a boat to collect them.

Too many what-ifs. Too much waiting. Too many troubling messages coming from Laura, telling him something wasn't right. Too much reliance on other people. The only people he relied on were his commando team—and he wouldn't trust some of them to babysit Theo's pet turtle.

Had Gabriel already started Theo's training? The thought socked him in the gut. The beatings, the emotional abuse, the humiliation—an unbearable onslaught that would flip the boy's understanding of right and wrong, and leave him convinced no one gave a damn about him but his commander. How quickly could Gabriel brainwash him into believing his papa didn't care, that he was all alone, with no choice but to succumb?

Rafe closed his eyes. Theo would know that wasn't true, wouldn't he? Rafe hadn't prayed since his English missionary-school days. *But, God, if you're up there, give me another chance to be a father.* He'd held out longer than most when he'd been inducted into the Lost Boys. But he'd already been toughened up by a lifetime of forced independence—trucked from refugee camp to refugee camp as the soldiers closed in, wishing always that at the next stop he'd find the parents he had no memory of, he'd find out where he came from and where he belonged. Until the militia had taken him and Gabriel, they'd survived by polishing shoes in villages near the camps, mostly for food or coins, but sometimes in exchange for lessons in English—the language of movies and escape and dreams. They'd vowed to never leave the other alone in that hell.

No wonder Gabriel sought revenge and had taken the only thing that mattered to Rafe. Deep inside, Rafe could still feel the hatred and violence the militia had beaten into him, like a core of molten lava. Every day he fought to keep it dormant. The last time he'd lost control, had allowed himself to retreat into that dark place of numbness where he could disengage from his conscience and do unspeakable things, an innocent woman and child had died. More than twenty years on, he could still smell the spilled blood, could still feel the anguish and self-disgust that had ripped through his chest when he'd come back into himself, when he'd realized what he'd become. It had turned him into a coward who broke a promise to his only friend.

Oh yes, he knew exactly what fueled Gabriel. The one thing that separated them was that Rafe had found a way to control the demon, by shutting himself off from anger and fear—the dangerous emotions that led to the dark place. If other feelings were shut off at the same time, so be it.

"Don't suppose you have any cards?" In the hammock, Laura linked her arms behind her head.

Doing nothing would do his head in. He never let his company rest for too long. Rest invited doubt, bickering, impotence. What would he do if his men were sitting here, instead of the heiress? Article five of the Code of Honor: *Soldat d'élite, tu t'entraînes avec rigueur, tu as le souci constant de ta forme physique.*

As an elite soldier, you train rigorously and you take constant care of your physical form.

"Do you run?" he said.

"Run?"

"As in jog, sprint…"

"Have been known to. Is this you making light conversation?"

"Get some running gear on." He began yanking on his socks and combat boots.

She swung her legs onto the floorboards and took him in with blue eyes so bright they were almost painful to look at. "Seriously? It's a gazillion degrees out there."

Which made running an even better prospect. "It'll be cooler under the canopy. And the snakes will be sleepy."

"Isn't there some law against torture of prisoners? The Geneva Convention or something?"

"Only if we were at war." He tied the lace on his second boot and leaped up, welcoming the energy sparking in his veins.

"Some might argue that we are."

He marched inside, grabbed her sneakers and backpack and threw two bottles of water in it. Then another two, followed by nut bars and chocolate, though it'd probably melt after a minute. As he stepped back outside, he yanked off his T-shirt. No point creating dirty laundry.

He sensed her stillness before he saw it. She was staring at his chest, her mouth open. What was it—a spider? His gaze darted down, his throat drying out. Nothing amiss.

"Why are you looking at me like that?"

"I'm not." She spoke too quickly, casting her eyes down. Pink flushed her face, from neck to forehead. Because he'd removed his shirt? Oh. A grin tugged at his mouth. He clamped down on it. She hadn't struck him as the blushing type. She was more *I've seen it all, and I don't give a damn.* Perhaps it wasn't just *his* body that was responding in inappropriate ways.

All the more reason to run it off. He tossed her sneakers over.

He'd stashed the comms gear in a place she wouldn't dare go hunting, but he'd learned the hard way not to let her out of his sight.

"Put on sunscreen. And a baseball cap. I don't want you dying of sunstroke before the day's out."

She leaned down and pulled on a sneaker. *"Oui,* Capitaine."

His stomach knotted. One offhand comment from Uriel and now she had a clue to Rafe's identity. If the guy wasn't already dead, Rafe would have wrung his neck. It wouldn't take a genius to narrow down the options—a non-French native with a French rank. He jumped off the veranda.

She stood. The blush had settled, leaving her skin the color of pale honey and just as smooth. Her blue tank top intensified her eyes, and her frayed denim shorts ended far too soon. He turned his back on her.

"Hurry it up," he said.

Footsteps padded down the steps. "Where are we going?"

"A trail circles the island." Recon plus a workout. That should stop his mind straying to places it shouldn't.

He set off down the hard-baked path behind the villa, going slowly for Laura's sake, though his body urged him to push harder, to the point physical effort consumed thought. As a child soldier he would spend weeks on the move, hauling a rifle, his legs whipped if he slowed. His Legionnaire training had him marching eighty kilometers from the Pyrenees almost to Carcassonne in full patrol gear, and then every year the two hundred kilometers from one end of Corsica to the other with a fifty-kilogram backpack. After Simone died, he would spend his rare leave days running near-marathon distances. Anything to get out of that haunted house with a silent son and a mother-in-law whose stoicism thinly veiled her heartbreak. Losing a child had almost broken her. Losing the grandson who'd kept her functioning would be the death of her.

That wasn't going to happen.

"Hey, Usain Bolt, slow down. Some of us like to breathe occasionally."

"You go in front," he said, hanging to the left to let her pass. He stared at the back of her head, forbidding his gaze from trailing down her body again. He hadn't even looked at a woman that way since Simone. Their relationship had been a failed experiment, and that part of him had died with her. Or so he'd thought.

After his upbringing, he should have known better than to drag anyone into the twisted debris of his life. Not only had he dragged a woman into it, but a child, too. He wouldn't let it happen again. He'd rescue Theo, then spend the rest of his life doing nothing but protecting him—even if it meant disappearing with him and leaving behind the Legion and Simone's family. He might never be able to show Theo the love his mother had, but he could keep the boy safe, which was more than Rafe's own parents had been able to do.

He frowned. But a kernel of hope was still buried deep in his chest—that he could placate Gabriel, that Theo could return to Simone's family, where the boy was safe and loved, and Rafe could go back to the Legion, where he could do the most good—and the least harm. Was he deceiving himself?

He settled into the heiress's pace. She wasn't tall, but her strong, regular stride was comfortable enough to follow. As they ran, she seemed to relax, as if she was equally relieved to do something physical.

The trail was reasonably clear, at least. Whoever owned the island must employ someone to keep nature from reclaiming it, though gnarled tree roots snaked across at intervals. Intended more for romantic strolling than hard running, no doubt. The jungle smelled of overripe fruit, rotting leaves, rich dirt. Nothing like the deserts and plains he'd grown up in. He closed his mouth, breathing solely through his nose to let the scent wash through him, as if it could clean the muck from his brain.

The jungle eased out into a clearing. Laura bent double and clutched her thighs. He hurriedly pulled focus from the bottom of her shorts, which had ridden up almost to her butt cheeks. *Merde.*

"I need a rest," she panted.

"We've just started." He lowered the bag to the ground. "Two minutes. Have a drink."

As she recovered, he dropped to the dirt and started push-ups, willing his muscles to burn, keeping a silent count in French. A couple of hundred followed by the same in *abdominaux* at the next stop would make up for the leisurely jog.

"You're a freak," she said, still breathless.

You have no idea.

Holly's damn eyes wouldn't stop staring. It was an anatomy lesson, at the least. Muscles pumped and rippled across Jack's slick back like some kind of hydraulic machine. His biceps looked like they would burst like balloons, though he was jerking up and down so quickly she struggled to get a fix on him without bobbing her own head in time. Two greenish stones swung from leather cords around his neck, bouncing against his chest.

Just watching was exhausting. She stretched her arm in front of her and bent back her hand to ease the ache in her forearm. What was that from—holding onto the inflatable last night? Wow, this time yesterday she'd been sailing across the ocean, congratulating herself that for once something good had happened to her, and now she was on a deserted island with He-Man. One day this would be a story for her grandchildren.

Grandchildren. Hardly. She'd have to have children first, and no child deserved to share her life. And given that the only man she'd been stupid enough to love had used and betrayed her, she wasn't gagging to start dating. Loneliness was a small price to pay for safety and freedom.

No, she'd stick to her plan, pirate kidnapping or not. In the new life she'd create, she wouldn't be trailer trash fresh out of prison. Hell, she might even shave some numbers off her age— wipe away the lost years. She'd rent a cabin by the sea twenty miles from Nowheresville and live like a hermit. She'd find an honest job to pay the bills, and spend her free time fishing and sailing and watching movies, needing no one else to make her happy, and letting no one ruin that happiness.

Finally—finally—the *capitaine* sprang to his feet, barely sweating. She might as well be showering in hers. The air was so thick you could almost grab a handful and squeeze out the water, like a sponge. So much for the seduction act. She felt as sexy as a slug.

"After you," he said, zipping up the bag.

He wasn't even having a drink? She'd sunk half a bottle. She set out on the trail, scanning the path for snakes. He was military, no doubt, but not here in an official capacity—she'd seen no gun, he wore no uniform. A mercenary? Maybe he was part of some international security company, the kind former soldiers joined to earn big money.

There was at least one thing that might tempt a man like that to defy orders. If she enticed him to break a few rules, would his tight self-control begin to disintegrate? Sometimes, picking at a fraying end could loosen an impossible knot.

Determined as she was to leave her old skill set behind, right now it was her only weapon. Her idea of lighting a bonfire on the beach last night had come to nothing when she'd failed to find matches or a lighter. Besides, she'd fallen into a deep sleep while waiting for him to doze off, and had woken well after dawn—her best sleep in months. She'd felt oddly secure with him on guard. How dumb was that?

Throwing herself at him would be too obvious. The men she'd seduced on the job had either been so unaccustomed to female attention they couldn't resist, or so arrogant they didn't question it. Jack wasn't arrogant or insecure. His confidence came from deep within, but he had troubles down there, too. And with troubles came weaknesses.

The path began to climb. After a few minutes her breath became ragged. The canopy lightened up and the air temperature seemed to surge with each step. She slowed to a walk, clutching her sides.

"I'm done."

"Good timing." He gestured to a rustic park bench, just off the path.

"You think of everything."

As she stumbled over the crest of the hill, the lagoon spread out below them, a pool of turquoise spilling into a mass of liquid sapphire.

"Wow," she breathed. "You really do think of everything."

"Sit," he said. "Drink. Eat."

He unzipped the bag and handed her water and a nut bar. As she unwrapped it, he glugged from his bottle, then scuffed around on a patch of long grass behind the bench.

He met her quizzical look. "Checking for snakes."

Evidently satisfied, he dropped, rolled onto his back and tucked into swift, noiseless stomach crunches. Oh, good grief. She pried her eyes away from his abs and gratefully flopped onto the seat, sucking in the sea view instead. The line marking the horizon was fuzzier than it used to be—her eyesight had shortened in prison. Too much time staring at cinder-block walls.

She bit into the nut bar. Maybe she could seek out a spot like this in her new life and live on fish and freedom. People just brought problems—especially people with washboard stomachs.

After Jack had done about a thousand sit-ups, he sat on the other end of the seat, the musky scent of dirt and exertion wafting from him. She sneakily inhaled. What was she, a cave woman?

"You know you don't have to impress me, right?"

He scoffed. "I don't want to impress you. I just want to watch you. I mean, *need* to watch you." She raised her eyebrow. "*Guard* you." He clenched his fists.

Oh yeah, that armor was chinking. "Looks to me like you're punishing yourself. Guilty conscience?"

"I'm keeping fit."

"It's more than that." She knew that urge for physical oblivion. In prison, hard exercise was the only thing that had blotted out the anger. She'd run around the yard until she was emptied of everything—every thought, every regret—counting her steps to stop herself from thinking, like a meditation. "You've got issues."

"Only Americans talk about 'issues.' The rest of us just call it life."

"You kidnapped the daughter of one of the most powerful men in America. I'm thinking your *issues* are bigger than most."

He studied her. Flecks of caramel swam in his chocolate irises. "And you've been captured by a bloodthirsty pirate. Also not the kind of problem normal people face."

"Ever met a normal person?"

"I married a normal person."

His bitter tone suggested he was no longer married. Nothing on his ring finger, and no band of pale skin. "How'd that work out for you?"

He shrugged, and turned to the view. His profile was so finely etched she had an urge to sketch him—and she couldn't draw a passable stick figure.

"She have trouble dealing with the whole pirate thing? Wanted you to settle down, take a nine-to-five job, get a regular paycheck, take the kids to their ball games instead of going marauding with your wooden-legged pirate pals?"

His jaw set in stone. He stood. "Break's over."

Okay, that had struck a nerve. Was it regret that brought the hard edge to his eye, or anger? It didn't look like heartbreak. She sipped her water. Maybe he did have kids who played sports on Saturdays. What would make a seemingly decent guy—a guy some woman had loved—do something like this? And what would trigger him to lose his nerve and let Holly go? She pushed up to standing. Press the right buttons in the right order and she might just find out.

The path curled into the jungle and narrowed. As she ran, leaves brushed her arms, and the air filled with rustling and scratching. She hadn't had much use for trail running in California, but she'd imagined dusty, quiet paths. Here, it felt like a million insects and other writhing creatures were hyped up and waiting for the signal to swarm her.

Behind her, Jack's boots pounded a rhythm that matched her footfalls. How long did she have to get to the bottom of him, before the ruse was blown? And what would he do then—kill her? She had to start with dissolving some of the tension between them—or, even better, cranking it up.

A force wrapped around her stomach, yanking her backward. She squealed. Jack's arms were circling her, lifting her off her feet, his hot chest hard up against her back. Her nerves buzzed, even as her heart pummeled.

"Watch where you're going, princess," he growled.

He eased her down, his hands coming to rest either side of her waist. A web hung across the path, with a fist-sized spider in the middle, its hairy legs raised to strike. Her cheeks prickled. Another step and it would have sunk into her right eye.

"Is that dangerous?" she squeaked.

"Wouldn't have killed you, but its bite hurts like death. And you don't want to risk an infection out here."

She exhaled, trying to force her body to relax. Between the sudden stop, the spider and the body contact, little explosions were spreading through her nerves. They skirted around the tree the web was strung from, Jack keeping a hand on her side until they were clear.

"Drink," he ordered, handing her a fresh bottle.

She took it blindly.

"Come on, princess. You can fight off two six-foot pirates, but a little spider scares you?"

Oh, she'd pretty well forgotten the spider—not so much the shock of Jack's body smacking into hers. That body was the far bigger danger, in all sorts of ways. She forced down a mouthful of water and handed back the bottle.

"You go first," he said. "And concentrate. It might be a snake next time, and I'd rather not be sucking venom out of you."

Whoa. Lucky her face was already about as pink as it got, because *that*... Damn, who was seducing who here?

After another few steps the foliage cleared. They were on a cliff top, overlooking a sparkling cove nestled between steep bluffs. A boat was moored in it, close enough to make out the faces of the three Asian men aboard. One looked up, straight at her. Holy shit, this was her chance. She inhaled, ready to scream.

CHAPTER

7

Jack spun Holly and captured her in a bruising kiss, his hands pinning her neck. Laughter floated up from the boat. He was making them look like the honeymooners they were supposed to be.

She scratched at his back and kicked out, but he drove her backward. Her spine hit a tree, the shock spinning out through her torso. He flattened her, one arm pinning her right elbow to her side and enclosing her left wrist, immobilizing her upper body, while his other huge hand held her head in place like a neck brace. His eyes were focused on the boat below them, scoping out the men.

If he could play dirty, so could she. She drove her knee toward his groin but he turned his hip, deflecting it. He hooked a foot around her calf and captured it, leaving her balanced on one leg. She tried to wriggle, but she was stuck to him like glue. Her lungs stung. With her one free hand she clawed his waist, regretting her stubby fingernails. His skin flinched but he held firm.

She bit his lip, hard. He grunted. Warm metallic liquid seeped into her mouth. He pushed against her lips until she could do nothing but concentrate on inhaling desperately through her nose. His eyes were so close to hers, so fierce, that she shut her own. The spicy, sweaty scent of him mixed with the ripe aroma of the jungle and the fresh hit of sea air. She felt woozy, like she would pass out.

An outboard motor spat and blatted into life. Damn. The

sound crescendoed, then faded, and still Jack kept her pinned. As disappointment coursed through her, her muscles relaxed. She became aware of his strength and heat, his hips driven into her, his arm flattening her breasts, his hand cradling her throat. She couldn't move, but he wasn't hurting her. *Fight me, and I will win*. No shit.

Okay, Capitaine, *you win this battle. But I'll win the war.* She inhaled deeply through her nose, softened her lips against his, sinking into him, returning the kiss as she flattened her palm onto his hip, her fingers splayed over thick, tight muscles. Time she seized some control.

The rattle of the boat became hard to discern. Abruptly, he stumbled back, wiping blood from his lip. She slid down the tree trunk to the ground, panting.

His dark eyes were on fire. "Not the kind of men you want to attract, princess."

"And you are?" She could barely spit out the words.

"Remember how I threatened to hurt you? I might show mercy. These men? They wouldn't."

"Who were they?"

"Pirates. The real thing."

"How do you know that?"

"You see any fishing rods? Around here, the locals don't go boating for pleasure. Especially not with an AK-47. My guess is they were scoping us out."

Her eyes widened. A gun? "Can they get onto the island?"

"If they've got this close in a boat that small, they're familiar with the currents and reefs. But the only place to land anything bigger than a surfboard is the lagoon right on high tide, and the entrance to it is dangerous. And they've lost the element of surprise."

"I thought you said this was a honeymoon island? Being kidnapped by pirates isn't my idea of romance. No offense."

"Usually they post armed guards here. We waived it."

"*We?* Who's 'we'?"

He pressed his lips together. They were flushed dark red, with a crack of scarlet where she'd bitten him. She licked her own lips, tangy with his blood. So now she was a *vampire* cavewoman?

"We need to be vigilant. If they've figured out we have no security guards, they may come back." Parallel lines stamped into the skin between his eyes. "Let's keep running. I want to get around the island to check they're gone, before it gets too hot."

Sweat trickled down her cleavage. The air got hotter than this? He strode up and swung a hand at her. She flinched, shielding her head, her pulse racing.

Silence. The blow didn't come.

She shut her eyes tight. *Idiot. Of course it didn't.*

"I'm not going to hit you, princess, just help you up."

"Oh, right." She swallowed as she uncurled and took his outstretched hand, willing hers not to shake. The kiss had thrown her off balance, that was all. He lifted her, so effortlessly she felt weightless.

"For the record, I wouldn't strike a woman, or force myself on one." He didn't release her hand right away, just held her there, her face inches from his collarbone, his breath grazing her hair. "That was a unique situation."

She lifted her chin. *Seize some control.* It brought their faces awkwardly close, but she squared her focus on his eyes. His expression was so serious she was at risk of melting. She smiled, slyly, ignoring the dart of guilt over milking his concern. "I thought you couldn't care less about returning me in one piece."

He lowered his brow, glowering. "Depends how well you behave."

And if *she* was playing *him*, why did that look make her heart skip like a stone across a pond?

They ran for another half hour, far enough around the island to satisfy Rafe that the pirates were gone, for now. He concentrated on following Laura's stride, holding himself back as the track descended to their drop zone then looped toward the lagoon. *You're punishing yourself*, she'd said. Maybe so. All he knew for sure was that he could lose himself in physical exertion, the same way he used to lose himself in sex.

Sex. Holding Laura against that tree, his body had begged to mutiny and seek that escape again. If the perfume she hawked in those ads was anything near as intoxicating as her own scent, the men of America were in trouble. What did she call it? Laura Hyland—Spark, or something.

"Pick up the pace, princess," he said. This was the price of easy running—thoughts found a way in.

Laura stumbled on a root. He shot out a hand and grabbed her arm. She shook it off and kept running. He'd expected a far more fragile woman than this. She was way out of her comfort zone, with her life in danger, and yet strength radiated from her. It fed into every word she spoke, her every gesture—as if she expected the worst from life and knew how to twist it to her advantage. How did her breeding prepare her for that?

But she'd flinched when he'd gone to pull her up. He knew that instinct—as did everyone who'd known violence too well as a child.

His gaze wandered up her body, lithe and relaxed, the muscles in her legs clenching rhythmically with her easy stride. She'd known fear. At whose hands—Logan's, her father's or Jasper's, whoever he was? Fear had created the tough shell around her. And what was underneath? Whenever she met his gaze, it was unflinching. Until that moment, she hadn't let down her guard, her wit hadn't wavered. A sharp brain inside a goddess's body.

He forced his eyes away, focusing over her head onto the path in front. Too much time and energy to think, that was his problem. And his lack of backup was eating him up. For now, he had no choice but to go along with Gabriel's plan. In the meantime, he'd figure out just what Laura's game was, and what kind of threat it posed. Recon and surveillance. Not his preferred mission, but if it kept him out of a flag-draped box…

He sprinted the last fifty meters to the villa, passing Laura as she jogged to a halt. He brought them each a can of cola from the fridge.

Her cheeks were crimson and she clutched her side. Maybe he shouldn't have forced someone who wasn't used to hard running to go that far, in the heat. He could go again, twice.

She opened the can, took a swig and planted it on a picnic table on the lawn. "What I really need is a swim." She slipped off her shoes, hopping, already heading to the water. "Coming? Or are you scared of sharks—or rock fish?" Her shorts and tank followed, leaving just her underwear, transparent from sweat. Lucky he only had her back to contend with.

"Stone fish," he corrected, numbly. Oh yeah, he could do with a whole lot of cold water right now.

She walked in ahead of him, her curves swaying against the pull of the water, then dived, her round *derrière* popping up for an instant before it disappeared. He strode in up to his chest, before she could surface and see the effect she was having on his body. The run had charged him up, that was all—and one part of him in particular was refusing to forget their encounter on the cliff. He prided himself on professionalism, so what in hell was going on there?

She broke the clear film of water and stood, facing him. She might as well not be wearing a bra. He could use more of that cola, but no way could he get out now. She splashed him. "Loosen up, Capitaine."

"You're supposed to be afraid of me."

She splashed him again. He half expected the water to sizzle as it hit his body. "Is that in the pirate rule book?" She stroked lazily past him, the water skimming her back, her hips, her ass, her legs. "Look, it's obvious that for some reason you're as happy to be here as I am. This battle isn't between the two of us, is it? So relax."

So that was it. She wasn't afraid because she was waiting—expecting—to be bailed out. Was that what life with money and power was like—Daddy would bail you out of any situation, even a kidnapping? That accounted for her nonchalance, if not the other intriguing questions he wanted answers to. *Okay, mademoiselle, I'll play along.* He splashed her back and she grinned, her eyes gleaming as blue as the water.

He dived, the cool hit a tonic for his edginess. As he surfaced his lip stung where she'd bitten it. He touched it. No more blood. It'd been torture to ram his body against hers for so long, to press his lips to hers, having already wondered what that would feel like.

"I gave you a pretty good fat lip," she said, twisting and sliding around him like a seal. "I'd say sorry, but it's kinda part of the deal."

He shrugged. "It was a smart move."

"It didn't work."

"Of course it didn't."

"Race you to the jetty."

She duck-dived and pulled away with the same languid strokes he'd watched that morning. He was surprised she still had energy for it. He powered through the silky water. As he neared, she upped her stroke rate. He matched it, and put on a surge of his own, glad to stretch a different set of muscles. Tension dissolved from his chest for the first time in days. They sure looked like a couple of carefree newlyweds.

They reached the end of the jetty together. "Check out the fish," she gasped, treading water.

A school of angel fish flitted under their feet, with parrot fish circling farther down. The water was clear as vodka right to the grains of sand far below, a break in the coral that bloomed and swayed around them. Yep, it was goddamn beautiful. *She* was goddamn beautiful.

"Oh, look!" She touched his shoulder. "Turtle!"

He dived out of her reach, eyes stinging against the salty water, and surfaced several meters away. Turtles. Theo was crazy about turtles.

And Rafe was just plain crazy. *This* was crazy. *Tu agis sans passion.* What the hell kind of game was he playing? He needed time out—from her.

"Do you think there's snorkel gear?" she said. "I've love a closer look."

"You know this isn't really a honeymoon?"

"Are you always this dour?"

"I'm heading in. I need to eat." *And get my head straight.*

"I'll stay out for a bit. Save some for me, *honey.*"

Damn. She'd struck out.

Holly starfished in the water, eyes closed against the high sun, her body rising and falling with the lagoon's gentle swell. If only the movement would unknot her stomach. Just when she thought she was gaining ground, he'd pulled away.

Where could she get some of his self-control? Even in the water her body throbbed, from the run, and from the shock of feeling nearly every muscle in his body taut against her—and he seemed to have more muscles than regular people. She sure was screwed if she got charged up at an encounter like that. Normal people didn't react like that, did they?

Normal. Whatever that was. He'd been married to a "normal" woman, was possibly still not over her. Maybe Holly just couldn't compete with normal.

She swam for another twenty minutes, to collect herself and for the sheer chest-bursting liberty of it, then breaststroked to shore, her stomach still swirling.

Under a tree on the clipped lawn, he'd set the picnic table

with the kind of food she'd forgotten existed. He sat on the bench seat with his back to the table, facing the ocean, wearing shorts and a deep blue T-shirt, one leg folded across the other. Wet clothes hung from a rope he'd strung up between two palm trees. He'd done laundry?

After a cursory glance her way, he reached for a towel that was draped over the seat, and tossed it to her. She took the hint, and wrapped it around her torso. Crap, her underwear didn't leave much to the imagination. She hadn't meant to be *that* obvious. Maybe she'd pushed it too far, too soon. They had a few days on the island, he'd said. A few days to take his defenses from rock to Play-Doh.

If the ransom was paid, she could go on her way without him being any wiser to her deception. If not, she wanted him on her side when the shit went down. Maybe then, she could come clean. In the meantime she was safer to play princess and hope for the best.

"You shouldn't have," she said, shoving her hair into what she hoped was a sleek style.

"You were right," he said, raising a glass of juice. "We may as well make the most of a bad situation. Cheers."

She poured herself a juice and sat at the other end of the bench. Hmm. Just what did he mean by that? A bird plummeted into the water, a flash of orange and electric blue.

"Salute," she said. "Or is it *santé*?" High school French hadn't covered drinking etiquette.

He cocked his head, frowning.

"You speak French when you're surprised. Or turned on." She swiveled to focus on the food as heat rose up her face. What was that about? She never blushed, especially when she was on the job. Had to be the air temperature. "Are you French?"

"Uh." He uncrossed and crossed his legs.

Stifling a triumphant smile, she began to assemble a sandwich—ham, lettuce, tomato, olives. Anything basic and relatively fresh made her drool like a mastiff after prison food.

"*Are* you French, Jack? I can't pick your accent. And I swear your English is better than mine."

He swallowed, his Adam's apple rising and dipping. "I'm a lot of things, and nothing. If I was a dog, I'd be a stray mongrel."

Just like her. "Guess that makes me a prize Chihuahua."

The bench shook with his laughter, deep and throaty, and only half-bitter. It did gooey things to her stomach. Man, that was so wrong.

"Pampered but scrappy as hell," he said.

"That's me." Half the truth, at least.

"Your foot—it's bleeding."

"Really?" Blood trailed from the arch of her foot, mixing with water and grains of sand. "It's nothing. You should have seen what I did to the shark."

He raised one eyebrow.

"I cut myself on the coral. No big deal."

His forehead crinkled. "We need to wash it. Coral carries dangerous bacteria and toxins. And in the tropics the last thing you want is an infection. I'll find a first-aid kit." He disappeared into the cabin.

She bit into her sandwich, closed her eyes and tilted her head back. The sea washed in and out, the breeze teased her face. No matter what became of her in the next week, at least she'd had the simple pleasure of this moment. In prison right now she'd be lying sleepless on her bed, trying to zone out the unvarying soundtrack of cries, groans and jeers of the other inmates. If the senator's people hadn't approached her, she'd be fighting a bunch of other homeless people for a spot under a freeway bridge. Here there were goddamn frangipanis. There were worse places to die—not that she planned to.

We may as well make the most of a bad situation.

Yep. They might as well.

CHAPTER

8

After a couple of minutes Jack's footsteps trailed back from the cabin. "You're not supposed to be enjoying this."

Holly opened her eyes. He stood over her, a wry half smile imprinting a dimple in his cheek. A pirate with a dimple—who'd have thought? "You're in my sun."

"Sorry, your highness."

He settled on the grass in front of her feet, his long legs sprawled, with a bowl of water and first-aid kit beside him. Crap—he intended to play doctor?

She pulled her foot under the bench. "I can do it."

"You eat. I like having something to do with my hands. Doing nothing drives me crazy."

She blew out a breath. When was the last time she'd willingly let a man touch her? An hour or two ago, he'd pinned her to a tree. She could let him clean a stupid cut. Laura would have no problem with someone worshiping at her feet—and it was a chance to get close to him, maybe draw him out.

"Come on, I won't bite," he said.

The run and swim sure had relaxed him. She inched her foot forward. He grabbed the heel and pulled it onto his knee. Awareness reverberated up her leg and pooled in a part of her that hadn't seen action in a long time.

"Doesn't look too bad," he said, all business. "But I'll give it a thorough clean."

He poured a cloudy liquid into the bowl and directed her foot into it. It was as warm as the air surrounding them.

"This might hurt." With a piece of gauze, he gently brushed over the wound.

She flinched.

"Painful?"

"Ticklish," she said, through a mouthful of baguette. Thank God boredom had prompted her to raid Laura's bathroom supplies on her last layover and wax her legs and paint her toenails, for the first time in six years.

"Suck it up, princess. The guy who taught me to do this ordered us to spend a good ten minutes cleaning coral wounds."

"Is first aid something you were taught in the military?"

He froze. Dark eyes flicked up to meet hers. Bingo.

"Don't look so scared," she said. "It's obvious you're some kind of military man—you don't smell bad enough to be a real pirate. I won't tell, I promise. But I can't help wondering how you got caught up in all of this."

"If I told you I'd have to kill you. In fact, I'd have to kill *me*."

"I'm not asking for name, rank and serial number. Just a, 'Once upon a time there was a nice young pirate called Jack...'"

"Consider ignorance your ticket to freedom."

"Consider disclosure your insurance."

"What does that mean?"

"Ever thought about what might happen if they catch you? If you're nice to me, maybe I'll lie and say you weren't involved in the kidnap. That you rescued me and saved me from a shark and a horde of pirates—and from death by coral."

"It's not going to happen like that."

"How can you be so sure? Maybe those men today recognized me."

"If they did, they won't be putting in a call to your daddy—they'll be back here later to steal my captive and take the ransom for themselves."

"You don't really think that's a possibility?"

"I'm trained to think in possibilities."

"Then why don't you have a gun? Or a phone? I don't get why we're unprotected."

"You fed the protection to the sharks, remember?"

"Only one of them."

He tightened his grip on her foot.

"Ouch," she said.

"Meaning?"

"As far as I can tell, it was in your best interests to lose those guys as much as mine."

"Shoving a guy into a shark's mouth isn't my style. He tripped." He scraped the wound, too hard. She bit her gums. "And we're not unprotected. I'd bet on you against a shipful of pirates. Where did a rich girl learn to fight like that?"

"I'll tell you something about me if you tell me something about you."

"I don't play games, or make bargains."

"I'll go first, then. So I like to be able to take care of myself—maybe because I've been so protected. It's empowering to know you've got your own back."

She'd finished her sandwich and was wiping her hands by the time he responded.

"How did you learn?" He sounded pissed, like he was being forced to ask the question, like he itched to know but was reluctant to risk starting a real conversation. She'd have to take her time with it, draw him slowly into her confidence.

"Just picked stuff up, I guess. My father's bodyguards gave me pointers. I think they enjoyed it."

"I bet they did. Did your father stop beating you after that?"

"What?" Her cheeks chilled.

"Your father. Did he stop hitting you once you learned how to fight back? Or was it Jasper who did the beating?"

She swallowed. "What are you talking about?"

"When we were up on the cliff you flinched when I approached to help you up, tried to hide yourself. Someone's hurt you, in your past. Repeatedly."

"I was scared of you. What did you expect?"

"Scared of me? If only that were true. I don't think much scares you at all. No. It was more than that. It came from within."

"What are you, a psychiatrist?"

"I've learned a few things about how the mind works. Who was it?"

He settled into a rhythm of slow strokes over the arch of her foot. She forced her leg to relax, in case he could feel her tension. If he could see through that much of her facade, what else had he picked up on? She hadn't given him enough credit. Rookie mistake. She took a swig of juice, stalling. This was meant to be about drawing him out, not her.

But you had to give something to get something back, right? Maybe if she opened up, gave him as close a version to the truth as she could without giving the game away, he'd start to give a damn about her.

He didn't press her, just continued brushing the wound, firing tingles up her legs with every stroke. She sure could use a topic of conversation that took her mind off his touch.

"My father. He'd get drunk, and start accusing me of all sorts of stuff. I think he genuinely thought he had to beat the evil out of me. His parents—" She gulped back the words. Jack had done his research on Laura. She couldn't claim the senator's parents were crazed religious zealots, like her grandparents. They were probably upstanding regular Baptists. She fought to remember details of Laura's life, gleaned from the same internet sources Jack might have seen. "My mother died when I was a baby, and I guess he took her death harder than he wanted to admit."

"Is he still violent?"

"No, not to me. Not to anyone, as far as I know."

"Not since you learned to fight back?"

"Something like that."

"Tell me about that."

How far should she take this? He was skating dangerously near the truth of her. But he was also looking at her differently—like an ally, not a princess. "I've never talked to anyone about this before, except my shrink." That, at least, was true. He didn't need to know it was a prison shrink.

"Who better to tell than someone you won't see again after this week?"

She released a shuddering breath. "Okay… I was about fourteen, but small for my age. I used to hang out a lot in the gym at school, trying to stay away from home—before school, after school. I'd join in with the wrestling team, the boxing team, try some martial arts. Picked up something from all of them. I learned to use momentum and accuracy to make up for what I lacked in body mass, learned the strongest parts on a woman's body and the weakest parts on a man's, learned that the body only moves in certain directions—reverse those and you cause pain. Simple, really." She left out the no-holds-barred fight club. Laura's private high school probably hadn't had one of those. "My fighting style was never very pretty—I wouldn't have won any competitions, but I wasn't in it for that. It was unpredictable, at least."

"That's a good strength. Didn't your father wonder where you where?"

"He was too preoccupied with his…political ambitions to notice. He thought I was in dance class." She grinned. Nice touch. Truth was, her parents had never cared where she was, as long as she wasn't asking anything of them, or cramping their drinking habits. They only wanted her around for the welfare checks.

"I waited about a year," she continued, "taking the beatings, keeping myself sane and strong by imagining myself rising up to him, imagining what I'd do to him. Stupid, really—it got to the point I was taking on guys much bigger and stronger than him in the ring, and slaying them, but I just had this block when it came to my dad. I was serving up the beatings out of the house, and meekly taking them at home. I was scared that if I took him on before I was ready he'd bash the life out of me, literally. I had it in my head that I needed to be unbeatable by the time I took him on, so I'd train and train till my knuckles bled." She clenched and unclenched her fists. "Pretty sure I broke a few bones in my feet, too. Kids at school started calling me Trinity. I kinda liked it."

He frowned.

"You've never seen *The Matrix*?" she said.

"What's that—a movie?"

"Are you even of my generation? You've got to see *The Matrix*. Trinity's this kick-ass girl fighter."

"I'll put it on my must-see list," he said, drily. "What tipped you over the edge?"

"One night he came after me, worse than before, because this time he had something else on his mind. Like he'd suddenly realized I wasn't a kid anymore, and there were whole other ways he could use me." She rubbed her palms into her eyes. Crap. She'd gone too far—forgotten she was playing a role. Accusing a senator of *that* put her in dangerous territory, even if there was no one Jack could tell.

"You don't have to go into details. I just want to know what you did to the bastard." Jack's jaw was set, his eyes glimmering dangerously, like he hated her father as much as she had, like he was right there with her in the cramped living room of her childhood home. If only.

"This goes no further, right?"

"Of course."

She swallowed. "I just let him have it, like this thing that had been building up inside me for all those years just…exploded. I used everything on him—punched and pounded and kicked and scratched and—" Pain cut into her palms. She released her fists. She'd been clenching them, driving her fingernails nearly through the skin. "And he was so shocked he balled up in a corner and cried. And I just kept on going. Until suddenly I got it. I got it that..."

"That what?"

That the same thing had happened to him when he was a kid, and in that moment he'd gone back there. That I was beating up on someone who was just like me. "That it was over. That he'd never do it to me again. That he was just a coward who'd been picking on an easy target, and I wasn't his punching bag anymore."

"Why didn't you tell anyone? You grew up in America— don't they have laws?"

She scoffed. Laws didn't do a lot to protect poor kids from abusive parents. Everyone was too busy just surviving to get involved in other people's business, and those who were paid to care didn't have enough time or money to get around to everyone. Half the time kids were given straight back to their abusers—she'd seen it a dozen times.

But she'd survived. That day, she'd walked out for good, sick to the stomach about how exhilarating it'd felt to be the person dishing out the violence. Not long after she'd started living on the streets, her boxing coach had become concerned at the anger she was pouring into her training, and suspicious of her dirty appearance at school, and had taken her down to his sister's sailing club to learn a less-confrontational way to let off steam. For three years she'd lived in an attic above the club rooms, earning her keep by maintaining boats after school, waiting tables and, eventually, teaching kids to sail. She got a sailing scholarship to college.

And then she met Jasper, and was so shocked to get so much apparent affection from another human being that she dropped out. He'd figured out from the beginning she'd do anything to earn the crumbs he threw. He'd recognized her straight away for the damaged, cowering child she'd been, just like Jack had up there on the cliff, and had spent four years exploiting it. Jack wouldn't do that.

Right. Because she knew him so well.

"Laura?"

"Huh?" She blinked the moisture from her eyes. "Did you say something?"

"How is it you can go campaigning for him, now? Why would you wish a man like that on a whole country?"

Her mind whirred. Good point. She'd gone too far. *Shut up about yourself and channel Laura. This is all an act, remember?* "I think he regrets it. I think in the end the experience made him a better man, more aware of his weaknesses, more empathetic. That moment I turned on him, it changed him. He repented and apologized, and has spent the last decade or more making up for it. People can change." Like hell. She'd seen her parents once since she'd left home, in the street, and they'd called her the kind of names she bet Laura's privileged ears had only heard in an R-rated movie. "And he's terrified of me turning against him, going public with the truth. He never says no to me any-more. What I want, I get—like this trip."

In fact, as far as Holly could tell, the real Laura had practically blackmailed her father to indulge her whim to sail around the world, when her only experience of sailing was on a mechanized luxury yacht with a skipper—and probably a cocktail waiter. After he'd forbidden her, she'd announced her plans publicly, in a joint press conference with the grateful environmental char-ity she'd chosen to patronize. Hamstrung—and aware she was bringing good publicity to his planned presidential run—he'd folded, on the condition they find someone to secretly sail the dangerous parts.

And imagine his relief, now. He could cut Holly loose, know-ing he'd left no paper trail, and the story was too far-fetched for the media or authorities to believe, should she approach them.

Still, he had an awkward problem on his hands, with his

daughter's kidnapping broadcast live on the internet. Maybe the truth had already come out and Jack was the only one who didn't know it yet.

He leaned back, supporting himself with one hand on the grass, cradling her foot with the other. Turned out she liked the contact, dammit, and not just because it fit her plans. It felt good to have someone touch her in a way that suggested he cared— even if only because he needed to keep her alive for his own reasons. Her body was happy to take what it could get. Didn't mean her mind had to buy into it.

"It's not something you can escape that easily," he said to her foot, so gently it made something ping inside her chest. No one spoke to her like that. "It's still inside you, still eating at you. As tough as you get, inside you're still that beaten puppy."

How the hell could he read her that clearly? Unless… She tilted her head. "We're not just talking about me here, are we?"

His eyes flicked back to find hers, fine brown lines bunching at his temples. For the first time he looked less than impenetrable. That was encouraging.

"I showed you mine," she ventured, softly. "Did your parents give you hell, too?"

He frowned, his gaze barreling into hers for a full minute. A pair of dragonflies shimmered and shot through the air between them. She stayed quiet, setting her expression to neutral.

He broke eye contact, and gazed at the jungle bordering the clearing, slowly shaking his head. She guessed it wasn't the trees he was seeing. She didn't dare even breathe aloud.

"I don't remember my parents, don't know if I had brothers or sisters," he said, finally.

She silently filled her lungs. *Breakthrough.*

"We fled a civil war when I was a child and got separated, or so I was told. I figure they were killed. I got to a refugee camp, and became prey for whoever could find a use for me. I got involved in bad things."

Her heart twisted. Jesus. He'd been as vulnerable as she was when Jasper came into her life—so starved of love and company she didn't recognize when it came with a hidden agenda. And she'd been an adult, a nineteen-year-old who'd already seen too much. Jack had been just a boy. "What kind of things?"

"A good girl like you wouldn't want to know."

"But you became a good man. How?"

"Why would you think I'm a good man?" Bitterness darkened his voice. "I kidnapped you. I'm holding you for ransom."

"You're putting a dressing on my foot. It's kind of ruining the whole Captain Hook image."

He flinched and looked down at her foot, as if he'd forgotten. He let it go, and shuffled away.

She leaned back, her elbows on the table. "Or maybe you're just waiting for me to drop my guard and then you'll break out the nasty juice." Not far off what Jasper did. Right there was a good reminder to keep alert, no matter how gentle Jack had been just now.

"I'll do what?"

"You'll get mean."

"You'd better watch out, then." He jumped to his feet. The sun had moved around and she squinted up at his towering frame. "It's shower time, princess."

"What?" Heat struck her cheeks.

"For you." A smile played at his lips. "Alone. I'm not that kind of pirate, remember?"

"Of course not. I didn't think you were… I wasn't meaning…" For a split second there she'd totally imagined him naked and wet—and pressed against her. Good grief.

He laughed. "You need to wash off any remaining toxins."

Damn. He knew just what had been going through her mind. This seduction really was flowing the wrong way. "You need me out of the way for five minutes. Would this have anything to do with your secret hiding place for a certain sat phone and laptop?"

"Like you said, trust is an *issue* between us. I want to see the media chatter about your disappearance."

Crap.

"You've been looking for the comms, haven't you? Believe me, you won't find them. Bathroom." He pointed. "I'll clean this up. We'd be *crétins* to let this food spoil, and we don't want to attract vermin. A slow loris would literally kill for a leaf of spinach."

She hoisted and retucked her towel, stacked a bunch of plates in her arms and headed to the cabin, going easy on her foot. "There's something making you do this. Someone."

"Making me tidy up?"

"You know what I mean." She glanced over her shoulder. "You're not denying it."

"Let's just say it's in everybody's interests if everything goes to plan this week."

Which it wouldn't. No way was that ransom going to be paid. But surely a search would be launched, assuming the senator wouldn't just come clean and risk the political fallout.

Meanwhile, here they were, swimming in the lagoon, picnicking on the lawn, about to do the washing up and then some googling. Oh, God, what if the internet revealed that the real Laura was safe? She stumbled on the steps. He caught her elbow, as she steadied her load. Her towel gave. With no hands to spare, she could only let it slip to the ground.

"Don't worry, princess. I won't look." She stood to the side as he passed her on the narrow step, his chest brushing the damp lace covering one of her nipples. It immediately tightened, the traitor. She caught her breath.

"I don't know if I can handle it," she said, quickly. "Watching the coverage on the net, I mean."

At the screen door, he turned, an eyebrow raised. "I thought we'd established you're not the sensitive type."

She maneuvered her elbows to hide her body's absurd reaction. "I thought we established you weren't going to look."

He quickly turned, bending slightly as he battled to keep his own armload in control. Interesting. So maybe he did feel the chemistry between them. She'd feel better if it wasn't just her long-neglected hormones spinning out of control.

"Seriously," she said. "Can we not google?"

"Shower," he ordered huskily. "I'll tell you the highlights."

He disappeared into the cabin. She stood there, paralyzed. Damn. Could she distract him, invite him into the shower? No—too soon, too obvious, and it would just delay the inevitable, not prevent it. Surely, if the truth had been revealed on the internet, someone would have turned up to tell Jack by now—and possibly to kill her. She had to take a gamble that her cover was still intact, that the senator was still trying to figure out a course of action, that she still had time to drag Jack over to her side.

She'd know soon enough.

CHAPTER

9

Seated at the picnic table, Rafe connected the laptop and sat phone. He brushed a thread of spider silk from the phone battery and clipped it in. Laura would never think to look in rocks directly behind a web guarded by a hairy palm-sized spider. Even now, the creature would be recreating the broken strands. It'd do the same after he put the gear back shortly. Nature covering human tracks.

No response from Flynn. Not what he'd hoped for, but just as he'd expected.

He typed in *Laura Hyland* and *Jasper*. A few fan sites brought up random hits, but nothing that would indicate a boyfriend by that name. The woman had vulnerabilities from her childhood, so it would make sense for her to come under the spell of the wrong man. But she'd grown up in the public eye, and somehow the media had missed a boyfriend she was so obsessed with that she'd tattooed his name on her back and left it there the entire ten years she'd been with Logan? And somehow everyone had missed the fact her father had abused her? He tried *Laura Hyland* and *tattoo*. It brought up a hit on a fan who'd tattooed her face onto his shoulder. But nothing about Laura having a tattoo. She had to have been photographed in a bikini. How could no one have noticed?

He got up to the *b* of *Laura Hyland* and *bikini* when she emerged from the villa, dressed again in the too-short shorts and the blue tank that echoed her eyes. He hurriedly closed the page and opened a fresh one.

"Find anything?" There was a skip in her voice. Perhaps she *was* choked up at the thought of reading about her kidnapping. She was good at hiding her fear, but she had fear, all right.

"Just about to search."

The bench squeaked as she sat beside him. If he relaxed his knee a fraction it would touch her smooth thigh. He made a show of moving, as if getting comfortable, and settled farther from her. She shuffled closer. Damn. Her hair smelled of coconut.

"You're lead story on CNN," he said.

"So are you."

The top photo was a split frame—Laura on one side kneeing Uriel's face, in a fuzzy still from the yacht's above-deck webcam, and Rafe on the other, snapped as he sprinted across the deck in a blur of black clothing. His shoulders relaxed. They couldn't identify him from that.

"That was a nice move," he said.

She rubbed her knee. "I'm out of practice. Still feeling that one." Her posture had deflated a little, as if the coverage brought her relief, too. Was she flattered that her kidnapping was such a big deal? Twenty-four hours ago he'd have believed that of Laura Hyland, the vain publicity seeker. But he didn't believe it of the woman sitting far too close to him right now. That woman had her head on straight. *You can't believe everything you read*, she'd said. No kidding.

He scrolled through the story. The false trails Gabriel's men had laid were working—the official search was centered in the wrong place, assuming they'd escaped by boat alone. There'd been sightings of Laura in places he'd never heard of. No one was looking for a couple of newlyweds at a honeymoon resort a hundred kilometers from the kidnap site.

"You're quite the sensation," he said. "Candlelight vigils all over America."

Further down was the photo Gabriel's soldier had taken of Laura after the kidnap, blown out badly by the flash, and a picture of her at a glamorous function, her eyes ringed in her trademark dark makeup and her skin pale as paper.

"You look very different without makeup." He had an urge to touch the freckles scattered over her face. They didn't deserve to be hidden.

"Do I?" She touched her cheek, her forehead screwing up. She didn't know how beautiful she was? Had her father made her feel that worthless? Rafe couldn't abide any injustice, but an adult who tormented a child...

"I mean that in a good way."

"Oh."

"Your eyes look bluer without it. You look healthier. I'll never understand why beautiful women wear so much makeup." Simone would never leave the house without lipstick on, even when they were going windsurfing.

Her eyelashes flickered down. "It's a mask," she said, so quickly he could barely pick out the words. "You'd wear makeup, too, if photographers were outside your door 24/7."

"Would I?" he said, a smile pricking at the corner of his mouth.

"Well, maybe not you, but..." She grinned, the flirt returning. A cover for the hurt? "Plenty of men wear makeup."

"Another thing I don't get. Ready to scroll down?"

She nodded. A second later she stiffened. He read quickly, catching up. Her father had called a press conference and announced he wouldn't pay. *"America does not negotiate with terrorists. My baby girl will come home, alive, I promise you that. But these evildoers will not get their way. They will feel the full force of American justice."*

Great. So Rafe was a terrorist now, as well as a kidnapper

and pirate. A day earlier he might have felt a pang of pity for the senator—after all, Rafe was doing to him what Gabriel was doing to Rafe. But not now, not after Laura's confession.

"He's bluffing," Rafe said. "Governments will always deny they pay ransoms, to be seen to discourage other kidnappers. He'll be negotiating privately." He'd better be.

"You think?"

"Believe me, a father would do everything he could to get his son back."

"Son?"

Merde. "Daughter."

A beat of silence. "Holy shit, Jack. How old is he?"

"Who?" His chest tightened.

"Your son. They've got a hold over you, something big. I've been wondering what it is. Not your wife—she's out of your life—and you said you don't have other family. They've got your son."

"Enough." He shut down the laptop and switched off the phone. How could he make such a basic mistake? She was getting under his skin. He'd never let anyone in, not even Simone, to her endless frustration. So why did he feel as if he could spill his secrets to Laura, of all women?

He wasn't used to people showing an interest in him beyond what he could do with a gun. Maybe he'd spent too much time around legionnaires since Simone had died. In the Legion no one asked questions, no one gave a damn about where you were from or what you'd done in the past. Everyone had something to hide. When you joined, your history was wiped. That's why he fitted in, when he couldn't fit in to normal life.

"You've been blackmailed to do this—to kidnap me—haven't you? To get your son back."

"Get back in the bathroom," he said, shoving the equipment in a thick plastic bag, his back to her.

"What does it matter if I know this? In fact, isn't it better that I know this? It explains *a lot*."

"The less you know about me, the better. I can't afford to have my identity revealed."

"You're safe there. All I know is that your name is not Jack, you're not a pirate, you speak French and English and another language I can't identify, you're a captain in some military organization and you have a son."

Imbécile! He needed to shut his mouth. "Bathroom, now."

"Jack, maybe I can help, maybe we can work together. We don't have to be enemies."

He spun. "We are enemies, whether we want to be or not. The only way you can help is to do what I tell you." Big blue eyes blinked. He'd roared the words, lost control of himself. She held her stance strong, her gaze steady and glittering with defiance. If he stepped half a foot closer he could capture her pink lips, press her body against his once more, feel alive again, human again, wash away his fear for Theo and his anger for Gabriel and escape into this woman who played him and stood up to him and intrigued him and made him feel things he hadn't felt in a long time. "Bathroom, now," he repeated, his voice as dark and loaded as he felt.

She cocked her head, then silently turned and strolled to the villa, her spine straight as a legionnaire on parade. He exhaled. Wise woman.

Holly's heart thrummed as she closed the bathroom door and leaned on it. So that explained the haunted expression that occasionally flickered over Jack's face—his son had been dragged into this mess, and Jack was being forced to keep Holly captive. His silence was as good as written confirmation. What would happen to the boy when the senator didn't pay? What would happen to her, and to Jack?

Should she come clean to him? She jammed her fingers into

her hair. What would that achieve, besides making him even more worried about his son—and furious at her? He might seem honorable, but he was also trained to kill, and they were on opposite sides of this. She hadn't had much experience of fathers who loved their children, but Jack was evidently one of them. What would he do for that love?

She'd thought she was in love, once, and she would have done anything Jasper asked. She had, in fact—which had launched the chain of events that were likely to end with her death on this false Eden, wherever the hell it was. And even if Jack didn't kill her, someone else from the gang behind the kidnapping likely would.

Keep it together. For now, at least, her identity was safe, going by the media coverage. It wasn't over yet. And she was getting somewhere in her strategy. She'd seen Jack's desire, she'd felt his anger as she'd related the story of her father, she'd sensed his competing urges. Just how far was she prepared to take this?

She'd done plenty more shameful things to survive. He'd said it himself: *we are enemies, whether we want to be or not.* One more con, and never again. There had to be a better life waiting on the other side of this—she just needed to figure out how to get there, alive. She owed him nothing—less than nothing.

She dragged her fingers through her scalp to her neck, unleashing the smell of coconut, a carefree scent at odds with the danger her life was in. Man, this would be so much easier if she despised him. Trouble was, she was beginning to admire more about him than just that goddamn Renaissance statue of a body.

She of all people should know that falling for the wrong man left a woman vulnerable. Perhaps it wasn't such a good idea to mine information from him. When he'd let slip the danger his son was in, she'd had to shut down her urge to reach out to him, to remind herself that she was playing a dangerous role and he was her adversary, no matter how much pain he was in. She'd always had a weakness for another underdog—growing up, on the streets, in prison. Top dogs, not so much.

Could she outright seduce him, to turn him from enemy to ally? That's what Jasper would tell her to do. If she'd learned one thing from him—the hard way ultimately—it was survival at any cost.

She sure wouldn't have to fake her desire for Jack. Pretending to him that she felt something would be easy. Pretending to herself that she didn't? That was a whole other story.

For Rafe, the afternoon passed painfully. Without a weapon to constantly clean and maintain, his fingers itched to be busy. He dragged a Windsurfer out of the shed, but there wasn't enough of a breeze to even get it out onto the lagoon.

Every time Laura came near he backed off and zipped his damn mouth, replying to her attempts at conversation in grunts. He couldn't risk giving anything else away. When she tired of bugging him and went out snorkeling in her bikini he made it a personal challenge to look anywhere but at her, to shut down any thoughts that weren't directly related to Theo's survival. Even when she lay on a mat on the grass two meters away and smoothed sunscreen *all* over her body he managed not to look. Eventually she got bored, found a fishing line and reeled in a couple of good-sized yellow snapper, while he stole a look at the internet. No word from Flynn. Not prepared to trust her with the knife, he did the filleting.

After an age, the sun began to drop. Bats glided overheard and squawked and fought in the coconut palms. He grilled up the fish and they ate at opposite ends of the picnic table in silence, both facing the darkening lagoon. Even then, his peripheral vision and battle-honed hearing gave him hell, feeding his brain unwanted information about the graceful way she folded and unfolded her legs, the slap of her hand on taut skin as she chased away mosquitoes, her frustrated sighs at his reticence.

His every nerve seemed to buzz at her slightest move, his every muscle tensed at her slightest sound, sweat sprang to his chest at every waft of that damn shampoo.

It was as if denying himself the pleasure of looking at her cranked up the reaction—overreaction—of other senses. But at least he wasn't betraying any more secrets. The important thing was to keep Theo locked away. *Au combat, tu agis sans passion. In combat, you act without passion.* This had become a combat of sorts, if only inside his body and mind.

He downed the last forkful of fish, wishing they had more, and stood, abruptly, to clear the plates. She rose at the same time and reached for the same plate. He found his gaze impaled on hers. Under the warm light of sunset, her skin glowed. He could swear more freckles had sprung up across her face than when he'd last looked. His resolve failed him, his eyes drinking her in. He stood caught in her magnetism like an imbecile.

"Hello?" she said, waving her palm in front of his face.

He flinched and returned focus to stacking plates. She laid a firm hand on his wrist.

"You cooked, I'll clean," she said.

He extricated his hand, and didn't make the mistake of meeting her eye again. "I'll have a swim. Don't answer the door to any pirates."

"Depends how polite they are."

She stacked a pile of plates on her arm like a seasoned waitress, as she had earlier that afternoon. Where did a woman who was accustomed to being waited on learn to do that? No doubt she'd hosted her share of elite parties, but surely it'd be the staff cleaning up? He added it to the tally of surprising discoveries about her, then tried to forget it, along with everything else about her that wouldn't let his brain be still.

Eventually, the sky turned a deep metallic blue. Evidently giving up on him, Laura retired into the villa, leaving him to settle in the hammock. The day had been too leisurely. Sleep only came easily when he'd pushed himself to the point of physical exhaustion. One run and two swims were not enough to settle the humming of his body, to exorcise the awareness of *her*. Tomorrow he'd have to triple his run, quadruple the swim. He had to keep the dark thoughts out.

He hadn't realized he'd fallen asleep until he woke, his instinct on red alert. Noise drifted in from the lagoon—clinking, low voices. He slid from the hammock and slipped off the veranda into the shadows. Gabriel's men, already? Had the ransom been paid?

The full moon lit the outlines of men creeping along the jetty. Behind them floated the pirate boat from earlier in the day. They must have crept in under oar. *Putain de merde!*

CHAPTER
10

Rafe had to get Laura out of the villa. They'd see him if he went in the front door, possibly open fire—the easiest person to rob was a dead one. Unless kidnap was their plan. And no one was kidnapping his hostage. He backed around to the brushwood fence encircling the outdoor bathroom, scaled a timber post and dropped noiselessly, knees bent. Inside, he pulled aside the mosquito net and held his palm over her mouth. Her eyes flicked open, her fist shot up to his jaw. He caught it.

"Pirates. Let's go."

She started, blinked.

"Shoes, quick. You'll need to run." He handed over her running shoes and grabbed the flashlight, his mind whirring.

Out the back, he hoisted her over the fence. She landed with a soft thud. A second later, he followed and pulled her into the shadow of a tree.

"There are five of them," she whispered. "I see guns."

"Five against one. A fair fight."

"Five against two."

"This is not your battle, princess—but I could use a diversion, if you're up for it."

"Of course."

"Take this." He placed the flashlight in her hand. "Don't turn it on yet. Go halfway up to the cliff and make a noise—a gasp, a scream—like you've slipped and hurt yourself. Shine the flashlight around, then turn it off and keep running. Count to two hundred and find somewhere to hide. Somewhere good. Don't leave tracks, like you did last night. And stay there until I come."

"What will you do, take on all five?"

"Just the guy with the AK."

Her mouth fell open.

"Soon as I get that, I'm in charge. But I want you to split them up. And be careful. It's in my best interests to keep you alive."

"Mine, too."

"If they get you, don't struggle and they won't kill you yet— you're too valuable. Worst-case scenario: try to tell them who you are, if they understand English."

"*Yet.* Nice. Got it." She frowned. "Be careful."

He raised his eyebrows.

"Like you said, I'd get lonely." She scurried off into the darkness behind the villa.

He welcomed the surge of adrenaline in his veins. The men trudged up the sand, not bothering to hide, having evidently established from their afternoon's recon that there were no guards. One AK, plus one handgun, maybe two, between them. In seconds they'd be at the villa. He'd have to isolate them and take them out one by one, by hand if necessary.

He picked up a rock, assessed its weight, then lined up another three. He stilled his breath and watched the men approach the villa. Three disappeared onto the veranda, out of sight. The locked door would buy him a few seconds. Another guy crept around the back, coming within a few feet of Rafe, a pistol barrel glinting in his hand. Motionless under his veil of darkness, Rafe let him pass and disappear around the corner. Save him for later. The guy with the AK stood isolated, five meters away. Rafe hefted the rock. *Clonk.* He went down like a tree, and was still. Rafe took a run-up and lobbed the second rock across the lawn. It crashed into a bush, short of its target. He waited. They didn't seem to register the noise. He grabbed another, adjusted his angle and hurled it with more grunt. It clattered onto the shed's iron roof. Quick words were exchanged, and one of the men who'd been on the veranda ran off in pursuit of the noise.

Crack. The remaining two men on the veranda had forced the door. With one guy around the back, two inside and one checking the shed, Rafe sprinted for the AK. He rolled the still-breathing gunner over, yanked the weapon from his arms and retreated into the darkness. Shouts rose up from inside. They'd discovered the empty bed.

Footfalls approached—the man who'd run past Rafe earlier, now responding to the calls from the villa. Rafe laid the gun down, let him pass, then tore after him, bare feet silent on the damp grass. He caught him from behind, planting one hand over his mouth, and jerked him back. Before the guy could register, he tore away the pistol and clocked him on the temple. The guy went limp. Rafe dragged him into the bushes. He had a rope strung around his waist. How thoughtful. In seconds he was trussed, gagged with his own shirt and frisked.

Rafe examined the guns. The AK-47 was ancient, dirty and empty. Just for show. The pistol was a Makarov, probably Cold War. These guys were on a budget. He cocked the hammer and pulled the slide back. A few rounds in the magazine. He released the slide and dropped the safety. The three remaining men assembled on the grass, whispering and gesturing all at once. One kicked their unconscious friend. Another pistol caught the moonlight.

Sheltering behind a palm trunk, Rafe lined up the biggest guy in the Makarov's sights and pulled the trigger. A click echoed around the compound. Dead round? One of the men called out, scanning the darkness for their friend. Rafe pulled back the slide, ejected the round and took aim. Click. *Putain.* He hurled the piece-of-shit weapon, boomerang-style, and missed. He was back to using his hands. The guy called out again, panic flecking his voice.

A scream. Laura. Light flickered through the trees on the

track above. Perfect timing. He scooted under the cover of the canopy toward the path, sprinted fifty meters and backed in behind a stand of bamboo, willing his pulse to slow.

He let the first two guys go ahead and disappear around a corner, including the guy with the other pistol—another Makarov, by the look of it. Laura had better be hiding. As the last man passed, Rafe sprang out, smashing an elbow into his face. The guy bounced back into a kung fu pose and flew like a bullet. His boot thumped into Rafe's solar plexus and Rafe sank to his knees, his lungs suctioning air. Shit.

The guy backed up and flew into the air, a blur of shadows. A crack of fire burst through Rafe's jaw. A punch, but it felt like a gunshot. The guy drew back his boot and drove it into Rafe's kidneys. Waves of pain engulfed him, his vision prickling with black spots. He'd singled out the wrong opponent, hadn't taken the time to size him up. Not a mistake he normally made.

And one mistake was all it usually took for things to go to hell.

Footsteps closed in on Holly—more than one pair. If they'd taken Jack out, she was done for. Sooner or later, they'd find her.

But she wasn't helpless yet. *Hide somewhere good*, he'd said. And she would, just as soon as she unleashed her secret weapon. She maneuvered into position and stood on the path, waiting, her pummeling heart nearly drowning out the pulsing insect noise. No need to shake the flashlight around to make out she was running—her trembling hands took care of that. The footsteps neared. She gave another girly shriek. Baiting the trap. Sweat trickled down her back. She shivered, despite the throbbing heat.

Two figures rounded the corner. They saw her and shouted. She aimed the beam into their eyes, switched it off and sprinted, straining to make out the track. Damn, the flashlight had killed her night vision, too. An inhuman scream split the air behind her. Boom—the first guy had run into the spiderweb. He wailed like a prison siren. Hell, Jack wasn't lying when he said those things caused pain.

She left the screaming man in her dust, but another pair of feet pounded the track behind her—not Jack's stealthy tread. She upped her pace, ignoring the sting from her coral cut as she veered left and right around the twisting trail. A branch clawed her arm. She didn't dare look behind. Her pulse thundered in her ears. Shit, this guy was fast. Too late to hide now.

He was so close she could hear him panting, though his breath wasn't as strangled as hers. A stitch stabbed her side. Her foot caught on something, jerking her back. Crap. Her knee lurched to the side, white-hot with pain. She rebalanced but too late. *Boof.* A solid weight drove into her back, and she skidded onto the ground, dirt grating her cheek.

Rafe heaved for oxygen, getting only strawfuls. Kung Fu Pirate's boot came in for the death hit. At the last second Rafe rolled, and the boot glanced off his side. More screaming, up ahead. What in hell were they doing to Laura? He had to get to her, push through the pain, push through this guy.

"Okay, okay." On his knees, Rafe clutched his stomach with one hand and held up his other palm, cowering in apparent surrender, playing to the guy's expectations. He wouldn't be anticipating much of a fight from a honeymooner, and so far Rafe hadn't given him cause to think he was anything but.

The guy spoke sharply, in an unfamiliar language. Rafe leaned back, groaning. The guy unfurled a rope, shouting to his friends. No chance of them hearing over the damn screaming. Laura. He had to get to Laura. He pushed himself to his feet, doubling over as if he were done. The guy whacked the back of Rafe's neck with the rope. He pointed down the path, evidently planning to herd his hostage like cattle.

"Okay," said Rafe, again. Still he didn't move, making out like he was catching his breath, while he furtively checked his surroundings. The guy was evidently a trained fighter, but Rafe had two advantages—size and surprise. The guy pushed his shoulder.

Rafe spun and charged, driving him into a tree like a freight train. The impact shuddered through them. As the guy wheezed, Rafe dropped him and slammed both feet into the small of his back, his full 240 pounds thudding down on the lower spine. The guy grunted, clawing at the leaf litter. He released the rope. Rafe clamped the back of his opponent's neck, pinning him like a flipped cockroach. He caught an arm, twisted the rope around it, yanked it back, caught the other one and knotted them. The screaming up the path invaded his head as he hog-tied the guy's feet, using far more force on the rope than he had the previous night with Laura. He secured the rope to the tree. He didn't give a damn if this *bâtard* was comfortable, as long as he couldn't come after them.

He checked his knots and patted the guy down. No oversights tonight. The guy was clean. Rafe took off uphill. The screaming suddenly stopped. Shit. His world narrowed to the path ahead.

Holly lay pinned, pawing the earth for a weapon. Nothing but dirt and the snaking tree root that'd tripped her. The man lurched to his feet. The screaming had stopped. Had the other guy recovered? Would he be coming after her, too? She scrambled to her feet, palms out. He had a handgun pointed at her chest. She swallowed. He was about her height, but all sinewy muscle. There had to be a way out.

The goon spoke quickly, waving the gun to indicate she should walk ahead of him. She shrugged, as if she didn't understand, letting her hands come to rest on her pockets. He shouted, jerking his head toward the path. When she didn't move, he stepped closer, reaching out with his spare hand to coax her forward. His finger left the trigger.

She pulled the flashlight from her pocket and rammed it in his face. As his neck snapped back, she aimed a kick at his nuts.

He caught her foot and twisted it, sending lightning up her leg. With a yelp, she hopped backward, wrenching out of his grip. Something slammed into her temple. The butt of the gun. Her legs wobbled, the world turning over like a wheel. She crumbled to the dirt, her injured knee twisting under her, the other stuck out in front. She began hyperventilating. *Sort yourself out, woman. You can take this guy.*

Click. He'd cocked the gun. He aimed it at her knee. Head spinning, she threw herself at his legs, collecting only air and earth. Something big and solid thumped down next to her, thwacking dirt into her eyes. The air exploded. Gunshot. She froze. No pain. She dared to look, blinking her vision clear.

Jack. Her soul soared. Jack had tackled her assailant and was wrestling him. The bullet must have gone into the trees. He slammed the attacker's gun hand down. The weapon skidded away. She pulled to her feet and limped after it. Jack drove his fist into the guy's face. Crunch. And again. She winced. Muscles the size of his had to cause serious pain. She aimed the gun at the men, her finger light on the trigger. Guns weren't her thing, and she was as likely to hit Jack as the pirate. The man lay still, groaning. Jack searched him, jumped to his feet and held out a hand for the gun. She tightened her fingers. Could this be an opportunity? Could she get away in the pirates' boat? But what about Jack? What about his son?

Don't overthink it. The guy kidnapped you. Pull the damn trigger.

In a beat, Jack had her in his grip, his chest flush against hers, an arm locking down her torso, a hand wrapped around the gun in her fingers. His dark eyes glittered. "Give it up, princess."

Crap. She was better when she didn't have time to think. Turned out smacking the shit out of someone in self-defense was a whole other thing from pulling a trigger on a guy who was looking straight back at you. Instinctive reactions were easy, but making a conscious decision to end a life?

"You don't want to do this, princess. Believe me." It wasn't a threat—more like…sincere advice. From someone who knew how it felt to kill.

She loosened her grip on the gun. Damn right she didn't want to do it. He released her, taking the weapon. She staggered to regain her balance, limping to take the impact off her injured leg. Like she could choose to end Jack's life, when a kid needed him. Like she could live with that.

He caught her around the waist, his arm pressing into her back to steady her. His gaze flicked down her bad leg. "Are you hurt?"

"Just twisted my knee. You look terrible." Blood trickled from a wound on his forehead. She resisted the urge to wipe the dark trail before it reached his eye.

"I heard screaming."

"Not mine. I unleashed Shelob."

"She-what?"

"The spider. It bit one of the pirates."

"How…? Forget it—tell me later. I have cleaning up to do." He released her and checked the gun, then nudged the guy on the ground with his foot. "Get up," he said, gesturing. "Time for you to hide, princess. Somewhere good, this time. I'll come back for you when I'm done."

"I can help."

"I don't want to have to worry about you. I have it under control."

The pirate spat out a gob of blood and God knew what else. With the gun, Jack pointed at the path. "Go," he said to the guy.

"What will you do with them?" she said.

"Give them what they deserve." He withdrew something from his pocket and held it out. Her pocketknife. "Just in case."

She took it quickly. "You trust me with this?"

"No."

He disappeared around a corner, the pirate stumbling ahead of him. Relief washed over her. She had no doubt he would "clean up," one against five or not. Hell—he wouldn't kill them in cold blood, would he? She limped over to the flashlight. It still worked. Good. She didn't fancy crawling around the jungle blind with those spiders around. What a coward she was, running off and hiding. But Jack was right—she'd proved she wasn't much use. And it was nuts she even wanted to help. He was only protecting her because she was his ticket to get his son back. And once he discovered her real identity, she'd be of zero value to him.

Her damn conscience. She might need to find the override button before this week was out. Would Jack hesitate before pulling the trigger on her, if he was ordered to? That was what soldiers did. How many people had he killed in his job?

But he had a conscience, too.

Overthinking, again. She limped along the track, away from the evidence of the scuffles, in case it wasn't Jack who returned for her. She pushed through a tangle of vines and found a palm tree to sit against, surrounded by a relatively bare patch of dirt that didn't seem to be crawling with bugs, or worse. With her shoes, she swept away a pile of sticks and leaves. Were snakes nocturnal? Scorpions? Reluctantly, she switched off the light. For an age she sat in the shadows, ears straining to catch any noise that wasn't explained by the ocean slapping and sucking at the bottom of the cliff, or the wildlife infesting the jungle.

A couple of times she thought she heard footsteps and froze, praying for them to be Jack's. A coconut thudded to the ground a few feet away, making her flinch. Occasionally, a shout filtered up. But no gunshots, thank God. If they got Jack, she'd follow his example—try to separate them, and pick them off one by one. She screwed up her face. Not that her fighting skills had been much use tonight.

Her knee throbbed like a jackhammer, her cheek burned, her cut foot itched. Sleep pulled at her eyes, and she yawned. An hour must have passed. Had Jack been hurt, or worse? Her neck prickled. A noise, behind her. She flicked on the flashlight. A face. She screamed.

CHAPTER

11

A hand wrapped over Holly's mouth, muffling her scream. A laugh rolled around her, low and deep. Jack. Oh, thank God.

"You jerk," she mumbled. His skin tasted earthy, possibly bloody. He released her. "What happened?"

"Our guests left, with some encouragement. Bad manners to interrupt a honeymoon. All but one guy."

She stiffened. "What do you mean?"

"No sign of the guy you fed to the spider. But I have a theory about where he is. Until we confirm it, keep quiet." He stood, ducking under a branch. "Good hiding place. You're learning."

"You found me."

"I'm good at finding people."

"And creeping up on people. Calling my name would have been just as effective."

"And nowhere near as fun."

"I've got a weapon. I could have used it on you before I realized who it was."

"This one?" He held up her knife.

She patted her pocket. How the hell?

"Before I realized who it was..." he repeated, slowly. "You're saying you wouldn't pull out a knife if you knew it was me? An hour ago it looked very much like you were going to shoot me. You're a complicated woman."

"We have a complicated relationship."

He checked the path and held back the vines for her. She followed, testing her weight on her shaky leg.

"How's the knee?"

"Feels like it's filled with glue."

"Lean on me."

He wound his arm around her waist and lifted her slightly, leaving her with no choice but to coast a hand up his back and over his sweat-slicked shoulder. They made slow, silent progress down the track. Dang, it felt good to feel those muscles tighten under her fingers as he stepped, to feel his body slide and shift against hers. Stupidly good. If she ever had another relationship—and she wouldn't—she'd like to get her hands all over a body like his. The tough-guy-with-a heart thing was also doing it for her, in entirely different ways. The kidnapping and threatening to maim—not so much. Was that her problem? She was attracted to men who wanted to hurt people—hurt her?

As they approached the former spiderweb, he stopped and disentangled himself, giving her a moment to find her balance before he stepped clear.

"Flashlight."

She handed it over. He tracked the beam along scuff marks in the dirt to where they disappeared off the cliff, and dropped to his knees to peer over the side. She shuffled to look. In the weak far reaches of the light, she could just make out a crumpled pile of clothes and limbs on a tumble of rocks.

She scooted out a breath. "Dead?"

Jack called out to the guy. Not a twitch. He dropped a large stone, which landed with an echoing crack a few yards from the body. Nothing. He trained the beam on the guy's chest and narrowed his eyes—watching for movement? "By the way he's lying I'd say his neck's broken. He must have stumbled off the cliff in panic, or pain. He sure screamed for long enough before he went over, but then it stopped suddenly. I guess that's why." He looked up at her. "I thought it was you screaming."

"You must have been worried sick."

He shrugged. "Hard to secure a ransom for a dead hostage."

He stood, brought an arm across his chest and pulled it into a stretch, like he had when they were running. Her gaze flicked down his dirt-smudged torso, all the way to the trail of black hair that disappeared into his shorts. Oh, dear lord, he was fine. She blinked hard. *Really? You've just seen a dead body—a guy you had a hand in killing—and this is your reaction? Truly screwed up.*

"So you've killed one guy with a shark and another with a spider," he said. "What are you planning to do to me?"

Oh, the things she could do to him, none of which involved any wildlife except herself. "Any tigers on this island?"

"It's too small."

"Death by slow Doris, then."

His teeth gleamed in the moonlight. "Loris. Slow loris."

"Whatever you prefer." She cocked her head. "I'm surprised you let those pirates go."

His jaw tightened. "Never kick a stray dog. I gave them one chance to get away and they wisely took it. Poverty will be driving this. They'll have families to provide for. Maybe this will shock them into going straight."

"You don't really believe that people like that can change?"

He studied her, unblinking. "I believe in redemption, yes— that you can leave the mistakes of your past behind."

Her heart skipped a beat, for some stupid reason. "So that's what you meant when you said you'd give them what they deserved. They deserved a chance."

"In my experience the line between good and evil is blurry." He slid in next to her and gripped her waist. Her breath quickened. "And dead bodies make a hell of a mess, which wouldn't make for a romantic honeymoon. Let's go."

"We're just leaving him there?"

"I might be able to retrieve the body at low tide but not now. Don't worry, princess. He's sleeping very peacefully."

She slid her hand up to find that sweet spot on his shoulder— purely for balance, of course. They settled into a rhythmic stride,

Jack taking the weight off her bad leg. So he, too, had a weakness for the underdog. That could come in useful, if he discovered just how much of a stray she was. "Would you give the people who are threatening your son a chance?"

His shoulder tensed. "Would you, in my situation?"

"I guess if I had a child I'd do whatever it took to get him back."

"There's your answer."

Whatever it took. Her gut curled. Including harming his hostage? Killing her?

Once, Holly had cared strongly enough for a man to do anything for him. Would she have eventually gotten over her qualms and killed for him? She'd done a lot of other things she'd never before considered herself capable of, getting more brazen with each hit. But she'd always assured herself her crimes were victimless—she was screwing banks and big business while they were busy screwing the American people. She was just an underdog snapping at the top dogs.

What if Jasper had continued to escalate their crimes, had pressured her to hurt someone physically? She'd been so addicted to his approval and terrified of being abandoned, she would have done anything—not that she'd been able to rationalize it so clearly at the time. Oh no, perspective had taken six long years to find.

Perhaps it was just as well the Feds had pounced when they had, just as well Jasper had immediately betrayed her. The spell had broken that day. Never again would she let a man—or anyone—have that much influence over her. Needing someone made you vulnerable, and she was safest in her own company. Prison had given her that gift, at least.

As they crested the hill that led down to the lagoon, the strain of a motor drifted in over the ocean. Jack stilled. After a minute, it faded completely.

"Do you think they'll return?" she said.

"They've been burned. They'll look for an easier target."

"Aren't you worried they might ask questions about the kind of bride and groom who can flatten five goons in the space of a half hour? Make the connection with—" Her face heated. She'd been a fingernail away from saying *Laura*. She swallowed. "My disappearance."

"They won't advertise this defeat. And I doubt they're following your kidnapping on a live web stream. People out here live simple lives—not like you're used to, princess. Survival is their only ambition."

Holly grimaced. She understood that, all right. "I guess the drive to survive can lead to desperate acts, huh, Jack?"

"This is too slow," he growled. In the flicker of an eyelash he scooped her up like a baby. Again.

"You like doing that, don't you?" And getting out of any conversation that might dent his armor. Sighing in resignation, she wrapped her hands around his neck—and immediately regretted it. It brought their skin too close, with only her thin top separating them. As he strode, the friction created a reaction under the fabric she hoped to God he couldn't feel. She tried to pull her torso away, but he adjusted his grip to hold her closer. Or would it be good if he felt it? That's what she wanted, didn't she—him to feel something for her? Her top rode up, leaving his bare arm flush against the skin of her lower back, his fingers pressing into her waist. His other hand was firm under her knees. He smelled of fresh sweat, salt, spice.

Whoa. There'd better be vodka in the cabin. She hadn't touched alcohol in years before yesterday's champagne, but she sure could use something to numb her overstimulated mind and body. Or would a drink make it worse?

Hell, maybe it was time to act on the things instinct was badgering her to do, take the game plan to its next logical phase. She'd never crossed that line before—was it crazy that she wanted to now? But they'd bonded tonight. It made sense to take advantage.

Trouble was, she'd only ever seduced men she didn't give a

damn about, even men she despised. Certainly no one she was genuinely attracted to. This would be a whole different experience.

She splayed her fingers on his hot skin. She'd have to make sure she didn't screw herself over at the same time. Somehow.

Mon Dieu. This woman was doing dangerous things to Rafe. Five thugs—four, once Laura had dealt with one—had proved much easier to control than his body's response to a woman he had no business being this close to. He upped the pace, ignoring the strain in his thighs, the heat of her body pressed into his, the fire on the back of his neck where her fingers pressed, the fresh scent of her. The sooner this torture ended, the better.

"I can walk from here." Her shuddering voice did nothing for his self-control. There was no reason she should be out of breath, unless she, too, felt the... *Don't go there.* A woman like that should feel nothing but disgust for a lowlife like him.

"We're nearly there." *Thank God.*

As much as common sense urged him to let her walk, he knew knee injuries needed rest. Without that, he'd be carrying her everywhere for the next few days. Not what he needed.

The path bottomed out on approach to the villa. He adjusted his grip, his fingers sliding further up her smooth back, confirming what the skin on his chest was already broadcasting— she wore no bra.

At last, blessedly, he staggered up the steps to the veranda, sidestepping the insect screen, which was hanging from a single hinge, and stepped over the broken door. The pirates had torn down the mosquito net, which at least made it easy to lay her on the bed. He switched on a lamp. It illuminated pink lips and far too much creamy skin.

Focus. "How's your knee?"

"Okay, I think. Maybe I just twisted it."

"Keep off it, and keep it elevated. I'll find something cold, to stop the swelling." He slid down the bed, untied her laces and slipped off her shoe. The dressing over her coral cut had slipped off. He pulled the flashlight from his pocket and examined the wound. It didn't look red or inflamed. "I'll replace the dressing, too."

He ejected the clip from the Makarov and laid the two pieces on the kitchen bench. There was just enough ice left in the cooler to wrap in a cloth and slip around her knee. He was tempted to throw some down the front of his shorts, to send a message to his body that this wasn't a woman to be desired. He filled a bowl with water and sat on the bed, beside her foot. If it wasn't for her twisted knee limiting her reach, he'd let her do it herself. But it was true what he'd said to her—keeping active kept him from going mad. Sleep wouldn't return easily, anyway. Perhaps he could dive into the lagoon again, to cool off—she couldn't come in after him, at least.

His call to let the pirates go free, along with a potentially very useful boat, better not come back to kick him in the balls. But hell, he had more than enough to handle with one hostile hostage—four more could have been the death of him, and Laura. *Tu respectes les ennemis vaincus. You respect defeated enemies.*

With the language mismatch, he hadn't even been able to interrogate them on Gabriel's local operations, though it was likely they knew nothing, given the reputation of *Les Pirates Fantômes*. And what if he and Laura had escaped in the boat—to God knew where—and the militia had returned for them? It'd be goodbye, Theo.

He repeated the sequence he'd performed earlier—sponging her wound with an antiseptic, smoothing on antibiotic cream and sticking on a dressing. "Done."

"Thanks." She propped herself up on her elbows, her eyes gleaming in the low light. "I bet you're a great dad." She smiled wistfully.

The note of sympathy kicked at him. "Believe me, princess, I'm not."

"You love him, don't you?"

"I'm his father."

She nodded. "You love him, all right. That's more than a lot of kids get."

Was she talking from her own experience? "Actions, not words, that's what's important." Like being there for your family, not just sending money every payday.

Her eyes took on a faraway look, a sad look. "True enough."

"You have a graze on your cheek. And a lump on your forehead."

The corner of her mouth curled up. "I have a lot of things going on. Those are not a priority."

"Still, I may as well wash your cheek while I've got the antiseptic out. You don't want a cut to get infected in this climate. Especially on a face…"

She raised her eyebrows at his unfinished sentence.

A face as beautiful as yours. "A face as expensive as yours."

He scooted up the bed. She pushed up into a sitting position and turned toward him, chin tilted, eyelids heavy, like she was fishing to be kissed. He clenched his stomach muscles. *Don't even think about it, Angelito.*

He dipped a fresh cotton pad in the solution and patted it along her freckled cheekbone. Her warm breath coasted over his hand. Her gaze dropped, her expression hidden under long eyelashes. She trailed a finger along his stomach. He flinched. *Mon Dieu.*

"Looks like you could do with medical attention yourself," she murmured. "Is that seriously a boot print?"

"It's nothing," he said, quickly.

"Yeah?" She focused on his eyes. "You know… I don't think you're as tough and mean as you look, Capitaine."

She flattened her palm onto his stomach. He froze. That touch—it wasn't innocent. *Pull back*, his mind urged. His body rebelled.

CHAPTER

12

Laura swallowed, without breaking eye contact, as if her mind and body were battling as fiercely as Rafe's. Her shell-pink tongue darted out to lick her lips. His mind went dark. He dropped the gauze, cupped her face and kissed her, hard, before his brain had time to catch up. She melted into him, her hand sliding around his stomach to his back and pressing him closer. Like he needed the invitation. He threaded his other hand into her hair, angling her head up. She parted her lips and he dipped in to taste her. Sweet, fresh, smooth. She stroked her tongue against his. *Merde*, he was in trouble.

She wrapped her other hand around his waist and drove her fingers up either side of his spine, digging into muscles that ached for release. Moaning, she urged him down until they lay side by side on the bed, not a whisper between them. As his tongue explored her silky mouth, he glided the fingers of one hand down her hair, her neck, onto her shoulders. Her skin was as sleek as water. Her hands left his back and dug into the sides of his neck, freeing him to explore her. And he did, with the hunger of a man who hadn't eaten in a month.

He slid a hand around her waist, to keep her close, and ran the other down her side, stopping at the point her top gave way to the satin skin of her lower belly. He dipped under the fabric and ran his fingers up her stomach to palm the swell of her breast. Her nipple was budded hard, like he already knew it to be. *Mon Dieu*. He longed to suck it into his mouth, but settled for grazing his fingertips over it—for now. She groaned, the sound ratcheting the tension in his stomach—and lower. This was about as wrong as wrong got. So why the hell did it feel so good?

Like she said, this war wasn't between them. So what if they gave in, right this second? He released her mouth, panting, and lifted away, just far enough to create room to slide his other hand under her top. He paused, testing for any sign of resistance. The slightest flinch and he'd stop. She groaned and arched. *Yes.* As he drew up her top, she raised her arms to help him slip it off. He threw it aside and swept his gaze down her, his jaw dropping.

"Mon Dieu. Tu es très belle."

Beautiful didn't begin to do her justice. Her pupils were huge, her swollen lips open in a breathless smile. No sign of anything but the same urges pumping through him. She pushed his shoulder, coaxing him onto his back, and rolled on top, propping her forearms either side of his head. She leaned down and nipped his lower lip. A moan escaped him. As she played with his lips, darting her tongue and scraping her teeth against them, he glided his hands down her back, molding their bodies together, fitting his erection into her cleft. Ah, the smoothness of her. The softness. He could just rip their remaining clothes off. He slid his hands down the dip of her lower back, under her shorts, and planted his fingers in the flesh of her *derrière*, pushing her right where he needed her. She took the hint and began rubbing into him, a torturous slow rhythm. She left his mouth and trailed her tongue to his ear.

"Do you think there are condoms in that first-aid kit?" she murmured.

"There'd better be." His voice sounded like it came from far away. "God."

"I'll check."

She pulled back, grimaced and clutched her knee. "Ow. Shit, I forgot about that."

Fighting every urge in his body, he gently rolled her onto her back. *Shit* was right. "We've forgotten about a lot of things." His gaze caught on one of her nipples, his mouth dropping open. If he leaned in just a few inches...

No. A force field had sprung up between them. He couldn't go through with it, as much as he hungered to.

"Jack, I want to forget. Seriously. Let's forget this whole insane situation. Let's do this. I want this."

He forced himself to sit, swinging his legs onto the floor so he faced away from her. Maybe starving his eyes of her would lower the heat in his body. *Jack.* She didn't even know who she was about to sleep with. "I apologize. This was inappropriate." Hell, it went far beyond any definition of appropriate.

"Who cares?" The bed shifted. She shuffled up behind him, slipping her hands around his waist. "I know this is crazy. The whole situation's crazy. But I know you want this as much as I do. You *need* this as much as I do—I can feel it. And I'm not just talking about what's under your shorts."

He gently removed her hands. "I will not take advantage of this situation."

"Who says it's *you* taking advantage?"

"Tu agis sans passion," he said under his breath.

"What does that mean?"

"It means this is not going to happen. Good night, princess."

Without daring to look at her, he strode out the door, sweeping up the Makarov on the way out. After checking she wasn't following, he stashed it under the veranda. Once on the sand, he yanked off his shorts and underwear and surged into the lagoon. The water swelled around him like warm cognac. Damn Indian Ocean. He'd need nothing less than the Arctic to chill the heat racing through his body.

He dived and settled into a punishing stroke rate, surging through the black water. Self-control, that's what he had to reclaim. That was the number one thing separating him from the monster he'd become as a boy, when fear and rage and pain had opened the dark place in his mind where his conscience and his feelings couldn't reach, where he could hole up and make his body do whatever it took to survive. If he lost control over himself again, there was no guessing what demons could erupt from his subconscious, destroying the years of rehabilitation, plummeting him back into that nightmare world where black was white and white was black, where a child's cry or a woman's scream meant nothing, where the innocent suffered and the guilty drank it up.

He wasn't going back there. He had a code of honor now, and he would not break it, no matter how much he wanted to walk into that villa and take that woman into his arms, to make the tension between them detonate. This was a woman who challenged and taunted him, who dug to the bottom of him and touched parts of his soul that had long ago withered and blackened.

Tu agis sans passion.

Giving in to temptation would be the end of him.

Shit. Holly scrabbled through her bag for a cleanish T-shirt and boxers and yanked them on. *Shit, shit, shit.* She finger-combed her hair, wet from the shower she'd stumbled into after he'd walked out. The water had done nothing to calm her—body or mind. If that stunt was supposed to seduce *him*, why was *her* every nerve fizzing? Now would be a very good time for a squad of US Marines to rappel down from a Black Hawk and rescue her. But then, what would happen to Jack? He'd be arrested, possibly as a terrorist. What would become of his son?

And why should she care?

That right there was the problem. She and Jack were on opposite sides of this. His loss would be her win, his win her loss. Giving a damn about him was dangerous. He'd kidnapped her from a yacht, potentially ruining her shot at a new life, and here she was worrying about him and his son. He sure as hell wouldn't sacrifice his goal for her sake. Why should she?

A rust-colored moth the size of her palm battered the bedside lamp. She limped over and switched it off. Moonlight beamed through the window. Movement outside caught her eye—Jack, rising out of the lagoon like Neptune, his strong, naked shape in silhouette. Desire pulled at her. Now she knew just how good those muscles felt under her fingers. She linked her hands behind her head. Goddamn. She guessed what the prison shrink would say—she was attracted to his size and strength because subconsciously she sought the protector she'd never had.

She needed no protector but herself. She *trusted* no protector but herself.

He pulled on his shorts and strode out of view. It was more than the physical that attracted her. It was his strength in so many ways. It was the decency that underscored his every gesture—looking after her wounds, defending her against that creepy pilot and now pulling back from sex because he refused to take advantage. She'd never known anyone with a moral compass that unwavering—if you didn't count the kidnapping. Always a catch.

A mosquito whined in her ear. She slapped at it. Better get that net back onto its frame, especially now the cabin had no door. Malaria was all she needed right now. She stood on the mattress, favoring her good knee, grabbed the loose corner of the net and reached to hook it up. She was too short. "Damn."

"Need help?" Jack leaned against the busted door frame, his jaw grim.

"I'll be fine." *If I can just grow a couple of inches.*

He strolled over, stepped onto the mattress and reached over her to hook up the net, his skin glistening and fresh from the water. Didn't the man believe in T-shirts? He looked down at her, his forehead creased. He'd enclosed them both in the net. He threw it over his head and bounded backward onto the floor.

She lowered herself to the mattress. "Thanks."

He nodded and walked to the door.

She had to say something, to cut through the thick air. "Awkward, huh?"

He stopped, locking serious eyes onto hers. "It won't happen again. I'm…sorry." His voice cracked.

Her chest ached. So was she, for entirely different reasons. "Do you think if we'd met under different circumstances—?" Was she still playing him? Even she couldn't tell anymore.

"We didn't," he snapped. He jammed a hand in his hair. "Don't even think about it."

It wasn't a no. What if they'd met on the Metro in LA, struck up a conversation, he a tourist, she an office worker, no life-and-death complications—would she feel the same surge of electricity she did now? Would they have eased into a relationship, the way she guessed it happened for everyday people? Got married, had kids?

Like hell. She knew better than to believe in fairy tales.

"Sleep well, princess." He walked out. The hammock squeaked as he settled into it.

Fat chance.

Holly woke with a dust-dry mouth, breaking out of wild, hot dreams. So she'd slept, after all the twisting and turning? What a miracle. She pulled up the net and padded to the fridge, her knee stiff but taking her weight. She drank from a bottle of water, her throat giving a little with the cool liquid. Voices filtered in from outside. She froze, wiping her mouth. Too tinny to be real. Jack must be checking the internet.

She opened the screen door—Jack must have fixed it while she slept. He sat on the boards of the veranda in a tight black T-shirt and khaki shorts, his long legs stretched out in front of him, laptop resting on his thighs. Her mind dished up a reminder of how his muscles and ridges and dips had felt under her hands. *Mamma mia.* She rested the bottle against her cheek, to cool her skin. He paused the video. How was this going to play out, after last night?

"Morning, princess. Just in time for the news."

"What's the time?" She squinted at the sun, about a quarter of the way up the sky.

"Early. I thought you'd sleep longer. Fighting off pirates can be tiring."

"Are you talking about our visitors last night, or yourself?"

He laughed, his dimple marking one cheek. He looked younger, relaxed. More Bruce Wayne than Batman, like he'd slept soundly, like he wasn't humming with tension the way she was. "Both. You're one hell of a pirate slayer."

"I can't help it if they keep getting in my way." The humor eased the tightness in her belly. She settled her butt into the hammock behind him, taking another sip of water. Blinding sunlight bounced off the lagoon. Even the crimson bougainvillea climbing the veranda was too bright to look at. Just another perfect day on honeymoon.

"How's the knee?"

She bent it back and forth. "Good. Swelling's gone down."

"Take it slowly and you'll be okay."

The laptop was paused on a close-up of the senator's face. Underneath scrolled the words: *A father's worst nightmare.* Her stomach knotted. "What's the latest?"

"They're still searching, still saying they won't pay. Your father has shot up in the polls, though he's put his campaign on hold."

She exhaled. She'd live to see another day. "They'd do a poll at a time like this? Vultures."

"Ah, everyone's out to make a buck."

"So is a platoon of US soldiers about to rush out from the trees and rescue me?"

He studied the screen, frowning. "Several companies of Marines are after you, along with local authorities, but they may as well be looking in another continent. No radars picked up our plane leaving the kidnap zone so they've started searching in the vicinity of the yacht."

Damn. What could she do next? Lighting a pyre on the beach was out, now that she had firsthand experience of the "help" it might attract. But it was good news they were at least searching. What was Laura doing now? Lying low, while her father figured out how to handle the change in plan? Perhaps he'd pay the ransom just to make the problem go away. He'd be happy about the bounce in the polls—maybe that'd be worth the outlay.

In the meantime, what choice was there but to sit still and try to burrow further under Jack's skin? Last night she'd gone a step too far with the seduction, for her sanity as much as her survival. Today she'd try the subtle approach, play on their obvious connection beyond the physical. When hell descended, as it would, she needed him on her side. He'd make too good an enemy.

"Have you eaten?" she said.

"Didn't want to wake you."

"Man, I was having some crazy dreams." *Featuring you.*

"This kind of heat can do that to you. I'll find some food." He shut the laptop, reeled in the phone, and removed and pocketed the sat phone battery.

"Still don't trust me?"

"I trust you as much as you trust me."

"That little, huh?" Stupid thing was, she *did* trust him. She felt it in her heart, even if her mind flashed neon warnings. Was that a natural response after someone saved your life? Or a textbook progression toward Helsinki Syndrome? Whatever— she sure as hell shouldn't trust him. His love for his son would trump any protectiveness he felt for her.

He stood. "What do you want to eat?"

"I'll come in and have a look."

She followed him into the cabin, limping slightly, the floorboards smooth and cool under her feet. Her gaze fell on the bed. Had they really come so close to sex? God, he'd fired her up, with those sure hands sliding down her belly and up her back, and gripping her butt. A few more minutes of that and—

"Laura?"

"Sorry?" She caught his eye, heat rising up her neck.

He scratched his buzz cut. "I asked if you wanted smoked salmon and capers on a baguette. There's enough food in here for a royal banquet."

Her stomach growled. Good to see hunger for food trumping her other cravings. Her survival instinct still worked, at least. "Guess they figure honeymooners need to keep up their energy."

He laid the ingredients on the bench. He must have been on a honeymoon himself, once.

She pulled up a bar stool. "What happened to your wife, Jack?"

His eyes met hers, shot with danger. He broke a baguette in two and split each half. "Don't you get it? The less you know about me, the better your chances of survival."

"I take it she was the mother of your son." Her stomach flitted.

"Laura, drop it."

"Sometimes you're not very good company, you know that?"

"I'm never good company."

She quirked an eyebrow. "You were pretty good company last night."

He stuffed shaved salmon into one baguette, then the other. Her mouth watered. "Last night was a mistake. We both know that."

"I don't regret it, for the record." That, at least, was true. She just regretted that right now she had an urge to slide her hands up his T-shirt and feel the ridges of his muscles shudder at her touch again.

"You should."

"Do you?"

He added capers and a chunk of white cheese and handed it to her. "It was unprofessional."

"You make it sound like we're operating under a set of rules. I'm guessing you don't have a job contract that specifically forbids contact with me."

"I don't need a piece of paper to tell me what's wrong and what's right."

"So it's right to kidnap a woman off a yacht and hold her against her will, but it's wrong to give in to your feelings?"

"It's all wrong, everything about this situation. But there are lines I'm forced to cross, and lines I can choose not to."

"You were pretty close to the line last night."

"Too close." He spat out the words, as he shoved the ingredients back in the fridge and slammed the door.

"It's not all on you, Jack. The attraction's mutual, as you may have noticed. I can make my own decisions."

"You're not in a position to give consent, no matter what you might feel—or pretend to feel."

Ouch.

He took another bite and marched to the broken door, still lying across the entrance. He heaved the wood aside as if it were cardboard and disappeared into the light.

She chewed her lip. She was sure hitting some nerves—but were they the right ones?

"Stay inside until I say you can come out," he called, back to being the *capitaine* barking orders.

She crept to a window. Was he hiding the laptop and phone? She had no sight line out to him. She peeped through another window, then the doorway. Nothing. He could be stashing it anywhere. She wiped her forehead with the back of her hand. The heat was creeping up already. She probably stank after a sweaty night of troubled dreams. She stripped off her T-shirt and shorts, and pulled on Laura's bikini. Her gaze rested on the tube of sunscreen, a smile catching her mouth.

* * *

Sweat trailed down Rafe's spine as he returned from stashing the comms. The air was as still outdoors as it was inside. There'd be no respite from the heat today, in any sense. He needed a swim. Christ, he needed to spend the whole day in the water.

Laura stood by the picnic table, wearing the damn bikini again. She smoothed sunscreen down one shapely leg, then moved her hand back up, massaging it in. He stopped, still, in the shade of a banyan tree. He shouldn't watch. Her hand circled up the back of her calf and knee, and along her quad, before sliding around to her inner thigh. He stifled a groan. The skin would feel like satin, like her stomach and back had last night. He cleared his throat. He needed water.

She looked up, and he hurriedly resumed walking. "I told you to stay inside."

She squeezed cream into her hand and rubbed it into her neck. "I wasn't looking… Ow!" She lowered her arm and rubbed her shoulder.

"Something wrong?"

"I must have strained something. I can't reach around to put sunscreen on my back. Would you mind?"

Rafe marched to the washing line, yanked his T-shirt off it, and threw it at her feet. "Try covering up, instead." For both of their personal safety.

She sat on the table and swiveled to face him, her breasts barely contained by the bikini, nipples outlined in the thin fabric. Where did he leave his damn water bottle?

"You're really not in a good mood, are you?" she said.

"Give me one reason to be."

"Am I right in thinking that at this moment there's nothing either of us can do to resolve this situation?"

He tightened his jaw. That was the damn problem. He wasn't used to being powerless. He was used to being in the center of the action, controlling it—or at the very least actively responding. With no word from Flynn and no one else he could trust, he couldn't do a damn thing. He wanted to go for a punishing run, but she wouldn't be able to keep up, with her injured knee. And God knew what she could get up to left alone for too long. Build a raft and drown in the swirling currents? He needed to get away from her, before he got too close. But the job entailed staying close.

She used her toes to pick up his T-shirt, pulled it over her head and knotted it at her stomach, leaving a sliver of skin visible above her bikini bottoms. The neckline slipped over one toned shoulder. How did she manage to make a black T-shirt six sizes too big look just as sexy as a bikini?

"So come out for a snorkel with me," she said. "Clear your head. Cool off. Try to relax. It'll be good for both of us."

"Are you always like this?"

"Like what?"

"You've been kidnapped. You're being held for ransom. You should at least be afraid."

Her flirty expression dropped. "Jack, I'm terrified. I'm very well aware that these could be my last days alive. And I could panic and scream and fight. But what for? How will that change anything? Or I can go out there and seek oblivion in beauty and innocence and goddamn fish. And do something that's not sitting still and worrying about a situation I have precisely zero influence over. It's either that or raid the alcohol cupboard and get stupidly drunk. Which would you recommend?"

Every minute that passed, she got more intriguing—less like the high-maintenance girl he had thought he'd be stuck with, and more like some alluring fantasy woman.

"Was that what last night was about?" he said. "Oblivion?"

Her forehead creased. This was no longer an act, like the sunscreen had obviously been. "Possibly. My mind wasn't really doing the thinking."

"Mine neither."

She eased off the table and walked toward him, hips swaying. "So." She stopped inches away, and squinted up at his face,
releasing a waft of citrus, sunscreen and woman. Jesus. "I'm
thinking there are a few options here. Option one—we could
sit around and drive ourselves crazy wondering what the hell is
going on somewhere out there in the world." She waved aim-
lessly at the ocean. "Two—you could strip me naked and screw
me senseless, right here on this picnic table, right now. Which,
for the record, I wouldn't mind in the slightest because, oh my
God, last night..."

His mouth dropped open. There wasn't a hint of teasing in
her voice, just a calm invitation, as if she was suggesting a game
of basketball. He could close the gap between them in a mil-
lionth of a second, plant his hands on her hips, pull her against
him, taste her, strip her naked. If last night was any indication,
the result would indeed blow his mind.

"Or, three, we could do the sensible thing and go snorkeling."

"Three." His voice caught. He swallowed. "Three," he said,
louder, clearer. She only needed to look at his shorts to see that
his body had stopped listening at option two.

She laughed, the sound husky and hearty. "Don't know about
you, but I need to get into that cold water soon."

She turned her back on him, mercifully, and sashayed to the
edge of the veranda, where she'd left her snorkeling gear the
previous day. "See you in there."

An hour later, Rafe kicked past the point where the coral
gave way to the sand rising up to the beach, and stood, facing
backward in his flippers. He pulled off the snorkel and mask.
Laura had been wrong. The swim had done nothing to ease
his state of mind, and had barely made a dent on the traitorous
state of his body. He'd spent too much time in his head, thinking about how shameful it was to swim around looking at fish
when Theo was being held captive. And too much time notic-

ing how the water washed around her legs as they powered and twisted through it.

She stroked lazily up to him and pushed her mask onto her forehead, letting the snorkel hang from it. She treaded water, too short to reach the sand. "Nice, huh?"

He fought the urge to smooth his fingers over the mark the mask had left around her eyes.

"Your shoulder seems better now," he said.

"Must have loosened up in the water." She smiled.

Was she playing him, or was he reading a genuine attraction? He was wrong about a lot of things to do with humans, but could usually tell when a woman was paying him undue attention. But he'd never before met a woman like this one. He was drawn to her, body and mind, whether he liked it or not. The possibility she was faking made his gut tighten. Why? Why did it matter that she should want him that way? He hadn't sought that from any other woman. Whenever a woman took an interest, he wanted to shout: *Can't you see what I am? How can you want this?*

In fact, he had said that to Simone once. She'd answered truthfully, bitterly: *I don't know.* As if he was some evil addiction she wanted to shake but couldn't. Like cigarettes.

Something buzzed in the distance. A plane. Chest constricting, he looked up to the east. He sensed Laura following his gaze to the dot of an aircraft, low in the sky, on approach. He grabbed her from behind, trapping her elbows so she couldn't signal.

"Just a precaution, princess."

She thrashed, trying to kick him away, but he had all the balance. Her flippers and the force field of water around them stopped her doing any damage. Beating up on him wouldn't help her, anyway. He knew this plane, and what it meant.

He squinted into the brilliant sky, willing his instinct to be wrong, willing it to be just some tourist plane. Or could it be a search plane, looking for her? *Merde.* Time for evasive action,

just in case. As it neared, he spun her, pinned her torso and arms
with one arm and steadied her head with the other. He crushed
his lips to hers, too forceful for her to free her teeth and bite
him again. It wasn't supposed to be for pleasure, this time, but
that instruction didn't make it to his shorts. What a psycho, getting turned on while restraining a woman. Thankfully the tide
pushed her hips away from his.

The engine's roar drilled into his head, growing louder every
second. He sensed it heading for the lagoon, dropping altitude.
A single-engine Cessna flew into his peripheral vision. *No. God-
dammit.* The noise rose into a whine as the aircraft gained altitude, its nose sweeping upwards. The signal. He released Laura's
lips, his arms dropping to her waist to hold her up. She could
fight all she wanted now. The plane shot straight up in the air.
Gabriel's damn show-off pilot. What was his name—Chamuel?
They could have just dropped a note.

"Is that the same plane tha—?"

"Yes."

"What are they doing—a loop-de-loop?"

The plane leveled out, upside-down, then dived again, before
righting, banking and returning from where it came.

"What's it doing? Checking up on us?"

If only. He tightened his arms around her waist. He had his
orders.

CHAPTER
13

In the thick, black moment when Rafe discovered Theo was gone, he'd wanted to throttle Gabriel and his entire militia, neck by neck. Right now, he ached to seek release from the darkness by carrying his captive up to the villa, laying her on the bed, stripping the wet clothes from her and finishing what they'd started last night.

Instead, he pulled her away, a little too roughly, and released her. She flipped onto her back, the black T-shirt outlining her breasts, her arms and legs stroking as her eyes strained to make sense of his expression.

The choice was simple—kill her, or throw Theo into a lifetime of pain. Twenty-five years ago he would have slaughtered her without blinking. But now? How could he bring himself to do that? He'd have to overthrow the years of therapy and dehumanize her, like he'd been trained to do with his victims when he was a child. How could he live with himself afterward? But how would he live with himself if he didn't do everything in his power to get Theo back?

Innocent people suffered every day, all over the world. He turned and strode out of the water, unable to look at her.

"Jack? What is it?" Holly kicked until she touched sand, and yanked off her flippers. "Jack?"

Her lungs tightened. The water felt like ice. For an hour he'd relaxed, even smiled and laughed, as they'd explored the lagoon.

He'd seemed almost boyish, and she'd felt both their straitjack-
ets loosening. Then came the plane.

She splashed through the shallows and caught up to him.
"Stop. What is it? Was that a message? Did something happen
to your son?" She grabbed his arm, but he shrugged it off and
continued marching up the sand. She dropped the flippers and
mask, charged around him with a desperate, hopping limp, and
planted both hands on his chest, pushing with all her strength.
"Jack."

He wouldn't meet her eye. "That's not my name." His voice
cracked.

"What did that mean—the plane? Tell me."

He closed his hands around her waist and lifted her aside. As
he set her down, the sand tipped. Damn sea legs were back. She
gulped back a surge of nausea.

"Talk to me, Jack. Please."

He strode ahead. "My name is not *Jack*. This is not a game
anymore."

"It never was." She pressed together her lips, bruised from
his kiss. Not that it met anyone's definition of kissing. "Something's happened. What?"

"I'm going to find out."

He strode into the clearing and disappeared down the track
on the far side, just as she reached the grass. Getting the laptop
and sat phone? She froze. Was the game up? Should she hide?
He'd find her, as surely as if she had a GPS tracker nail-gunned
to her forehead. Could she arm up? He'd hidden the kitchen
knives, the gun, the pirate's knife… Last she'd seen her pocketknife, it'd gone into his shorts.

Too late. He was back, with the gear. He laid it on the picnic table beside her and hooked it all up, without bothering to
sit. Seconds ticked into minutes. Goose bumps pricked her wet
skin. He leaned over the computer, drumming his hand on the
table, muttering in another language. She closed her eyes, im-

patience curling her stomach, the world swaying. The rhythmic crash of surf drifted from the other side of the island. In the clearing even the birds had quieted. The computer trilled. She flicked her eyes open.

"Technology's a bitch, huh?" she said.

His black eyebrows dived together. He'd gotten serious, all right. Why? He clicked open the internet and flicked to a news website. The headline screamed in bold: HEIRESS RESCUED. Fuck. A photo below began to load, then jammed. She swallowed.

Jack stabbed at the mouse, unleashing words that would've got her expelled from high school French. The cursor froze. He staggered backward, shoving his hands in his hair. The laptop screen blinked, then the photo trickled down the page—a close-up of Laura hugging a man in dark combat gear, his face blackened, a dozen cameras surrounding them. The senator, playing the soldier he'd once been. A choked gurgle escaped Holly's throat. He'd staged a rescue?

Jack swung around, breathing fire. He caught her upper arms, fingers digging into her flesh. "Who the hell are you?"

She gaped. Time to come clean. There was no other way out of this. Hell, there was probably no way out at all. "Holly," she squeaked. "My name's Holly Ryan."

"Holly." He spat her name like it was a curse. His skin flushed red, veins cording in his neck. "Are you in on this? Talk!"

"Let me go. I'll tell you everything I know—which isn't much, I swear."

He didn't move. His fingertips dug into her arms.

"Jack, please. You're hurting me."

He looked at his hands. His eyes widened, as if he hadn't noticed he was holding her. He released her with a jerk and stepped away. She clawed her toes into the grass, shooting her arms out to stabilize. The ground was rocking like an earthquake.

"I was—I was paid to pretend to be Laura, to do some of the sailing for her. I'm the hired help here, just like you."

His eyes were popping, his jaw so tight it looked ready to explode. Fisting his hands, he stalked toward her, muttering some kind of chant. She backed away, hit the picnic table and stopped, trapped. Icy fear flooded her stomach. He raised his hands robotically and closed them around her neck. Spittle slipped out of a corner of his mouth.

She clawed his wrists, but his grip held, cutting off her air supply. He stared at his hands, white showing all around his dark pupils, like he'd morphed into someone else—something else. She pummeled his face with her fists. He closed his eyes and took it until her hands weakened, like they'd turned into noodles. Pinpricks of light swam in her vision. *Oh, God, was this it? The end?* She tried to scratch him, but her nails swiped air. She felt like she was slipping underwater. The world blackened and swayed.

When all else fails, play dead. Her fight club teacher's words filtered into the darkness. Yes. She closed her eyes, let go of effort, dissolved into jelly.

His grip eased, his hands forced to abandon her neck and catch her waist before she fell. She let her head loll, let him take her whole weight. He froze, then swung her limp body into his arms and slumped on the ground, tangling his fingers in her hair and pulling her into his chest, cradling and rocking her like a baby. "*Non, non, non.* What have I done? Dear God, what have I done?"

He laid her gently on the ground and pressed his fingers into her throat. It wouldn't take long to find her hammering pulse. She sensed his face leaning into hers, his warm breath trickling over her cheek, her own breath ricocheting off his skin. A drop of liquid landed on her nose, then another.

"*Mon Dieu.* Laura, please." Another splash. Holy shit, he was crying? Something soft and warm pressed lightly on her temple.

A kiss. He cradled her cheek, touched his nose to hers, then his forehead. "Laura… Holly. Please be okay. I'm sorry, I'm sorry. That…that wasn't me. Holly!"

Her belly flipped. Her real name. He'd said her real name. His touch was achingly gentle. A twisted part of her wanted to reach for him, pull his body onto hers. That had to be a good sign the immediate danger had passed. She allowed herself a groan. Pain thumped behind her eyes.

He flinched. "Lau—Holly! Holly!" He threaded an arm under her legs and the other around her shoulders and sat her up, gently urging her head between her knees. He rubbed her shoulders and smoothed his hand down her back. The sensation of safety washed through her like warm honey. She let herself drink in clean, beautiful oxygen.

Once her breathing had evened out, he drew her onto his lap, wrapped his arms around her and pressed his lips to her forehead. He smelled salty. Her eyes stung and watered, and she had to hold back from throwing her arms around his waist and holding on, tight. Black clouds whirled in her brain, heavy with memories of another man who used to hurt her, then be racked with guilt.

But that just then…that was worse than anything her father had dished out, far worse than Jasper's manipulation. Jack very nearly squashed her like a bug. She'd thought he was so controlled and calm, but maybe she was just seeing the mammoth effort to contain that rage.

"Honestly, Jack, I don't know what's going on here." She couldn't speak above a whisper. "All I know is that I was supposed to be paid to sail around the world."

"I kidnapped the wrong woman." His voice was flat.

Tentatively, she rested a palm on his chest, as if it would imprison the demons inside, and bring back the Jack she'd thought she knew. His heart pounded. "Yes," she said.

Would she would snap, too, if her child had been plunged into danger—into even more danger? People always broke along the same fault line, and she'd just located his.

"That footage?" he said.

"I'm guessing they've staged some kind of rescue with the real Laura." And cut Holly adrift.

His pecs bunched up, under her hand. "This is fucked up."

"So what happens now? That plane—it spooked you. Was it a message?"

"An order."

She swallowed. "To do what?"

His arms tightened around her.

"To…kill me."

"Yes."

"And will you?"

He buried his face in her hair. The water rushed over the sand below, in and out, in and out, like the world was just spinning on as normal.

"Wow. You have to think about it?"

"I didn't think it would come to this. I thought I could keep you safe. Killing innocent people in cold blood is not what I do. Not who I am." His voice wavered. It wasn't a no. It sure seemed like he'd been ready to kill her a few minutes ago.

"That's reassuring." She should wriggle out of his embrace, but her nerves craved his touch, her body ached with the comfort of being tucked between his chest and arms and bent head. "Your friends obviously think you're capable of it."

"They don't know me so well anymore."

Anymore? "If you kill me, will your son be okay?"

"There are no guarantees."

"But that's the deal, right?"

"I'm not sure anymore. The game has changed."

No kidding. It didn't feel much like a game at all. Reluctantly, she unfolded herself and sat cross-legged, facing him. His eyes were shot with tiny red veins. He was evidently fighting some internal battle. Without thinking, she rested a hand just above his knee—not to manipulate him this time but because…because the thought of him hurting drove daggers into her chest. Oh shit. She cared. She cared about a guy who'd just come one squeeze away from killing her. Would she never learn?

She had to think, to reassess. If the whole of America now knew Laura was okay, no one would be looking for her. Her chances of rescue had plummeted from slight to zip. Her gaze rested on the laptop. Maybe she could get out a message. But who to? No one on Earth gave a damn about her. She'd never felt so alone.

But then, there was Jack. They were alone in this together.

"You've been playing games with me from the start." His tone was dead calm.

"I've been trying to preserve my life."

"So all that stuff about your father hurting you, and learning to fight so you could defeat him, that was a lie designed to make me feel sorry for you?"

"That was true. But my father is not a senator—not even close. And I don't need anyone feeling sorry for me."

"Seducing me—was that all part of your plan? To get inside my head, force me to feel something for you?"

"Yes."

He made a scoffing noise. She stared at her legs, feeling like the fraud she'd been for too many years. But this…this had been different. She couldn't let Jack think—

"Initially," she added weakly, raising her head.

He narrowed his eyes. "Initially."

No—what was she doing even admitting that? This was complicated enough. She should have stopped at "yes." Whatever irrational feelings she'd been developing for him should have dissolved the second his hands closed around her in anger. Her fingers floated up to her neck. It felt tender, bruised. He closed

many corrupt bureaucracies. You must understand, this militia has operated underground for forty years, at least. Any authorities they can't evade they buy off or blackmail. Gabriel would find out, he'd know I betrayed him, and he'd run, taking my son with him. In the space of a day they could be anywhere in the world." He dug his knuckles into his temples. "No. This is between me and him. I can still resolve this. I'll have to."

"Gabriel?"

He dropped his head back and groaned in self-disgust. A slip.

"You might as well come clean. Who would I tell?"

He studied her grimly.

"I told you my story," she continued. "Why don't you start with your name, and we'll ease on in from there?"

He stared a long minute. "Raphael," he muttered, finally. "Rafe, now."

Rafe. It suited him. Masculine and heroic, though he wasn't angelic in the slightest.

"And you're in the army—the French army." She took his silence as confirmation. "So who's Gabriel? Hang on—Raphael and Gabriel? Are you brothers, with God-fearing parents?"

He shook his head, slowly, like the movement hurt. "No one remembers the names we were born with. We were in the same militia, many years ago, before I became a real soldier. Our commander beat our names out of our consciousness and gave us new ones. His little joke. Gabriel and I had grown up together in refugee camps, both orphans, the closest thing to family we each had. We vowed to protect each other, and we did, for years. Then one night all the orphaned and abandoned boys in that camp were rounded up and taken away, and forced to fight for the militia. Gabriel hid from them. He might have escaped, but he saw them drag me away and came to my aid."

"Because of the vow."

"Yes."

"And you were both taken."

"Yes."

Crap. It took a lot to make her own childhood look rosy, but that… "So you were forced to fight. Like conscription."

"Of a sort. But this wasn't a real army, with rules. There was no code of honor, no Geneva Convention, just the word of the commander at the top of the chain."

"How old were you?"

"Nine."

"Holy shit, really? I thought you were talking sixteen, eighteen. Nine? How can a nine-year-old be a soldier?"

"In some ways a nine-year-old makes a very effective soldier. Frighteningly effective. You don't question authority, you don't understand consequences—guilt, remorse. You're more malleable. Any scruples you might have are swiftly beaten out of you."

"What did you have to do?"

"Whatever I was told to—intimidate, threaten…kill."

Kill? "How can a nine-year-old kill someone?"

"We were well drilled in the use of weapons."

"No, I mean, not *how*—not in the practical sense. I mean, how could a *child*…"

He nodded, grimly. "I couldn't, at first. They threatened to execute me because I couldn't bring myself to be violent. But I found a way to switch off my conscience. I found I could will myself to fill up with the rage and the anger and the pain and the suffering and the loneliness and the fear, until something gave and I came out the other side, into a—"

"A trance," she said. "Like just now." She rubbed the back of her neck.

"Yes, like now. A trance. A place of refuge, from which I could do whatever was necessary to survive, however despicable. Where I could stop myself feeling anything. Just now, I felt that first warning that it was happening—I *saw* it—and I was still powerless to stop it. After all these years, I'd thought…"

Leaning forward, he clasped his hands across his knees, and stared at them.

She wanted to grab them, link her fingers through his. She didn't. "What was it, that warning? What did you see?"

"When I was in the militia, my vision would go shaky, like everything was diving into everything else, and that was the last thing I'd know." He rubbed a callus on his thumb, absent-mindedly, it seemed. "That's what happened, with you. Next thing, you're unconscious at my feet and I feel like screaming. That hasn't happened to me in more than two decades. I didn't know it still could. I saw it coming and I couldn't override it."

"That terrified you."

"Yes." It sounded like he was repenting, like in confession. Not that she'd know about that.

"That tells me you have a strong conscience, not a weak one."

"Not strong enough, as you discovered."

"Sometimes it's healthy to recognize your weaknesses, so you can at least begin to patch them—find that kill switch. It's when you're unaware of them that they bring you down."

Like with Jasper—if she'd been aware that she was vulnerable to obsession, she might not have lost most of her twenties. Her path wouldn't have brought her to this predicament.

But suddenly, she didn't regret being here, with Jack—*Rafe*. It seemed right, somehow, that she'd wound up on this island with this man. She blinked, hard, reactivating her headache. What an insane thought.

They fell silent. She sneaked a glance at him. His brow was knitted, as he stared out to sea. The things he'd been through. He had to be the strongest man she'd met.

"How long were you a child soldier?" she said.

"Five years. I got out, eventually. It was during a firefight—I was separated from the others and was found by a group of Spanish aid workers. They had to hold me down to prevent me from going back in. I wouldn't leave Gabriel. They said they would

look for him. I described him—he has disfiguring scars." Rafe
touched his nose. "They said they'd seen his body. And then
the only thing I felt was relief, that I wouldn't have to be that
monster anymore. They found me a place in an English missionary school, where I could be rehabilitated."

"But he wasn't dead."

"No."

"So where is he now?"

He sighed, as if giving up a great effort. He was really letting her in. Only, instead of her chest filling with triumph at
breaking through his walls, there was only...sadness, for the
abandoned orphan he'd been, for the weight he must still carry.
"No one knows, exactly. At some point he became the militia's
commander. Six years ago I was stationed briefly in the Indian
Ocean, brought in to help the French and American navies bust
a human trafficking ring that was targeting former French col-
onies, among other countries. We'd intercepted comms of the
traffickers talking in my native language. It's an ancient dialect,
almost extinct after waves of invasion and genocide in my country. They called themselves a name that translates as the Lost
Boys—also what the militia was called when I was a boy. It's a
common enough nickname for child soldiers, but that plus my
native language..."

"You think it was Gabriel?"

He linked his arms behind his neck and stared at the jetty.
"No. I still believed he was dead, and they never used his name.
But I wondered about others I'd fought with. One of the conversations I intercepted was about me—about 'Raphael.' They'd
spotted me and knew who I was—who I used to be. That was
confirmation it was the same militia. I believe it was also how
Gabriel tracked me down. We nearly got them once, but they
were tipped off. All we found were the bodies, still warm.
Twenty-six women and girls, the youngest barely ten, destined
to be sold as sex slaves. The things they did to them, before

they killed them…" His jaw tightened. "It bore the hallmarks of the militia."

"They never got caught."

"They're too well organized. Before the French navy lost interest, they called the militia *Les Pirates Fantômes*—the ghost pirates. If the authorities get too close, they vanish. Your kidnapping suggests they're involved in a lot more than we gave them credit for. I had wondered if they'd come for me one day—no one willingly leaves the Lost Boys. I…I didn't think they'd come for Theo, too, didn't think they could possibly know about him. They must be holding him somewhere near here, but I have no idea where, which is why I have no choice but to follow orders, for now."

"Theo." A regular kid with a regular name. "How old is he?"

"Nine."

"Oh, man. The same age you were." No wonder Rafe was haunted. Nine. Jesus.

"But he's much younger, in a lot of ways. I was old before my time. Theo—I've made sure he's stayed young."

"Given him the childhood you never had." *Breaking the cycle*, they called it in the States. Was there a time her father had wanted to save her from the childhood he'd had, instead of inflicting it on her?

Rafe rubbed his face. "This is getting us nowhere."

Us. Including…her? "Does Gabriel want you to join him again?"

"Either that or he wants me dead. But first, I suspect, he wants revenge. He wants to break me. That's the way they operate. They force you to do the thing you think you'll never do, to turn you into one of them. In my day, they made you kill an innocent, preferably someone you loved. They need you to burn bridges with your former self, ensure your family no longer accepts you, ensure you can't live with yourself in your original form." He fixed sunken eyes on her. "If I have to, I'll take Theo and go into hiding—for the rest of our lives, if necessary—after getting you to safety."

"What did you have to do when you were taken from the refugee camp?"

"Kill Gabriel."

"But you didn't, obviously."

"No." The word was twisted with disgust. Regret? "But I did find that place of darkness."

"And now you have to kill me."

"Yes."

"He thinks you're capable of that—killing an innoc—" She cleared her throat. "Killing a relatively innocent woman?"

"I was, once." His eyes widened, as if inspiration had caught him.

"You are speaking past tense, right?"

He swiveled, and grabbed her shoulder. "If they believe I've killed you, we'll have a chance."

"I thought we established you weren't going to do that. Never strike a woman, remember?"

Life glittered back into his eyes. "I'm not killing anyone, not when you've already done it for us."

"I'm not following."

He jumped up and strode toward the shed. Okay, so he probably wasn't going to kill her. What would he do—let her go? What then? For six years, the only thing she dreamed about was freedom. Now, freedom seemed empty and lonely, and lacking in funds. Her past and her future were two scary gaping holes. Which left just the present. She had nothing and no one to live for, but one thought gnawed at her: somewhere nearby a child was in danger of growing up like she had—like Rafe had. Alone, unloved and vulnerable.

Right now, that at least was something to live for. And fight for.

CHAPTER

14

Rafe yanked open the door to the shed, blinking impatiently while his eyes adjusted to the gloom. He tossed several ropes into a pile outside the door. No tarpaulins—the parachute would have to serve as a body bag. Laura—Holly—kept her distance, eyeing the haul. What else could he use?

"What are you going to do?" She looked ready to bolt. She really did think him capable of killing her—and why not, seeing as he'd nearly strangled her fifteen minutes ago. So much for all the years of turning himself inside out and endlessly reliving the hell for a parade of psychologists and psychiatrists and psychotherapists. After all that prodding and picking over his brain, after all their attempts to reprogram him, the dark place still beckoned. If Holly hadn't played dead and jolted him to his senses, she'd be dead for real. God knew what the next twenty-four hours would hold—whatever happened, he needed to keep a hold on his emotions.

"Ja—Rafe?"

Task at hand. He'd been staring at a corrugated iron wall. "They want a body? I'll give them one." He scanned the shelves, and riffled through some boxes. Duct tape. He lobbed it outside, onto the coil of ropes.

"Oh! The pirate. Right. Of course. I thought..." She closed her eyes for second, and huffed out a breath. Yep, she'd thought he was about to kill her. "You think we can fool them?"

"Bodies decompose quickly in this heat. The smell alone

should be enough to deter them from looking too closely." He tested three carabiners. Rust flaked off them and fluttered onto the packed-dirt floor, but they held—strong enough to take his weight in a cliff rappel. "If I wrap the body up tight, I'm guessing they won't feel the need to confirm it's the right one."

Outside, he crouched over the ropes, separating out the strongest and longest to be his main and safety lines. He'd lower himself down and carry the body out around the shoreline. That way he wouldn't need Holly's help. He'd handled enough bodies to want to save her the trauma, princess or not. His jaw tightened. *Not* a princess. A stray like him.

"When will the militia come?"

He shook the dirt off a pair of gardening gloves. They'd do for protection against rope burn. The parachuting gloves were too thick.

"High tide tomorrow afternoon," he said, "assuming they're sticking to the contingency plan. But I'm not taking chances. We'll get what we need from the villa and sleep rough tonight."

"The contingency plan?"

"The fallback position if the ransom wasn't paid."

She grunted. "Right. Get rid of the…evidence and get out of here. Will you go with them?"

"That'll be their plan. Even if Gabriel intends to have me killed, he'll want to be there to see it—perhaps to do it. That should buy me time." Enough time to overcome the entire militia and rescue Theo—alone? He'd had some long-shot missions, but this had to be the most impossible—with the most at stake.

"You'll leave me here?"

"Yes. Hiding in the forest. You'll be safe here until I can come back and get you. If I don't come back… I'll leave instructions for my guy to get you. If neither of us comes within a couple of weeks, you'll have to assume I'm dead, and take the risk of showing yourself to the next honeymooners. It's that or live wild on the island." She was chewing her lip, processing the instructions. Maybe he should have sounded more upbeat. "But I will come back for you."

"I want to help."

"Here." He threw her the safety rope. "Untangle this. No knots, not even a kink."

"I mean, help you get your son back."

He strode into the shed. "This isn't your problem."

"In my experience it's always useful to have another set of hands, another pair of eyes. Someone you can trust."

"Trust? I don't even know who you are. No need to play mind games anymore, *princess*. As I say, I have a guy."

"Who you haven't heard from."

"I'm well aware of that." He hauled out the Windsurfer's sail. It'd do as a shelter for a jungle camp. "You're on your side, I'm on mine. Best we keep it that way."

"It's not about playing games, Rafe. I think we understand each other better than most people who've been acquainted a day and a half."

Had it only been that long? Just hearing her say his real name injected a warmth into his veins that threatened to melt the ice around his heart. He needed the ice, to trap all those dangerous human emotions inside. The avalanche had very nearly released a few times in the past twenty-four hours. Christ, he'd messed up this mission. "I just tried to kill you. Why would you want to help me?"

"But you didn't. I don't believe you're capable of it."

"I am capable of it, believe that. If you hadn't collapsed..." He screwed up his face. What was wrong with her? She should be running from him, not volunteering for duty. "I'm letting you go. What I did just then... These men wouldn't hesitate to finish the job. I have enough on my conscience without getting you hurt, or worse. You've been dragged far enough into problems not of your making. Go back to America—live. Life, liberty and the pursuit of happiness—that's all you need to worry about."

She stared at the rope in her hands. After a minute, she began to unpick it, slowly but deftly. A change had come over her since he'd discovered she wasn't Laura. Relief, possibly, but something else, too. She'd let go of the act of playing the heiress, the spirit of defiance had broken, and she seemed…lost. He had to be careful—vulnerability never failed to fuel his protective instinct.

"Princess. I'm letting you go. You'll be safe from me, and from them. You can go back to America—your family, your job, your home, your Facebook page. Isn't that what you want—your freedom?" Wasn't that what anyone wanted from life? He wouldn't know. The freedom he sought was from a past that haunted him, and that would never come.

She blinked up at him, evidently lost in her own thoughts. "Freedom," she repeated, as if the word was unfamiliar.

"You're worried the senator's people will come after you?"

She shook her head. "The world's a big place, and I'm good at hiding. If I stay quiet and out of sight, they'll have no reason to make my life difficult." A wry, sad smile settled over her.

Don't ask. You don't want to get involved. He collected his cache and strode down the track to the clearing. He took the steps to the villa in one leap, grabbed the parachute bag from beside the gaping doorway and ducked inside to get a couple of towels. Truth was, he itched to know more about her. Where did they make women with courage like hers? There was something very different about her—he'd sensed it from the start.

He shouldn't care. *He didn't.*

When he returned to the clearing, she was slumped at the picnic table, the rope between her teeth, tugging at a knot as if it was Jasper's balls she was tearing apart. Or Rafe's, more likely.

"All right, fine," he said, walking up. "I speak English but I don't speak woman. You're going to have to spell out why you're looking as if being free is worse than being dead."

"Oh, it's not worse," she mumbled. "I like being alive, very much. God knows why. It's just…freedom's not something I'm used to. Family, a job, a home, a Facebook page. I don't have any of those things."

He stuffed the duct tape, gloves and carabiners into the side pockets of the bag, and picked up the other rope. "How is that even possible? I'm guessing your real father's house isn't an option and this Jasper guy is out, but you can't have nothing—you're American." Rafe knew what nothing was. He'd started with nothing half a dozen times before he turned twenty—the refugee camps, the militia, the missionary school, the Legion. But even he had a family now, and a job, and perhaps a home, if the barracks counted. "What's your story, Holly? Who are you?"

Her face screwed up, as if she was bracing for a reprimand. "I've been in prison for the last six years. I'd just been paroled when the senator's people approached me."

He froze, the rope half coiled in his hands. Something snapped in his chest and came out as...a laugh.

"Why is that funny?"

"I'm not even sure." The sound of his own laughter was as unfamiliar as the sensation. "All this time I've been thinking you were a pampered, beaten-up little princess and...*oh la vache.*" He shook his head. "What were you in jail for—murdering Jasper?"

She grimaced. "I wish. Try identity theft, criminal imperson-ation, fraud, grand larceny, cybercrime, conspiracy, counterfeit-ing, money laundering... I'm just your basic twenty-first-century bank robber."

Ah. She was an expert at fooling people. That explained a lot. "Doesn't sound so basic. A balaclava and a shotgun would have been much simpler."

"And more likely to cause collateral damage. I don't like to hurt people."

"Oh, so you're a pacifist now. And those bruises you've given me...?"

"Self-defense, in the heat of the moment, if you remember. And each one deserved."

"What about all your training?"

"To defend myself. Never to attack. Even in self-defense, I can only bring myself to hit back if there's no other choice, and if I don't have time to think about it. I know too well..." The parallel lines appeared between her eyes.

"...what it feels like, to be hurt," he said. "That's why you couldn't shoot me back there, on the cliff. You gave yourself too much time to think."

"That was part of it, yeah." She studied him, her head angled. "You must hurt people, in your job. How do you deal with that, after the pain you've suffered?"

"Usually the people I hurt are threatening others, so it's in defense of the innocent. I try never to cause people pain. The most successful soldier manages a situation without violence."

"But it's your job. What if you're ordered to hurt someone you don't want to hurt? That's got to happen, right?"

He winced. "Those moments are the worst. I don't—what's the English phrase? *Come off lightly.* None of us does." In those moments he could feel the slide back to the devil he once was. Every time, it took all his presence of mind to stay focused.

Enough about him. As usual, she was digging too deep. "So if you didn't use shotguns, what did you use?"

She stayed silent half a minute, the rope slack in her hands, no doubt seeing his change in subject for what it was—a deflection. He grabbed the parachute and began folding it.

"We found more subtle ways to get around bank security," she offered eventually, getting stuck back into the knots. "It wasn't about hoarding wads of cash. It was about changing numbers on computers, and preying on people's greed and gullibility. It's incredible how vulnerable greed can make people. I don't think we ever targeted anyone you'd call 'innocent.' I hope not, anyway."

"We?"

"Me and Jasper. He betrayed me, ratted me out to the Feds and took all the money."

"Ah. True romance."

"More like the film than the real thing. Though Jasper was no Christian Slater, it turned out."

"Huh?"

"You need to watch more movies."

"Life gives me all the drama I need."

"Good point."

"What happened to Jasper?"

"He got everything. I got worse than nothing." She slammed the rope onto her thighs. "Fucking knot," she whispered.

"Give it to me." She relinquished the rope. He scooted up onto the bench beside her, drew her pocketknife from his shorts and eased it into the knot, just hard enough to loosen it, without fraying the fibers. "I see why you have an *issue* with trust."

She leaned back, propping her elbows on the table. "The great, stupid irony is that he was one of the few people I ever allowed myself to trust. Turns out love can make people even more gullible than greed can."

"Ah, love. It's a dangerous emotion, I am told. Possibly the most dangerous thing in the world."

"You are *told*? Are you saying you have no firsthand experience?"

He shrugged.

"But your wife, your son."

"Ah, my son. Wait until you have children—then you become truly vulnerable."

"Like now, you mean." She twisted to study him, squinting against the sun. "But you don't strike me as the kind of man who regrets becoming a father."

"Never," he growled. His protectiveness for Theo was a beam of light in the darkness of his soul. "Theo... His very existence makes up for my half life. If I do nothing else to make up for the pain I've caused so many people, at least I'll leave one good, innocent, pure thing behind." He stabbed the knife into the table. And, by God, he'd keep Theo that way—if it wasn't too late. "But that kind of love—if that's what it is—it makes you weak. It opens you up to fear, and there's no more powerful driver than that. Fear can drive a man to do things he thought he wasn't capable of."

"Like kidnap." Her hand fluttered to her throat. "And worse."

He ground the knife into the table. Whenever he thought of his son, of what Gabriel was doing, his chest churned like a lava pit—fear, anger and the instinct to protect swirling ever faster.

She swung around to straddle the bench, and rested her hand on his thigh. He knew this was some kind of sympathy, but she was entering the red zone. A touch like that could ignite the whole combustible cocktail. But looking into her eyes seemed to settle him, too, their coolness and sincerity offsetting the heat. He didn't dare let his gaze stray.

"I think I understand," she whispered, her voice tight. "There was a time I would have done anything for Jasper. I hadn't really thought about it before, but you're right, it comes down to fear. My fear was that he'd stop wanting me around, and then I'd be back to having nothing and nobody to live for." She stroked his leg, firing up the skin under his shorts. "I know it's different for you—I don't mean to compare it like that. A man like you—you don't have a choice whether or not you're going to love a child. And you can't walk away."

"Is love a choice?"

She lowered her gaze, eyelashes brushing her cheekbone. "I don't think so, but I'm not the person to ask. Maybe some people just can't love, like my father. My mother tried to protect me sometimes—I don't know if that counts—but her fear of my father was greater than any feeling she might have had for me. Jasper's the only person I've loved—thought I loved—and that was so destructive it's hard to even remember what it felt like, beyond an all-consuming desperation." She met his gaze.

"Is that what love is, for normal people? Is that what it was like for you and your wife?"

"You forget, princess—I'm far from a normal person. I was wrong to think I could be. Simone and I..." He leaned his head back and stared into the cobalt sky. What was he doing, telling all this to a stranger when he'd never spoken to anyone about it before—never even allowed his own brain to process it? When he dropped his head, those blue eyes were holding their position, waiting for him to return to her when he was ready. She wasn't playing him now—she genuinely wanted to know. And for some reason he ached to tell her. Somehow, talking to her calmed him, right to his soul. He could do with a bit of calming—a lot of calming.

"She loved me, but I could never love her back, not the way she wanted. She got pregnant not long after we met, and I married her because it was the expected thing—her family is very traditional. I guess I liked the idea of having a family, after yearning for one as a child, and I tried to choose to love her, but it didn't work like that. I discovered I'm the kind who's not capable of loving a woman. And for her...it could be dangerous, as you might have figured out."

"So she called it off?"

"She died, suddenly."

Holly's eyes widened. "Oh."

"Natural causes," he added, quickly.

"Oh, I'm sorry. I'd assumed..." She bit her lower lip.

"You assumed my wife had given up on being married to such a difficult man? You were right. If she hadn't died, she would have divorced me eventually. I think she believed that if she tried hard enough she'd dig to the bottom of me, that I'd let her in. We were together five years, and she didn't even get under my skin." He frowned. Yet, here he was talking to a con woman like she was a psychiatrist, or worse, a friend. "I made a mistake by dragging Simone into my life, and I messed up hers. It won't happen again."

"What if you meet someone else, and feel whatever it is people feel?"

You mean someone with eyes as blue as the sky, who gets in under my defenses and creates an itch that begs me to abandon self-control and plunge into her, body and mind and soul? "Far too dangerous, for both of us." Time to detour the conversation away from him. "How about you? What if you meet someone—would you take the risk again?"

He smoothed out the crease between her eyes. A habit he was developing. She dropped her gaze to his leg and yanked her hand off it, as if she hadn't realized it was there.

"No, too dangerous," she said.

"You must have been very angry, when Jasper betrayed you." He should stop asking questions, get on with the job at hand. But talking to her, it made him feel...*good.*

Merde. Good was not good.

"Oh, believe me, I was angry. Afterwards, the prison shrink explained that a situation like that...it's like going through grief. I guess you would know this—there's this series of stages you're supposed to pass through. It's some psychological theory. You start at shock and denial, and then you get the pain, and then anger, and then you really crash—loneliness, misery. But after a long time down there at the bottom, there comes an upswing. You kind of accept that this is what's happened, and you're supposed to get all energized with hope again."

If that was his journey, he was stuck at denial and anger. The only hope he harbored was that Theo would grow into a good man, and one day a good father, and perhaps that small thing would absolve some of Rafe's sins.

He frowned, catching up to her last words. "*Supposed to* have hope? You don't have hope?"

"I did allow myself a little, I guess, when I left prison." Her mouth softened, looking as if it might turn up if she let it. "But then some bastard kidnapped me from my yacht."

"Ah. Yes. Don't worry, princess, I'll get you back your hope. Maybe you'll even meet someone who surprises you, one day." Not that any man could be a match for her, criminal record or not.

"I don't think I could bring myself to give in like that again."

"Not every man's like Jasper."

"I know that. I know there are good people out there. I guess it's not even about him anymore, it's about the person I became when I was with him. I got too needy, too desperate, and that made me vulnerable. I don't want to be that person again. I like being in charge of my mind and my life—at least, I think I will, when I get a life again. It's just safer to be alone. Anyway, I don't think I could let myself give in to someone again—and you can't love halfheartedly, can you? You can't keep something back, or it doesn't work. It's an all-or-nothing thing, right?"

"You're thinking aloud? Because there's no point asking me." He picked up the knife and resumed working the knot. *Safer to be alone.* No shit.

She laughed, the sound filtering in through his pores and warming him up. "I'm having a philosophical conversation about love on a tropical island with a pirate who kidnapped me, and I'm wondering why my life isn't normal?"

"Maybe you could find 'normal.' And when you do, tell me what it's like."

"That's my plan. When this is over, I'll become someone else—literally. Move to some forgotten place somewhere in the world where my old life can't catch up with me, and start again. Number one rule: keep my distance."

That's just what he'd done. Only his old life had caught up.

"People only mess up your plans," she continued. "As you have demonstrated. That's if…"

"...if I haven't ruined it for you. You were relying on getting paid for your mission."

"'Normal' will be difficult without some cash, yes."

"Do you have *any* money?"

"Not enough to pay you a ransom, if that's why you're asking. But I do have a little. I insisted the senator give me a down payment. No more than pocket money, really—it was a pay-on-completion deal—but if I can get to a big enough town around here I should be able to access it. After that, I don't know. Go off the grid, I guess, and figure it out from there. There's nothing for me back in the States."

He pocketed the knife. He didn't have a lot of money, didn't need a lot—it all went to Theo and Simone's mother—but he couldn't leave her stranded. "I will give you the money you need."

"I don't want your money."

"You're getting it. I'll go on the internet now and wire it to your account."

"Buying off your guilt?"

"Something like that."

Money was a small price to pay for getting her off his conscience. As soon as she was taken care of, he'd block her from his mind, lock away the memory of licking her salty skin deep in the vault in his soul where he kept everything that had the potential to harm him.

"Here, I've loosened it. You can do the rest." He held out the rope.

She grabbed his hand instead, letting the rope fall to the grass, and threaded her fingers through his. The touch ignited sparks up his arm, as if his nerves were still undecided about whether she was a threat or an opportunity.

"I can be of use to you, Rafe. We're a team—you said that." A new note rang in her voice. Desperation. Precisely what she'd just said she feared.

"On this I work alone. I've seen what Gabriel's militia do to their victims. Best way you can help is to get out of here and live your life—or someone else's life." He should break contact. So why the hell did he trace one finger of his free hand up her throat and tilt up her chin? "You're afraid. You haven't shown fear—real fear—since I grabbed you from that yacht. Now your eyes have lost their bravado. Why now? I know I don't deserve your trust, but I promise you I'll keep my word."

"I believe you will. And I'm not afraid of anything. Except death. I'm kinda afraid of death—just for the record." Her eyes creased into a smile of sorts, but her voice wavered. Trying to cover for the rising panic?

"That's a healthy fear. But there is something else you fear. Nothingness. Loneliness."

"I'm very good at being alone."

"Big difference between being alone and being lonely. Tell me you have someone you can rely on."

She tried to shake her head free, to look away. He held her gently but firmly. Her eyes had proved more honest than her words.

"Really? No one at all?" he said. Shit. Even he had Flynn, and maybe a few other guys. Not that he and Flynn usually discussed anything more personal than ammunition and targets, but a fractured soul could sense another. One night many years ago, after a few too many whiskies, they'd shared their sorry histories, trusting each other with deep secrets and then burying them forever. Flynn's eyes had the same dead look Rafe saw in the mirror every day. In all the time they'd served together—maybe nine years—the guy had never failed Rafe, as a lieutenant or, yes, a friend.

"Come on, Rafe. I'm on your team, remember? You could use some help, I can help."

"No, princess. Very soon, we part ways and you start over. You're a remarkable woman. You could live a remarkable life."

For the first time, he knew he was looking at the real Holly—
the fragility that lay behind the strength. The fragility fired up
his protective streak, the strength drew him to her like a magnet
snapping to metal. He wanted to explore her in every way possible. It was more than just an urge for physical release—every
piece of him wanted the corresponding piece of her. His mind
wanted to know everything about her, his body wanted to feel
every part of her against him. There was an unfamiliar pull in
his chest that made him want to...

Her gaze floated down to his lips. Her mouth parted. *Yes, that.*

CHAPTER

15

Slowly, Rafe lowered his mouth to Holly's, closing his eyes at the moment of contact, so he could channel his senses into just that one silky touch, like taking a last sip of water in the desert. She stilled. He waited. She squeezed his fingers and slid her other hand up his thigh, over his shorts, settling on his hip.

He cradled her neck, urging her closer. A bead of sweat trailed down his back. She dug her fingers into his waist, giving him all the invitation he needed to explore her mouth. She tasted salty and sweet. The breath of her sigh danced over his tongue. She untangled their hands and swiveled onto his lap, wrapping her bare legs around him, linking her feet behind his back. *Mon Dieu*. It was too much—and not nearly enough.

He pressed the finger pads of both hands into her scalp, not trusting himself to go lower, as much as he yearned to explore the scrap of fabric that barely covered her *derrière*, to dig his fingers into that soft flesh and press her against the part of him that begged for more. Instead, he concentrated on the kiss, groaning as she responded with equal urgency. She trailed her fingers up his back, over his shoulders, down his chest and settled again on the sides of his waist. She found his belt loops and tugged him closer. Every nerve and tendon and muscle strained with the craving to lose himself in her, to find that blissful state where he was both hyperaware and beyond the reach of reality. The point he lost control.

The point he didn't dare go. He reared his head, breaking the kiss, sunlight searing his eyes even through his eyelids.

"Rafe." Her voice was velvet with desire.

If only he could lay her gently on the grass, slip off the clothes that separated them, and taste and touch every part of her, filling the air with her sighs and groans, atoning for everything he'd done to hurt her. But if he allowed one kind of emotional release, what tsunami of darker urges would flood out?

He drew away his hands, skating them down to rest on her hips. Unable to speak, he touched his forehead to hers, his chest still heaving. She closed her eyes and linked her fingers behind his neck. They stayed like that a minute, two minutes, waiting for the world to return to equilibrium.

"I need to know you're safe," he said, once the roar of his desire had faded into the buzzing of insects and lapping of the tide. "From people who want you dead, and from me. I don't want the responsibility of this." And he didn't want to be her next Jasper. She needed a normal man, as much as she claimed she didn't. Someone who could teach her how to love without the fear she carried—of violence, of being abandoned. Rafe would destroy her like he had Simone, even if it was the last thing he wanted.

He eased her backward on his lap, closer to the more neutral territory of his knees. Not that any territory felt neutral under her touch. She unlinked her legs and let them fall either side of him. With the fingers of one hand he smoothed the reddened skin around her neck, where he'd gripped her in a fury he hadn't known he could still feel. If only he could erase the mark, erase the event. He pulled her into an embrace, inhaling her salt- and coconut-scented hair. She rested her cheek on his shoulder.

"I think I've proved I'm not to be trusted," he said.

"Then why do I feel safer right now than I have in my entire life?"

"Because you're just as screwed up as me."

She laughed, her breath tickling his neck. A cool breeze

floated in from the lagoon. He pulled her tighter, and she responded. A real hug. Two people seeking nothing but comfort from each other. When was the last time he'd been able to enjoy the simple pleasure of holding a woman? Had he ever?

"Does this feel as unreal for you as it does for me?" She stroked her fingers down his arm.

"You feel unreal. Everything else feels far too real. Maybe it's the tropics driving us mad. You know what the local name for this island translates as?"

"What?"

"Deception Island. Appropriate, yes?"

"Ha. I'm guessing they don't tell the honeymooners that."

He eased her away, far enough to cradle her face and look into her eyes. "Holly, I'm sorry, for before, what I did when I found out about Laura. It was unforgivable."

"Like you said, it wasn't you."

"It was me—a part of me I keep buried—but it was me. And it was a warning, to you. I'm not a safe man. I have urges—dangerous urges. No matter how deeply I bury them, no matter how much concrete I pour over them, they can still break through. You don't want to be there when it happens."

"I understand. I forgive you," she said, quietly, tracing a finger across his pecs. He caught her hand and moved it away. No more of that.

"You shouldn't."

"But you're right. Perhaps it's just as well we might not see each other again after tomorrow—for both of us." Her voice held no humor anymore. "It's not so much the physical threat of you, but what you could do to my heart. Because…" She linked her fingers through his and squeezed, looking at their entwined hands. "*This*. It kind of works, right? We *work*, somehow."

He nodded, an unfamiliar feeling drying his throat. "I don't want to hurt you. And I would eventually. Two wounded souls will only wound each other deeper." He leaned in and kissed her grazed cheek. "Speaking of tomorrow, princess, we have work to do." He inhaled her scent one last time and, reluctantly, lifted her off him.

"Can I help?"

"Body retrieval isn't pretty work for princesses."

"Lucky I'm not a princess."

"Closest I'll get to one." He stood. "But since you're not a princess, you can start gathering everything we'll need to set up camp—food, water, clothes…" He walked away, his tread less certain than it should be, retrieved the safety rope from where it had fallen, shoved it into the bag along with the parachute and hoisted the main line onto his shoulder.

"I'll be back in an hour."

"*Oui,* Capitaine," Holly said from the picnic bench, her back to him.

At least a dead body would sort out his priorities. Because that kiss sure didn't.

For a long time after Rafe disappeared up the path to the cliff, Holly sat motionless on the picnic bench, staring unseeing at the lagoon. Holy crap, that was intense. Her chest ached with an emotion she hadn't felt since the early days with Jasper—desperation, churned up with need. The kind of feeling that got her in trouble.

Somehow, she'd landed in the dangerous situation of trusting Rafe—worse, of freaking *caring* about him. Instinct should be screaming at her to run the other way. Instead, it was urging her closer. So much for being older and wiser. Talking to him just now…it'd made her realize that though she'd long ago shaken off her anger for Jasper—because what was the point?—she was terrified of becoming that obsessed again. And she could so easily get obsessed with Rafe. The way he kissed her, the way his words and his gaze cut right into her… She leaned forward, elbows on knees, fingers to temples, staring at the flattened grass at her feet.

You're just as screwed up as me, he'd said. Was that the problem? She felt connected with him because he seemed to understand her—and she thought she understood him. What would a life with him be like? She and Rafe and Theo, all living some harmonious existence in... Hell, she didn't even know what continent he lived on. Yep, they sure weren't normal people. Did that make them perfect for each other, or as wrong as it got?

Two wounded souls will only wound each other deeper.

She pushed herself up. The ground swayed. She grabbed the bench, willing her land legs to return. Wrong. It was all wrong. She straightened, warily. No, that wasn't quite true—one thing had gone completely to plan. She'd been wildly successful in her mission to get Rafe to feel something for her, enough to stop him killing her—just—and enough to make him kiss the bejesus out of her. Trouble was, now she wanted him, too, so badly, in all sorts of ways she shouldn't be imagining.

She wandered into the cabin, running a finger over her lips. She'd have to pack her ChapStick. She was out of practice at kissing—and she'd never been kissed like that. His stubble had felt so addictively masculine, rasping against her as his earthy scent filled her airways. A sweet torture for her body, but real torture for her skin. He'd kissed her like he'd meant it, his initial gentleness making her ache with the pleasure of being needed and wanted, and needing and wanting in return.

Then she'd yielded to the need to crank things up, and he'd responded, except that he'd kept his hands on her face, instead of exploring the parts of her that screamed for his touch. Through her bikini bottoms she'd felt his thick, hard need pressing into her as strongly as she'd felt her own desire—yet he'd kept the action above her neck, as if it was more than just her body he was interested in. And, God, that was sexy. If a little frustrating.

That was one thing she'd never felt with Jasper, or the few other men—boys, really—she'd been with. And Jasper would never have let his conscience pull him away. He didn't have a conscience. Rafe was all conscience—well, aside from the whole kidnapping thing.

She began throwing her scattered belongings into a heap. His few clothes were folded into perfect flat squares. He even did laundry with military precision.

Damn, he *kissed* with military precision. She'd lost herself for several long, sweet minutes. That one wasn't like their kiss last night, on the bed. Her body had responded then, sure, but her mind had been driven by a strategy that had little to do with desire—emotional, or physical.

The kiss in the water and the one on the cliff had been all strategy on his part. But that kiss just now, it was both of them stripped naked. No pretenses, no defenses. It'd seemed natural to open up to each other physically, after opening their souls and sharing their secrets.

Why the hell did she think she could trust this guy? She hadn't known him forty-eight hours. The number one lesson of her last decade? She was better off alone than putting her faith in anyone else. Twenty miles from Nowheresville—that's where she belonged, that was the dream that'd kept her sane in jail.

But now that she had a chance to make it real, its bleakness and emptiness made her stomach curl. Dammit. *There is something you fear—nothingness, loneliness.* She hurled a sneaker at her collected clothes. It plowed through them like a bowling pin and bounced off a wall. No. No way. Those were the things she craved.

But talking to Rafe, kissing him, being with him—it made her feel...alive. The buzz of bouncing flirty banter off a man with a quick mind, the rush of connecting with someone, the pull of physical attraction...

She kicked everything back into a heap. Dang, she needed to get out of this crazy place that screwed with her head, and away from the man who made her feel so raw and exposed, and...

goddamned hopeful. Deception Island, huh? Looked like the person she was deceiving was herself.

The white light of the midday sun had given way to the gold of late afternoon by the time a splashing in the shallows heralded Rafe's return.

"Ugh. I smelled you before I saw you," Holly said, as he trudged up from the sand—shirtless again, of course, the low sun warming his skin to the color of burnt caramel. Pity the improvised body bag over his shoulder ruined the view.

He laid it on a patch of shaded grass, as gently as if the guy was merely injured. He'd wrapped the body in the parachute and secured it with the ropes and about a roll of duct tape so nothing was visible, though liquids she didn't want to think about seeped through dark patches in the fabric. She shuddered, and yanked the last of the clothes from the washing line.

"It'll be worse by tomorrow," he said, strolling over, "but hopefully they won't stop to distinguish between a one-day-old body and a two-day-old one. Can't imagine they're going to want to ID this guy before they dispose of him."

"It looks pretty bulky—will they believe it's me?"

"I've wrapped it in a couple of towels, to soak up some of the fluids."

"Fluids. Oh, God." She retched, shoving her palm over her mouth.

"Sorry, princess." He dropped the parachute pack and pulled his forearm across his chest, stretching his shoulder. She didn't even pretend she wasn't checking out the straining muscles—it took her mind off the corpse, at least. He repeated it with the other arm, too lost in thought to notice her attention.

"Here," he said, pulling something out of his pocket and laying it on the picnic table.

"An iPhone?"

"Counterfeit, and an older model, but it seems to work. Faint connection to a network, but no GPS. It was switched off, so it's got a little battery left—enough for an email or phone call or two, if nothing else. Take it. We'll be able to remain in contact once I'm off the island."

Remain in contact. That thought really shouldn't appeal like it did.

"You're not leaving me the sat phone?"

"I have to risk taking it, in case my guy responds. Can I trust you not to murder me in the night if I return this?" He placed her pocketknife on the table.

She met his eyes. "You can trust me."

He held her gaze for a few seconds, assessing her, then gave a swift nod. "You done packing?"

Before he could change his mind, she zipped the knife and phone into the pockets of her cargoes. "I've packed pretty much everything—which took all of about two minutes." She waved a hand at her backpack, now stuffed with clothes and leaning on a pole on the veranda, next to a pile of bedding and towels and kitchen stuff, and the first-aid kit. "I figure we'll only take as much food as we need for the night, and leave the rest refrigerated for now."

"Good plan." He grabbed a towel from the pile. "Time to make the princess a castle. I found a spot that should work—sheltered enough to provide cover from the weather and human eyes, but with a good view of incoming traffic. I'll shower, then we can go. I smell like a zombie."

Hell, if the undead looked like that, bring on the zombie apocalypse. But no kidding, he stank. He disappeared into the cabin. The screen door to the bathroom squealed open and snapped shut, the gas hissed as the hot water fired up. She let her eyes close, picturing a less sensible version of herself following him, stripping off his shorts and her clothes, lathering him up and picking up where they'd left off. She opened her eyes.

Fortunately, she was the sensible type. She picked up the parachute pack and stuffed the clean laundry into it.

A weird kind of domestic bliss settled over the afternoon. She imagined it was the equivalent of what real couples did—working in the yard, pottering around in the house. They strolled to their new hideaway on the arm of land that hugged the eastern side of the lagoon. Now they'd opened up to each other, conversation came easily, though they didn't stray into the deep territory of earlier that day. He talked about his son, she talked about prison and the bliss of sailing across the Pacific.

Maybe she'd played things wrong earlier. Maybe the way to get to him hadn't been through physical temptation but through honesty. Who would have thought? She'd fallen back on the mind games Jasper had taught her, rather than trusting her instincts and respecting her adversary. She was better than that now. At some point, her connection with Rafe had become genuine—and she'd wager Jasper's sizeable fortune that the feeling wasn't just at her end.

Together, she and Rafe slung the hammock between two palm trees. Straight out of a tropical postcard. Not that anyone had ever sent her one, so what would she know? They hung a mosquito net over it and he rigged a Windsurfer sail with rope so they could haul it up if it rained. Real cozy, though he'd stressed the hammock was hers and the ground was his.

He found wooden boxes in the shed and carried them to the hideaway for storage and seating, refusing to let her do anything physical. Her knee felt okay, if a little stiff and puffy, but he made it clear he wasn't taking chances.

To stop herself from spending the entire afternoon goggling at his physique, she changed into her shorts and took the fishing rod to a rocky outcrop, having been banned from the jetty in case the bad guys came. She left his T-shirt on, though it was stiff with salt. After throwing back an aquarium of tropical fish, she finally landed two snapper. While she scaled, gutted and filleted, he figured out the number of the fake iPhone and went online to create a new email account for each of them, so they could keep in contact—she noted he wasn't trusting her with access to whatever means he was using to communicate with his buddy. "Just until I'm sure you're safe," he said. Yes, just until then.

As the sky blazed pink and orange, with a blue-black cloud blanketing the horizon, they set up a campfire. Rafe stripped a leaf from a banana plant, wrapped the fish in little green packages tied up with a flax-like fiber, and placed them in the embers to steam.

Holly lay back against one of the boxes and bit into a wild banana, still warm from the sun. Its sweet tang danced in her mouth. Rafe leaned on the trunk of a palm tree, long legs crossed in front of him, laptop on his knees.

Weird to think this time tomorrow he'd be gone. Then what? She wasn't fazed by the idea of being left alone—it sure beat being surrounded by several hundred women slowly suffocating from incarceration. As long as she was alive and not locked up she wasn't about to complain about anything. But her gut took a dive at the thought of not having Rafe around. How could she feel so goddamn comfortable with a guy she'd only met two days ago? Her skin fizzed with anticipation whenever he came near, her insides went gooey at his voice, her brain fired up as they discussed even the most banal logistical issue. Was she just deranged after being denied male attention for so long?

No. She was old enough to know this was real. Temporary, and disturbing, but real.

"Weather report says we'll pick up the edge of that typhoon within a couple of days," he said. "If it gets severe, shelter in the villa—they won't navigate these waters in a storm."

She tossed the banana skin into the undergrowth. "How bad is it?"

"The equivalent of a category three or four hurricane, but it should skirt to the north of us. Hopefully you won't get anything worse than swaying palm trees and falling coconuts."

"Beats swaying parachutes and falling pirates."

He tapped on the keyboard some more. And then sat straighter. *"Mon Dieu."*

"What is it?"

"Fl—my guy. He's sent a message." His pupils raced across the screen. "He's on his way to Bali. Nightmare of a route—via Paris and Singapore, but it gives us a backup."

"Will you wait here for him?"

He shook his head. "I'll go with the militia, as planned, and tell him to lie low and wait for my say-so. I'll contact my guy when I know the location."

"What if they confiscate the sat phone?"

"I'll make sure they don't find it. They have no reason to suspect I have one." He tapped out a reply. *"Merde, princesse.* This plan might actually work."

He slid the computer and sat phone into its plastic bag and let his gaze fall lazily on her, the sunset lighting up amber tones in his eyes. She stared right back—it seemed the comfortable thing to do. At some point that afternoon the nature of the nervous tension in her belly had changed. The fear of being found out had given way to pure attraction—that delicious awareness that something *could* happen between them, heightened by the uncertainty of when or if it would. The idea she could have a future with him was laughable, of course. But they had tonight.

CHAPTER

16

"Where did you grow up?"

Holly blinked at the sudden question. Rafe really didn't ease into small talk, did he? "Ah, a place called Carterville. On the outskirts of Los Angeles."

"What's that like?"

"No one lives there by choice, if that's what you mean. It's a rough neighborhood—a different kind of rough from what you knew, I guess. Why do you ask?"

He pulled a baguette from their food store, cut it open and began spreading butter on it. She liked how he assumed it was his job to feed them. Her father had only ever gone into their kitchenette to get beer. She and Jasper had lived on fast food and TV dinners—or flashy restaurants, when they'd pulled off a con.

"When I was in the refugee camps, America was the big hope. I used to get myself to sleep by imagining the UN coming to choose me and Gabriel, and give us to an American family, who lived in a house in Phoenix with a basement and real beds in the rooms." He wrapped the bread in banana leaves and laid it in the embers. "I don't think I knew what a basement was and I don't know where I got Phoenix from. We thought everyone in America was rich and safe and happy."

"That wasn't far from the dream I had."

"And all this time I've been calling you princess. Are your parents still there, in Carterville?" He perched on a box, and began ripping salad leaves.

"I don't give a damn where my father is, as long as he's no-where near me. My mother went missing a few years after I left home." *Home.* Huh. She couldn't even say the word without it sounding ironic. "Rumor was that my father had killed her dur-ing one of their epic fights and dumped her body. Sounds like the cops investigated for all of about half an hour."

He'd frozen and was contemplating her. She must sound like a psycho, talking about her mother's likely homicide as if the woman had just moved to another town but she'd long ago stopped thinking of her parents with any emotion. Well, hey, if anyone could understand the urge to block out feelings and bury the past, Rafe could. She felt like she could talk to him all night, though her body hummed with other ideas. Would he make a move? Could she—without him thinking it was a ruse? Because, holy crap, she wanted to feel that body against hers again. Just the thought of it—

"Brothers or sisters?" he said.

"No, lucky for them," she squeaked.

He leaned forward, legs bent and forearms on thighs, and studied her. "So we both bypassed the happy family. This is why we…understand each other."

She swallowed. "Wait—you didn't find your happy family, with your wife and son? Not even early on?"

He pulled a mango from the cooler. The aroma of the fish, the fire and the steaming bread swirled around her, better than any perfume she'd swiped from Macy's as a teenager. Her mouth watered.

"I stumbled into one," he said, as he sliced mango onto the lettuce. "Not just my wife and son but her big Corsican family. They welcomed me—they are good people—but I never felt a part of it. It wasn't something I sought, not after my history. Si-mone and I, and Theo—we had this pretense of a happy family, but I never felt it, not inside. All I got was this overwhelming urge to protect my wife and son from evil. There was no room in me for anything else. I could never enjoy the things you were supposed to enjoy—the football games, as you said—because I was always waiting for the soldiers to come and take it away. And they did, eventually. I should have known my past would catch up, that my family would suffer because of it." He threw the mango skin into the trees, with more force than it warranted.

"But you love Theo."

"I believe so, yes. It's hard for me to understand this emotion, but I feel it here." He planted his fist on his chest. "It's like a dagger that sits in my heart and twists whenever I think about him, especially now that he's..." He shook his head. "I'd want to die if he died—and I'd die for him. I call that love—I don't know if it really is. Those feelings—they're the only way I know I'm alive."

Her throat gummed up. She never cried but that...*that*. She blinked hurriedly.

"The thing you must know about me, princess—the thing I must warn you about—in some ways I'm more machine than man. After I was rescued from the militia, a platoon of psychologists did their best to reprogram me. They called me a 'fascinating' case, a curiosity. They wrote papers about me, like I was some rare zoo specimen. The rehab took almost as many years as I'd spent as a soldier. Sometimes it felt like another ceaseless round of torture, but eventually they restored the basic functionality of a human being—confidence, self-control, the understanding of right and wrong. But some emotions and instincts are too complicated to replicate. Fear, happiness, empathy." He shrugged.

"Seriously? You never feel any of those things?"

"I know that if I threaten someone they feel fear, because that's what the psychologists told me—not because I feel it. It comes from my brain, not my soul. I don't even yawn when other people yawn—that would require true empathy. My wife...she cried a lot after Theo was born. I would hold her, because I figured that's what a husband did, but inside I felt empty. I didn't care—not because I didn't want to, but because I physically couldn't. I didn't understand how she could be sad and complain that she felt alone, when she had a home and a family, and she was safe. My son healed me, in some ways. It was a relief to feel something for someone. But that doesn't seem to transfer to anyone else. This is why I can never be with anyone."

She exhaled raggedly. He would only be telling her this if he felt what she felt. Her heart ached—for what would never be, for Rafe and Theo. That poor fucking kid. "I understand," she managed to say.

"I believe you do. I don't usually talk this freely." With bare fingers he plucked one of the fish packets from the embers and untied it. Steam puffed out. "We should eat."

"You'll get Theo back."

He grunted, tipping the fish onto a bed of mango and lettuce. He drew out the baguette and unwrapped it, broke off a section and added it to the plate. "Voilà," he said, handing it to her. "It seems wrong to be taking pleasure from this..." He swept a hand. This? Meaning the food, the setting...her? "When he is in hell right now."

"But you see, your guilt shows you are a good father, and you care deeply for your son."

"If guilt was the only test of being a good parent, I would pass." He stared at the empty plate in front of him, as if wondering how it came to be there. "Do you think you'll have children, one day?"

"Hell, no. Not that I have anything against them—I just wouldn't wish my life on them. Kids deserve parents who've got their shit together." She popped a cube of mango in her mouth. Its silky sweetness exploded on her tongue. She nearly choked as her words caught up with her. "I didn't mean... Your son's very lucky to have a father like you. Any kid would be."

"I agree—parents should have their shit together."

"I bet he idolizes you."

"He does." His voice was flecked with surprise, as if he wondered how she could know that. Like it wasn't obvious. "I don't know why. Maybe it's because I'm never there."

"You're away a lot—soldiering?"

He plated up his dinner. "For most of the year."

"And your home is in Corsica."

"My son lives on Corsica, with his grandmother. It's where I lived with Simone, and it's where I'm headquartered. I suppose that makes it a home. The regiment I'm in—we're not your normal military. Most of us are the only family we have. We're sent on long, remote missions."

"Ha. It sounds like the French Foreign Legion."

He shot her a look, his eyebrows hunkered.

"Okay, you're giving me your neither-confirm-nor-deny look, which usually means confirm."

He dropped his gaze to his plate, and stuffed a piece of bread in his mouth.

"You mean…what? That's not actually a thing anymore, is it—the French Foreign Legion? I'm getting images of Brendan Fraser in *The Mummy*. All floppy hair and seriously sexy shoulder holsters." Rafe with floppy hair? No. That didn't work at all. His buzz cut suited him—masculine and no-nonsense. Not styled, no forethought, just pure unadulterated man.

"Not familiar."

"Actor, played a guy who was ex–French Foreign Legion in *The Mummy*. Which is a movie. But that was set in the 1920s or something. So it's seriously still a thing—the French Foreign Legion?"

"It's a thing, as you say, though in France we call it the *Légion étrangère*."

Was it her imagination, or was his voice huskier when he spoke French? It did twingy things to her belly. God, he could recite her rap sheet in French and she'd have to restrain herself.

"You like movies, don't you?" he said.

"The best escapism there is. As a kid I used to sneak into the movie theatre and watch whatever was on. In prison, it was one of the few things that would transport me out of there, for a couple of hours. I guess you wouldn't have seen movies, growing up."

"Some. There was a hut in the last refugee camp I was in, with a satellite dish on top. You'd spend an entire day searching the nearby village for a coin, so you could squeeze in with everyone else—usually it was the film *The Karate Kid*. Have you seen it?"

"Maybe once or twice."

"Or we'd watch football, what you call soccer. That's what we played, all day, at the camps—there was nothing else. This was before the soldiers came. We heard once of a kid who got picked straight out of a camp for the English Premier League. I doubt it was true, but it made us train like the scouts were watching. This is why Americans will never win the World Cup—kids like that grow up with a ball attached to their feet. I cleaned shoes every day for months to afford a Man U shirt— counterfeit, of course."

He sounded wistful. She smiled. "Man U?"

"Manchester United. English football team."

"Oh, wow. Globalization, huh?" She wrapped chunks of fish and mango in a lettuce leaf. Cutlery would spoil the joy of it— and she didn't want anything ruining the simple pleasure of this last supper, with this man. "Have you tried to find your family— your birth family?"

"Without even knowing my real name, it's impossible. So many of my people died, I'm not likely to find more than a mass grave. When you have a past like mine, it's easier to leave the whole thing behind."

"Oh, yeah—I get that." She nodded at the rectangular scar on his forearm. "Do you remember how that happened?"

"I remember very clearly. I did it."

"How?"

He covered the scar with the palm of his other hand, as if to heal it. "I was fourteen. I heated up an iron bar and pressed it into the skin."

She choked on a lettuce leaf. "And I thought I was a messed-up teenager. Why would you do that?"

"Same reason you got rid of your tattoo. Erasing the past."

"Hey, I had a local anesthetic—and that was painful enough. What were you erasing?"

"When I was inducted into the militia I was branded with the initial of our leader. An S. After I left, I needed to get rid of it—it was the mark of the devil. I found the bar in a pile of rubbish in a wasteland near my school, lit a fire and heated it up. I had to do it several times, to get rid of the outline of the letter."

She pressed her lips together. She got that—the urge to erase your miserable past—but branding yourself? "Holy shit, Rafe. That took a lot of guts."

He shrugged. "It was necessary. It made a hell of a mess, and the smell… The smell is something I'll remember all of my days. But at least it was my mark, my choice. It was almost a…pleasure to get rid of it, to feel that pain and anger but not give in." He poked the embers with a stick. "I imagined the fire forcing its way into the dark part of me that had allowed me to do all the unspeakable things I had done as a child soldier, and destroying it. I hoped that place had been destroyed, or that I at least had the strength to never return to it, no matter how tough things got." He threw the stick in the fire and linked his hands behind his head, staring into the flames. "When I snapped, today, when I went for you, I knew for sure. This place is still there."

She swallowed, tasting smoke. "Place? You think it's a physical part of you?"

"That's the way it makes most sense. A place my conscience retreats to while the anger takes over, so I don't have to feel anything."

"Did the counseling help?"

"Hard to say. I've twice had my brain reprogrammed—for evil, and then for good. After that much messing around, I had no hope of a normal life."

"Is that why you joined the Legion?"

"Yes. That's when my life began, when I finally found a place I could belong, where I could do good."

She stared at a flame curling around a piece of wood, as if it was embracing the thing it was destroying. "I'd like to find that place. I'll consider my life starting when I get off this island. Hey, maybe I could join the Foreign Legion."

"They don't take women."

"That's not very twenty-first century of them."

A flicker of a grin slipped past his facade. "Half the legionnaires join up to escape women—their ex-wives, their lovers, their lovers' husbands. If you wish, you can take a new name to make it harder for people to hunt you down."

"Did you?"

"I did change Raphael to Rafe. In some languages this name means 'wolf.' It seemed more truthful than masquerading as an angel. Perhaps if I had changed completely, Gabriel might not have found me."

"Are you sure there isn't a way I can help you? For your son's sake."

In the fading light, his expression darkened. "*Ma chérie*, you don't know these people. Knowing you are safe will help me do what I need to." He sipped water. "I apologize for the rudimentary accommodation while you wait for rescue."

"Compared with what I'm used to, this is heaven. Seriously."

"Wait." He laid down his plate and drew a champagne bottle from the cooler. He popped it, poured it into two cups and handed her one. "To our futures. May they be better than our pasts and our present."

"To rescuing Theo."

They leaned forward and clunked cups. She closed her eyes as tiny bubbles tickled her throat. Now that she could associate the sensation with Rafe, and not Jasper, she would forevermore let champagne be a small pleasure. "The present isn't so bad. It's the future I'm having trouble seeing."

"Don't worry about that. I will fix things for you."

And how would he fix the fact that Nowheresville no longer seemed like the sanctuary she'd clung to for so long? She pushed away from the box, stretched out on the ground with her head on her backpack and closed her eyes. The sounds around her amplified—the rush of waves on sand in the lagoon, the occasional pop from the fire, a rustling in the undergrowth behind her, the call of a cricket nearby, backed up by a chorus of millions. Wood smoke mixed with sea air and the aroma of cooked fish and Rafe's soapy-clean skin. Hey, if this was Nowheresville, it wasn't so bad. Was twenty-nine too young to become a hermit? How long could she hide on the island, living on fish and bananas and coconuts, hiding from honeymooners, raiding the cabin for matches and sunscreen and medicine, and whatever else she couldn't do without?

ChapStick. She'd run out of that pretty quick. Even the thought of it made her lips sting. She patted her pockets. Damn, she'd left it in the cabin.

A rush of movement jump-started her heart. She sat bolt upright, eyes wide. Something smacked her back down—Rafe's body, on top of hers. What the hell?

"Wow. You're not at all subtle." She tried to sound casual, but her pulse jackhammered.

"Not with snakes."

"What?" The word caught in her throat. She followed his gaze to the ground beside her. Holy cow, a snake. She flinched, but he had her pinned. "Do someth—"

"I already did."

She peered closer, tracking the blue coil of its body up to

an unnaturally blunt end. In Rafe's hand, a knife gleamed. He flicked the creature away—first its body, then its severed red head.

"Was it poisonous?"

Silence. Stillness. She turned back to Rafe. His eyes focused right on hers, dark and deep. He held himself up on one forearm, his chest brushing against her breasts each time he drew in air, his hips pressing into hers. Oh, God.

"Remind me to tell you how to deal with snake bites." His husky voice heated her up from the inside. He stabbed the knife into the earth. "Later."

He didn't freaking move. His eyes didn't even flicker. Nervous energy wet her mouth. She swallowed and tentatively planted her hands either side of his waist. Under his T-shirt, thick knots of muscle flinched. He blinked, once, slowly, a wash of dark lashes.

"Will you run away this time?" She barely recognized her own voice, it was so low. "Because I don't think I could bear it."

"You genuinely want this? Because I would never take adv—"

"I want this, like you wouldn't believe. Rafe, we don't know what's going to happen tomorrow—we'll find out soon enough. Let's just do what our bodies are telling us to. No strings, no awkwardness. We can wake up tomorrow and remember how screwed up our lives are, but tonight I just want to forget. I want to feel nothing but this—you, right next to me. You inside me."

"Mon Dieu."

Sea water lapped. An owl hooted. She held his gaze until her eyes watered. He eased his full, delicious weight onto her, achingly slowly, moving his hands up to frame her head, smoothing her hair away. She closed her eyes—this was going to be all about the feel of him, the earthy, salty smell and taste of him. And the feel of her—her breasts pressed into his chest, their stomachs and thighs flat against each other. She slipped her hands under his T-shirt and slid them up his back, her fingers exploring the ridges and dips.

"I need to forget everything but this…but you," he said, touching the hollow at the base of her neck. He skated one finger slowly up her throat and over her chin, leaving her nerves somersaulting in his wake. He rested a finger on her lips, charging them up with a ticklish awareness. She parted them, slipping her tongue out to taste his finger pad, tracing the grooves of his prints. Mmm, wood smoke and mango. If only she could explore every part of his body this intimately, pore by pore, over days, weeks, months. She'd have to settle for hours.

"How do I say 'kiss me' in French?" she whispered.

"Embrasse moi."

Oh yeah, even that sounded better in French.

CHAPTER

17

Before Holly could repeat the words, Rafe covered her mouth with his. Stubble scraped her chin, the sensation competing for attention with the silkiness of his lips and the wet rasp of his tongue. He explored her slowly, sending her the message that he was prepared to take his time. This wasn't the hot, desperate need for temporary oblivion, as on the park bench. It was the next step in their unfurling of secrets.

He shifted slightly, and his erection pushed into the dip between her thighs, igniting desire deep inside her. Water whispered in and out of the lagoon as waves of arousal rippled through her, swirling and building.

She moaned and drifted her fingertips up the curves of his back and shoulders to the soft suede of his hair, as he moved his hands down. As they kissed, he scooped under her butt, drawing her up so her damp heat ground into him, unleashing rivulets of hot, liquid pleasure through her, lighting her up to the soles of her feet. With both hands he kneaded her butt, slipping a couple of fingers under the hem of her shorts, and following the line of fabric to her sweet spot. Thank God she'd worn her shortest pair. He massaged her through the Lycra of her bikini as his tongue laved her mouth, exploring her top and bottom. Tiny explosive charges peppered under his fingers. She ached to feel his naked body against hers, but the effort of undressing seemed too great, with all her neurons focused elsewhere.

She pulled her mouth away. "Take my clothes off," she said, the words coming out half plea, half order.

He hissed something in French, his eyes half-hooded.

"I hope that means 'yes.'"

"*Oui, princesse, avec plaisir.*"

She could have melted at his pronunciation, low and gravelly. "Call me that again."

"*Princesse, princesse, princesse.*"

He eased down until his mouth was level with her waist, un-knotted her T-shirt—*his* T-shirt—and pushed up the hem, just far enough to reveal her stomach. Oh, man, he *was* going to take this slowly. Capturing her hips in firm hands, he flicked his tongue over her navel. She shuddered. His lips traveled over the curve of her belly to her hip. He gently bit the bony part. How could *that* be erotic? But—oh, man. As his mouth meandered to the other hip, his hands glided up her waist, bunching her T-shirt. She sat and raised her arms. He knelt, his thighs flanking hers, and smiled lazily as he swept the T-shirt over her head. He yanked his off with one hand. Better and better.

His mouth returned to hers, gently urging her back down. He palmed her breast, but the padded cups of Laura's bikini were doing nothing for her. As if reading her mind, he slid his hands to her shoulders and eased the straps down, his fingers tracing their former path to the curve of flesh pushing up from the tightening cups.

"You're gonna have to take that off," she murmured.

"*D'accord.*"

How did he get that sexy low *R* sound? He threaded his fingers behind her and navigated the clip, giving her an opening to arch up and lick his sweat-slicked collarbone. The tang hit her taste buds. So far it had been his tongue doing the explor-ing. That was going to change. In a little while.

"How do you say, 'Mmm, tasty,' in French?"

He released the clip, his torso reverberating with a laugh. Discarding the bikini top, he swept his tongue over her nipple and caught it gently between his teeth. "Mmm, *délicieux*."

Her thoughts dulled as he teased and pulled and tongued her, first one breast then the next. A groan rolled through her. His hands slid south, and she closed her eyes, only vaguely conscious of deft fingers flickering over the fly on her shorts and pushing them over her hips. She arched, her hands seeking his shoulders, feeling his muscles contract and release as he moved over her. He stroked the front of her bikini panties, strong and deliberate, and sucked a nipple against the hard roof of his mouth, lighting up a fuse between her breast and the apex of her thighs.

He hooked a finger under the Lycra and drew circles deep into the flesh, the silky slide of his path and his deep growl telling her how slippery she was. Like she didn't already know. With every slow circle, she rose to a new plateau. The sounds around her muffled, her own moans and sighs coming from a misty distance.

He released her. Damn. She'd almost been there—what was he thinking? He yanked down her bikini and buried his mouth in the spot his fingers had just left. *Oh, that's what he's thinking.* His tongue resumed the circling motion, round and round, licking and lapping and sucking and sending her head spinning along with the rest of her. He plunged his fingers deep into her, moving inside to match the rhythm of his mouth. Heat and pressure and light built, sending her higher and higher and higher. With a crack, she exploded, bucking and panting and screaming and—holy shit, she didn't care what else.

As the world re-formed she realized he was laughing, a sexy chuckle so deep it might as well be subterranean. "Wow," he said.

"Wow, indeed." She lay back and stared up through palm fronds to a black carpet powdered by stars. "When did it get dark?"

"Somewhere between here..." He rose over her and kissed

her. "And here..." He traced a path through her cleavage with his lips. "And here..." He slipped a finger over her most sensitive spot. She shuddered; the touch bordered on painful. He moved down and planted a line of kisses down her hip, her inner thigh, her outer thigh. Suddenly, he reared back. "Eugh," he said, wiping his mouth.

"What is it?" She propped herself on her elbows. She'd had enough of nasty surprises in this jungle.

"Insect repellent."

She laughed. He stretched over her, retrieved her champagne glass, long since knocked over, and refilled it. He took a gulp and leaned in for a kiss. She tasted the spark of champagne, the sting of Deet and the tang of...her. Wow was right. She'd had good sex before, but she'd never felt anything like that. Not just the violent orgasm but the feeling that she could surrender herself to him and trust that the memory wouldn't be ruined by a future betrayal. As they kissed, she drifted her fingertips up the stubble on his jaw and cheek, to the smooth skin of his temple. Was she being naive?

Whatever. She didn't need to overthink it, not tonight. Tonight was an escape, for both of them. A delicious—*délicieux*—escape, but just an escape. A mosquito whined in her ear. She smacked at it, breaking the kiss.

"Our defenses are down," she said, nodding at the darkened fire pit.

"Way down." His gaze slid down her body.

"I'm talking about mosquitoes." She tugged his waistband, drawing him in, and coasted her hand over his tented shorts. "Though it does seem you're still wearing too many defenses."

"Feels like it, too," he said, huskily.

His eyes shifted and narrowed, focusing on her shoulder. He raised a palm, hovered it a second and swiped at her.

"Got it. We need to retreat, stat."

He stood, and pulled her up. "Hammock? Will that, uh..."
She looked at his shorts. "Work?"

"We'll make it work." He fixed his focus onto the first-aid
kit, his hand still holding hers. "Go, now. I'll meet you there."

She raised an eyebrow.

"Why are you looking at me like that?"

"You make it sound like a military operation. *Rendezvous
HQ ASAP. Over.*"

His face relaxed into one of his rare full smiles. Dimple city.
Her heart pinged. Was this beautiful, fascinating man really
all hers, if only for tonight? "I'm not used to my orders being
questioned."

"Who made you commanding officer?"

In a blur of movement, he planted his hands on her butt, lifted
her clean off the ground and drove her back into something
solid—a palm tree. She giggled and wrapped her legs around
his waist, feeling drunk—on a few sips of champagne, on *him*.
Feeling *happy.* Wow.

He kissed her, his tongue bruising, his erection jammed into
her sensitive cleft. Oh, God, she wanted to feel that filling her.
The fabric of his shorts had to be getting soaked with her re-
newing desire. She squirmed. Mosquitoes be damned. She wriggled her legs free, let her feet find the earth and ripped at his fly.
Gracelessly, she dislodged the button and lowered the zip. He
was blessedly commando. She gripped his hard, engorged length
with one hand. His tongue eased off, and he groaned into her
mouth. She shoved the shorts over his butt, letting them fall.

"Finally," she said.

He released her mouth and hoisted her back up. "Hold tight,"
he said hoarsely, as if talking was too much effort.

She tightened her thighs around his hips and wrapped her
arms around his shoulders, as he stepped out of his shorts and
carried her away. If she lifted her hips a fraction and eased them
down, he'd be right where she needed him.

"How do you say, 'I want to screw you into next month'?"

"That doesn't need a translation," he growled in her ear. "Grab the first-aid kit." He crouched, hovering over the kit, his quads straining under her butt. She plucked it off the ground, a giggle bubbling up in her.

As they reached the mosquito net, he stopped to allow her to pull it open. He stumbled the last few steps, dumping her out onto the hammock. It swung wildly, forcing him to shoot out a hand and stop it. "Sorry, princess. I'm wound a little tight."

She shuffled back on the hammock, allowing room for him. Earlier that evening, he'd laid a soft blanket over the strings. "Me, too. It's been…a while."

"How long?"

He removed a packet from the kit, knotted up the net, and sat straddling the hammock, facing her. His eyes were black, his erection shot up like an invitation.

She crawled to him, until his lips were so close that his hot breath trickled into her mouth. "Six years." His jaw dropped. She licked his open lips and plucked the packet from his hands. "I know. Believe me, I know. And you? Have there been other women since…"

"None that I…" He traced a finger down her cleavage and circled it around her nipple. She felt the pull as it tightened. "No one important."

No one important. She frowned. Did she come under that category?

He lifted his finger and smoothed it between her eyes. "No one as incredible as you, *mon ange.*"

She clenched her teeth on the corner of the condom packet. God, it was a shame they had no future, but she'd damn well make the most of the present. Tonight, she would just enjoy breaking her drought with the most *délicieux* man she'd ever met.

CHAPTER
18

Rafe's quads tensed as Holly rolled on the condom, her firm grasp threatening to undo him. Sure, he'd had flings with a couple of women since Simone's death, but he'd never allowed himself to connect with them at any level but the purely physical, to their frustration. He had to be careful. He actually felt something for this woman, right in his soul. If he opened himself up to her—no matter how good it felt—what would stop him losing control of his emotions and sliding into the dark place where impulse and instinct took over from logic?

She straddled his lap and replaced her fingers with her wet *chatte*, sliding along the length of him, back and forth, back and forth, as she slipped her tongue in and out of his mouth in a matching rhythm. Enough foreplay. He'd been in the red zone too long already. He gripped her waist and lifted her. She groaned as she sank onto him. That alone threatened to end things before they began. Nothing sexier than an aroused woman. He pushed up to the hilt and held still, restraining himself from roaring as she squeezed her muscles around him.

She wrapped her hands around his neck, her nipples brushing his chest. He began moving his hips and hands, setting a slow pace. He wanted this to last forever, to begin to make up for all the years that no one had loved her. She slid up and down, in time with his thrusts, squeezing and releasing, squeezing and releasing, pushing her hips to rub herself against him with each slide.

"Faster," she whispered. "Harder."

He breathed out slowly. "Patience, princess." First, he wanted to hear the urgent panting that told him she was close, because once they sped up, his satisfaction was inevitable. He wanted to take her with him, to hear her cry out again.

He scraped his teeth against her smooth shoulder and kissed it. Leaving his thighs to hold them up, he wandered his hands up her body and cupped her breasts. He flicked her nipples with the pads of his fingers until they tightened, then rolled them between thumb and finger, his fingernails grazing the tips. Her breath became husky, somewhere between a groan and a plea.

He pulled her head down and kissed her deeply, increasing his rhythm in concert with his tongue's plunder. She took the hint, her fingernails biting into his shoulders as she held on, the pricks of pain at the burning in his thighs bolting lightning into his groin. His quads were about to cramp. *Merde.* He reluctantly left her mouth and lay back on the hammock, gripping her hips as she drove him ever closer to the edge.

He closed his eyes as the fog of oblivion descended, muffling her crescendoing cries, the ocean, the wind, concentrating his every sense on the place they were joined. He kneaded her *derrière*, the skin slippery with sweat and her wetness. She tipped forward and balanced her hands on his pecs. Too late for control. If she wanted to be in command, he'd let her. His desire wound tighter and tighter as she rode him, the darkness closing in.

A strangled cry burst through the haze—Holly, toppling over the edge, her muscles milking him. He exploded, the shock spiraling through him, scalding the muscles in his thighs even as it gave release, and shooting up his chest to release a yell of pressure from his throat. He bucked with the aftershock, swearing loudly as they wound down to stillness. No anger. No darkness. Just release, as sweet and cleansing as absolution. He took a scraping breath.

She slumped onto him, panting. He drew up his legs, wincing, and hooked them around hers. A shudder racked her body.

"Cold?" he said.

"Hell, no."

"Didn't think so." Full sentences in English would be beyond him for a while.

He kissed the top of her head and wrapped his arms tightly around her, as she flattened into him, her cheek on his chest. A fresh breeze played on his face. Their skin was slick and hot, the blanket under his back was soaked. His body begged him to push her away, to let the air cool his sweat. He didn't move. He wasn't one for embracing after sex, especially in heat like this, but a release like that called for a slow comedown. His head spun. Was it the otherworldliness of the island, the knowledge that they were alone in the jungle, just a forgotten part of the ecosystem? Was it the craziness of the whole situation? Was it because he was tenser than he'd been in his life, in every possible way? Because sex had never felt like that before—like it meant something beyond the physical, like more had entwined than just their bodies.

"*La petite mort,*" he muttered.

"Meaning?"

"It's a French saying. 'The little death.' The—I don't know the English—*transcendant* feeling when you lose yourself in an orgasm."

"Transcendent? Oh yeah, I get that—I got that, just now."

"I'd always thought it was exaggerated. But now..." He'd died a little, lost control and brought it back. Not a risk he should have taken with Holly, but it was a positive.

"*La petite mort,*" she repeated, awkwardly. "I like it."

They lay there for five, ten, a hundred minutes, silently melting into their surroundings. The wind was beginning to turn, the breakers booming ever louder from the other side of the island, the water of the lagoon surging onto the sand, the temperature dropping as a breeze cleared out the humidity. Goose bumps sprang up on her back as his hands skimmed it. He drew in the edges of the blanket, cocooning them. She purred in lazy approval.

"Early birthday present," she murmured.

"When is your birthday?"

"In another month. I'll be thirty."

He bit his cheeks to stop himself making promises.

"When's yours?" she said.

"I don't know what my birthday is, or my exact age. The Spanish aid workers who rescued me from the militia gave me one—December twenty-five."

"Wholly unoriginal."

"They also gave me my surname."

She pushed up onto her hands and knees, astride him, jolting the hammock. "Oh, God."

"What? What's wrong?"

She slumped beside him, her skin reconnecting with his—all the way down—and slung an arm across his stomach. "I just slept with you, and I don't even know your surname."

"It's just made-up, so what does it matter?"

"All names are made-up—some just more recently than others. It matters."

He cupped a satiny shoulder. What was the harm, now? He'd already let her in far deeper than he should have. "Angelito."

She played with the hair around his nipple. *Mon Dieu*. Much more of that and he'd be ready to go again. "You've got quite the angel thing going on. What does it mean, angel what?"

"Little angel, in Spanish."

She laughed, her belly quivering against his side.

"What's so funny?" He rolled over her and took her mouth in a kiss, pinning her arms above her head as the hammock rocked. Stifled, her laugh became a groan.

"You are an angel," she said, when he released her mouth.

"But not the harp-playing kind. More of the kick-ass demon fighter."

He sure felt more demon than angel right now. He stretched down to untie the net. "Come on," he said, easing to his feet. He held out a hand for her. "Swim. I need to cool off."

Her gaze wandered down his body. "You sure do." She reached for her shorts.

"What do you need those for?"

"Good point." She grabbed a couple of condoms instead. "These might be more practical."

The moon was high by the time they settled back into the hammock, Holly's body tucked into Rafe's under a blanket. The gentle sway reminded her of being on the ocean, of freedom. The man in it reminded her of the simple joy that came from togetherness and intimacy. But it was different from the flippy-stomach feeling she remembered from the early days with Jasper. More mature, more knowing, more equal.

And this time she knew just how to extract herself without getting hurt. Later. She trailed her hand over the rises and dips of his chest, letting her fingers come to rest over his rib cage. She would walk away with good memories of this day that would never be sullied by the inevitable heartache and disappointment. Rafe nuzzled her hair, and his lips pressed against her forehead. He held the kiss a long moment. She closed her eyes, soaking up the buzz. One perfect night with an incredible man was more than some women got in a lifetime.

Slowly he sat up, pulling off one of his amulets. "Here." He pushed it over her head. She swallowed, her eyes stinging. Great. Just as she'd tried to convince herself there was nothing lasting about this moment, he went and gave her something older than civilization.

"For protection," he whispered. He bent over her, tracing the cord's path from her collarbone to where the stone rested between her breasts. It felt heavier than the couple of ounces it weighed. Oh, God, she couldn't afford to get any more attached to him.

"That looks kind of personal." She grabbed the stone and went to remove it. He caught her hand, and the amulet, in both of his.

"It is—very." He frowned. "My son wears one, too. It will keep you safe until I come for you, until I deliver you to your new life." He pressed her hand against her chest, enclosing the stone. "Please."

Her eyes burned. "I'll give it back when I see you again, when we're all safe." She couldn't speak above a whisper. The amulet…it made their connection tangible, somehow. Like their fates were entwined—hers, Rafe's and his son's—and they would find a way back to each other.

"Deal."

"We should sleep."

He cradled her cheeks and kissed her, his lips soft and lingering. "We should. We'll take turns, just in case. You first."

"Sure?" she said, yawning at the thought of sleep. Sleeping curled up with him? Forget frangipani and mango—*that* was paradise.

"I don't think I can sleep just yet."

She wasn't about to argue. He drew the blanket around them and she snuggled in to his rough body, surrendering to the warmth and comfort he offered. Amulet or not, she felt irrationally safe. Prison had taught her to appreciate the rare moments when life was good, even if the bit before sucked and the bit afterward was sure to suck. This was one of those moments.

This melty feeling in her chest, her stomach, her bones—it was just tiredness, right? It wasn't…she couldn't be…? No. Holly Ryan, convicted felon, falling in love with her captor, Capitaine Rafe Angelito of the French Foreign Legion? Ridiculous.

She yawned so wide her jaw hurt.

"Fais de beaux rêves," he murmured, his chest vibrating under her cheek. "Sweet dreams, *princesse.*"

For once, she didn't need dreams. Right now, reality was sweet enough.

Rafe shifted, and the hammock swayed. Cool air played on his face, tempering the warmth of Holly's body. How could a day in which he'd hauled a stinking corpse for an hour end in such a magical way? His stomach twisted. Was Theo sleeping, too, taking respite from whatever hell he was in? He drew Holly in tighter, his chest stinging with the craving to do the same for his son.

He closed his eyes, pulling up like a slideshow in his mind the look of delight on Theo's face when he'd won his football team's player of the day award, on Rafe's last visit home. He was so proud that Papa got to see his game, for once. The boy's cheeks still hadn't lost the cherubic chubbiness of his early years, spent in the bubble of warmth and safety and plenty every kid deserved.

"J'arrive, mon fils," he whispered. *I am coming, my son.* Holly murmured. He kissed her salty hair. Why did he get the same urge to protect her that he had for Simone and Theo—and even Gabriel, once? He'd lost Gabriel, then Simone, and now Theo was in danger. He traced the leather cord of her amulet down to the stone, warm from her body. He'd committed to keeping her safe, but he couldn't open up his life to her, even if it were logistically possible. She'd only be another person to disappoint and lose.

It was nearly time to set her free. Once he did, they would never meet again. It wouldn't matter if he never again had this feeling with a woman—he knew now it was possible. That was a victory.

Sleep had fallen heavily on her. His eyes felt no compulsion to close. Good. He had no intention of waking her so he could take a turn at resting. He was trained to operate on little sleep.

He'd make do with spending the night reveling in the touch of her smooth, lithe body against his.

Many hours later, as the black melted into gray, before the sun returned colors to the world, she stirred and began to move against him, and they drifted into the unhurried sex of people who had all day to do nothing but explore each other's bodies.

As she eased back into sleep, birds began their morning routines. He'd raised the sail in the night, and wet tropical fronds scratched the plastic, as a shower lightly drummed. Water surged and slapped in the lagoon as the tide crawled out. That gave him six hours until Gabriel's men had another window of opportunity to access the lagoon, more if they were forced to wait until the seas calmed. And Flynn was on his way. He allowed his eyes to close.

"*J'arrive, mon fils,*" he whispered, again.

Dang, nature could be as noisy as a prison siren. Holly hunkered her cold shoulders down under the blanket, turning her body so her stomach and breasts lay flush against Rafe's side, and her cheek rested on his thick shoulder. He must have pulled on his shorts in the early hours, the spoilsport. She slung her knee over his legs and squeezed her eyes shut against the early morning light.

She didn't need sight to know the picture around her had changed. The ocean roared as unrelentingly as the freeway she'd grown up beside. Ten thousand tropical plants brushed and squeaked and scraped against each other. Gulls cried like human babies as they circled the lagoon, cutting through the cacophony of squawks in the jungle. Whoever named it birdsong had never been here. More like bird scream. So much for six years of fantasizing about sleeping in until noon. Ever since her release from prison, her eyes had snapped open at dawn, the same time her cell light had flickered on each morning.

She inhaled—spice, man, salt, wet earth. Someone should

bottle that. She swept her fingers through the soft curls on Rafe's chest. He grunted in his sleep. Would the hair on his head curl like that too, if he grew it? Delicious dark-chocolate swirls she could lose her fingers in—and use as traction to rein him in. If he'd been in the French Foreign Legion since his teens, his poor hair probably hadn't been allowed to grow longer than a buzz cut for a decade or two.

Not that she'd ever see him looking any way but this. She pressed her lips together. If they'd been chapped before last night they were pretty much grated now. Not that it hadn't been worth it. And, dammit, she'd left her ChapStick in the cabin. Surely she could risk going back to get it? With a strong onshore wind she'd hear any boat's engine before it came into the lagoon, and the tide would be too low to make the jetty serviceable. Rafe wouldn't be expecting the militia for hours.

Muting her body's protests, she eased off the hammock. Nothing sexier than a hunky man sleeping, the masculinity tempered by innocence. No need to wake him—yet. She closed the mosquito net behind her and yanked on her closest clothes. Her pocketknife and the pirate's phone weighed down the baggy pockets of her cargoes.

She shivered, missing the heat of Rafe's body, and hunted through her backpack for the outsized sweater she'd barely worn. It was about the only clothing she had that wasn't stained, ripped or dirty. Her hair was thick with salt and she could feel it sticking out in several directions, but at least it was out of the way. If she didn't have a mirror, what did it matter?

She walked slowly, giving her swollen knee a chance to ease up. Last night's acrobatics hadn't helped it, but the odd bolt of pain had only intensified the other feelings. Muscles ached in her inner thighs and all sorts of other forgotten places.

At the clearing, she sheltered for a moment under a stand of palm trees, their heads tossing in the wind, to convince herself a boat wasn't about to round the fingers of land that hugged the lagoon. The wind carved salt spray off the water, the mist sting-ing her eyes and lips. The generator hummed. A drop of rain splattered on her eyelid, and more pattered on the leaves and ground around her. She hurried up the steps to the cabin—she ached to be back in the hammock, in Rafe's warm arms.

She found the ChapStick, eventually, on the floorboards under her bed. The generator grew progressively louder, the noise ris-ing from a hum to a rhythmic thumping even louder than the wind, like it was about to blow. Weird. She'd better tell Rafe. If it exploded, their food would rot in hours.

She smeared on a thick coat of the salve. Ah, better. Her eye caught movement outside—the shape of a man jogging across the clearing. Rafe must have heard the generator. He'd sure gotten there quick.

She walked to the screen door and pushed it open. "Rafe, the generat—"

He looked up, straight into her eyes. Her scalp tightened. Not Rafe. The creepy pilot from the other night, dressed in a jumpsuit. That thumping—it wasn't the generator. A helicop-ter hovered above them. It must have come from the west, its approach masked by the easterly. Shit, shit, shit.

CHAPTER

19

The man closed in. As he reached the steps, Holly sprinted along the veranda and leaped on the grass. Her knee split with pain and collapsed under her. The guy followed, landing with a thump inches behind.

She pushed herself up, but he tackled her, his full weight punching her down and knocking the air from her lungs. He shoved her face in the grass and wrenched her arms behind her. She gasped for oxygen, thrashing like a fish on a line. Something cut into her wrists, yanking them together. Cable ties. Too late, she remembered her knife. Something clicked, right behind her head. A gun. She tried to sweep her feet around behind her, but he grabbed a handful of her hair and wrenched it back. *Dammit, Rafe, I need you.*

Another man's voice sounded behind her. A dark figure in heavy boots stomped past in the direction of the body, shouldering a big black rifle. They yabbered loudly in the staccato language Rafe had used with Angry Birds and the other goon. More shouts pelted from the helicopter. She'd messed with their game plan. Would they kill her now, or take her with them? Wait—would they think Rafe was in the tarp? It was padded enough they might not realize the corpse was too small.

"The body—it's not Rafe," she shouted, her voice a squeak against the helicopter's roar.

The pilot ground her nose and mouth into the damp earth.

It was all she could do to breathe through her one clear nostril.
"Quiet, whore. Or I make you quiet."

He returned to the argument, ramming the gun barrel into
the back of her skull in time with his shouts. She picked up the
word *Gabriel*. Would they seek new orders, buying time for
Rafe to get there? And even if he did, what the hell could he
do against these guys?

Rafe sprinted through the undergrowth, his pulse in over-
drive from the shock of lurching from sleep to action. Where
the hell was Holly, and why hadn't he thought Gabriel's men
might bring a helicopter? *Imbécile.* He'd assumed they'd stick to
the plan and use a boat. But if Gabriel had his own plane, Rafe
should have figured he had a helicopter, too. He had more funds
than anyone had given him credit for. Just because there was
no room to land a plane on the island, didn't mean there wasn't
enough to hover a helicopter. Perhaps they'd made the call to
come early, before the storm peaked.

Holly had better have just gone for a nature call, and be hiding somewhere. In a matter of minutes, he'd be on that helicopter and on his way to his son. He had to get there before they
started looking for him, in case they found Holly first. He'd secured her safety, for now. Time to secure Theo's.

The helicopter whined and rose, its metal glinting sunlight
into Rafe's eyes through the canopy. Why was it lifting? They
wouldn't give up on him that quickly.

"Hey!" he bellowed, though they had no chance of hearing.
"Stop!" He pumped his arms to increase his pace.

The helicopter hovered. The scene strobed by in flashes between the overhanging branches and lurching palms. They were
winching something up. The body? No, two bodies, clipped
together. Live ones. The smaller one jerked around, spinning
in circles while the other grabbed at it. Holly. *Putain!* With that
son of a bitch Chamuel.

She screamed Rafe's name. He changed direction, shoved through the undergrowth, and skidded to a halt on the beach. "No!" he yelled, jumping and waving. They had to take him, too. Up in the air, Chamuel's fist flew out and smashed into Holly's face. Her arms and legs went limp.

Rafe roared, his hands fisted by his sides, the muscles in his torso and arms snapping tight. Two men leaned out of the chopper, too intent on pulling in their cargo to notice him. The machine tilted and headed off to the west, disappearing from view behind the canopy. He raced after it, his breath heaving in and whooshing out. By the time he reached the island's western fringe, the helicopter was a speck against the gray sky, way out over the horizon. He sank to his knees, clutched his head and swore so loudly his throat burned.

Holly's cheek was shoved against the dimpled rubber floor of the chopper, a hand tight around the base of her neck, a knee in her back. Her lungs struggled to fill under the guy's weight. Her head throbbed. She couldn't tell if it was coming from inside her brain or from the thrumming of the chopper. She woozily recalled being punched. The burn in her temple backed it up—right on the spot the pirate had pistol-whipped her. Had she blacked out? For how long?

The men shouted at each other. Speckles of light zipped and zapped through the blackness. She opened her eyes a crack. A shard of pain shot into her brain. She counted two men, plus the guy flying the chopper and the guy on top of her—the plane pilot, no doubt. No point struggling, for now. What could she do—overcome four men and learn to fly a helicopter? Jump in the ocean?

The man shifted his weight, long enough for her to inhale deeply. She gagged on the smell of rotting flesh, and fought to shut off the impulse to vomit. The body was laid out next to her, still wrapped. Maybe they'd wait to open it until they reached their base. Then they'd have to go back for Rafe, and there would be two of them, if they didn't kill her straight off. Two against how many?

Or could Rafe's friend get him off the island? But then what—they wouldn't know where she was being taken.

"It's not him," she cried, but her words came out as a hoarse mutter. "It's not—"

The plane pilot bore down on her neck, threatening to cut off her windpipe. Another man dropped down next to the body and flicked open a switchblade. They'd find out in a second, anyway. The plane pilot shoved him with his free hand and barked a few words. The guy shrugged and folded the blade. The third man tossed him something white and plastic. He unfurled it on the floor. A body bag? Grunting, he rolled the corpse into it, and hauled it to the open door of the chopper.

His friend heaved something up from the middle of the floor, staggering under its weight. A piece of machinery, red-brown with rust. He dropped it onto the body, with a squelch. Ugh. Holly's gut heaved. Just as well she hadn't eaten.

He repeated the process with a second piece of junk, then a large rock. The guy beside the body bag zipped it up and shouted to the helicopter pilot. Burial at sea—a routine they were evidently familiar with. They weren't going to ID the body.

"Stop!" she gurgled. "It's not Rafe."

The plane pilot shouted at one of the goons, who chucked him something. A piece of fabric. He forced it into her mouth, and tied it around her head.

The two men each took an end of the bag. They chanted in unison, and on the third count they swung it out the door. She let go a breath. Had Rafe carried out his instructions, that would have been her funeral.

The pilot shifted his weight, bringing his face to her upturned cheek. "No *capitaine* here," he said, the words barely decipherable through his accent. "You and me. My name Chamuel. Your name Mrs. Chamuel." He slid down her back and humped her butt. The other men laughed. She clenched her teeth. The creep had an erection. "Later, Miss America. You and me."

Rafe fired up Google Maps on the laptop, drumming his fingertips on the picnic table as it loaded, ignoring the flashing battery light. He'd charge it in a minute. First he had to figure this out while it was fresh in his brain, then brief Flynn about the change of plan. The helicopter had flown west, not toward the mainland. That narrowed it down. What was out there? He typed *Penipuan* into the search. The screen froze. The computer's fan whirred, as if the effort was too much. He leaped up and linked his fingers behind his head, his teeth grinding.

If Gabriel thought Rafe was dead, there was nothing to stop him beginning Theo's induction. He'd do it personally—induction was an intimate relationship between the commander and the boy. He'd start with the first beating, telling Theo it would release his demons. Afterward, he'd ritually wash the boy and dress his wounds, chanting blessings over him as he nursed him back to health. As soon as he was healed, the beating would begin again. The cycle would repeat until the mental breakdown equaled the physical. The visible wounds would heal but the psychological harm was intended to last. Then would come the test. The first kill. The moment Rafe had held the machete over Gabriel as his friend had looked him in the eye and begged for his life was the moment Rafe became one of them. He'd wanted to earn the commander's respect more than he'd wanted Gabriel to live. That fucked-up decision would haunt him forever. No wonder Gabriel wanted revenge.

And what would those sons of bitches do to Holly? They had no reason to keep her alive, long-term. His jaw tightened. He knew just what they did to their female victims. He'd been lucky to be rescued from the militia before he became old enough to be forced to join their rape squads. He'd never forget the day Gabriel returned from his first one. He'd pushed past Rafe and headed straight for the scrub on the outer edges of the militia's compound. Rafe was sure his eyes had been wet with tears. Hours later, when he returned, the last drop of goodness in him had evaporated. Rafe knew enough about the gang's activities in recent years to confirm their modus operandi hadn't changed.

Anger throbbed in his chest. *Control yourself.* He couldn't lose it. *Tu agis sans passion*—even with two innocent lives at stake. Especially with two innocent lives at stake.

Holly must have left the island with the iPhone, at least—it was nowhere to be found in their camp. Last he saw it'd gone into her trouser pocket, with the knife. She was smart enough to make the most of the smallest advantage. Damn, he should have programmed the sat phone number into the iPhone. He'd have to text it to her—she'd have no reason to have memorized the full fourteen digits.

The computer screen blinked. He clicked onto satellite view, closing his eyes as it loaded. *Breathe. Think.* The helicopter was an older model Russian Kazan. Maximum range with a full load would have to be four hundred kilometers and they must have already flown half the journey, which gave him a starting point for the landing zone of within two hundred kilometers. They wouldn't want to push that, with a storm brewing, so he could count on a shorter trip. He opened his eyes. At least three dozen islands showed up on the map—but Gabriel's headquarters likely had an airstrip. He zoomed in, forcing his brain to stay in charge, tamping down the pressure under his ribs. The picture trickled onto the screen.

After a patience-testing half hour, he narrowed the possibilities to four islands, slung over a territory of forty thousand square kilometers. Two were resort islands, one larger with several villages on it and a whole lot of jungle. One was a smaller inhabited island, another an abandoned World War II base. Factoring in the time it'd take Flynn to acquire a boat and pick Rafe up, it could be another two days before they could search them all.

He changed screens and starting typing a message to Flynn. Once he was done, he'd text Holly.

The screen went white. An error message: the internet had dropped out. The sat phone also showed an alert. *This device has been blocked by your service provider. Please contact your provider.*

He froze. The Americans had cut the connection. *Putain de merde.* He was stranded.

CHAPTER
20

Chamuel shoved Holly out of the helicopter, his hand clamped around the back of her neck. She landed awkwardly on hard sand, pain scooting up her blown knee, forcing her to juggle her feet to maintain balance. They'd landed in a compound—a ring of simple thatched timber huts, dominated by a bigger building. He pushed her forward, shoving her head low.

Once they'd escaped the radius of the blades, the chopper's whine changed pitch and the machine lifted, pelting a million grains of sand into her face. She ignored the sting in her eyes and the drilling pain in her temple. She had to get a handle on her surroundings, figure out where she could be, find opportunities for escape. The sandy ground meant they were near a beach. A hazy blue-green mountain rose in the distance, its peak shrouded by cloud. A volcanic island, or the edge of a continent? Didn't look like Australia, but it could be anywhere in Southeast Asia.

Damn, she should have grilled Rafe about where their island was—it would at least have given her a starting point. One of the many things she should have sussed out, rather than getting distracted by his glorious body. As the helicopter noise receded, crashing surf and thrashing trees took its place. A dozen dull-eyed men and boys sat or stood on the balconies of the huts, some smoking, every one decked out with serious firepower. One guy had skin as dark as midnight, two were Asian, the others had Rafe's coloring. The Lost Boys? She'd pictured them in uniforms—but why would an underground militia advertise itself? Chamuel shouted to one of them, gesturing. He used Gabriel's name.

Tears streamed from her burning eyes. She fought to keep them open as far as a slit. Through the blur that was left of her vision, she picked up the outline of a man walking to her with an unhurried, confident stride. He snapped out a few words, directed at Chamuel. Her heart raced. Rafe?

Not Rafe, you moron. This guy had a similar build and walk, and his language and commanding tone sounded the same, but he was shorter, his voice raspier and nasal. Gabriel? The footfalls of another guy thumped away through the sand and clonked up the steps leading to one of the huts.

The man loomed over her. He placed two fingers under her chin and raised it. The sun pierced the cloud cover, searing her corneas. Someone jogged up—the guy who'd run into the hut— and handed him something small and white, too bright to look at. The man brought it toward Holly's face. She flinched and shut her eyes tight. Chamuel gripped her hair with one hand and her waist with another, yanking her backward into his body.

"Relax, my dear," whispered the man holding her face, in a thicker version of Rafe's accent. "This will help."

Something cool and wet touched her eyes. A washcloth? The man squeezed it, sending water running across her eyelids to pool in the hollow by her nose and slide down her cheeks, soaking the gag. He swept the thick, soft cloth across one eye, from temple to nose, and then the other, dribbling out water as he went. A peppery cologne drifted from him. His fingers left her chin and alighted on her forehead, coaxing her head down. He pressed the cloth across her eyes, while cradling the back of her head, dislodging Chamuel's hand.

"Better?" said the man, drawing the cloth away.

She opened her eyes, tentatively, wincing at the light bouncing off the guy's white shirt. Fighting the bright, blurry haze, she forced herself to focus on his face. Intelligent brown eyes crinkled. Dark curly hair touched the open collar of his crisp shirt. Late thirties, she guessed. His nose was disfigured, as if it'd been cut cleanly straight across and had joined back together wrong. If not for that, he'd come under the label of classically handsome. He wiped a rivulet of water from her cheek with a delicate finger. *This* was Gabriel?

"I can see how Raphael had trouble killing you." He smiled, revealing unnaturally perfect teeth.

He spoke sharply to Chamuel. Holly picked out the name Raphael. The pilot answered with a single word. Gabriel's neck flushed, corded veins sticking out. As their conversation heated, spit peppered Holly—Gabriel's on her face, Chamuel's on her neck.

Gabriel had to be getting the news about Rafe's apparent death. He bared his teeth and clawed at his hair with his fingers, like he was morphing into an animal in some paranormal movie. So he'd wanted Rafe alive. Would he blame her for messing up his plans? Her stomach curled. With her hands bound and her knee busted, her defenses were flimsy.

Chamuel pushed her, pitching her into Gabriel. Her vision cleared, just in time to see Gabriel raise a hand. Instinctively, she tried to pull her arms over her head, but the cable ties gouged her wrists. He shoved her head sideways, wrenching her neck, then kicked her hip. She smacked into the sand, pain bouncing around her body. He stood over her, shouting indecipherable words, like he was insane. With anger or grief? Safe to say Rafe was central to his plans, whatever they were. She squealed into the fabric jammed in her mouth, widening her eyes. *Take off the fucking gag.*

He yelled instructions toward one of the huts, as she pushed up into an awkward sitting position. A guy on the porch relayed the directions inside. It could have been English, but the wind and waves masked the words. A whippet of a young Asian woman appeared in the doorway, wearing a dirty pink dress. From behind her emerged a boy, clasping her hand, brown eyes wide with fear. Oh, God. Rafe, in miniature. An amulet hung from his neck—a match for the pendant hidden under her sweater.

Gabriel shouted at the woman, and she hurriedly nudged Theo down the steps, whispering to him. He sauntered to the boy and knelt, brushing the kid's hair back with his palm. Theo froze.

"Tell him his father is dead," Gabriel hissed to the woman.

Holly went cold.

The woman slapped her hand over her mouth. The guy on the porch behind her jabbed her with the point of his rifle.

"*Ton papa est mort,*" she said, her quiet voice wavering.

Mort, like *la petite mort*. Meaning, death.

The boy stared at the ground, trembling. A strangled whimper escaped him. Holly's eyes stung as she watched the hope drain from his little body, leaving it slumped. She shouted into the gag. A force punched into her lower back, smacking her belly-first onto the ground. Someone had kicked her. Chamuel? She swayed to her knees, her injured one tight and protesting. Rafe's kid at least appeared physically unharmed—clean and healthy, and his T-shirt looked new, still creased with the manufacturer's folds. But those wild, scared eyes...

"Tell him *she* killed his father." Gabriel took his eyes off Theo long enough to nod toward Holly.

Crap. The woman's mouth dropped open.

"Tell him," Gabriel ordered.

As she translated, Theo slowly raised his head and stared at Holly like he couldn't absorb the information. She yelled but it came out as a strangled whine. All she could do was shake her head. *Don't believe them, kid.* His mouth contorted, the edges of his lips sinking. He blinked hard to clear the tears. Oh, God, he thought his father had died and he was trying *not* to cry? That was one tough kid. Or maybe just a terrified one.

Gabriel cradled Theo's cheeks with both hands, forcing the

boy to meet his gaze. "Tell him this is his home now, with us.
I am his father, and these are his brothers."

The woman stammered out the translation. Theo whimpered, his eyes huge.

"We will start his training tomorrow. Tomorrow he begins
to be a man." Gabriel kissed Theo's forehead. "Tell him!" he
shouted at the woman, adding what sounded like a string of
curses.

Fat drops of rain spattered on the ground and on Holly's head.
As the woman translated, Gabriel issued instructions to the men.
He strode into the largest building. The woman herded Theo
back to the hut, her butt nudged by a soldier's rifle. Shit. Holly
would have to find a way to tell him the truth, and soon. A kid
shouldn't have to feel that kind of pain.

A small dusty truck raced into the clearing. Holly made out
dive tanks and surfboards in the back. Weird. She couldn't see
these guys catching waves.

Chamuel kicked Holly's lower back. "Up," he said. She staggered to her feet, testing her knee. He shoved her in the direction of the building Gabriel had entered. She collapsed into the
sand and had to haul herself up. Two armed men on the doorstep separated just far enough to let her squeeze through, one of
them grabbing her ass as she passed. She gritted her teeth. Better they get a handful of that than the iPhone or knife. Thank
God she'd pulled on her cargoes that morning, not her shorts.

Water pelted the tin roof. In the distance, thunder rolled. She
stumbled into a large room with a dark timber floor, the pitched
roof held up by roughly hewn wooden columns, with sliding
shutters around the perimeter for walls. Most of the shutters were
drawn back, leaving three sides open to the outdoors. Several
long dining tables were lined up, their chairs neatly pushed in.
Lounge chairs were arranged in a nook. Through an internal
door, she glimpsed a gleaming commercial kitchen. Another
door was closed. This was no rustic camp.

Chamuel pushed her onto her knees. Rain cascaded down the hut's open sides, creating walls of water. With his back to her, Gabriel surveyed a blur of green jungle and charcoal skies, his hands slung in the pockets of sharply pressed chinos.

He spoke to Chamuel, who clicked open a knife. She swallowed. Shit. He yanked her neck back and sliced off her gag, nicking her jaw in the process, then shoved her forward and sawed off the cable ties. Something wet and soft touched the nape of her neck. His tongue. Creep. She flipped around and scooted backward, out of his reach. He checked Gabriel wasn't watching and made a show of circling his tongue, leaving a strand of saliva drooping from his lips. "Later, Miss America."

He left. The two guards leaned against the doorway, eyeing her with casual arrogance.

Gabriel sauntered to a table, poured two glasses from a bottle of mineral water in an ice bucket, and, using stainless steel tongs, clinked in ice cubes. "You must be thirsty, my dear. Please, sit." He nodded at a bamboo lounge chair. She sat warily, rubbing her wrists. A dull ache gripped her head. He handed her a glass and sank into a chair opposite, resting snakeskin shoes on a leather ottoman. She downed the water, her throat so dry it hurt to swallow. Gabriel looked like a millionaire on holiday, not the dangerous warlord Rafe had painted him as. She wasn't fooled— the appearance of respectability could be an asset to a criminal.

"I have seen many killers in my life. You do not look like one," he said, his words sounding careful and clipped.

"Neither do you." She chewed her cheek. "And I'm not a killer. He's still alive."

"You are lying. My men disposed of his body."

"That wasn't his body."

Gabriel lifted an eyebrow.

"It was a pirate, who came to rob us."

"Pirates do not rob my islands."

His islands? "Well, they tried. And a guy died, and that was his body your men got rid of. Rafe is back on the island."

"*Rafe...?*" He grunted. "I do not know why you tell me this lie."

"It's not a lie, I swear. You have to go back and get him."

"You are trying to trick me, somehow. You think I would believe your word over my men's?"

"You seriously don't care that your friend is alive?"

"He was no friend." His eyes narrowed. "You think I care."

"I see you do."

A flash of darkness crossed his face. The werewolf in him, ready to lunge. "I set Raphael a test and he failed. It is always disappointing when people fail me. His death is of no consequence."

A test. So he *had* wanted Rafe back in the Lost Boys? "He was supposed to kill me."

"He was ordered to kidnap a senator's daughter. His first failure. His second failure was not killing you. And I see he told you far too much, including his new name. He is no good at following orders, these days." He waved a manicured hand. "It does not matter now. I suspected he would let me down. It is a shame, but I am very good at adapting."

"Do you plan to kill me?"

"Ah, so that is your intention, in lying to me. You think it will buy you time."

"I'm telling the truth. Do you really believe I could kill someone like him?"

He pressed two manicured fingers to his lips, his gaze landing on her wounded temple. "You have had the misfortune of suffering a blow to the head. That may account for your confusion. My lieutenant confirmed the identity of the body. He is a...*troubled* man, but I will believe his word over yours.

"My cleaning staff will arrive at the island in a few days, weather permitting. Maybe Raphael will give them a surprise."

He shrugged. "And maybe he will not. Do not worry, my dear, I would rather not kill you. Where is the profit in that? There are many uses for a woman like you, and I have costs to recoup." He smiled, his eyes dead—a man practiced in faking emotions. "You may come to wish Raphael had done his job, my dear."

She jammed her fingernails into her fisted palms. A few days. She just needed to stay alive for that long. "People are looking for me."

He smiled. "That is the curious thing. I have eyes all around the Indian Ocean and Asia. As soon as Laura Hyland was…*found*, all activity to find her stopped. No one is looking for you, there is no mention of another missing woman in the global media. The senator and his people have returned to America, and a crew is sailing the yacht back. Whoever you are, you are of no value to your country. I believe very few people know of your little deception, and those who know do not care. That makes you very valuable to me—there is something very appealing about a lost person, do you not think?"

Holly inhaled slowly and steadily. *Don't show fear.*

"How is such a pretty woman not missed? I am very curious. Who are you?"

"A close friend of Laura."

His smile didn't waver. "Not so close, I think." He nodded to a TV mounted on an internal wall. "Her celebrations at being rescued were not ruined by any concern for you. No. I think you have served the purpose you were hired for, and they have abandoned you to your fate. Do not be sad, you will be worth something to me. A beautiful white American whore will fetch me a record price."

Her cheeks iced over.

"Do not worry, my dear. You will enjoy it." His voice dropped to a whisper, barely audible above the rain. "American women love being tied up in dungeons and whipped and raped, yes? It is the fantasy you all read about in your safe lives, in your expensive houses. In other countries, women fear this treatment. You Americans crave it. I find this strange."

She swallowed. Where did he get that whacked-out impression? He pushed up to standing, casually crossed the space between them, and ran a finger over her temple. The skin near her eye felt puffy and numb under his touch. How many seconds would it take to whip out the knife, unfold it and plunge it into his throat? Too many. His observant thugs in the doorway would be on top of her in a blink. She'd lose the knife and the phone—and possibly her life—before she got the blade anywhere near him. Better to bide her time. If they were planning to search her, they'd likely have done it before now. No point relinquishing the best defenses she had.

His finger traveled to the bruise on her forehead, where she'd clonked heads with Rafe on the inflatable. "How about that? Did that give you a thrill?" She jerked her head away. He laughed. "My lieutenant, Chamuel, would love to show you some more good times. It would be a shame to have my stock defiled, but a good commander keeps his men happy. I can ask him not to leave any marks—you are worth more to me in good condition. What is your name?"

"Does it matter?"

"Not where you are going. Your new...*employer* will no doubt give you something he finds suitable."

He gripped her chin and yanked it up, forcing her to meet his empty gaze. His fingertips ground into her jaw. "Do not think that because you have a value to me I will not kill you if I discover you are too much trouble. I like to give people choices, and this one is yours—live or die, it is up to you." He rapped an instruction to his men. "Now, my dear, my soldiers will look after you carefully while we find a more permanent home for you, with someone who will give you all the attention you desire. A pity your American girlfriends will never find out what became of you. They would be envious, yes?"

CHAPTER

21

Even in the foaming shallows of the ocean beach, the undertow tugged at Rafe's legs, forcing him to sidestep to stay upright. *Merde*—was he really going to attempt this? Gusts snapped at the Windsurfer's sail. If he let go of the boom it'd be airborne in seconds.

Crossing open ocean on a Windsurfer was a crazy risk. And in a cyclone? Insane. But if the militia hadn't come back for him by now he could assume they wouldn't. And Flynn would hold out several days at least between losing communication with Rafe and defying orders to come after him. Several days was several days too many. Now that Gabriel's plans had been disrupted, he'd change them, fast.

Somewhere beyond the cloud-smothered horizon was Rafe's first target—an uninhabited sandy cay that marked the northern end of the island chain he'd set his sights on. It wouldn't offer much shelter, but it would allow him a breather before he searched from island to island. How long would it take to get there? Three hours, best case? Six, if the wind turned against him?

He tugged the backpack straps, tightening them. The dusty life jacket he'd strapped on was two sizes too small but it'd do in an emergency. The Windsurfer harness hugged his waist. It'd be a miracle if the laptop survived the trip, even inside the plastic. Not that it was any use without the phone. He did a mental stocktaking—water and food, clothes, boots, bug spray, the

Makarov, the sharpest of the kitchen knives. Holly's portable GPS was taped to the mast, just above the boom, its little LCD screen already smeared with salt.

He tightened his grip on the boom. If they hurt Theo or Holly he'd slaughter the lot of them, code of honor or not. He squinted out to sea. Isolated gusts skidded over the shallows, marked by dark patches in the dull water. Nothing predictable enough to ride. With the gale-force easterly shooting over the island and hitting the water five hundred meters out, he'd have a bitch of a time getting started. In the distance, the wind announced its descent with a mass of black sea torn with white-caps and whipped by spray. That's where he'd pick up the pace.

He blew out a breath. Time to see if this contraption worked. And to find out if he remembered how to windsurf. He closed his eyes, hearing over the surf the soft music of Simone's southern French accent, peppered with Corsican expressions. The summer she'd taught him the sport while he was on leave was the best of his life. Her lilting voice and those carefree days had lured him into thinking he could attempt a normal existence in which he flirted with a woman, fell in love and lived a regular life.

Like hell. With one foot on the floating board, he looked over his shoulder, fixed his gaze on the tops of the palm trees and waited. However strained his relationship with Simone, she at least had given him the skills he needed to save their son right now. And to save his…captive? Ally? Lover? What exactly was Holly? A few days ago she'd been a stranger. Until yesterday he'd believed she was someone else entirely. Now, the thought of her being in pain and danger delivered the same sickening kick to his gut that he got at the thought of Theo in Gabriel's control.

He'd never felt that strongly about anyone but his son. It wasn't just the guilt that he hadn't prevented her capture, or that he'd dragged her into this situation to begin with. He didn't just want to save Holly for her sake. He wanted to save her for his sake, because a world in which he knew she existed, in which he might see her again, was better than a world where he'd never known her.

The palm trees doubled over in a bolt of wind. He gripped the boom with both hands. Showtime. As the gust punched into the sail, he lifted his anchor foot onto the Windsurfer. It took off, skipping over the water. His forearms tightened, fighting the strain from the bucking sail. Then, bam—the fin spun out, sliding the board sideways. He wobbled. The edge of the board caught the water, and the whole thing flipped, thumping his skull into the mast and catapulting him into the water. He staggered to his feet, spitting out a lungful of ocean. *Putain.* The water wasn't even up to his thighs.

He slapped the surface. He was a specialist in amphibious warfare, a parachute commando, and he was letting a Windsurfer defeat him? He lifted his gaze to the heavy blue-black clouds. Somewhere out there, two people waited for him—the only person he'd ever loved and a woman who'd cut right to the center of him like no other. The two people who proved he could still be human. If he couldn't save them, his life would be worthless.

La mission est sacrée, tu l'exécutes jusqu'au bout et si besoin, en opérations, au péril de ta vie. The mission is sacred, you carry it out until the end and, if necessary, at the risk of your life.

On his second attempt, he made it past the lee and settled into his harness. His forearms were burning already. Half an hour later he was still upright, syncing with the rhythm of the waves, with a strong, consistent wind pushing him on. Heading hard downwind at high speed, he only had to pull out the occasional jibe—and just as well, because the surging swells were enough of a challenge. At this pace the slightest error could somersault the board end-to-end.

The rain intensified, smoothing the water into a moonscape and blurring gray sea into gray sky for three-sixty degrees. Lucky he had the GPS to track his position because he couldn't see shit.

But just skidding across the water felt like progress—flying off the crests of waves, launching into the air. Every wave brought him a second closer to the people who, right now, needed him most.

The people he needed most.

Holly limped across the compound and followed Gabriel's doormen down a sandy path through the jungle, with Chamuel behind. Water vapor rose around them, from the downpour. Every time she hesitated or stumbled, the pilot groped her ass. Lucky her get-out-of-jail-free cards were in her *front* pockets. She dug her fingernails into her palms, longing to spin around and smack him one in his leering face. But then what? Limp away into the jungle, pursued by three armed men? She'd get a better opportunity.

They reached a clearing dominated by a dirty concrete hut. Two more men sat on the porch, rifles slung across their laps. One spoke into a walkie-talkie. A reply crackled back. She was losing count, but that made at least twenty Lost Boys. Right now, right here, it was five against one. Four big-ass assault rifles and at least one handgun against one pocketknife. The guard in front pointed with the tip of his gun toward the hut and yabbered something at her, gesturing. Shit. What exactly did they plan to do with her in there? She climbed the steps. If Gabriel considered her more valuable alive, they'd be reluctant to pull the trigger, at least. If they planned to use her in other ways, the best she could hope was that they'd take turns. She'd have more chance against them one at a time.

One of the men shoved her through the doorway. She sidestepped to avoid tripping on something. A leg. The floor was carpeted with bodies—live ones, thank God—sitting cross-legged. Twenty, maybe thirty pairs of fearful eyes stared up at her. All women, all Southeast Asian. Gabriel's trafficking victims? She dry-heaved on the stench of week-old sweat, unwashed hair, stale urine—and worse. The women had left a wide arc around a bucket in the corner. The toilet? Next to it was a dark red stain that could be only one thing. She swallowed.

Another guard sat in a corner by the door, his chair tipped so he could lean back against the wall, his nose and mouth covered with a red bandanna. Beady black eyes leered at her. The guy from the plane. Holly gritted her teeth. How many shipments of women had been channeled through this place? Her problem had just got a whole lot bigger.

He shouted and the women shuffled. A guy behind Holly prodded her with his gun barrel toward a gap that materialized on a dirty woven mat. She picked her way through the women and sat. Was it selfish to be grateful she wasn't alone?

As the men talked, the women cast her surreptitious looks. The woman beside her clasped her hand roughly, and squeezed. Holly gave her a grim smile. The room was a bunker with a couple of barred, insect-screened windows, one next to the heavily guarded door. Greasy-haired women with glassy eyes rested against the grimy walls. In the middle of the room, they sat back to back. One slept sitting up, her head slumped. How long did Holly have here? Given she'd come as a surprise, it could take Gabriel a while to find a buyer.

Outside, several pairs of boots receded. The woman released Holly's hand, rose stiffly and waved at the guard, pointing to the bucket. He nodded slightly. She shuffled her way through the crush of bodies. As she neared the bucket, half a dozen women stood and formed a semicircle around her, facing outwards—masking the guard's view. After a minute, the woman emerged. She met the guard's eye, raising the bucket and nodding at the door. He waved dismissively, revealing an S-shaped burn scar on his forearm. The woman was gone for a minute, before returning with an empty bucket and reassuming her seat.

An hour passed, in silence. Maybe two. Holly itched to ask someone what was going on, but the guard shouted at any woman who as much as cleared her throat. The women gave up staring at her and instead studied their hands or the floor or the walls. A girl wearing a Justin Bieber T-shirt sobbed into her neighbor's lap. The older woman rubbed her back in listless circles. The air thickened and heated as the insect chorus intensified outside. Now and then, a coconut thunked to the ground. The guard hosed the room with insect spray, and stepped out for half a minute while the choking fog cleared. Holly pulled up the collar of her sweater and breathed through it. No doubt the women were worth less if they had malaria.

Women went to the toilet, one by one, others forming a wall each time. The younger guard appeared with bottles of water, which the women passed around. A G was burned into his forearm—for Gabriel?

When she could no longer stand the heat, Holly took off her sweater and laid it over her lap to cover the bulges in her pockets, ready to pull it on again in an instant.

It was prison all over, but with no laws governing her treatment, no path to parole, no trial—fair or otherwise. Her only chance at surviving was to break out, with zero idea where she was, a child to protect and a couple of dozen women she could hardly leave behind. She couldn't even be sure what ocean she was hearing.

One of the men—the dark-skinned one, marked with a G— appeared in the doorway and gestured to his mouth, miming eating. Four women pushed to their feet and filed out. Holly gripped her sweater, searching the women's faces for signs of fear. Nothing but listless resignation.

She let maybe ten minutes pass, then pulled on the sweater. Time to put Plan A into action, which really wasn't much of a plan. Even if she could get a message to Rafe, what could she tell him? *Theo's alive, but they think you're dead?* No one was going back for him. Could Rafe get word to his guy and get off the island that way? She stood, gesturing to the bucket. The guard nodded. As before, the human shield went up. Facing the wall, she crouched over the bucket, and pulled out the phone. The senator's people had briefly entrusted her with an iPhone so they could keep in contact while arrangements were made for her trip, so she was familiar with its basic functions. She switched it on and wrapped it in the sweater, anticipating the trill as it fired up. Her stomach muscles clenched. She bent double over the muffled phone, and coughed loud and long as the first beep came. She froze. No footsteps, no shouts.

She extracted the phone and switched it to silent, blowing out her cheeks. It had a signal—only one bar, but that could be enough. A low battery warning flashed. She dismissed it. Feet shuffled up the steps to the hut. She hit the internet icon. The women around her muttered, and began to move off. Shit, her protective wall was crumbling. Sweat prickled her forehead. She pressed the phone's sleep button and shoved it in her pocket.

Rain pelted Rafe's skin. The waves surged like a roller coaster, the constant rebalancing straining his quads and abs. He could do sixty chin lifts and carry a two-hundred-pound man five kilometers, but this demanded a strength and agility his body had forgotten.

He peered at the GPS. He'd been out three hours, averaging fifteen knots. He was maybe two-thirds of the way across, making good time but being swept too far northwest.

Salt spray burned his throat. Could he risk pulling out a water bottle? The board crested a swell and hit air in a gut-flipping flight, before skidding back onto the choppy surface. Teeth clenched, he strained to keep the Windsurfer from landing flat and killing the power.

He adjusted his grip as the board righted. That was too damn close. The drink would have to wait until he was in the lee of the archipelago. The waves were getting bigger, slamming him down and pushing him toward an island he hadn't intended getting anywhere near. He jibed head-on to the swell—he had no choice but to cross it and head southwest.

He launched off a crest, too high. *Putain*. The harness dropped away. He didn't need to wait for the landing to know he was in trouble. Gripping the boom, he tried to angle the board to ease the nose in first, but it slapped flat onto the water, the boom twisting with his weight. *Crack*. Shit.

The boom slipped from his fingers and he plunged backward into the water, his bag dragging him down. Everything muffled. Bitter seawater swamped his airways. He fought to the surface, broke through with a surge and spluttered: spitting out water, sucking in air. The board was already being pushed away by the current, its limp sail dragging in the white-flecked water. The mast had snapped at right angles. Christ. He was screwed. He powered through the water and grabbed the edge of the board. The GPS had slipped off. No sign of it in the surging waves.

He unclipped the rig and dragged himself up to lie on the bare board—just a worthless surfboard now. Panting, he peered at a smudge of gray on the horizon, between the charcoal sea and the concrete sky. The cay? The island to the northwest? Or a trick of his eyes?

He'd have to paddle for it and hope for a miracle.

Holly yanked the sweater down to cover her pocket and turned, fists clenched. The four women had returned with two large metal platters. One was heaped with rice, the other noodles.

Lunch. Just lunch. She'd have to bide her time. She released her hands. The women settled the dishes on the floor. The others surged at them, snatching handfuls of food and shoving them into their mouths. The guard stood, stretched and ambled to the doorway. Facing out, he spoke to the other goons.

A woman wearing a grubby yellow dress grabbed Holly's sleeve and urged her toward the food. Holly shook her head.

She'd been eating like a princess for days—she had plenty of reserves. By the way the women were sucking up the food, she guessed they needed it more. The woman sank her fingertips into Holly's biceps. "Come!" she whispered, her eyes wide with meaning, yanking Holly toward the dish furthest from the guard.

Holly stumbled after her. The woman knelt, grabbed a fist-ful of rice and held it over her mouth. Holly copied. "You are English?" she muttered into her hand.

"American. You speak English."

"Yes. You are here to be trafficked, too?"

"So I'm told. Who are these women? What happened to them, to you?"

"They are from Cambodia. Some of them were sold by their families, some are from the street, some paid a lot of money to be secured factory jobs in other cities, other countries. You see that girl?" She nodded to the girl in the Justin Bieber T-shirt. "She is twelve."

"Twelve?" Holly's throat dried.

"Her name is Devi. She was sold by her mother, who has too many children and cannot afford them all."

"Her mother sold her."

"Many girls are sold by their mothers. The mothers convince themselves they are sending the girls out to work, just like in the fields, but they know the truth."

"And you?"

"I am not like these women. I was born in Cambodia but I am an Australian national. I work for an aid agency trying to stop human trafficking. I was working undercover to find out what was happening to women like these, and I was kidnapped, too." She shrugged. "The plan worked a little too well."

"What will happen to them? You?" *Me?*

"We will be sold to brothels, probably in Asia or Europe. We will be told we can earn our freedom, earn money for our families. But that won't happen. We will be kept in servitude for as long as we are useful, then we will disappear."

Holly bit her lower lip. Hell, compared with that her own life had been sheltered. "Where are we?"

"I don't know. We left Cambodia from the Port of Siha-noukville, but we spent so long locked in the hold of a cargo ship that I lost track of night and day, let alone direction. When I was taken, I tried to leave behind a message for my colleagues to at least tell them which gang we were dealing with, but I was caught. People will be looking for me, but they won't know where to start."

"I was taken from Indonesian waters. It was a short flight—maybe half an hour, plus a helicopter ride—but I don't know which direction."

"Still, that suggests the boat came south, putting us in Malaysia, maybe, or Indonesia."

Holly swallowed. "Would it help if your colleagues knew that?"

"They would at least know which authorities to pressure." She shook her head. "But it is hopeless."

Holly ate a few grains of rice. Maybe not so hopeless. Could she trust this woman? "How long have you been here?"

The woman paused. Noting the change of subject? "Two weeks, I think. They are breaking us. Forcing us to accept our new fate, showing us we are worthless."

Holly nodded at the bloodstain on the floor. It glistened—still wet. "They're being violent?"

The woman followed her gaze. She crossed herself. "One woman...she...stood up to them, last night. These men are monsters. I've never seen men like this. They are dead in their eyes."

"Are you let out of this room? Other than to empty the bucket and to bring in food?"

The woman eyed the guard, who was paying scant attention to the scrabbling women. "Only to be raped."

Holly choked on the rice. She coughed and swallowed, her eyes watering. "Have you…?" The words stalled in her windpipe.

"We all have, except the youngest ones." She indicated the girl in the Bieber T-shirt—Devi. "They are virgins, so they are worth more intact, but the threat is still there. These men—" She shook her head, her lips pressed tightly together.

Anger flashed hot in Holly's chest. "How long will you—we—be kept here? Do you know?"

"We believe women are usually kept in holding areas for a few weeks. Just long enough to break their spirits."

Holly made a snap decision. "Do you have someone you can text? Do you know how to use an iPhone?"

The woman's brown eyes widened. "You have one?"

Holly chewed her lip. She could be jeopardizing her only means of contacting Rafe.

"Please. I can contact my agency."

Holly glanced up at the door. The men were still talking. She caught the eye of Devi, who shyly averted her gaze. Quickly, she reached under her sweater and pulled out the phone, keeping it covered by her hands. She pressed it into the woman's stomach. "What's your name?"

"Amina."

"Be careful, Amina. Don't get caught."

The guard turned, and shouted at the women. He strode up to the nearest dish, and kicked aside a woman who was leaning over it. Lunch was over.

"I won't get caught." The woman—Amina—teared up, as she slipped the phone down her top, into her bra. "God bless you."

The four women who'd brought lunch removed the empty platters. The guard in the bandanna returned to his chair. Another water bottle was passed around. Holly leaned against the wall. Across from her Amina did the same. She'd better have made the right call. Amina had people looking for her, which was more than Holly could claim.

After the room settled into silence, Amina stood. Holly's heart hammered. She tipped her head back against the cool concrete wall and focused on a mouse-sized cockroach creeping along the ceiling. In her peripheral vision, she tracked Amina as the woman approached the bucket. Her mouth filled with saliva, forcing her to lower her head to swallow. She didn't dare look at the women who stood sentry around Amina. Minutes passed. Holly pulled off the sweater. It caught on the amulet. At least she had less to hide for a while. She pressed her spine into the concrete, allowing the rough surface to cool the sweat seeping through her T-shirt. *Hurry up, Amina.*

Footsteps and voices sounded outside. Several men had arrived. The woman next to Holly hugged her knees, letting out a whimper. Devi hid her face. With a clatter, three men appeared in the doorway. None of the women looked up. Those standing around Amina remained frozen to the spot, fear pulling at their faces as they dropped their gazes to the ground.

One of the men stepped forward, crunching on a woman's foot. She screwed up her face, internalizing the pain. His gaze moved from woman to woman, then he advanced on one and yanked her to her feet. She cried out and tried to pull away, but his grip was sound. Holly made to stand, to defend her, but the woman beside her caught her shoulder and yanked her down, with surprising strength. The guy hoisted his quarry over his shoulder and carried her outside. She cried out, pleading. Holly's neighbor sank her fingertips into her shoulder. A second man grabbed another woman. Her face was set in solid hatred, but she shook him off and rose of her own accord, her spine rigid.

A shadow fell on Holly. Her nape prickled. Chamuel stood over her, sneering. He presented his hand with a flourish. "Miss America."

CHAPTER

22

Rafe's head felt like it was jammed in a slowly tightening vise. Groaning, he tried opening his eyes. Daylight shot bolts of pain into his skull. Pain was good. Pain meant life. He was on a beach, fringed by thrashing palm trees. How did he even get here? He remembered thirst, muscles about to explode, an overwhelming urge to sleep.

Water surged around, sucking at his legs. He commando-crawled out of its grip. His muscles seemed to be working, at least. The only real pain was in his head. Dehydration, probably. He spat out salt and sand and unclipped the life jacket with fumbling fingers. Had he made it to the cay? It felt like he'd paddled to Singapore. *Merde.* He was a lucky bastard, of sorts—with all that open ocean he could have been paddling for weeks. But now he was stranded, again. What was that English expression the missionary school cook was fond of? Up shit creek without an oar?

He eased off the backpack, swung it around and yanked a piece of kelp off it. Soaked. Seawater poured out of the laptop bag. No sign of the board. He chugged from a water bottle, closing his eyes against the brilliant white clouds.

He sensed movement to his left. A boot flew toward his face. He rolled as it whooshed past, and tried to drag himself up. What the fuck? Something hard smacked into his back, knocking him flat—another boot. Groaning, he staggered to his feet and swiveled, just in time to see Kung Fu Pirate launch a foot into his stomach. *Oof.* He careened backward and landed on his ass. His pain neurons ping-ponged.

Half a dozen men surrounded him, a couple with shotguns aimed at his face. Where the hell had they come from? One of them grabbed the backpack. If he could get one of the gunmen, he could take them on. But both were several meters away, and his body wasn't at its finest—or his mind, evidently, if he'd missed six men creeping up. And if their firearms were as shoddy as the ones they'd brought to Penipuan, he might only have a couple of bullets that may or may not fly in the right direction. He held up his hands. Better to live, for now. At least he wasn't shipwrecked on a deserted island.

"Never!" Holly spat.

Chamuel sniggered, and said something to the bandanna-clad guard, who raised his eyebrows, in uneasy deference. One of the goons from the veranda darkened the doorway, holding his gun loosely but in a clear warning to Holly.

Bandanna Guy stood, letting the teetering chair fall, and advanced on Holly. Chamuel grabbed her wrist. Panic bubbled in her stomach. Her brain lit up with a memory—another man grabbing her, planning to use her like this. She could still smell the whisky on her father's breath.

Chamuel yanked her up, wrenching her arm nearly from her socket. Instinct told her to pull away, but she overrode it. Cowering, as if in submission, she steadied herself to balance on her bad knee and fisted her left hand.

His grip loosened, slightly. "Good g—"

She smashed her knuckles into his eye socket and powered her good knee into his groin. He stumbled back, clutching north and south. Bandanna Guy flew forward and tackled her. She landed face-first on the thigh of a woman next to her. He kneed her in the sacrum and pulled back her arms. She thrashed. Someone else cable-tied her wrists. Shit. Bandanna Guy and another guard wrenched her up by her armpits, and she hung between them, her feet swinging off the floor. Chamuel's face darkened. He made to step toward her, then backtracked, glancing warily at her unshackled feet.

"Okay. I take you later. Now, I take her." He pointed at Devi, who was still hiding her face in her hands. "For now, she is you."

"No," said Holly, thrashing against her captors. Not the girl. Not anyone—but definitely not the girl. "No! Fine—take me!"

Chamuel advanced on Devi and wrenched her hands from her face. She wailed and turned away, hyperventilating. The woman who'd been comforting her grabbed her hand, yelling at the pilot. He kicked the woman in the chest and shouted over his shoulder. Holly bucked, but she was powerless. Another goon charged in, grabbed Devi's friend and dragged her out. Chamuel heaved the sobbing girl over his shoulder and glared at Holly. "Next time, you to come."

"Take me now. Not her."

"Yes, you want this. You like Chamuel. Next time, Miss America."

She glowered back, teeth clenched. So the Lost Boys would allow a captive to lose her value, if it meant maintaining discipline. Which meant there was nothing empty about Gabriel's threat to kill Holly if she proved difficult.

Bandanna Guy shouted at Chamuel, dropping Holly and striding forward to block his exit. She found her balance just as the other goon let go, gesturing with his gun that she should sit. She stood motionless, her mind spinning as the two men yelled at each other in rapid fire, their faces contorted. Bandanna Guy shouted Gabriel's name.

The goon rammed his rifle butt into her stomach, slamming her into the wall. Gasping for breath, she slid to the floor, ignoring the rip of pain as she tried to follow the argument. Chamuel charged for the door, Devi's legs bouncing over his shoulder.

Bandanna Guy clamped a hand around the girl's ankle, pulling Chamuel up short.

Chamuel's face contorted, turning the color of sangria. Snarling at Bandanna Guy, he threw Devi across the room. Her skinny limbs flailed and she landed with a thud and a smack, sprawled over several women. Chamuel grabbed the arm of the nearest woman—the one whose foot had been crushed—and dragged her out instead.

Devi crawled, wailing, back to her spot, her companion gone. The woman next to Holly clutched her shoulder again, her quick breath heating Holly's cheek. The adrenaline had got to her, too.

Damn. Holly should have gone with Chamuel. Not only would she have saved that woman from being raped, but she could have pulled the knife on him. She'd let her urge to defend herself override the bigger goal of escape, as futile as it might be. And she'd transferred the punishment to someone else— something she would never knowingly do. God, she should have clawed Chamuel's eyes out and smashed her knee into him ten times as hard, really put him out of action. Hell, she should have pulled out the knife and cut his dick right off. Next chance she got...

Devi inhaled a heaving sob. That poor, terrified child. Across the room, Amina met Holly's gaze and nodded, quickly and grimly. Sometime in the fracas she must have got her message away. That was something. Had the iPhone been in Holly's pocket, the men might have it by now. Thank God they'd been too distracted to spot the less-obvious outline of the knife.

Holly shuffled into the least uncomfortable position she could assume with her hands tied. When could she get the phone back—at the next mealtime? She located the cockroach and resumed following its journey across the room. Not for the first time in her life, she found herself envying an insect. Cockroaches didn't entrap and abuse each other, for kicks or for profit. They just got on with their simple lives, each to his own. Humans really were the lowest life form.

It seemed like hours before the women returned. The others moved aside as they limped back to their places. Devi's friend walked in, her head high, meeting no one's gaze. She lowered herself to her spot next to the girl and clutched her, fiercely. The woman Chamuel had dragged out gulped air in strangled whimpers. Holly closed her eyes, each cry spearing her.

Even if she died doing it, she'd find a way to make Gabriel and his men pay for what they'd done to these women, and to Theo.

Rafe allowed the men to march him along the beach, his hands tied with coarse rope. With his strength returning, he could shrug off the bonds in five seconds and take out at least the two armed men, but it was wiser to cooperate until he'd scoped out which island he was on and how he could get away. The sun was low and fading, and nightfall might offer a better chance of escape.

They trudged up into soft sand and took a well-trodden path through beech forest. After about a kilometer they reached a village. Rafe's shoulders ebbed. Kids, chickens, pigs, vegetable plots, weathered men with red betel nut–stained teeth and conical hats… Ropes and nets were lined up on the dirt, decaying seaweed and drying fish scented the air, worn clothing hung from washing lines, huts were tacked together with traditional and Western materials. This wasn't the headquarters of a gang of bandits. This was a bunch of people trying to survive.

A bunch of people who probably held him responsible for the death of one of their sons. If all went to hell, perhaps he could escape into the dense bush behind the village. Assuming this was a fishing community, finding a boat wouldn't be hard.

Shouts rose up, and a woman in a batik hijab ran into a hut that had a large satellite dish propped on its roof. A middle-aged man emerged, wearing a khaki Che Guevara T-shirt and shorts. He pulled a pair of scratched glasses low on his nose and studied Rafe, as Kung Fu Pirate gave a rapid explanation. Rafe spoke a little Indonesian, but couldn't pick up any words. Could it be Javanese? Sundanese? Hell, he could be in the Philippines, for all he knew.

After a lot of questioning and nodding, the man cleared his throat and addressed Rafe. "Do you speak English?"

"Yes."

"You came from Penipuan?" His accent was clipped and precise—the voice of a man who'd been educated by the English, like Rafe.

"I was swept off my Windsurfer. I washed up here." Better to be frugal with the truth, for now.

"That is a long way to come on a Windsurfer. You became lost?"

"I went off course."

"You are a lucky man, to wash up here and not..." He trailed off.

Rafe frowned. Not where?

"You were windsurfing in a cyclone?"

"Best time to windsurf."

"With a laptop and a knife?"

Rafe shrugged. No mention of the Makarov—had it been silently pocketed? "In case I got blown off course."

"I see. And your name?"

"Jack."

"Jack," the man repeated, as if testing the likelihood it was the truth. "You may call me Mr. Buana. Perhaps you would like to come inside and tell me the entire story, including what happened to my son, with whom I believe you were briefly acquainted."

His son. Oh, shit.

Mr. Buana bowed slightly, sweeping his hand toward the hut's doorway. He spoke softly to the woman in the hijab and followed Rafe into a living room with a vaulted dark teak ceiling and a concrete floor patchworked with rattan mats. Woven bamboo partitions veiled other rooms. A bead curtain to their right was swept aside, revealing a rudimentary kitchen with walls of blackened brick and bunches of sweetcorn and purple shallots hanging from the roof. The scent of charcoal and coffee hung heavily in the air, spun lazily through the room by a ceiling fan.

"You must be very thirsty," said Mr. Buana.

The woman swept past them into the kitchen and brought out a carafe of cloudy water and two earthenware mugs, which she placed on a tabletop covered with yellow plastic. Rafe's throat burned at the sight of water. Shooting pains in his head warned of dehydration, but he couldn't risk catching a waterborne bug.

"Can I drink the water I brought with me, in my bag?"

Mr. Buana nodded. He spoke to the woman, who left.

Rafe noted a wall of photos, mostly in yellowed black and white. In the darkening room, his eyes strained to catch details: solemn framed portraits of men in fine suits, alongside pinned snapshots printed from a computer of children in Western settings and a postcard from Paris. A progression of framed certificates marched along the top of the wall, all headed up University of Oxford, with dates going back decades.

Mr. Buana stepped up beside him, sipping from a mug. "That is mine." He pointed at the last degree along the row. "That is my father's. My grandfather's. My great-grandfather's. Every eldest son in our family, for four generations." He indicated an empty spot on the wall, next to his certificate. "It is a luxury we could not afford for my eldest. We are a noble family. Unfortunately, there is little money in that anymore. Now, we are just poor fishermen."

"Your son—he came to Penipuan?"

Mr. Buana's mouth tightened. "You speak of my youngest son. He causes me many problems."

Rafe winced. *Causes.* Present tense, when his son was re-soundingly past. "He was the one who didn't come back?"

"He is dead?" The man's voice wavered.

"I'm sorry, yes. He fell from a cliff, in the dark."

Mr. Buana nodded, the skin around his eyes bunching, sending deep parallel lines across his cheeks. "Ah." He fell into silence. A minute passed.

"His body is still on the island?" the man said, quietly. "I would like to bury him."

Rafe swallowed. The mechanism in his throat felt rusty. Which version of the truth should he tell? It would be honest enough to say the body was swept out to sea and lost—Gabriel's men would have disposed of it quickly. The pain in Mr. Buana's eyes decided it. He'd lost a son. Rafe owed him the truth. *Au combat tu respectes les ennemis vaincus. In combat you respect defeated enemies.*

"I brought your son's body to the villa on the island." He paused. How much detail should he go into? "A helicopter came this morning and removed it. I wasn't there. I don't know where they took it, but I imagine he was buried at sea."

Mr. Buana lowered his head. Rafe gave him time. He didn't know this man, but he well knew the greatest fear of a father. After a few minutes, Mr. Buana looked up and spoke. His eyes glistened. "This helicopter, it was red, with a white stripe?"

Rafe's eyes narrowed, the movement firing pain through his brow. "You know it?"

Mr. Buana frowned. "You must be tired. Please, sit."

Before Rafe could press the issue, the woman returned with his backpack. Nearly falling on her, he dug out a bottle of water and guzzled. He had the hunger of a wolf, too, but that would have to wait. Sure enough, the pistol was gone.

"Please, excuse us," Mr. Buana said to Rafe, bowing.

He ushered the woman into a room behind one of the partitions. Soft words filtered back, then quiet sobs. The mother, presumably. Rafe pressed his palms into his salt-whipped eyes.

"I must thank you," said Mr. Buana, returning.

Rafe withdrew his hands, quickly. Mr. Buana was looking older by the minute. He closed the partition behind him.

"What for?"

"For sending my other sons home." Bitterness skewed his tone. Rafe hoped it wasn't sarcasm.

"They were all yours?"

The man sat heavily on a worn flower-print couch and closed his hands around his empty mug. "Two of them were, in addition to my youngest. One of the others—he is a cousin of my wife, from Jakarta. He thinks he is a ninja. Ninja Turtle, more like. He stirs up trouble with my sons, but he has connections to people I cannot afford to insult."

Rafe filled Mr. Buana's mug. He wanted to ask about the helicopter, but first the man deserved answers.

"You must understand, this is not the people we are. Not the people we were. They tried to rob you? I have been trying to see through their lies."

"I suspect that was their intention. Or possibly to kidnap us. In the end, they did us no harm."

Mr. Buana rattled off a string of words in his own language. Swear words, Rafe guessed.

"Us?" the man said, suddenly. "Many honeymooners go to Penipuan. Your wife is still there? She must be worried about you. You may charter a boat from me, so you can return."

A charter? The man planned to make money out of this? Rafe blew out his cheeks, torn between the desire to enlist his help, and protect the mission. How much should he let on? Maybe he could buy a boat outright—and go where? But this was a good man. Desperate, but good. "She also left in the helicopter, not of her choosing."

The man's eyes widened.

"Mr. Buana, you know whose helicopter this is, don't you?"

"Why do they have your wife? Are you one of them?" He struggled to mask the hatred in his voice.

Rafe took a punt. "They are no friends of mine."

Mr. Buana nodded, his lips tight. "Ah. We are agreed on this."

"Do you know where their headquarters is?"

His mouth turned down. "They do not stay long in one place. I hear they work on many different islands. Sometimes I see their helicopter and plane, and I know they're back, but I don't know where they hide. They have many resources. They are destroying us."

"How so?"

"You know the business they are in?"

"Human trafficking—women and children."

"Not just women and children. Also men. They sell their slaves to the big fishing boats. These men are forced to live aboard, working, working, working, until they fall off and drown. Or are pushed. Or jump. We cannot compete in the marketplace with people who have slaves. They are shutting us out—the resorts and wholesalers only buy from these boats now, to save money. And the consumers in the countries they export to—they don't care how food gets to them, as long as it's cheap." His focus had trained on something unseen in the distance, beyond the walls. Now, it returned to Rafe. "But this isn't your problem, is it? You need to get your wife back."

"And my son." Rafe's voice cracked.

Mr. Buana's face turned hard as concrete. "They have your son? They took him as well as your wife?"

"They took him earlier. I came out here to get him back."

"They are making him a slave?"

"In a sense, yes. I believe they want him to join them."

"Ah." He pushed his chair away from the table and folded his arms. "It is hard to keep our young men honest. How did he get mixed up with them?"

"He was kidnapped from his home. He is nine years old."

"Nine?" In the low light, the whites of the man's eyes gleamed. "Now I understand why you would wish to take a Windsurfer out in a cyclone. But you do not know where they are being held? They could be anywhere."

"I've narrowed it down." Rafe's eyes fell on the ruined laptop in his bag. There was still one remote chance of making up for lost time. "Is there anywhere around here I can access the internet?"

"Of course."

"Will you take me there? I will pay."

The man pushed off the sofa and crossed the room. He pulled up a blind that had been screening a room: an office, with a carved teak desk, a phone—and a computer. "My internet rates are reasonable."

"I have no cash."

"No problem. I have PayPal."

"Do you have weapons I could buy?"

He winced. "For that you will have to speak to the Ninja Turtle. I refuse to deal in weapons. But I will sell you an iPhone. Genuine. Good price."

Rafe guessed it would be neither.

CHAPTER
23

Dinner in Holly's new prison was a repeat of lunch, though the rice and noodles were served with unrecognizable sinews of meat and a peppering of something green. It looked a lot liked chopped grass.

Amina assumed the job of feeding Holly, giving them cover for a whispered conversation. Holly got her new friend to slip the phone into the front of her underwear. With her hands bound, she was unable to pull on the sweater, though that was a relief in the sauna-like heat. The guards changed, and the tension in the room seemed to lighten. Women began to move and whisper to each other.

"Did you get your text out?" Holly said.

"Yes. I took a—what do you call it?" She frowned. "A *selfie*, and texted it to my sister. I told her to send it to my agency's Twitter account, with the details we have and ask people to retweet it. We have almost 400,000 followers, from all over the world, and many of our sister agencies have ten times that, so…" She shrugged. "It was good you kept the guards busy."

"Wow. That was quite a…public thing to do. I thought you'd just text someone in your organization."

"That was my first thought, but no. It could take too long. My sister spends all day attached to her phone—she'll get it sorted out in seconds. Believe me, this way we'll get more attention, faster. A face is much harder for people to ignore than a name."

So right now word could be getting out. That was something. "Could we get the other women to do the same?"

"These are simple, poor women. Most would not have anyone to contact online. Others would fear putting shame on their families, or forcing harm on them from the traffickers." Her gaze flicked to the guard. "They would also be putting their own lives in more danger. My agency will help. This could be the breakthrough we and many others like us have been seeking for many years. The authorities cannot turn a blind eye if the pressure comes from the public."

"Good. I will need you to do me a favor later. I don't have your contacts, but there's someone I need to get a message to." Not that she had much to report, except that she and Theo were safe—relatively. Rafe would be frustrated enough to try swimming for it, by now. "When I go to the toilet, can you help?" She indicated her bound hands.

Amina nodded. "I'm sorry, the phone battery is low. I turned it off, to save power."

Holly nodded. She just needed enough juice for one email.

Amina placed her palm in the middle of Holly's chest, over the amulet, which was tucked into her T-shirt. "You are a brave woman."

"Not as brave as you. Do you mind if I ask: What do you think they will do with me, if we don't get out?" She cringed. How selfish did that sound?

"Hard to say. I've never heard of a white American woman being trafficked in this region, though I do know that white women fetch higher prices. Usually traffickers have a hold over these women—perhaps threats against the family—to keep them compliant as they work in brothels. What do they have on you?"

"Nothing. I have no family." She thought of Rafe, of how right it'd felt to be wrapped up together in the hammock. For one of the few times in her life, she'd believed that somebody else gave a damn whether or not she existed. She sure as hell wanted him and Theo to survive this. That was the only thing Gabriel could hold over her—she'd have to be careful to hide it from him.

"Sometimes the women are sold as slaves to men who keep them locked up at their homes or somewhere nearby. Maybe this is what will happen." Amina gripped Holly's knee. "But I am sure you will get out. You have courage. And I will help if I can."

The guard shouted. Dinnertime was over.

Amina ate the last grains of rice off her fingers. "You must tell me your story, later—how you came to be here, so far from your home."

The dishes were removed and water was passed around. Amina held a bottle to Holly's lips so she could drink. A guy sprayed the room, the chemicals itching Holly's airways.

"Now?" Amina said, after he left.

Holly nodded. She cleared her throat and jerked her head toward the bucket. The guard stared at her, unmoved. Damn. What if he just let her pee her pants? He grimaced and jutted his chin in permission. Holly eased out a breath. Amina mimed pulling Holly's shorts down and gestured to her bound hands. He shrugged dismissively.

They slipped behind the human bathroom wall. Holly nodded to her pocket. Amina found the knife and sawed through the cable tie.

"I'll take the bucket out for you, when you're done," Amina whispered.

She peered out from behind the women before joining their ranks. Holly pulled down her shorts and switched on the phone. She really did have to pee, so she did it as noisily as she could, while she brought up email. The battery icon flashed. It took its time loading. *Come on, come on.*

A message popped up: an open wireless network was in range. Could be a faster connection. Hands shaking, she accessed the settings and turned on Wi-Fi. The search icon spun, round and round, round and round. The low-battery warning flashed again. *Just a few more minutes.* Her thighs burned from crouching, her knee tight enough to burst. Round and round, round and round. *Come on.*

Bingo. The network flashed up—Suaka Surfing Lodge. Her mouth dropped open. Holy shit. She had a location. She could give it to Rafe.

After forever, she got to the compose screen. She keyed in the address Rafe had set up and swiped quickly, with the name of the lodge, an update on Theo and a brief rundown. Her fingers shook and slid all over the screen. Sweat pricked on her brow. She clicked Send. The screen went black. Her stomach lurched. Oh, God. No. She swiped it. Nothing. She tried the power button. Nothing.

She screwed up her face, shaking with the urge to throw the thing against the wall. She bit down the frustration, shoved the phone back in her underwear and returned to her spot, pretending her hands were still tied. Amina took care of the bucket, then settled in next to her. Amina's message had better work—it was all they had.

The guard was picking at his fingernails with a dirty knife. She leaned right over to Amina's ear. "Have you heard of a surfing lodge called Suaka?"

The women shook her head. "Why do you ask?" Her eyes widened. "That's where we are?"

"It came up as a Wi-Fi network."

"I've heard the word before—Suaka. It sounds Malay." Amina grabbed Holly's hand. "We can tell my agency. They can find us."

Holly winced. "The battery's dead."

Amina slumped. Then her grip tightened. "But you got your message away? I'm so sorry, I hope I didn't—"

"It's fine," whispered Holly. "The message went."

Sometimes there was mercy in a white lie.

They sat in silence until the guard switched off the light, plunging the room into a deep charcoal. From outside, the door was bolted. The clonk echoed around the room—the sound of hope shriveling. Holly bit her lip to keep from crying out. After six years inside, she'd promised herself she'd never be locked up again. Now, she faced being locked up for the rest of her life.

No. She wasn't giving up. Amina's sister might already have seen her text. Maybe the lobby group could trace it somehow. In the meantime, Holly just needed to stay alive, maybe create a chance to escape and get to Theo. She chewed her lip. What if the post did go viral and word got to Gabriel?

She lay awake for hours in the increasingly stifling room. Late into the night a thunderstorm hit. The lightning illuminated the women's faces, many of them equally sleepless. Bolts shook the ground, as if a giant drew ever closer. She willed a bolt to strike the hut. Either she'd die or escape in the chaos. Rain followed, furious but brief, leaving the air washed clean and cooler. The heady jungle fragrance floated in through the window, relieving the stench of stale breath and sweat.

Had she really been sleeping in Rafe's arms only twenty-four hours ago? She forced her mind to clear away its fears and create an image of him, lit by the moon, his finely sculpted face sharp with desire. She squeezed her eyes shut. At the very least, she'd fight for a chance to see that beautiful sight again, no matter how briefly. She imagined the touch of his skin on hers and his deep voice whispering in her ear, in French.

She wasn't stupid enough to believe in fantasies in the cold reality of day, but she'd long ago learned to go along with whatever promised to get her through the night. And Rafe... Rafe could get her through anything.

Mr. Buana's eldest son eased back on the throttle of his fishing boat, leaving it rocking in the swell. Between the boat and a strip of white sand, a dozen wet-suited surfers bobbed on their boards, like seals guarding the beach. "You go now," he said to Rafe, without turning around.

"This is Suaka?"

"Yes. You go." The man pushed Rafe's shoulder, his eyes scanning the beach in the gray predawn, as if expecting a dozen men with assault rifles to materialize from its row of shabby huts. His nervousness was a good sign—evidence they weren't dropping Rafe at any old island just to be rid of him.

Rafe fit the mask over his eyes, plugged his mouth with the regulator and took a slow draw of air. Shielded from the beach by the small boat's cabin, he sat on the bulwark, gave a thumbs-up and rolled backward into the water. He sank like a rock, watching his bubbles dissipate in the wake of the departing boat.

At ten feet, he gained neutral buoyancy, taking stock of the crappy rig Buana had sold him. The buoyancy compensator could be a Jacques Cousteau relic, but at least the getup wasn't leaking air—yet.

The villagers might be taking a risk in helping him, but they'd also taken everything but the eyes from his head for it. Damn PayPal. They'd even forced him to buy their entire catch that morning, which they would attempt to sell to the lodge as cover while he slipped in.

But, hell, money was easier for him to come by than it was for a village of poor fishermen. He'd made only a token effort at bartering. He'd have handed them his life savings if it meant rescuing Theo and Holly. They'd better be on that island. After his near-disaster with the Windsurfer, he didn't want to risk stealing another one.

He kicked hard against the buffeting current. The strap on one of his fins was loose—he'd be lucky if it survived the swim. As he dropped deeper, his left ear refused to equalize, aggravating the headache that hadn't left him in twelve hours. At least he'd eaten and slept, though it'd been torture to wait until nearly dawn to set out, when the winds had settled and the tides were right.

The words of Holly's email played over and over in his head. "Theo's okay, physically," she'd written, the inference clear. And she was to be sold into slavery. She'd obviously had a hand in the photo of the Australian woman that had gone viral on the internet overnight, but he doubted it would do Gabriel's captives any favors in the short term. He'd just get rid of them quicker—kill them, if necessary. It might already be too late.

Rafe had never felt as tense as he had last night, waiting for his email to load over Buana's agonizingly slow connection. He'd told himself not to expect word from Holly—even if she'd re-mained alive, the Lost Boys could have confiscated the iPhone. But there it was: a short, clipped email, sent just a few minutes earlier. The relief had been so powerful it'd nearly broken him.

He'd managed to catch Flynn on live chat an hour ago. The lieutenant had landed in Bali with a plan, having caught up with the overnight explosion on social media. With the added intel from Holly, he had something concrete to work with—and he'd work it, all right. Flynn was like Rafe—never happy resting. That was when the demons caught up. But his plan would take time to arrange—several more hours, best case. And Gabriel would know by now his operation was compromised. Going on previous form, *Les Pirates Fantômes* were about to vanish, leav-ing nothing but bodies. This time, Rafe would not be too late.

After several minutes of kicking, the hazy outline of the drop-off appeared, growing more distinct as he neared. A coral pla-teau. Fish swarmed and darted around him, some peeking out from anemones. They reminded him of children in war zones, their fear battling their curiosity as giant armed intruders rolled past.

The current rose and fell. The crackling of a thousand tiny teeth on the coral mixed with the saw of his breath through the reg. The dark shape of a surfboard passed overhead. He kicked in the opposite direction from the jetty to which the boat had headed, aiming for a rocky outcrop between two white buoys he'd spotted earlier. It would screen his arrival and allow him to scout out the island.

Mr. Buana had doubted Rafe's assertion that this private island, with its simple surfing lodge and untamed jungle, could be the hideout for Gabriel's militia. The word *Suaka*, meaning "sanctuary," was used in the names of dozens of lodges. But this one had an airstrip and was within the helicopter's range. The sat map had shown little more than the row of beachfront huts, but it was several years out of date.

Rafe's gut call better be right. Otherwise he'd have to find a way to cross another forty kilometers of open ocean to the next most likely island. Knowing Gabriel, Rafe wouldn't have time for a leisurely tour of the archipelago before Holly was sold off or killed, and Theo was pushed beyond salvation.

Shouts outside tore Holly from sleep. She bolted upright, panting, seized with the instinct to run. Next to her, Amina sat up. No doubt sensing the same danger, Amina backed up against the wall, staring at the door. The lock clonked. The guard on the chair—Bandanna Guy again—scrambled to pull it open.

Crap, Holly was supposed to be still shackled. Behind her back, she wrapped the cut cable around her wrists, holding the severed ends in her palms.

Gabriel charged in, followed by five men. He shouted a command and the overhead light buzzed and clicked on, bleaching the room white. Holly blinked, resisting the urge to bring her hands to her eyes. Birds squawked in the trees. It had to be near dawn.

Gabriel held a smartphone and was looking from it to the women, searching for something—someone. As he turned his back to her, Holly caught a glimpse of the screen—a close-up of Amina's face. Holly stopped breathing. As Amina shrank into the wall, Holly shuffled in front of her, wishing she could make her disappear.

He grabbed a woman sitting along the far wall, yanking her hair to force her face up, compared her with the photo and shoved her aside. One of the men called out from the back of the room, pulling another woman to her feet. He hauled her forward. Like Amina, she had shoulder-length black hair and wore a dirty yellow dress.

Gabriel pointed at the phone. "You?"

She shrank back, but the goon clamped a hand on the back of her neck, forcing her face to within inches of Gabriel's. Gabriel spoke to his men. Two looked from the screen to the woman's terrified face. They grunted in agreement. Gabriel fisted her hair and hauled her across the floor. Her legs bumped over the other women as they scrambled aside. Her scream echoed off the walls.

Holly sensed movement behind her. She grabbed for Amina. Too late.

"It is me you look for," Amina said, standing, her chest heaving against her dress.

"No!" Holly shouted, as three men descended on Amina. Gabriel let the other woman go, and shook tufts of her hair from his hands. He spat an order, his face contorted. Holly stood, awkwardly, clutching her hands behind her. "I did it. I took her photo. She didn't know."

Gabriel advanced and gripped Holly's neck, crunching her head against the wall. She jabbed at him, but her fist glanced off his stomach. He shoulder-charged her. *Boof.* As her lungs sucked in air, he punched her in the gut. Red-hot pain shuddered through her torso. She retched and vomit surged into her mouth. She let it go, channeling it into his face.

He released her. As she slumped to the floor, he staggered out the door, spitting out her stomach contents. Hate filled her chest. If that was the last thing she saw, she'd die satisfied.

Two men grabbed Holly's feet—one each—and dragged her

out. Her spine bounced down the hut's concrete steps. She drew her arms over her head to protect her skull. No use pretending her hands were still tied. Her shaky vision relayed that they were doing the same to Amina behind her.

They shoved Holly onto a patch of wet grass, a boot shooting flames into her ribs. Amina skidded to a halt beside her. A dozen armed men closed in around them. Chamuel sliced a machete through the air in figure eights. Holly swallowed. Through the men's legs, she spotted folded white plastic, lit by a beam of light from the veranda. Another body bag.

CHAPTER

24

Holly grabbed Amina's shoulders. "You know what this means," she whispered. "Your message got out. Help is on the way."

Amina circled trembling arms around Holly. "Yes, this is good," she squeaked. "This is very good. Excellent."

An arm closed around Holly's neck and wrenched her back. Amina's wide, wet eyes locked onto Holly's as Bandanna Guy hooked back the woman's arms, pinning her. Holly felt the same happening to her. For Amina's benefit, she didn't waver her focus. She sensed the circle of men parting to let someone through—Gabriel, wiping his face with a handkerchief.

"Yes, you watch, American," he said, his voice shaking with rage. "You did this."

"People are looking for her."

"That is why she must die. Followed by you."

One of the men closed in on Amina. Holly smelled Chamuel's fish-oil breath.

"No! It was me who took the photo and posted it. She didn't know." Holly tried to twist out of her captor's grip, but he jerked her back.

"Then her death is on your conscience."

"Don't do this, you sicko!"

A tear slipped down Amina's cheek, but her lips set in a firm line. Holly's eyes watered as she thrashed. "No!" Through blurred vision she watched Chamuel lift the steel blade and slice Amina's neck. Oh, God. The woman whimpered briefly, then gurgled. Bandanna Guy released her, and her hands flailed at her neck.

No, no, no. Holly's vision streamed with crimson, the color melting into the yellow. She yanked against her captor. Gabriel issued an instruction and the grip relaxed. Tumbling forward, she gulped in a breath and scooped her arms around Amina, pulling the woman's head and shoulders into her lap. Blood bubbled from the wound. She could do nothing but hold Amina's cheeks as they paled, the liquid seeping thick and warm through Holly's fingers and clothes.

"You did it, Amina." Holly's tears dripped into the red river. "Help is coming. Hold on."

Amina's eyes lost their focus. Her body fell from weak to limp, her head lolling back to reveal a yawning wound. Blood rushed out. Holly buried a yelp and wrapped her arms around Amina, kissing her forehead, cradling her head and neck. She was gone. And Gabriel was right—this was on Holly's conscience. Tweeting had been too bold, too public. What would Gabriel do now he knew people were onto him? Kill all the women?

A sob sounded from among the men. Holly jerked her gaze from Amina. One of the Lost Boys was crying?

No, not a soldier. Gabriel crouched on the ground, hands sandwiching Theo's pale cheeks, forcing him to look at the bloody scene. The boy trembled, his eyes red and haunted. Gabriel spoke in his ear in a soft, fatherly tone.

"You made him watch?" Holly cried. "You're even more of a psycho than I thought."

Gabriel stood, holding the boy firmly by his shoulders. Theo dropped his gaze to the ground. Gabriel slid a hand under his chin and jerked it up. He couldn't see Theo had closed his eyes.

"I told him it was your choice the whore should die," said Gabriel, "like it was your choice to kill his father. And now it is his choice to kill you."

Gabriel held his palm out to one of the men. A handgun

was slapped into it. Gabriel enclosed Theo's hands around the weapon, threading the kid's finger onto the trigger and pointing it at Holly. Theo's eyes flew open. The gun clicked as Gabriel cocked it.

"Do not worry, my dear. He has had some training. It should not take him more than six shots to kill you." He stepped away from Theo, leaving the gun in the boy's trembling hands. "Woman!" he shouted.

Theo's translator shuffled into the circle. She swallowed, crossing herself.

"Tell him again that killing her will cleanse his father's soul and send him to heaven. That if he fails, his father goes to hell."

"His father is alive," shouted Holly, as the woman shakily translated. "You're a fucked-up whacko, you know that?" She should feel fear, but her body shook with anger. "A coward."

Gabriel's face darkened. "The only coward is the man who couldn't kill you in the first place."

He turned to the translator. "Tell him to do it quickly, before his father's soul descends. Tell him it will make the pain go away."

"No, tell him his father is alive." The woman hesitated. A man behind her planted a kick up her ass. She lurched forward and gabbled out the translation. Theo raised the gun and aimed it at Holly's chest, his downturned mouth trembling. Tears filled his eyes. The man behind Holly skirted out of the way. "Fire," said Gabriel quietly.

Rafe navigated by tide and current to the first buoy—an empty white plastic container, with a rope trailing down to a crayfish trap. In the cage, a tangle of creatures clambered over each other, antennae waving. He turned inland, kicking for the far side of the rocks while keeping clear enough that a surge wouldn't smash him into them. He rose to the waterline, crocodile-like, and spun in a three-sixty. Nothing but sand, rocks, trees and sky. He pulled off his mask and spat out the reg.

Moving swiftly and silently, he stashed his wet suit and dive gear in the heart of a near-impenetrable banyan tree and stole a green T-shirt from a cabin that faced away from the others. His shorts would dry quickly enough. He stuffed pilfered bottles of water into his pockets, along with the iPhone and Makarov, still in their dry bag.

He did a creeping recon of the lodge—half a dozen huts and a simple communal eating hall. A woman swept a veranda with a broom made from twigs lashed to a pole with homemade twine. Two men bent over a gutting table, scaling and filleting fish as they chatted in their own language. No prisoners, no guns, no Gabriel, no Theo. Rafe's stomach tightened. If it was cover for a people-smuggling operation, it was good cover. He might yet be looking for a Windsurfer.

He crept through the coconut palms until he found the narrow dusty road that linked the lodge with the airstrip. He eyed up a dirty van parked in a clearing. The airstrip was a good ten kilometers away, but he couldn't risk the engine noise alerting the staff. His greatest advantage—his only advantage—was surprise. He could use a run, anyway.

He unfolded the dry bag and checked the phone for messages. Flynn was still trying to pin down his contact. Too late, *mon ami*. Rafe pulled out the gun and checked it.

Son of a bitch.

Holly eyeballed Rafe's son, willing his gaze to lift from her heart—where he was aiming the gun—to her face. "No, Theo."

"Tell him not to listen," said Gabriel. "Tell him she is possessed by the devil."

Holly talked over the woman's translation, struggling to think of words Theo might understand. *"Non, Theo. Non. Papa...ah...* not *mort. Papa non mort."* All wrong, dammit. What the hell was the French word for alive? The phrase *vive la France* sprang into her mind. Didn't that mean long live France?

"Tell him to do it," hissed Gabriel. "His father descends to the devil while he waits."

"Papa...vive... Papa...vive." Holly scrambled for the amulet under her T-shirt. She held it out to Theo in her bloodied hand, like a talisman. She pointed at his pendant. *"Papa mi amore."* Shit, no, that was Spanish, or Italian, or something. There must be some French line she'd heard in a movie.

Theo's gaze fell on the amulet. He looked down at the stone on his own chest, rising and falling with his desperate breaths.

Gabriel yelled in Theo's ear: "Pull the trigger, you stupid rabbit."

Theo's bewildered gaze linked with Holly's. She didn't dare blink.

"She is the devil! Tell him!" Gabriel jerked a hand to the translator.

"Papa mi amigo," cried Holly. Oh, God, that really wasn't right. Entirely different language. What was that Shakira song, with the title that was French for "my love"? One of her prison guards had sung the damn thing for a year.

"Mon amour!" she yelled, over the woman's translation. That was it! *"Mon amour."* She pulled at the amulet, as if the words were hidden in it. *"Papa est mon amour. Papa est vivant."* *Vive* high school French.

Theo blinked, as Holly repeated her shouts. She'd probably bamboozled the kid, pouring mumbo-jumbo at him like the possessed nutcase Gabriel was making her out to be.

"Mon papa est encore vivant?"

Holly didn't so much hear the faint words as read them on Theo's lips, and read the hope bringing life into his eyes.

"Si... I mean, *oui... Papa est encore vivant."* God, that had better mean what she thought it did: *Papa is still alive.*

Theo's focus pulled back to the gun. He looked up at Gabriel, his hands shakily following the direction of his eyes until the barrel pointed at the warlord's face. A goon stepped toward Theo. Gabriel held up a palm, stopping the man, but keeping his eyes fixed on Theo.

"What did you tell him, you American bitch?"

"I told him his father wouldn't want him killing anyone."

Gabriel looked at the translator for confirmation. She nodded briskly, lips tight.

"Tell him I am his father now." Gabriel held his hand out for the gun, breathing heavily. "He belongs with us. He will have everything he needs here."

The woman spoke quietly to Theo, her focus darting between him and Gabriel. Holly got the feeling she wasn't so much translating as giving a pep talk. She'd better be telling him not to shoot. Theo's hands were too young to have blood on them.

Holly's, on the other hand...

With all eyes focused on Theo, Holly slowly laid Amina on the ground and launched forward. Her hand closed on metal. Theo's grip loosened and she pulled the gun away, fumbling to get her fingers in the right places. Shouts pelted around. A figure flew at her. She stumbled backward into the gap the men had left and her assailant landed at her feet. They didn't need to know she'd never fired a gun in her life. Could she take out Gabriel? She aimed it at his chest. She just needed to pull the trigger, right? Gabriel had already cocked the thing.

Gabriel snatched the machete from Chamuel and wrapped an arm around Theo, holding the bloody blade at the boy's throat, shielding himself with the kid's body. Shit. She'd hesitated and lost her chance. In her peripheral vision, she counted at least three rifles trained on her.

"Go on, American. You want to kill him, like you killed his father? Or should I kill him for you? Your choice."

Theo whimpered. Scarlet blood trickled down the blade, mixing with Amina's. Hot with fury, Holly tossed the gun at a goon's

head. Another guy shoved her to the ground. Gabriel lifted the
machete from Theo's throat and the boy ran to Holly, teeth
clenched. She threw her arms over her face, bracing for a pummeling for grabbing his gun and wasting the opportunity—or
would he attempt to finish her by hand? How far had his "training" gone?

He threw his skinny body onto her, threaded his arms around
her waist and…hugged her. Oh, God. She froze, then wrapped
him up, her arms overlapping his narrow back. If only she could
cast a spell that would transport him to safety. She took a shuddering breath, her body aching with the need to protect this kid.

"Papa est vivant, Papa est vivant, Papa's okay, sweetheart," she
whispered, cradling his head. This was a precious part of Rafe—
the most precious part. If she could safely deliver him to his father, any price she paid would be worth it.

Hell, if this was how protective she felt for the kid after just
meeting him, she could only imagine the deep hole Rafe was
in right now. He must be dying inside. No wonder he'd been
wound so tight. She hugged tighter, as if she could bridge that
gap between Rafe and Theo—yesterday she had been embracing the father, today the son. She felt like she had a stake in both
their lives. How crazy was that?

"We're wasting time." Gabriel gave orders to his men. A
couple of them closed in on Holly and Theo, and yanked them
apart. Theo's fingernails almost gouged Holly's arms as he tried
to hold on. "Death is too good for you. I want you crying over
that slant-eyed whore every day you're chained up for the rest
of your miserable life."

Gabriel relayed another order and a man began searching Amina—for the phone, no doubt. Holly yanked it out of
the back of her underwear and threw it at Gabriel's head. She
couldn't risk them searching her. It missed, dammit.

One of the men chucked the body bag to Bandanna Guy,
who stood over Amina. He tore off her clothes, ripped out her

small hoop earrings—taking chunks of her ears with them—and rolled her inside. With a zip, she was gone. Holly gripped clumps of grass. Inside, she screamed with rage.

Gabriel spoke, gesturing at the body bag. The helicopter pilot stepped up and lifted one end of the bag, shouting at another guy, who quickly took the other. How many white bags littered the ocean floor around here?

As they staggered away, Gabriel sought out Chamuel, giving what sounded like urgent instructions. Several men entered the hut, shouting at the women. They filed out, blinking. Devi stared openmouthed at Holly's blood-soaked T-shirt. A man shoved Holly. She took the hint and fell into line, frustration eating at her gut. What was the way out of this? At least five guns were trained on them. Would they all be executed?

"What are you doing with us?" she shouted at Gabriel.

"Moving my stock. Your training period is over. Time for you all to start paying your keep. If anyone comes to investigate your friend's claims, they will find nothing more than a modest tourist resort." He gripped Devi by the scruff of her neck. "And from now on, every time you attempt to defy my orders, my American whore, I will order my men to kill a woman. You are worth a lot of money, but they are not."

"Let Theo go. He's not one of you."

Gabriel turned to her, smiling, as he released Devi. He looked almost...sad. "He will be, in time. We will look after him, here—orphans are my favorite kind of children."

Holly gritted her teeth. For now, the odds were against her. But if they were to be moved out, maybe the Lost Boys would split up. This wasn't a federal penitentiary. Sooner or later, an opportunity would present itself.

Within minutes, the women were crammed into the small truck Holly had seen earlier. With no room to sit, they clung on as best they could as it jolted along a sandy path. Three Lost Boys followed on a quad bike, including Chamuel and Ban-

danna Guy. With two more goons in the front of the truck, and
at least three guns and a machete between them, Holly didn't
like the numbers.

A small hand enclosed Holly's and squeezed. Devi. Though
Holly needed her hand for balance, with her wobbly knee and
shaky hold on gravity, she squeezed back, hoping she wouldn't
fall and plow straight into the kid. She smiled. It felt fake as hell,
but the girl smiled shyly back.

Next to Devi, Theo's translator clutched at the side of the vehicle. Damn, the kid had lost the one person in Gabriel's camp
who'd offered some comfort. The truck flew into the air, and
Holly winced as her stomach muscles compensated, her belly
aching from Gabriel's punch.

After maybe fifteen bone-rattling minutes the truck forded
a stream, climbed a bank and skidded to a halt, sending Holly
flying into Devi, who took out a couple of women behind her.
A skull cracked into Holly's, triggering a headache. A woman
fell out with a cry, her spine smacking onto the ground. The rest
were ordered out. Bandanna Guy opened a gate in a tall wire
fence and they were herded through it onto an asphalt road, surrounded by trees. An airstrip? The lightening gloom of dawn
revealed a waiting plane—larger than the one she and Rafe had
parachuted from. Shit. They'd be untraceable.

CHAPTER

25

The truck accelerated away, leaving Chamuel, who'd grabbed the machete, Bandanna Guy and two other armed goons. The men began shoving the women toward the plane, pointing and shouting. Perhaps Holly and the women could overcome the soldiers once onboard? Surely the men wouldn't risk shooting in midair. And then what—bring the plane down? As Holly stepped into line, a hand grabbed the neck of her T-shirt and yanked. She scrambled to avoid falling.

"I wait long time for Miss America," Chamuel whispered into her ear. "You come or I pick little girl. She good and tight."

Oh. Shit.

Bandanna Guy shouted at Chamuel, frowning. He yelled back, gestures flying past Holly's face. She swallowed, to settle her curdling stomach.

"No fight me or I cut off your hands. You no need hands. Just mouth and cunt." He pressed the blade into her back, forcing her to arch, then threw her forward. Her knee wobbled, and righted. "Walk." He pointed to a patch of jungle fifty feet away. She walked, gingerly at first as her knee eased up, his footsteps dragging along behind. She slipped the knife out of her pocket and held it against her stomach. Pocketknife versus machete wasn't a fair fight, so her timing would have to be perfect. Saliva flooded her mouth. She could do this—whatever it took. She swallowed, hard.

"Stop," he said, as they entered the canopy. He sank his fingers into her upper arm and swung her around, as she swept the knife around to her back and snapped it open. "Down." He pointed to the ground.

She clenched her jaw. Doing what she was told would give him a false sense of security. She lowered herself to her knees onto the damp forest floor, keeping her hands behind her, as if she was propping herself up.

He stood over her, thrusting his tented groin toward her mouth. Ugh. If he made her do that, she'd bite the damn thing off.

"Down!"

She unfolded her legs and lay back, making a point of looking as scared as she felt. The knife handle was slippery in her palm. She just had to wait until he dropped his guard—and the machete.

"Take off." He gave her shorts a tug.

She couldn't do that one-handed—the button was too stubborn. Which meant neither could he. "No."

He sneered. "You like man do that?"

She turned her face to the side and whimpered, as if she were about to let him take what he wanted. He dropped to his knees and fumbled with her fly. Fighting the urge to recoil, she adjusted her grip on the knife. She wouldn't mess this up like she had with shooting Gabriel. No hesitation. Chamuel's life for Amina's. He tore at the button, muttering as it refused to rip.

Her hand shook. *Wait…wait.* Finally, it gave and he leaned over, ready to scoop his filthy hands into her shorts. Every muscle in her body tensed. She filled her lungs, scanning his neck and throat. He let the machete go.

"You will like," he said. A thread of his saliva dripped onto her T-shirt.

Bile shot up her throat. *Now.* She snapped upright and punched the knife into the side of his neck, angled down. For Amina, for all of them. The blade sank up to the handle. She twisted it.

Before he could react, she scooted out from under him, grabbing the machete.

He reared back on his knees and gagged, eyes bulging. Blood gurgled from his mouth. She circled him, holding the machete with shaky hands, panting heavily. Her heartbeat thudded in her ears. She'd done it. She'd goddamn done it. But now what? Fighting him off was one thing, but finishing him off with a machete...?

His hands flailed at the knife, still stuck in his neck. He yanked it out with a sucky, squelching noise, and stumbled toward her, its bloody point aimed at her chest.

She scrambled backward. Sunlight seared her eyes. He pitched forward. She sidestepped, and he swayed and thumped to the ground. He grunted, but stayed down. Shouts rose from near the plane. Shit, she was back in the open, in full view of three men with guns. *Run.*

The air cracked with gunfire as she loped into the jungle. Something punched into her upper arm, sending her careering onto the vine-covered ground. She grabbed at the spot. She'd been shot? She lurched to her feet and staggered further into the undergrowth, pain scorching her skin. Her arm still felt workable, just with a pulpy, bloody nick in it.

She scooted behind a tree and chanced a glance behind, buttoning her shorts. Chamuel's body was wrenched into an unnatural pose, a deep red gouge in his head. His friends had finished him off—by a stray bullet, or a targeted one? They'd been none too discriminating with that volley.

Bandanna Guy sprinted from the plane, gun leveled, yelling over his shoulder. His two comrades watched his progress, weapons aimed. One grabbed something from his waist—a walkie-talkie. Damn. As he raised it, a dozen women closed in from behind. Devi struck first, leaping onto his head and scratching at his eyes. Holly clawed the bark of the tree. *Yes.* A tide of women sucked him under. As the other soldier caught on, women swarmed over him like fire ants. The walkie-talkie and guns went flying.

Oblivious, Bandanna Guy bolted toward Holly, camo pants pumping, red T-shirt a blur. Right now, her job was to keep him from looking behind. She crashed through the jungle, crying out as if in pain. Gunfire rattled, popping as it hit trees and dirt. The guy was operating on luck—the sunlight shining in his eyes would obscure his view of her until he reached the canopy.

Crouching low, she turned sharply right. If she kept charging into the jungle she'd get lost and die out here—and he'd expect her to run away from the airstrip, not parallel to it. Her breath labored, as loud as Malibu surf.

She slid down a bank, trying not to think about what lay beneath the ferns, and splashed into a creek. A fog of mosquitoes zapped around her. She spat out a mouthful of the bloodsuckers. The stream had to be the one they'd forded to get to the airstrip. She could follow it back and double around to help the women. If they were holding their own, she could trek back along the trail to Theo.

She jumped from rock to rock, trying not to splash or leave footprints in the mud, her speed checked by her wobbly knee. The air was so thick it felt liquid and hot right down to her lungs. No sea breezes here. Sweat slicked the machete handle. She adjusted her grip. Where was Bandanna Guy? She hadn't heard him talking—hopefully he assumed his friends had radioed in.

She cleared a boulder and ducked behind it, pressing her back into its cool, smooth surface. The pulsing insect noise alternated with the pounding in her ears. She had no hope of hearing Bandanna Guy over that cacophony, but he'd be having the same trouble.

If he couldn't find her, what would he do? Return to the airstrip and start shooting, or raise the alarm, or both? Damn, this wasn't just about escaping—she had to take him out. She looked up to the tree-laced heavens. This really wasn't her thing. Give her a greedy dreamer and a get-rich-quick scheme and she'd come out the winner—or even leave her with her fists against a scumbag in a dark alley. But a machete, a jungle and a soldier who'd been trained to kill since childhood?

She peered around the boulder. Nothing but a blue-green haze of twisting jungle. She crouched over the stream and splashed her face. Rivulets of water mixed with blood and sweat ran off her clothes, clouding the stream pink. Stupid. She was leaving a trail.

Maybe she could circle back to the airstrip and get one of the guns. She pushed off, forcing herself to keep a steady pace. Too fast and she'd slip and screw her knee for good. Too slow and the guy would catch up. She rounded a bend in the stream. Ahead, light filtered through the tall canopy. A large clearing. The airstrip? Something scuffled in the trees. She ducked against the mossy bank, her neck prickling.

She transferred the machete into her left hand and picked up the biggest rock that fit in her grasp. She'd do this—for Amina, for all of them. She waited. Nothing. She peeked over the bank. Stillness. She loaded another rock into her pocket and, warily, resumed her trail.

An inhuman scream pierced the air. She stumbled and splattered into the water, stifling a scream of her own. What the hell? Another screech, overhead. Her heart constricted as she looked up. Half a dozen hairy brown monkeys flew through the treetops. If it was some primate alarm system, it was effective. Caution be damned—she ran, splashing. Overhead, the monkeys followed, signposting her journey.

A gunshot split the air and reverberated around the stream bed. To her right, movement flashed through the jungle—a red T-shirt, thirty feet away. Shit. Another boom. She ducked. Like that would do any good.

The banks steepened, the stream narrowed and deepened. She sank into water up to her thighs. She'd run into a canyon, with seven-foot walls of sheer rock on each side. The current pulled against her. She was an apple bobbing in a bucket, or whatever that saying was. Like she'd ever bobbed for apples. Ahead, the stream disappeared over a rocky waterfall. She'd slice herself to pieces if she slid down it. She swiveled and surged back through the water, fighting the current. There had to be another way through.

Bandanna Guy loomed above her on a ledge, jogging to a halt. Fuck. She heaved a rock. It bounced off a palm trunk and skated into leaf litter. Black eyes locked on her, followed by a gun barrel.

A boom echoed up the canyon, blowing all sound away. She didn't stop to check if she was still alive. As she cleared the pool of water, something large dropped down behind her—some*one*. She swung wildly, heaving the machete. He fended it off with his gun and it went soaring. As it clattered down the waterfall, her gaze met her attacker's. Not beady black eyes. Big dark-brown ones.

"Holy shit. Rafe!"

CHAPTER

26

Holly looked up. "Watch out, there's a guy—"

"I took care of him." Rafe grabbed her arm, right on the bullet wound. *Youch.* She shrank away. "Are you okay? *Merde,* the blood..."

"It's not mine." She looked down. What color had her T-shirt even been an hour ago? "Well, not much of it."

"Not much?"

"Just a little, right where you're..." She glanced at her arm.

He let go abruptly and pulled up her ripped, bloody sleeve. "Gunshot?"

She nodded, unable to take her gaze off his beautiful face. Rafe? Here? Had a bullet hit her and made her delirious—or was this heaven? "I'm guessing it's not bad. I can't really feel it. What the hell are you...? How did you...? Are you alone?"

"Yes, unfortunately. But I'm here." Gently, he touched the skin around her swollen eye. "It's a long story. I just met your friends—the Cambodians. They nearly blasted me straight to hell, before I talked them down. One of them spoke French, and briefed me."

"They're okay?"

He nodded. "They found cable ties on the soldiers and secured them. I disabled the plane and took them to a good hiding place in the jungle, with their captives. For which they kindly gave me a gun." He raised his shoulder.

"Gabriel and his men—they're evacuating."

"I know. And our backup won't get here in time. I'll hide you with the women, then I'm going after Theo."

"I'm not waiting around. I'm coming with you."

"No. I've put you in enough danger. Here." He pulled a bottle of water from his pocket. "I need to be sure you're safe."

"Don't worry about me, I'm a survivor." She ripped off the cap and glugged.

"We're all survivors until we're not. You are a lost girl looking for a cause, and I like you too much to want to drag you in any further."

Oh, boy. Here she was fighting for her life and her mind fixed on his "I like you" like a moth at a neon sign. *Of course he likes you, you moron.* "I know where he's being kept, and I know how to get there. It'll save time." She pressed her fingers to his lips, as he parted them to speak. "Don't say no, now. I think I've proved that two's better than one. Come on, while my adrenaline's still pumping."

"Wow." He grinned. "I'm glad you're alive."

"So am I."

His eyes drilled into hers. Why was he not moving? He caught her hips and pulled her close, taking her in a blessedly bruising kiss. Yep, she was alive, all right. She planted her hands on his waist, relishing the tautness of the muscle as she hungrily returned the kiss. Touching him again—she could cry, in relief.

He released her abruptly. "Theo—how is he?"

She palmed his cheek. "He'll be okay now."

Rafe's brow creased.

"He'll be very happy to see you," she added, slipping her hand down to his stubbly jaw, relishing the rasp against her palm that told her he was real—not even close to an angel. As if she'd ever make it to heaven. "I'm happy to see you, too." *Like you wouldn't believe.*

He grabbed her hand and planted a long kiss on her palm, his eyes tightly closed. Her insides went gooey. Oh yeah, she had it for this guy, bad. Her vision watered. She choked out a sob.

His head snapped up. "What was that? Are you okay? Need more water?"

"I cried, you robot." She swallowed the urge. It would be so comforting to give in, so easy to dissolve into his strength.

"Oh. Yes. It's okay, you know, to cry."

"I'm good. Moment's over." Her lip quivered. She clamped her jaw tight.

"I am sorry, Holly, for what you've been through because of me."

"Drop it." She held up a palm. "Seriously."

"Drop what?"

"Stop being kind."

He raised his eyebrows.

"Kindness kills me. Be as nasty as you want and I'm okay. But being nice… That makes me weak. You can be kind to me all you like once this is over." Because—wow—as much as she wanted Theo back with his father, and the women safe, she really didn't want this…*thing*…she had with Rafe to end.

He nodded slowly. "I once thought we were so different." He tilted up her chin. "It's okay to show weakness with me, princess. Because, believe me, I know you're not weak. You are the strongest, most loyal, most beautiful woman I've ever known."

The kiss came gently, this time. Tears ran down her cheeks. Happy tears? Sad tears? Kissing Rafe wasn't helping her mental state, but oh, God, her chest was filling with bubbles of goodness. She wound her hands around his neck. She needed him close. If she could fuse herself to him right now, she would.

He released her, all too soon. "I feared for you, Holly."

Did she detect a waver in his voice? For the first time he seemed less than 200 percent confident, like it cost him something to say that. He traced the path of a tear up her jaw, up her cheek, as if he was putting it back. He probably didn't understand tears. Hell, *she* didn't understand tears. Surely just a normal physical reaction after a stressful twenty-four hours. She'd cried the first night in prison, too. Then, never again—until now.

Truth was, she was terrified. Not of Gabriel—well, yes, she was terrified of Gabriel—but these tears were coming from a different place. She was terrified of this, of the knot in her stomach that wasn't going to let her ignore the truth anymore—she'd fallen in love, goddammit.

She grabbed his hand and pressed her cheek into it, then her lips. He groaned and pulled her tight. A dozen bruises and other injuries protested, but she clung on, wanting to give as much to him as he gave to her. He'd told her he didn't have the normal range of emotions, but he was obviously feeling something now. Relief? Or the same cocktail of emotion that churned in her belly?

Something crackled. She flinched. Bandanna Guy's walkie-talkie. Rafe scaled the bank, gesturing at her to remain silent. A reedy voice trickled out of the unit, in Rafe's native language. Rafe replied, muffling his voice with his hand, eyeballing her to remind her not to speak—like she needed the warning. A terse reply crackled back. Rafe responded briefly, then flicked a switch and slid it into his waistband.

"It's safe to talk," he said, lying flat on the bank and reaching for her.

She took his hands, and clambered up. "What was that about?"

"Gabriel's men at HQ were wondering why the plane hadn't taken off. I said we were fixing a maintenance issue, but everything was under control. They seemed to accept it."

"A maintenance issue. That's one word for it."

"At least we know no one managed to raise the alarm. We must go. We have to secure Theo. This will be over soon, princess."

Rafe relieved the dead soldier of his M16. *Merde*, the things Holly had been through. He didn't want to subject her to anything else, but she was right—he could use her help finding Theo. Then he'd force her to hide while he rescued his boy. He'd tie her to a tree and gag her, if necessary.

Theo. He was so close.

He passed the rifle to her. At least the militia could be relied on to keep their weapons in working order.

She raised her palms. "I have no idea how to use that."

"They don't need to know that. Use it as a decoy."

"Wouldn't it make them more likely to shoot me, if I'm aiming a gun at them? I'd rather take my chances with my right hook."

She had a point. And she wouldn't be facing the enemy at all, if he could help it. He pocketed the magazine, dumped the rifle and searched the guy's pockets, commandeering a packet of cable ties. They crept through the jungle, quietly swapping accounts of the last twenty-four hours and talking scenarios and tactics for freeing Theo, their voices hidden beneath the cicada screeches. The gunshots had scared off the macaques, at least.

The airstrip was silent and still. Rafe scanned the patch of jungle he'd led the women through. No sign of anyone, and he'd made sure they'd left no tracks. Flynn would find them right away, using the coordinates Rafe had texted him, but the militia would have to do a time-consuming grid search, once they'd even figured out there was a problem.

If, as Holly said, Gabriel had around two dozen soldiers at the compound, they'd immobilized four so far. It would help to get that number down further.

"Is it okay if I retrieve your knife? I'd feel better if you had it, if you don't want to use a gun."

She winced. "If it makes you feel better."

He jogged to Chamuel's body, twisted the blade out of the guy's clamped hand, and wiped it on the grass. If anyone deserved to rot, that *fils de pute* did. He checked that his walkie-talkie was switched off, as he had with the other soldiers. It was a matter of time before Gabriel became suspicious about that, but what else could he do? He dragged the body into the foliage. The longer the militia puzzled over what happened here, the better.

"Could we take that?" Holly said as he returned, jerking her head toward a quad bike parked beside the wire fence.

"Noise would be risky. Our best advantage is surprise." *Our only advantage.* "Can your knee handle it? You've been favoring it."

She nodded. "It's wobbly, but working."

He slashed the vehicle's tires and handed her the knife. She zipped it into her pocket. Her other pocket bulged with something heavy.

She stared at the plane. "Should we check on the women?"

"Believe me, princess, they are well in control of that situation."

They slipped through the open gate and splashed through the stream bed, taking refuge in the tree line. Once he was satisfied there were no immediate threats, they jogged along the rough road, ready to dive into thick cover at a second's notice.

It was the fence next to the airstrip that had first assured Rafe he was in the right place. Why would a rustic surfing lodge need a four-meter fence topped with barbed wire? Then gunshots had ripped out, and he'd sprinted and found the plane and the women. Figuring out who they were, he'd approached with his hands up.

The news that Holly had been shot had driven a dagger through his heart. Then another woman, the one who spoke French, hugged him, crying about Theo and how she'd comforted him as best she could. *That* he was grateful for.

"Water," said Holly, breathlessly, after about twenty minutes of jogging.

Ducking under the canopy, he handed her a bottle. Her face was flushed, the pink sheen from the heat and effort mixing with bruises in shades of red, purple and green. Her black eye was bloodshot, half-closed and rimmed with red, and her arms and legs were washed pink and brown with dirt, blood and sweat. And still she was beautiful as heaven—nothing short of an IED would rob her of that. "I don't think I'd recognize you without your bruises."

She touched her puffy eye. "I must look like a zombie."

"You look very much alive to me." So alive that she was prompting all kinds of reactions in him that didn't befit a man of his rank on an operation.

"That's encouraging. I can't wait to throw these clothes away."

He caught her waist in both hands. "I can't wait for that either." A lightness came over him whenever he looked at her, despite the fear he held for Theo. He wanted to kiss her again. He clamped his lips together. He'd been overcome with relief earlier. This time he would control himself.

She rolled the one eye she could fully open. "I meant get changed into something that isn't soaked with blood. Like, I don't know, a dress. I haven't worn a dress in six years. I'd very much like to get that chance again."

"I'd like to see that."

She frowned. He let his hands slip from her waist. He shouldn't confuse things between them. He was fooling himself that a future lay ahead in which he'd see her in a dress, or see her at all. There could be no future for him with any woman, no matter how tough she was, no matter how she appeared to be capable of handling the danger he posed. Not when he didn't trust himself to control the fire that burned in him. He'd messed with her life enough.

"You can email me a photo," he said, "in the dress."

She smiled, and handed back the water. "A photo. Sure. I'll do that." The phone in his pocket vibrated. A text from Flynn. He was at least two hours away. *Merde.* Gabriel could be on another continent by then.

They continued in silence. The air was marginally cooler on the track than in the greenhouse of the jungle, but his skin dripped, and sweat trickled into his eyes. Behind him, Holly panted rhythmically as she ran—a now-familiar sound he didn't want to think too carefully about. As they came to a corner, she tugged at his T-shirt. He stopped.

"I recognize this place, from being on the truck," she whispered. "The hut where they were holding the women is about a half mile from here."

He switched on the walkie-talkie at minimal volume and listened for chatter. Some logistical talk about moving out, but nothing to suggest any suspicions. He switched it off.

They resumed at a quick walk, following the tree line. As they neared the hut, voices filtered up the track. They came to a stop near a clearing, ducking behind undergrowth. The stench of chlorine bleach blasted him. Two soldiers stood outside a dirty concrete hut, smoking and talking, no weapons in view. The older one looked familiar. Scratches and thuds came from inside. A small truck waited out front, parked parallel to the hut.

"Can you hear what they're saying?" she whispered.

He placed a finger on her lips. He could have removed it—should have removed it—but he let it linger a bit. For several minutes they watched and listened. A man stepped out of the hut, shouting. The soldiers lazily stubbed out their cigarettes and disappeared into the back of the truck. They returned carrying dive tanks, which they heaved inside.

Rafe leaned toward her ear. "They're in a hurry. The guy who was inside is worried they'll hold up the boat. Another boat has already left. Gabriel's taking the helicopter—with Theo, I imagine. I haven't heard it, so it must be still here."

"They're cleaning up and clearing out. Making it look like a storeroom."

"How far away is Gabriel's compound?"

"Maybe another half mile, possibly less."

So he couldn't risk opening fire. "Stay here."

"What are you…?"

He held up a finger. "And I mean it."

He sprinted to the near side of the truck and sheltered behind it. He chanced a glance into the back. Diving and surfing equipment. They'd be unloading it awhile. Voices approached. He flattened against the side. Two guys came and went. A minute later, more footfalls closed in—a man on his own. The truck shifted as he stepped into the back. Rafe slipped his M16 from his shoulder and crept to the corner of the vehicle, giving the guy a chance to load his arms with tanks. As the guy backed out onto the dirt, Rafe stepped out and spoke a quiet, casual greeting.

The guy swung around, frowning. Rafe rammed the rifle butt into his forehead. He crumpled, out cold. Rafe caught the tanks and stashed them back in the truck. Boots thunked on the veranda of the hut. He dragged the guy out of sight, behind the truck, and raised his weapon, steadying his breath.

"Remiel?" one of the soldiers called. "Where did he go?"

"To have a wank. Lazy pig."

The pair loaded up with more tanks. Once they were back in the hut, Rafe threw the man over his shoulder and ran into the trees. He gagged him with his own shirt, and tied his arms and feet. This was Remiel? Little trace of the boy Rafe remembered. A year or two younger than Rafe, he'd killed his own sister during his Lost Boys induction. Rafe looped him to a tree trunk with a series of cable ties. He caught movement in the jungle—Holly, creeping his way. He lowered the M16.

"I told you to stay put," he hissed. "I might have shot you."

"I'm not good at following directions. What are we doing with the other two?"

"*You* are doing nothing."

She crossed her arms. "You don't have a lot of respect for me, do you?"

"I have too much respect for you—that's why I want you safe. This kind of thing—it's what I do for a living. Just sit back and enjoy the show, princess." He took her elbow and spun her around. "From a safe distance. Pretend it's one of the movies you like so much." He gently pushed her lower back.

She slung a backward glance at him, then retreated, shaking her head. *Mon Dieu.* He was used to people following his orders.

He planted his spine behind a large tree and bided his time until one of the men stood alone by the truck. Muffling his voice in his palm, he called out.

"Remiel?" the soldier replied.

"Come," said Rafe, quietly. "I've found something."

"Where are you?"

Rafe reached a hand out and flicked it, hoping the militia still used the same signals.

Apparently, they did. The man approached, and Rafe dispensed with him as cleanly as the last. Gripping his weapon, he ran back to the side of the truck. As the third soldier rounded the back, he leaped in his path, barrel aimed.

"Arms in the air, turn slowly."

The guy blinked, evidently as surprised to hear a stranger speak his language as he was to come face-to-face with a gun barrel.

"Do it, or I shoot."

He complied. Rafe yanked his wrists together and clicked on a tie. His forearm was branded with a *G*. The new generation.

"Stop. Lay down your weapon," said a deep voice behind him.

Putain. Where had a fourth guy come from? In front of him, yet another soldier stepped into view, from around the other corner of the truck. He wore a green beret and gripped an M16 like he knew how to use it. Surrounded. The cable-tied guy slunk to the side. How had Rafe missed two men approaching? A recruit's error.

"Gabriel sends orders," Rafe said, hoping confusion would buy him time. With one in front of him and one behind, neither could fire yet—the downside of flanking an opponent. "Hurry it up."

"Who are you?" said the beret guy.

"Reinforcements."

"He is Raphael. Shoot him," said the guy behind Rafe, his footfalls indicating he was moving aside. Giving his friend a clean shot.

By the time Rafe lifted his weapon, he'd be dead.

CHAPTER

27

The soldier in the beret aimed at Rafe's chest.

Rafe froze. "I think Gabriel would prefer to do that himself, don't you?"

The man frowned. A rock shot out of nowhere, smashing into his skull. As he dropped to his knees, Holly flew out from behind the truck in an airborne blur. Her shoe connected with the soldier's head. Lights out. The guy would be in for one hell of a headache.

Behind Rafe, the other gunman swore. Rafe spun and unleashed a liver shot to his gut, doubling down with an uppercut before he could lift his rifle. Rafe shoved him to the ground and yanked his hands together, behind his back.

"Rafe! One of them is getting away." It was the soldier whose hands he'd tied. "I'll go after him."

"Wait!" Rafe clicked on cable ties, at wrist and ankle. The guy could crawl, but not far.

Rafe took off after Holly, reaching her just as she launched herself at the soldier's legs. The guy smacked nose-first onto packed dirt. Rafe body-slammed his back.

By the time he and Holly had tidied up—locking the bound soldiers in the hut—they'd taken out five men. If more had left on a boat they might be down to half a dozen remaining with Gabriel. Better odds, but they'd be the elite.

"Didn't I say you needed me?" Holly bent double, hands on

her knees. He handed her water, adrenaline still rolling through his veins.

He more than needed her. He fucking loved her.

He shrugged. "I could have handled it."

She sucked down the water. A helicopter's blades thudded through the air. He drew her in under the canopy, holding her tight, sensing his heart rate calm at the contact.

"Crap," she said. "Maybe Gabriel's leaving—or is our backup arriving?"

"Too soon." The helicopter passed low overhead. He closed his eyes with relief. "It's coming in to land."

"I haven't heard it return since they took away Amina's body."

"They probably dropped her further out, in a trench. The ocean around here will be shallow coral reefs, and they wouldn't risk her body washing up near their operations."

Heat pooled between their bodies. He pulled her tight for a second, then let go. "We don't have much time. Someone will come looking for these guys."

Holly stabbed the truck's tires and those of two parked quad bikes, then led Rafe down a narrow path. His pulse quickened. Theo was close, he could feel it. After a few minutes she signaled and moved into the trees, pointing ahead. He crouched beside her. They'd come to a compound, a gathering of huts around a patch of sand and sea grass. Deserted.

"Could they have gone already?" she whispered.

He shook his head, pointing to the helicopter blades still spinning to a halt. "Someone was here a minute ago." His neck bristled. "I don't like this." He jerked his head, indicating they should retreat.

"Raphael!"

Tensing, Rafe swung his rifle barrel toward the familiar voice. Gabriel appeared in the doorway of the largest of the huts—a man, in place of the boy Rafe remembered. Two soldiers with M16s ambled out either side of him, taking up sentry positions.

Plants rustled behind Rafe. He swiveled. Two more soldiers eased to their feet, weapons aimed. A trap.

"You think I did not know you were here?" Gabriel said, in English. "You underestimate me."

"Where is my son?"

"Inside, with several guns pointed at his head. I suggest you stand very slowly, and lower your weapon to the ground. My men are under instructions to shoot Theo if you pose a threat. Your choice."

Son of a bitch. Rafe eased the strap over his head and laid down the M16, as Gabriel ordered three men to check the airstrip. Damn, Rafe should have hidden Holly—he'd got her captured, again, and now that Gabriel suspected the women weren't secure, time was ticking on them.

"Just so we are clear, Raphael," Gabriel said, "it is not just death that may come to your son. My men are under instructions to brand him before they kill him, so the devil will know he is one of us. This is not what I wish to do, but if it is what you choose…"

Putain. Rafe backed away from the weapon, empty palms upturned, nodding at Holly to follow suit. She was seething so hot she might explode. Filling his lungs, he strode into the compound and stood his ground. Holly stopped a step behind him.

"Let me see him," Rafe said.

On Gabriel's command, a soldier patted down Rafe, relieving him of the magazine, the phone, the Makarov and the walkie-talkie. At least they didn't bother searching Holly—making the same mistake Rafe did that first night. With her slight build, it was obvious she carried no gun. They'd find out soon enough about the damage she could do with a knife. He should have given her the phone.

"Patience, my good friend," said Gabriel. "We have a lot to catch up on, first."

"Theo!" Rafe's shout echoed through the compound.

"Papa!" The small voice trembled. "Papaaaa!"

Relief gripped Rafe's body, followed by a kick of fury. "Everything is fine, my son," he shouted, in French. "Papa is here to take you home." He switched to English, and dropped his volume. "Let him go. He is an innocent. He is not like we were."

"You forget, we were innocent once, Raphael. Perhaps not as innocent as your little rabbit in there, but anyone can be broken and turned into a good soldier."

"And anyone can turn back."

"Can they?" Gabriel sauntered down the steps, hands linked behind his back, the pose too stiff to appear casual. He was taller and leaner than Rafe remembered. Neither of them had properly reached manhood when they parted. "Is that what you told our American friend?" He switched focus to Holly. "I do not know what kind of man Raphael has convinced you he is, but I am afraid he seems to have led you astray. He is one of us, and always will be."

"He could never be the scum that you are."

"Holly, no." She was in trouble deep enough.

Gabriel laughed. "Ah, *Holly*." He rolled the name slowly around his mouth. Rafe glowered. "I like this name. Like Christmas. So you are on Raphael's side, yes? Passionately, it seems. And you are confident. Because of the message you helped your friend get out? I am afraid it was all for nothing, my dear. You thought you were helping her, but you killed her. Your friend's message has been interpreted in official circles as an elaborate hoax by a woman who had become obsessed with a lost cause, a desperate move to procure funding for a struggling charity. By now the media will be reporting that she is being held in an asylum, poor misguided woman. My most sincere thanks for helping me to eliminate her before she could cause real trouble."

Holly launched forward. The guards raised their rifles. Rafe caged her behind him with his arms. Gabriel wouldn't want Rafe dead, not yet, not until he'd taunted him a little longer, but there was nothing stopping him killing Holly, even just to spite Rafe.

"Then why are you running away?" She gestured at the chopper.

"No more than a precaution. We never stay long in one place. Adaptation is the key to survival in business. We are *Les Pirates Fantômes*—that is what your French navy calls us, is it not, Raphael? 'The phantom pirates,' and today we disappear." He smiled, his teeth so unnaturally white they looked blue. He was close enough for Rafe to throttle him. "I am grateful to them for this excellent name, and for leading me to you and your charming son, after all this time. Now perhaps, Raphael, you will tell me why you betrayed me all those long years ago."

"The aid workers who found me...they told me you were dead."

"And you believed it? Why?"

"I thought it was the truth."

"You did not. What truth ever existed for us? You let yourself believe it because you wanted to. You let yourself believe it so you could be released from our bond, so you no longer had to think about me, so you could start a new life."

"I wouldn't have gone if I..." Rafe shook his head. "I thought you were dead."

"You did not!" Gabriel's face darkened, and contorted. "You did just what we promised each other we would never do. You left me behind. You, who were all that I had. You knew what they would do to me, to punish me for letting you go, and still you left."

"No, Gabriel." The words came out in a heavy whisper. So they'd tortured him.

"Rafe?" Holly whispered, planting a palm on his back. "Are you okay?"

He arched, and stepped forward, away from her touch. He couldn't crumble now, and her gentle tone threatened to break him in two. Theo needed him to remain strong. *She* needed him to be strong. He had to let Gabriel's words brush over him, even if this was what he'd feared all these years—that he'd left Gabriel behind, alive. He shook his head. What had he known? What had he believed?

Gabriel might be the devil incarnate now, but back then he was only a year or so older than Rafe. Old and wise, Rafe had thought at the time. It was only as the years began to pass, after his escape, that he'd realized how young Gabriel had really been. Fifteen, at most? The nightmare Rafe had woken from that night had continued for his only friend.

"She cares for you, Raphael." Gabriel had regained control of his voice. He circled Rafe and approached Holly. "Why is this?"

Rafe swiveled. "Stay away from her."

"Do not tell me you feel the same. Did she seduce you, so you would protect her? She is clever, this one."

Gabriel reached for Holly's neck. Rafe stepped within striking distance, aware of the guards raising their weapons. Gabriel's fingers grazed the amulet resting between Holly's breasts. Without taking her eyes off Gabriel, Holly raised a palm to Rafe, signaling him to keep his cool. Her other hand hovered over the knife in her pocket. If she made any sudden moves, he'd have to get to her before the guards opened fire.

"My dear, either you are a powerful seductress, or my friend Raphael has become feeble. The boy I knew would never let a woman's charms weaken him, no matter how beautiful she was." He linked his hands behind his back. "Remember that woman in Hadad, Raphael? The one who offered herself to you to save her child?"

"Gabriel..." Feeling Holly's gaze on him, Rafe tightened his jaw, trying to block out the face of the woman he remembered as clearly as if his brain had photographed her.

"You want to know what happened to her, don't you, my dear? Shall I tell you?"

"No," said Rafe. It was not a story to share with Holly. Or anyone. He'd told every haunting detail to the psychologists. Then he'd buried it all. Or thought he had.

"He refused her, then slit the little girl's thr—"

"Gabriel!"

"Do not worry, my friend, Holly will not be telling anyone your secrets, where she is going." Gabriel narrowed his gaze, and pivoted to face Rafe. "Or is it that you care what this woman thinks of you? That is even more curious. What did these people do to you, Raphael, the ones you ran to? Did they brainwash you into believing you could live like normal people? We both know that could never happen, with everything we carry in our heads." He tapped his forehead with a long, slender finger.

"They turned me back into a human."

Gabriel tilted his head, gazing steadily into Rafe's eyes. "Impossible. They just created a different machine. One that says and does the right things outside, but inside will always be a Lost Boy."

Rafe didn't trust himself to speak. He couldn't let Gabriel free his ghosts.

"Did they tell you that you were not responsible for your actions, because you were a child? This is where our paths split. *I* claim responsibility for everything I do, everything I have done. I am at peace with it. You, my friend, are haunted, I can see it in your soul."

"Enough."

Gabriel laughed. "I do not believe it—they turned my fearless Raphael into a coward. The boy you were, the things you did—you cannot escape that. It is branded into you, as clearly as..." His gaze flicked to the scar on Rafe's arm. He spat on the sandy ground. "You have run away from everything you have done, you have reinvented yourself as a hero soldier and a father, but it does not change who you are."

Rafe sensed the recesses of his mind melting into darkness. *Non.* He must stay present. "What do you want, Gabriel?"

"Answers, Raphael. To start—I am curious about you being a father. How do you know what to do, when you never had a father? Theo says you do not beat him. Maybe this is why he is a coward, like you have become. But perhaps you do not see your son much. You ran away from him to join the French, like you ran away from me. You like running away. But you have found you cannot run from yourself, haven't you, my friend?"

Rafe swallowed. How could Gabriel read him so clearly, after all these years?

"Ah, I see there is truth to this. You feel deeply for this boy. This must make a man weak. It has already made you kidnap a woman. What else will it make you do?"

Rafe's gaze flicked to the weapons Gabriel's men had taken from him, now lying on the veranda of the large building. The men stood behind Rafe and Holly, M16s slung from their shoulders.

"Shoot me, Raphael? Yes, that is what you itch to do, isn't it? But then your son will die also. So this will not work. Besides, killing me would be too easy. You would only be finishing off what you started all those years ago."

Holly stepped up, level to Rafe. The muscles in her face were tight. What must she think of him? He should have told her the truth, opened up to her about what he'd done, warned her what she was getting into. And Theo—what had Gabriel told Theo?

"I don't want to kill you, Gabriel. I just want to take my son and my—and Holly—and leave you to do whatever it is you're doing. You've proved yourself the winner in this game. You've shown yourself to be the better man. Let's take the easy way out here, for everyone."

"Oh, I will give you a chance to save your son—and your girlfriend. But I will make it interesting."

"Gabriel—"

"Do not be in a hurry to leave, my friend, not after all these years." He wandered back to the veranda, dusted a wooden banister with a handkerchief and leaned back against it. "I have many questions. Such as, did you choose to play the hero or the villain when you were on Penipuan Island? I think the hero, considering that Holly is here, standing with you." He studied Holly, head to foot, slowly. "He has been practicing that a lot, lately, I think. Capitaine Rafe Angelito. Ah, this is not the Raphael I know him to be, my dear."

"You don't know him, then."

"Holly, no," Rafe murmured. Gabriel knew so much more about him than Holly ever would. She wouldn't stand by him like this if she knew the truth. He'd deceived her, endangered her. Unforgivable.

"I know precisely who he is," said Gabriel. "He is me. We were born from the same fires. Had Raphael not abandoned us, he would have become the leader of the militia, not me. He would have been very good, I think, much more ruthless than me. This man you see here, this *hero*, he is not real. He has been constructed out of evil, a mansion built of rotten sticks. He might present well, but when he crumbles, the real man will emerge."

Holly's hand flicked up to the purple bruises on her neck. Rafe's skin crawled. "Holly, don't listen," he said in an undertone too low for Gabriel's ears.

"But I think you have seen this real man." Gabriel pushed off the veranda and sauntered up to Holly, his guards shadowing him. He raised both hands to her neck. "This man placed his hands here and here, and squeezed."

Holly planted a hand on his chest and shoved. His expression darkened. Reading his intent, Rafe lurched forward. The guards caught him, one on each shoulder, as Gabriel plunged a fist into Holly's stomach. She crumpled, gasping. Rafe shrugged off one man and staggered toward Gabriel, the other guy hanging on his shoulder with his feet skidding along the ground. The son of a bitch was going down. As Gabriel retreated, shaking his hand, two more soldiers ran forward to close ranks around their leader, guns raised.

"Ah, yes, your anger is there, Raphael. Just like mine. You would sacrifice your son's life, just to get to me. Yes, this is the Raphael I know. I am glad to have you back."

"Holly?"

"I'm okay," she squeaked.

Bile rose from Rafe's stomach. Gabriel nodded at his man, and the guy released Rafe. Rafe bent over Holly and laid his palm on her back. "You're sure?"

She nodded, her freckles standing out against her blanched skin. He ground his teeth. Gabriel would pay for that.

"My dear, you fight for him, and look at him with respect, but you must know you can mean nothing to him. No one can mean anything to a man like this, a man programmed to feel nothing. Oh yes, I think you will enjoy the future I have in mind for you. You are one of these women who likes a violent man incapable of caring about you, yes?"

Rafe bowed his head, his chest tightening. *Focus*. He couldn't afford to direct his anger to the wrong place. Holly pushed to her knees, panting. She wouldn't want to let Gabriel think he'd broken her. Rafe gripped her waist and helped her rise to her feet.

"How are you imagining you will kill me, right now, Raphael? Blow my head apart with a bullet? Decapitate me with a machete? Pound my face into pulp with your fists? Cut out my entrails and watch me die? Or, yes, strangle me. Effective, if a little too tidy."

Rafe tightened his hand around Holly's waist. She hugged her arm around her torso and gripped his fingers. Seeking comfort, or warning him to stay grounded?

"I don't want to kill you, Gabriel," said Rafe. "This can end peacefully."

"Or do you order other people to do your killing now, Capi-taine? My dear, you should know he is capable of doing all these things I speak of. I have seen him do these things to women and children, to people who do not matter and cannot fight back. He was very good at it. Our commander would shout at the rest of us that we should be more like Raphael. I was proud he was my friend. Many years later when I learned this word 'prodigy,' I thought immediately of Raphael. He was a killing prodigy. Are you still?"

"You are lying," said Holly. Her voice was strong, and her grip on Rafe's hand was true, but she'd become still as ice. Oh yes, doubt was creeping in.

"Am I? Raphael, would you like to join this enlightening conversation?"

"What do you want me to say?"

"You will note, my dear, he does not deny it. He cannot, be-cause it is the truth, and he is an *honorable* man now, a man who does not lie, though his life is a lie."

Holly squeezed Rafe's hand, making him feel like more of a fraud.

"Somehow," continued Gabriel, "Raphael has manipulated many people into believing he is good—the aid workers, the French military, his dead wife, his son—and even you. But you know the truth, do you not? You are too smart not to have fig-ured it out."

He stepped out from between his men, his gaze fixed on Holly. She stared back, chin raised.

"You have seen the true Raphael," said Gabriel. "Yes. I see the doubt flickering in your eyes. You think I am the evil one here? No. Everything that is inside my head is inside his. He has just done a better job of suppressing it. The man he really is can be drawn out of him."

Holly shook her head, as if trying to shake Gabriel's words from her brain.

"My dear, you and I have something in common. We have both suffered the consequences of caring for this man. You see this?" He placed a finger on his scarred nose. "Raphael, tell her how I got this."

"Gabriel, stop this."

"Tell her," Gabriel spat. "Or I will have your son branded, this minute."

Holly's fingers tightened on Rafe's hand, strong as claws.

"Tell her who did this to me." When Rafe didn't respond, Gabriel shouted instructions to his men, switching languages: "Heat up the brand."

CHAPTER

28

"I did it," Rafe whispered, his chest tightening. "I was the one. Call off your dogs."

Holly's grip flinched but held.

"They will not act until they are ordered to. They know how to follow instructions, just as you once did." Gabriel turned to Holly. "Our commander ordered him to kill me—me who was like a brother to him—to prove his loyalty to the militia. I did not believe he would. I believed our friendship would triumph. You know what happened? The machete got stuck in bone." He stroked his nose. "If he had not struggled to pull it out and finish the job, he would have finished me. The commander only stepped in to stop him because he wanted me for his Lost Boys, too. He needed numbers that day, so I got…lucky. Oh, yes, we both bear the scars of this dangerous man, my dear. You are lucky yours are not permanent."

Gabriel fingered Holly's amulet again, his hands brushing her T-shirt. Rafe balled his fist. Lucky Holly was holding him so damn tight. He couldn't lose it, not with Theo so close.

"When I first saw you with this, my dear, I thought you must have taken it from Raphael's dead body. A souvenir, perhaps. I thought you merciless. You also used it to manipulate Theo and save yourself." He stepped back and called over his shoulder to one of his guards, ordering him to fetch a wooden box from his desk. "Now, I think Raphael *gave* it to you, which makes you even more merciless. You would steal a man's heart to save yourself."

Holly kept her chin defiant, though Gabriel towered over her.

"Ah, I see this is true. This amulet, it is a tradition of my people—of Raphael's people. You give it only to those closest to you. When you become betrothed, you chip off a part of it for your future wife. When you have a son, you chip off a part for him. The smaller the amulet gets, the more power it has. Only when there is dust left do you make a new one for the next generation. You must have made quite an impression on my friend."

A guard walked out and handed him a small carved box. Gabriel ran a finger over its grooves. "Most of our people in the refugee camps had these amulets. I once had one of my own, but it was stolen from me while I slept, when I was a very young boy. When I became the commander, I had our former camps searched for it. I found it hanging around a man's neck, a man a little older than me. He had taken it because he had lost his, lost his link to his past. I took his neck and the amulet in one."

Rafe swallowed.

"For a long time I have kept it safe in this box. A year ago, I began to wonder. These are unique stones—their coloring, their feel. I hired a geologist. She traced my amulet back to a rock formation near an abandoned village in the northwest of our country."

"Whatever game you're playing—"

"Quiet, Raphael. You will be very interested to hear this, I promise. Two months ago I traveled there. I found an old woman who had been there when the village was attacked by our enemy. She recognized my amulet—these are like fingerprints to our people. She remembered my family. She told me my father had been shot, along with all the other men. My pregnant mother was beaten and died slowly of her untended wounds. My older sister was taken to their rape camps and never seen again. This woman helped many children escape—I might have been one of them. She could not remember my real name."

"I'm sorry." Holly's voice trembled. It sounded like genuine sympathy.

Even Rafe felt a tug in his gut. For Gabriel to find his home after so long, to find out what had happened to his family after decades of wondering... A lump grew in his throat. That had to mean something, even to Gabriel. It would mean something to Rafe. He frowned. Was this also the village he came from?

Gabriel handed the box to Holly. "Open it, please."

Holly looked questioningly at Rafe. He shrugged. She released his hand, which he kept firmly on her waist, and popped open the box. Inside lay a gray-green stone.

"What do you make of that, my dear?"

She cradled it in her palm. "It...looks the same as the others, just bigger."

Gabriel instructed the guard to remove Theo's amulet and bring it out.

"Leave him be," said Rafe.

"Do not worry, *Papa*, I will give it back."

A cry of pain shot out from the building. Rafe released Holly and lurched forward, his face heating. Four guns were leveled at his face.

"If you want to protect your son, you must calm down, my friend," said Gabriel.

The guard returned, Theo's amulet strung from his fingers, the leather snapped where it'd been yanked from the boy's neck. Rafe balled his fists. *Les salauds.* Another thing they would pay for.

Gabriel held out a hand to Rafe. "Your amulet, too."

Rafe looked over his shoulder at Holly. She widened her eyes as if to say, *play along.* He ripped the leather from his neck and slapped it on Gabriel's palm.

Gabriel passed it to Holly. "What can you conclude from these, my dear?"

"They look like they were cut from the same rock." She took off the amulet she wore and cupped all four stones in her hand, their leather cords hanging between her fingers. "They form a complete ball."

"What?" said Rafe, stepping back to her.

Holly opened her fingers. The pieces huddled together in her palm. Each stone was worn smooth—Gabriel's bigger and a little rougher than the others—but they fit together.

"The missing pieces of our family, together for the first time in decades," said Gabriel.

"You are brothers," whispered Holly, looking sideways at Rafe, as if she expected him to explode.

"We are not brothers." Rafe could barely speak above a whisper. "He is manipulating us."

"You have already figured this out, have you not, my dear?"

"There are similarities," said Holly, tentatively. "Your walk, your bearing, your coloring. And your faces, from what I can make…"

"From what you can make out from my disfigured one?"

She exhaled. "Yes."

"It was the old woman who made me wonder. She asked if my younger brother survived—a dark, pretty boy with eyes like chocolate."

"You describe half the boys at the camps," Rafe said. "And you can't know that the stone you found was yours. There are many like that."

"I thought of that possibility, little brother. That is why I sent your son's DNA to a laboratory a week ago. I can show you the results, if you doubt me. A quarter of our DNA is the same. He is my nephew."

Rafe gaped. He searched his mind for evidence it was true—some memory, some flash of knowledge. All he knew was that

Gabriel had always been there, right from his scattered earliest memories.

"Tell me, Raphael. If you could get hold of the people who killed our parents, who took our sister, what would you do to them?"

Rafe shook his head, staring at the stones in Holly's palm. He could absorb none of it. He had long ago given up hope of finding his parents—but a sister? She could still be alive.

"You would track these dogs down, would you not? You would do the same to them as they did to our parents, to us, to our sister?"

"No." But, hell, he truly didn't know. He felt nothing. Even he should feel *something.* Some neurons should be connecting, figuring out what this all meant. He had a family, a place of origin—the pieces that were missing from the story of his life. *Gabriel* was his family. This should all mean something.

"You would do the same. I know this." Gabriel spoke almost pityingly. "You would go to that black place that beckons you."

Rafe's gaze snapped up.

"Ah, you know this black place, do you not? We all do, my brother."

"Don't call me that." Rafe's voice sounded distant, even to him.

"It is the truth. Yes, you would do the same as I did."

"What did you do?"

"What do you think I did? I found the villages of our enemy. I found them, their children, their grandchildren. I dealt with it." He smiled at Holly. "I think that is what you Americans call getting closure."

"You're an animal," Holly said, clutching the stones as if protecting them.

"No, my dear. I am human, and that is far worse."

"Papa!" Theo's voice hit a new note of anxiety. The dagger twisted in Rafe's heart.

"Courage, Theo. I will come for you soon," Rafe yelled, in French.

His urge to go to his son was like a tide pulling his chest. But Gabriel held all the power. His vision swam. *Putain*—the early warning sign. He closed his eyes, tight, and lifted his face to the sky. *Stay in control.*

"So you see, it has been an interesting year for me," Gabriel continued. "A *soul-searching* year. I like this English phrase. I found my brother, after many, many years of hunting. I found my nephew. I found the place I was born. I have spent many days thinking about all this, about whether I am glad Raphael is my brother, or whether it hurts more, to know it was my brother who abandoned me. Character building—that is what you Americans would say, yes?"

Rafe risked opening his eyes. His sight was fuzzy but improving. He dug his fingernails into his palms. He must stay anchored against the pull of the blackness growing inside, find the kill switch. He yearned to make Gabriel shut up, but the longer he talked, the longer they all stayed alive.

"And this?" said Rafe, darkly. "This is your revenge?"

"I will take revenge if I must, but I have moved beyond this need. I want more. I want to know if you are my brother in deed as well as in blood. You must prove your loyalty to me once more—your loyalty to your family, to your people. Otherwise, yes, I will settle for revenge. There is much comfort in revenge."

"I will not kill my son, if that's what you want."

"Why would I want that? Theo is precious to me, more so than you are, because he I can train. I can mold him into someone who can be trusted, who can follow orders, who can lead this militia into the future. A line of succession. Having said that, my earlier promise still stands—if you kill me, he, too, will die. Or, if you simply do not wish to join your brothers here, you will die and I will take him, anyway. Your choice."

"Don't do this."

"I want to show you that you belong somewhere, Raphael. I want you to know you have a family—is that not what any of us always wanted? It is too late for you to go back to your other life. These people you fooled—the French military, your wife's family—they have received evidence of the truth about you."

Rafe stiffened. "What have you done?"

"The people who turned you back into a human, as you say, they kept records. These things are supposed to be destroyed, but their systems were lax. My men found them, remarkably easily—our first step to finding you. All the evidence is there—interviews with you, in which you catalog every atrocity you committed. These are now in the hands of your colonel and the mother of your wife. I have several more copies, in case your girlfriend would also like to have a read. It is very enjoyable. Better than Hitchcock. In fact, maybe I will send a copy to Hollywood. Our Raphael will be famous. Or is *infamous* the right word, in English? I get confused with these two. Such a needlessly complex language."

Rafe clamped his mouth shut. The life he'd built from scraps had collapsed. He concentrated on filling his lungs, emptying them, filling, emptying. Nothing mattered now but getting Theo and Holly out alive.

"Do not worry, my brother. You do not need to return to that false existence—you do not belong with those people, with whom you must always pretend. You belong with me, with your many other brothers. But you have let me down before. You need to show me you will not do it again. We had an agreement of what you had to do to get your son back."

"I fulfilled it. Let her go." Rafe switched languages. "She's a mongrel, like us."

"She is a mongrel, yes?" Gabriel stuck with English. "This is what you think of your girlfriend? You kidnapped the wrong woman, and you failed to kill her when I ordered you to. You still have a little time to fix one of those errors."

"Never."

"Interesting. I thought Theo meant more to you than that. Perhaps I was wrong. Perhaps he is better off here, with someone who will take proper care of him. How can you care for him when you are not there in the night to protect him? Is that not the job of a father? This mission, to capture Theo—I carried it out personally, while my men restrained the old woman. He woke when I entered his room, and he ran to me, willingly, calling out in the darkness for his *papa*. He thought you had come home for him. I do not speak his language, but I heard in that voice his desperation to be loved by a man who cannot love. I felt his anguish at being abandoned by his father, just as I felt the anguish of being abandoned by my brother. At first, he embraced me. It was beautiful, to feel his young, thin arms around my neck, squeezing tight."

The scene felt as real to Rafe as if he was there right now, in the little room plastered with Captain America posters—Theo's voice calling out for him with all the delight of Christmas morning, those trusting arms flung around a man he thought was his father. And then the terror and panic… Rafe swallowed.

"He did not know his own father from a stranger," Gabriel said. "Or maybe he just sensed he was better off with me." He shouted at his soldiers to check if the brand was hot. "Join me, or you will die and I will make your son one of us, forever."

Either way, Theo lost. Rafe flinched at the sickly stench of burning hair and flesh. Was it coming from his memory, or was it real? *Put your brain in charge.* Theo wasn't screaming, and Gabriel wouldn't play his trump card yet. He was building to something Rafe was powerless to stop. *Stay present.*

"My brother, I understand you, like no one else does. I know the devil that lurks within you, constantly seeking a way out. You are too frightened to let your guard down, because that is when the demon takes control. It is always there, always threatening to split open your skin and slither out. Like now. Join me, join your brother. Let go of the struggle to keep the mask on. Shed it and be the man you really are. You will never need to leave your son again. He can be with his father and his uncle—with his family."

Rafe chose silence. To react was to make him vulnerable to the monster within. Gabriel understood him better than he'd thought possible. *Everything that's inside your head is inside mine.* Even after twenty-two years?

"Rafe," whispered Holly urgently. "You are not one of them."

He clenched his teeth. Oh, he was indeed one of them. He didn't want her pity, didn't want her making excuses for him. She knew now what she'd made love to.

"You don't know me," said Rafe, quietly. "What Gabriel says is true. I've killed more people than I can count. I still see their faces—every one of them, frozen in the terror of the last moments of their lives. I can run away from it—I did run away from it—but they follow me, these people, everywhere."

"You were under someone else's control. You were a victim, too."

"There can be no excuse. Those memories are my price to pay."

"You've already paid the price—you lost your childhood."

"What price have I paid? I got to wipe away the past and start again like it never happened. Those people and their families paid the price, not me." He hung his head, feeling every drop of weight in the humid air. "Only chance separated my path from Gabriel's."

"My brother, you are beginning to see the truth. Many, many people paid the price for your freedom. My dear American friend, do you want to see the price I paid?" Gabriel tore at the buttons on his shirt.

Rafe yearned to turn away, but he owed it to Gabriel to witness this. He owed it to his *brother.* His gut churned as Gabriel yanked off the shirt. Gouged white scars crisscrossed his chest and stomach, and trailed into his waistband. Rafe gagged. The ground seesawed. Gabriel turned, slowly, revealing the same pattern on his back. Rafe had seen many whippings, but none like this. There were more scars than skin. How was he still alive?

"I didn't kn…" Rafe's throat closed.

"It was a warning. No one ever left the militia again."

Gabriel slowly pulled his arms into his shirt and buttoned it, smoothing the iron-flat fabric. That was why he appeared stiff—the scars restricted his movement. His every move must remind him of the torture he'd endured, because of Rafe.

"I would have come for you, if I'd known," said Rafe, testing his voice. It was the truth he'd clung to all these years, but suddenly it felt like a lie. *What truth ever existed for us?* An ember deep in the recesses of his brain began to glow. Had he buried the truth, like he'd buried the monster?

"You knew." Gabriel's words were barely audible above the roaring in Rafe's ears. "My dear, can you guess why they whip you front *and* back? Because then you have no way to lie down, no relief from the pain. They rub dirt and shit into the wounds to infect them. The agony and the illness last for months. You cannot sleep, you cannot eat, you can only long for the pain to get so bad you will pass out. When it does, you wake to find rats chewing on the wounds. This pain…you cannot see a way out of it. It drives you mad."

Rafe's breath came in ragged gasps. His brain screamed at him to block out Gabriel's words, to protect himself from losing his sanity. But that was the coward's way. This was what he'd caused. This was what he'd face.

"To start with, I kept myself alive by imagining that Raphael would come with his aid workers to rescue me, take me to a hospital where they would do their doctor magic and take away the pain and sickness. Sometimes I would hallucinate and believe he *had* come back for me. Then I would regain consciousness and find myself propped up on the same filthy mat on the same floor, chasing away the same rats. Always chasing the rats. One night I was too weak to scare a rat off—it kept coming back and feeding. I could hear its teeth tearing, feel it tugging at my flesh, and, oh, the agony—this is nothing you will ever know, no matter how much I hurt you. And I did not have the strength to lift my arms or legs to chase it away.

"Weeks and weeks and weeks went by. Raphael did not come. My brother—as I know now he is—did not come. You see, my dear, he was trained to believe that caring about someone was a weakness. I thought our bond was proof we had won, we had retained a little of our true natures. I found I was wrong, just as I had been wrong about his will to kill me with the machete. I was a fool. His training had worked better than I thought— far better than mine. These injuries you see, these scars on my body—they don't stop at my waist. They left me unable to father children. They robbed many futures."

An anguished yowl surrounded Rafe, piercing his ears, his brain, his skin. His knees buckled and he slumped to the ground. The cry went on and on. *Shut up. Shut up.* He rocked, pinning his palms to his ears. Blackness circled his vision and closed in.

A voice echoed in his head—a voice he'd once known as well as his own. "Kill the woman and come home to your family, Raphael. Kill the woman and save your son. Kill the woman and show me you're sorry for my scars. Undo the past and be with people who will not judge you for what you have done. Let go the tremendous effort of hiding who you really are."

Cold metal touched Rafe's palm. His fingers brushed over the scars and nicks in the pistol's bodywork and settled into the firing position they knew so well. One shot, and he'd earn Gabriel's forgiveness and give Theo a chance at a future. A flick of his finger, a microsecond. He'd done it before, so many times. He opened his eyes.

CHAPTER

29

Her blood racing, Holly turned to run. Rafe had morphed beyond her reach, just as he warned her he would. Two guards caught her, one either side. She thrashed, but others joined in, dragging her to the ground. They cable-tied her feet and her hands behind her, and stepped away to form a perimeter. She flipped and wriggled onto her back. Laid out like a sacrifice.

Rafe knelt on the ground a few feet away, his head bowed. His strength seemed to be seeping out, as if he was mortally wounded. And maybe he was, in his mind. She had to bring him back.

"Rafe! Remember Theo. Remember what kind of man you are, what kind of father you are. Don't do this to him—don't do this to yourself."

He raised his head and eyeballed her, like some great beast. His eyes were dull and huge, just as they'd been when he'd tried to strangle her. He was right—she didn't know him, not this version.

"I nearly gave in to death," Gabriel continued, speaking for her benefit now—Rafe was beyond comprehension. "That would have been easy. But I survived by thinking of the many ways I could get revenge on Raphael, one day. In my head I'd measure each possibility, test it, visualize it. Each day my body and my will became stronger. By the time I recovered, after many months, I had been relieved of my one weakness—I no longer cared about anyone. I was truly alone. That's a liberating moment. In a strange way, it completed my training."

Rafe pulled himself up to standing, his gaze never leaving her, like a hunter tracking his prey. He began speaking, trancelike, in his native tongue. The same chant he'd used on the island.

"Rafe. Rafe! No!"

Nothing registered on his face. Nothing. The man she thought she knew was gone, replaced with this...robot. She wanted to leap at him and shake him until the good man returned, the one she'd been stupid enough to fall in love with.

He'd warned her not to get close. Love was the most dangerous thing in the world, he'd said. *I'm the kind who's not capable of loving a woman—and for her it could be dangerous.* He'd given her a chance to escape. Why the hell hadn't she taken it?

If she died now, at his hands, then maybe she deserved it. But Theo... And the women... If they fought back, with their sole weapon, they'd be mown down, or worse. So much of this was on her—she was the one who'd trusted Rafe, who'd brought him here, who'd given Amina the iPhone, who'd incited the women to rebel in a battle they couldn't win. Now they would all die, for nothing.

Rafe closed in on her, his face twisted way past handsome. She wouldn't shut her eyes. She would keep them focused on this unrecognizable creature, so he'd remember this, so she'd haunt him like all the others. How many faces were in the catalog of victims he carried in his brain?

"Rafe, don't do it."

Nothing.

"He is mine, my dear. He always has been."

Rafe straightened his arms and aimed the gun. She recoiled. This was it. Her last moment. *Click.*

Silence. He'd pulled the trigger but—nothing. She dragged in a breath. The men around her muttered. One laughed. How could that be? One of the goons had opened and checked the gun before he'd handed it to Rafe—she'd seen the bullets go back in, she'd heard him cock it. Rafe swore in French and tossed the gun onto the sand, striding to the veranda, rifle barrels trained on him. The guy who'd checked it picked it up, opened it, and shrugged, muttering to his friends. He cocked it, aimed it at the ground and pulled the trigger. *Click.*

Rafe picked up his rifle and slid something backwards, until it snapped. He strode back into position. Gabriel moved in beside him, smiling like he'd won.

He aimed. *Here goes.* The last seconds of her life and all she could think about was what a sucker she was. She wouldn't make that mistake again. *Obviously.* She let her eyes close, too beaten to be brave anymore. The only mental image she could conjure was of Rafe's face, of the intense look in his eyes in the seconds before he kissed her, in the moment he was at his least guarded, when she knew she was staring right into his beautiful, honorable soul. It had made her feel so wanted, so...loved. She would die a fool.

Gabriel laughed, and spoke to Rafe in their own language. Ick. So the last thing she'd hear would be the voice of that psycho. She tried to block out the sound, zeroing in on the crash of the nearby waves, ready to wash away her poor excuse for a life.

Click.

Really? What was this—Russian roulette? She opened her eyes to a squint. Gabriel had pushed the barrel aside, his hand still on it. He spoke quietly to Rafe, still smiling. Rafe's dead gaze swung from her to Gabriel. So that click—it wasn't the trigger, but Rafe disarming the gun, on Gabriel's order? Rafe pressed a button and the magazine dropped out into his hands. He slid something backward and a round flicked up and landed on the ground.

So Rafe had tried to kill her, and *Gabriel* had spared her? Not how she thought this would go. She slumped, her muscles giving up the effort. Life equaled hope. She would survive this, god-dammit, like she'd survived every other fucking mess in her life.

"I have a buyer for her and many costs to recuperate," said Gabriel, switching focus to her. "I would have gladly given up three million dollars for the privilege of watching you kill this sorry pig of a woman, Raphael, but maybe this is a sign I should take the money. Adaptability is the key to survival. We will take her with us and drop her at the transit point. She will be with her new owner in hours. This operation has become profitable after all, in many ways."

Rafe spoke to Gabriel in his own language, his words mechanical. Gabriel gestured at one of his men and rattled off orders, which were relayed into the hut.

Two men pulled Holly to her bound feet and dragged her backward to the helicopter, as Theo stepped, blinking, through the doorway of the building.

"Papa!" He scrambled down the steps and ran. Rafe crouched, and Theo disappeared into his arms. Rafe's voice rolled over her, in the same melodic, soothing French tone he'd murmured on the hammock. She'd thought it so beautiful. Not anymore.

Behind her back, she opened her fingers and dropped the four amulets. They hit sand with a series of thuds. Rafe had got Theo back. That was all he cared about—all he was capable of caring about. He'd warned her of that, from the outset.

An hour ago she'd have sworn the best place for Theo was with the father who loved him so desperately. But what was stronger—Rafe's parental instinct, or his preinstalled flip switch? How long until Theo saw that side of his father, if he hadn't already? She'd been so ready to believe the best of Rafe, despite all the evidence.

Theo's slight body shuddered with sobs. Rafe rubbed his back, his hand splayed across the kid's ribs, their heads bowed together. Tears pricked her eyes. At least the boy had found a place of comfort and security after all that turmoil, however temporary.

The goons slid open the helicopter door and threw her into the hollow shell at the back. Her elbow whacked a metal box, shooting pain up her shoulder. Awkwardly, she twisted herself into a sitting position on the floor, leaning back on the box. A man followed her in—the thug who'd held her back while Amina was killed. He sat by the open door, facing her, gun at the ready. She was out of options, out of ideas, alone.

Well, hell. Alone wasn't such a bad place. She was still alive. And she had the knife. With luck, Rafe would be past remembering that.

She closed her eyes and let her head fall back against the box—sending a signal to the soldier that he could take it easy. Her gut burned from Gabriel's punches, her arm throbbed from the gunshot wound, and she couldn't open her left eye even if she wanted to.

Urgent voices filtered in from outside, punctuated by quick footfalls and heavy thuds and scrapes. Out of the windows she could just see the tops of trees against the bruised sky, but occasionally a man would pass the chopper's open door, carrying a box or bag or some other item. They were moving out— before Rafe's backup could get there, if the guy even existed. She didn't know what to believe anymore. She strained to pinpoint Rafe's and Theo's voices. Nothing. The men had talked about leaving on a boat—had the *capitaine* and his son joined them? Her heart twisted. She'd never see them again.

Well, good. When she got out of this mess—and she damn well would get out—she'd find that cabin by the sea and grow into an old hermit. Maybe she'd adopt a dog. Yes, a stray mongrel, to remind her of the dangers of letting people in.

After a while, the noise outside subsided. The helicopter pilot pulled himself into his seat, put on headphones and started pressing buttons. A man ducked into the hull, striking up an animated but hushed conversation with her guard. Gossip—she'd recognize that tone of voice in any language. The confrontation between Rafe and Gabriel must have been quite the soap opera.

The new guy settled into a spot near the front, facing backward. More eyes on her. They fell silent as footsteps approached. The helicopter blades whined.

Gabriel climbed in, still fucking smiling, followed by Rafe, carrying a sleeping Theo. Relief washed over her. Hell, that was dumb—of any of her enemies, Rafe was the most dangerous. Not only physically, but because he knew how she fought, knew what to expect, knew about the knife. His gaze flicked around and locked on hers. His eyes had lost their white-rimmed wildness, but there was no hint of emotion. Just a cold, hard stare. Not the man she thought she knew. She dropped eye contact.

Rafe and Gabriel sat along the wall furthest from the door, Theo sighing as he resettled onto Rafe's chest. Yearning clawed her stomach. How stupid had she been to picture the three of them, together? The two of them were a unit, and she was alone. The whine climbed in pitch. The helicopter shuddered, rose and angled forward.

She curled her bound feet underneath her and let her bent legs drop to one side, ignoring the stiffness in her injured knee. Retrieving the knife would require a few gymnastic maneuvers. Her guard shot her a look. She winced and stretched her neck from side to side, feigning sore muscles. Looking bored, he fixed his gaze out the open door. They were heading over the sea.

If Holly managed to get away—*when* she got away—she'd track down Amina's lobby group. If she could cut the cable ties, maybe she could take a flying leap out the door as they approached land? Not her best plan ever, but options were few. She'd rather deal with the sharks down there than those up here.

She twisted her arms to bring her hands to the knife pocket, her muscles screaming with effort. Blood squeezed out of the bullet wound and dribbled to her elbow. She ignored the bite of pain. Her fingertips came up an inch short of the zipper. She drew her legs higher and tighter. Her swollen knee burned, ready to pop. If anyone looked right now, her contortions would look mighty suspicious. Rafe pointed to the windscreen of the chopper and spoke to Gabriel, taking his attention away. The other guard turned to look, too.

She pinned the zipper between two fingers and eased it open. The engine's roar and the whip of the wind masked the rasp of the parting teeth. She caught the top of the knife and worked it out of the pocket, every nudge straining her forearm to near snapping point. Finally, she closed her palm around its familiar shape. Hallelujah. She straightened her legs, hiding the knife in the arch between her back and the metal box, and inhaled crisp air. Her leg muscles pulsed, grateful for the reprieve. A breeze played with the clammy skin on her face. She closed her eyes for a second, willing it to cool her down.

Leveling her breath, she popped the blade, coughing to mask the click. With one wrist jammed over the other, the angles were awkward, like doing something tricky in the mirror. The tremble in her arms wasn't helping. She parked her face in neutral as she experimented. She jimmied the knife in under the plastic and flicked. It held. She repositioned it and filled her lungs, willing her strength to pool at her right wrist.

Flick. The knife slipped, slicing into something too soft to be the ties. Her left wrist. Shit. She bit her lip, waiting for the pain, to tell her what she'd cut. Surely an artery would spurt blood from the get-go? The sting came, clean and sharp. Warm liquid trickled into her left palm and seeped through her fingers. Ounces of it, not pints.

Change of tactic. Swallowing, she maneuvered the blade so it faced upward, away from her skin. She seesawed the knife, keeping it firm against the plastic. Slicked with blood and sweat, the handle kept slipping in her fingers. Finally, the bond released. She pulled it from her wrists and tucked it into her trousers. Last thing she needed was for the severed tie to go skidding along the floor.

She shifted position, scooting her feet as close to her right butt cheek as she could, and twisted her arms as far around as they'd go. Sweat tickled her forehead. No matter how much she strained, she was still a good five inches short of the ankle ties.

Unless she sat on her knees or tipped forward flat onto the floor, the logistics of freeing her feet while pretending her hands were bound were impossible. Either move would draw suspicion. Damn. She'd never make it past the guard and out the door with her feet tied, let alone swim. She'd have to risk sneaking her hand out from behind her. If anyone noticed, her plan was toast. She gripped the knife and inched her hand along the floor, her pulse drumming.

Rafe looked her way. She darted her hand behind her back, her cheeks chilling. His gaze rested on her pocket. The zipper gaped—she hadn't thought to do it up. Game over. Lines bunched on his forehead. His focus scooted around the cabin, to the faces of the guards and Gabriel. Checking if they'd seen? Dammit, was he on her side or not? He leaned toward Gabriel and the guy nearest him, and spoke in words she couldn't understand. Her stomach fell. *Not* on her side.

He pointed to a large polystyrene box beside the door, and addressed her guard. The guy shrugged, and reached for it. Gabriel and the other goon watched listlessly as he pulled out a bottle of water and handed it over. Rafe took a gulp, and passed it to Gabriel. Her guard got out another bottle and chugged, shutting his eyes. Diversion. She didn't know what the hell was going on with Rafe, but she wasn't about to waste an opportunity. She reached down, sliced the ties behind her ankles and resumed her position. If anyone looked too close, they'd notice the plastic lay too loose over her foot. Rafe *must* have known what she was up to. Had he distracted the guard on purpose?

His eyes pinned hers. Deliberately, he trailed his gaze to her guard, then back. He repeated the eye movement, this time following it with tiny movements of one finger—pointing to her, then her guard. He wanted her to take out the guard?

He drew the finger up to his neck and patted it against his skin. He rolled his eyes to Gabriel and then the other guard, then returned focus to her. He raised his eyebrows. A question—did she follow? Her face heated. So he would take out Gabriel and his guard while she was busy with hers? The pilot could wait—he couldn't fight *and* fly. Was Rafe planning to hijack the helicopter?

She gave him the slightest nod she could. Adrenaline prickled under her skin. His face reassumed its default robot expression. At some point it'd become a facade. When? No doubt about it, he was screwed up, but he was present enough to know working together gave them a better chance of escape. At least this meant he wasn't in league with Gabriel. Not that his loyalties lay with her, either. That stung, but she'd get over it once she was free.

Watching the men, he surreptitiously held up a palm. Wait for his signal. He nestled his face into Theo's hair and spoke softly in French. The boy jerked awake, rubbing his face and looking around him dully, before sinking back against his father. Holly could feel his relief. If she could help it, his ordeal would soon be over.

Rafe pushed the hair off his son's face. *"Tu comprends?"*

"Oui, Papa," Theo whispered groggily. His hair was plastered to his head in damp curls.

Rafe kissed his son's forehead, letting his eyes drift closed. A second passed. Two. His chest rose to full capacity and sank. Something squeezed Holly's heart. How hard would it be to knowingly put your child in danger when you'd just got him back in your arms? He'd do anything for that kid.

Including: betray and kill me.

Through the door, a fringe of snow-white beach came into view. Rafe wrapped his arms around Theo's back, so his right hand was visible only to Holly. He splayed his fingers. *Five.* He tucked in his thumb. *Four.* She gripped the knife. *Three.* She'd rather shove the guard out the door than spill more blood, but the blade was good backup, at least. *Two.* She filled her lungs. *One.*

CHAPTER

30

Holly leaped up and launched a flying kick at her guard's head. He stood, and her heel struck his stomach, the impact coursing up her leg and drilling him into the side of the chopper.

Over her right shoulder, Rafe was a blur. She registered Theo dashing into the corner she'd just left. Shouts echoed through the hull.

As the guard gagged, she powered a knee into his nuts. He squeaked but wrenched her arm, spinning her. Her back smacked into his chest, and his arm wrapped around her throat. Crap. She rammed an elbow into his belly. He flinched but tightened his grip, crushing her windpipe. Damn, she'd have to get dirty with the knife.

She jerked her right hand over her shoulder and stabbed at his head, cringing. She caught only air, but he raised his arms to defend himself, releasing her. She pivoted. The chopper banked, sending her flying backward into Theo, driving him into the wall. The guard grabbed a bracket on the other wall, his legs flying. Theo yelped, his face squashed against her back. G-forces pinned them.

"Sorry, kid."

The chopper lurched. The guard lost his grip and smashed on top of Holly—right onto her outstretched knife. His eyes widened. His hands went for her throat, as if he hadn't figured out a blade was sunk to the handle in his gut. She twisted it. His hands tightened, wringing the breath from her. Beneath her,

Theo wriggled. She tried to arch up—the poor kid was taking the weight of both of them.

The helicopter righted, but still the goon squeezed. She gagged, her vision pinpricking. Blood trickled from one side of his mouth. Finally, his hands weakened and he tumbled down her body and slumped to his knees, the knife still embedded. Air scraped back into her lungs. He teetered and collapsed forward. One twitch and he was dead.

In the doorway, Rafe and the other goon wrestled. Gabriel leveled a handgun at them. She launched forward, tackling the warlord's legs. Something dense slammed into her back—Theo, joining the fight. A gunshot exploded through the hull, followed by silence. The floor jerked. Shit.

"Rafe?"

The helicopter dropped, taking her stomach with it. Rafe yelled, his words gurgling in her blown ears. She looked up. His goon had vanished. The pilot lay slumped over the controls, the windscreen sprayed red. The recoil had shoved Gabriel into the fuselage. He juggled to regain his grip on the handgun.

Rafe shouted again. Her brain registered: *Jump!* He grabbed Theo and spun him up onto his back. A rifle hung from his shoulder. Holly listed toward them. Theo clasped his hands around his father's neck.

"Holly, now!"

Rafe held out a hand. As she stretched up to take it, the chopper jolted, plunging him out the door, with Theo. Holly went to follow, but the floor tipped. Bracing her thighs, she fought up the slope, like on a boat in high seas. The helicopter tossed sideways, thumping her onto her back. Gabriel slid into her, cracking the gun barrel into her injured temple. Her head burned. The chopper lurched again and righted. A mechanical wail rang through her brain. Or was it coming from her mouth?

She caught the edge of the door with her left hand. The helicopter dipped and bounced, sending her swinging as she grappled to get a grip with her right. The world went into a spin, g-forces catapulting her out the door, wrenching her shoulder nearly out of its socket. The chopper spiraled like some demented carousel. She should let go. Gabriel flew past, into space, his shout surging and fading. The polystyrene box pelted her face on its way out. *Let go, you moron.* Wind belted her eyeballs. The ocean rose up fast, whipped white by the churning air. She released her hand.

Her shoulder crunched into the skid, flipping her onto her back. She hit the surface of the water with a slap and plunged into cold liquid, jolted immediately by the force of the helicopter crashing down beside her. Kicking hard, she fought through the wash until her lungs caved, forcing her up for air.

Treading water, she spun, her head gyrating as though she'd been spat from a washing machine. Her panting sounded like it was coming from someone else, far away. The helicopter floated on its side. An island lay maybe a mile away. It looked tiny. She turned almost a three-sixty before she spotted Rafe and Theo, clinging to the polystyrene box. Rafe had a rifle aimed at her. He shouted something indecipherable.

Shit. She dropped under the surface and pulled herself down and away, in the direction of the island. A muffled series of explosions sounded above her—or did she imagine it? Rafe had lost the killer-robot face, but who knew what was going on in his brain?

She swam underwater until her chest pinched, surfaced just long enough to gulp in oxygen, then changed direction before popping up again. She braced for gunfire but no shots came. One of her shoes had come off. She yanked off the other, and continued toward the island in a crazed diving zigzag. A few times she thought she heard distant shouts, but with her buzzing ears and water slapping all around, she couldn't be sure—and she wasn't stopping long enough to check. Salt stung her wrist and her bullet wound and found a dozen other cuts and scrapes to torment. Her knee held together okay, as long as she kicked with straight legs.

After an age it felt like swimming through cement. She'd pass out if she kept rationing her oxygen, and the island didn't seem to be getting any closer. She'd have to risk a rest.

She heaved in a breath, then swam as far as she could sideways, underwater. She surfaced quietly, rapidly blinking the water from her eyes. Only a bump of fuselage remained of the helicopter. Next to it were three figures. A wave rose up, obscuring her view. She ducked under the swell and broached again. Her blond hair would be a beacon.

She squinted at the figures. Theo clung to the box. Rafe had one arm wrapped around the polystyrene, and the other around…Gabriel. She dived under another wave. When she surfaced, Gabriel was gone. Dead? Rafe raised his head, his gaze barreling into hers. Eyeing up his next target? She wasn't going to wait around and find out.

She dived. Her best hope was to get to the island and pray the inhabitants were friendly. Was she even getting anywhere? The outgoing tide tugged her backward with every stroke, her knee burned with each kick, and her arms ached. At least Theo would slow Rafe down.

She chanced a look behind. The choppy swell hid her from Rafe, most of the time. The sun opened a gap in the clouds, creating blinding reflections. Her muffled hearing somehow amplified her pulse, making it boom in her head. A wave slapped salt water up her nose. It burned its way through her sinuses.

The island looked further away than ever. Ah, screw it. She'd never make it at this pace. She'd have to break cover and swim freestyle. If she was having trouble spotting Rafe, he'd struggle to see her, too. No doubt he was a crack shot. If he intended to kill her, at least it'd be all over before she knew it.

She swam on, the events of the past few days rattling through her mind—the night Rafe grabbed her from the boat, the shark, the plane, the island, the pirates, the hammock, the helicopter, Gabriel, Amina, Devi, the explosion of relief in her chest when Rafe had appeared in the jungle. It was all a confused tangle.

She'd have plenty of time to figure it all out once she was entrenched in her cottage by the sea. Her number one priority was to get there.

The change of stroke upped her momentum. Instead of pulling her back, the waves surged her forward. Fatigue clawed her. She ignored it. She settled into a pattern—four or five strong strokes in between waves, then rest and ride the surge. Her eyes stung. Something scraped her elbow. She flinched. A wave picked her up and dragged her along a ragged rock, gouging her side. The pain barely registered.

Not a rock. A reef. She hadn't been paying attention to the changes in the waves. She scrambled to her feet before the next surge, and launched herself into a break in the coral, the water swirling light-brown with sand. Forcing her eyes open underwater, she navigated past swaying smudges of lime and burgundy. The water calmed, the going got easier. Ahead, orange and blue blurs flitted and darted.

A minute or two later, she beached in the shallows, her body pulsing with relief. She crawled to the water's edge and flipped onto her back, gulping air with a strangled sob, willing her burning muscles to cool. She'd be hurting tomorrow—if she saw tomorrow at all.

Movement along the beach caught her eye. Rafe pulled Theo clear of the waves and threw the box up the sand.

She stumbled to her feet. No time to rest. She no longer knew who was on which side. The world tipped. Damn. One swim and she'd lost the land legs she'd only just found. She staggered up the beach, eyes fixed on the tree line. A muffled shout—her name, close behind. She wasn't stopping to let him get a clear shot. A wave of sand seemed to rise up, and she pitched forward. A shadow blocked out the sun. She rolled.

Rafe leaned over her. Shit. She kicked out, ready to fight with whatever energy she could squeeze out. He caught her feet, flipped her onto her stomach and pinned her like a butterfly.

CHAPTER

31

"Holly, it's over," Rafe rasped.

No kidding. No way could she fight anymore. "Make it quick," she mumbled into the sand.

"Make what quick?"

"Kill me."

"Merde."

He eased his grip, and she rolled over, squinting as he crouched above her. He looked like Rafe again, her Rafe, his brown skin dappled with drops of water, his eyelashes wet. Her chest ached.

Her mind wasn't fooled. *You hear me? You're not fooled.* "Don't you plan to finish the job?"

"You're delirious. Wait here." He took off down the sand, toward Theo.

Wait here. If only she had an alternative, but her body was finished. Her chest and arms started to shake.

It seemed like Rafe was back before he left, Theo with him. He knelt beside her and wound an arm down her back, pulling her into a sitting position. Something touched her lips, wet and cool. A water bottle. She grabbed it with trembling hands and guzzled.

"Get away from me," she croaked, closing her burning eyes.

"Holly, it's me, Rafe."

"I don't know who you are."

"Mon Dieu." Warm skin touched her cheeks. She eased open

her eyes. He was cradling her face, so gently she could cry. "I'll get you help."

"I don't want your help." Dr. Jekyll had returned, but she wasn't buying it. "Just leave me. I'll find my own way out of here. I won't talk."

"*Mon chou*, you're not thinking straight. You've been through so much."

She pulled away his hands, feeling the fight return to her body, and forced herself up on her elbows, grimacing. "Oh, *I'm* not thinking straight? You just tried to kill me—twice. No, three times."

His jaw dropped. "You know I was faking, with that pistol? For Gabriel?"

"Don't give me that. You were going to that place you went to before—that...trance. You were descending, turning into the devil Gabriel said you would become, the machine you warned me about."

"You are right, I *was* turning, but—"

"You were going to kill me."

"Yes, but—"

"Sorry, I don't think there can be a 'but' when you're trying to kill someone. I could see it in your eyes. You pulled that trigger—on a loaded gun. If it hadn't jammed, or whatever—"

"Holly, I knew the gun wouldn't work. It was the same one the pirates had brought to Penipuan—to Deception Island. The sons of bitches double-crossed me—sold me a working one, then switched it with that piece of junk. It's old and crappy and not something Gabriel's men would bother with, so when they put it in my hands, I realized what I could do to get us out of there."

He planted his hands on her shoulders. She shuddered. Oh, God, did her body want his touch, his comfort. But she was putting her mind in control, for a change. She shrugged him off.

"How could you possibly have been sure? I saw the guy hand it to you. You had your eyes closed."

"I knew the gun, Holly. I know guns, and this one had nicks in it, scratches. I recognized them."

"How did you know they hadn't—I don't know—fixed it before they gave it to you?"

"All they did was check it was loaded. I knew it wouldn't fire. The mechanism's broken. Holly, you don't seriously think I'd kill you, after…everything?"

"Rafe, you were unrecognizable. And then you shot at me, after the chopper went down. If I hadn't dived—"

"Mon Dieu." He swiveled and sat, heavily, next to her. Theo nestled in beside him, seeking out Rafe's huge arm and dragging it around him. Rafe pulled him tight. Holly's heart tugged, despite her better judgment. "This is what you think of me. You think I am a monster." He pressed his free hand into his eyes.

She sat up. "What am I supposed to think?"

"I thought there was something between us that…transcended…" He shook his head, slowly.

"So did I." She didn't bother to keep the pain from her tone.

"You don't trust me."

"Well, Jesus, of course I don't. You kidnapped me, you tried to strangle me and you tried to shoot me—three times."

"Why do you think I saved you from that soldier, in the jungle?"

"I don't know—because you figured you might need my help?"

"Holly, I… I knew Gabriel would stop me from shooting you—you were worth too much to him. I knew his greed would win. I just had to be convincing enough to make him believe that I *would* do it. Gabriel wanted to believe me—to believe in me. If that hadn't worked I would have found another way to keep us all alive. I didn't think I would convince you, too. I believed—hoped—you thought more of me than that, after…" He rubbed the spot between his eyes, as if he was trying to clear a headache. Sand as fine and white as flour dusted his face.

"Oh, it was convincing, all right." She was in danger of believing his explanation. Hell, she was in danger of throwing her weary body on his and sucking up all the comfort she could handle. She straightened her spine. "And what about when you fired at me on the water?"

He dragged his hands over his stubble. The rasping sound made her heart twang with a memory of their night in the hammock. "I wasn't aiming for you."

"Sure looked like it."

He groaned. "I was aiming at Gabriel. He was behind you, about to shoot you. I told you to dive, and you dived."

She narrowed her eyes. Patches of salt were drying on his tanned forehead, pinching the fine lines together. He looked ten years older than the night they'd met—and he'd looked haunted then. Still imposing, but...hurt and vulnerable. She tore her gaze away and forced herself to focus on the white-capped ocean. *Don't fall for it.*

"You don't believe me." His voice was guttural.

Her throat tightened. She didn't want him hurting—how stupid was that? "I saw you with him afterward, by the wreckage."

"He was dying." Rafe's voice cracked. "My shot found its mark. I held him until death came. I couldn't get his body to shore as well as Theo, so I let him go."

Her eyes pricked. Theo stretched up and whispered something in Rafe's ear, eyeing Holly. Rafe murmured back. He had an answer for everything, and it sure sounded like he was telling the truth. But how could she know? She was a failure at reading men she'd fallen in love with. *Was* she in love with him? She wanted to be—which was the craziest thing of all—but a boulder was sitting right on her heart and not letting her breathe. She wanted to believe him, but she didn't want another broken heart.

Crap. Maybe the problem wasn't Rafe, but her.

"I told Gabriel..." Rafe trailed off. He stroked Theo's fringe upward and swept it to the side. The move looked habitual, and it probably was—a solo dad taming his kid's hair, like he might do each morning before school. His Adam's apple bobbed. "I said I was sorry, that I wished to God I'd taken him with me that day, when I was rescued from the militia. It was my biggest mistake—and I've made many. I should have gone back." His voice faded.

If she kept looking at him, it'd break her. But she couldn't help it. His eyes watered. Oh, God—Rafe, crying? She gulped down a squeak, her own eyes burning.

"He said, 'So do I, my brother.' There was no bitterness in it, just longing, and…regret. And that was it."

"I'm sorry," she said, automatically. And she *was* sorry—not for Gabriel's death, because he damn well deserved it, but for the pain and loneliness of his youth, and for the guilt and sorrow Rafe carried. "If you feel responsible, you shouldn't."

"Seeing those scars on his body—that nearly broke me. He's right. I abandoned him, just like I've all but abandoned Theo for most of his life." He leaned his forehead on his son's crown. Theo snuggled in deeper, as if claiming ownership. Her throat was too strangled to manage comforting words. Rafe remained still as a rock. After a silent minute, he turned to her, his eyes crinkled with concern. "It nearly killed me to pull that trigger on you, in the compound, even though I knew the gun wouldn't fire."

"It nearly killed *you*?"

He laughed curtly. "*Ma chérie*, you should know, I did nearly go into that dark place. So much of what Gabriel said was the truth, a truth I've hidden from myself for too long. But I knew I wasn't the machine he believed me to be—that you still believe me to be. I managed to stay present, because I found my kill switch. You know what it is?"

She shook her head, unable to talk.

"You. I *was* falling into that hole, I *was* battling these demons. But then I thought of you and I felt this lightness right here."

He punched his chest, making Theo flinch. He kissed the boy's hair. "This goodness. And it grew. It brought light with me into the darkness. I knew I'd fallen in love with you, and that meant I was truly human. With Theo, I've always doubted that feeling. I've always thought it was merely a basic animal instinct, no more than the protectiveness animals feel for their young. I once felt it for Gabriel—now I know why, because we are brothers. *Were* brothers." His glistening eyes captured hers. "And now I feel it for you, but in a wholly different way. More urgent, more powerful, more hopeful. I've never known whether I can trust that feeling of…love…as a real emotion."

The word *love* sounded unpracticed on his tongue. That alone made her stomach melt.

"Holly." He gulped. "Meeting you, knowing you… You make me feel something I've never felt. Now I know that what I feel for Theo is not just protectiveness, but real love. It goes so deep inside. It's the same way I feel about you."

She whimpered and clamped a hand to her mouth. He was laying *everything* out, and it was everything she yearned to hear. So what was stopping her blurting out what she also knew to be true—that she loved him with every atom of her body? That she did trust him, and she knew in her heart his version of events was true? Maybe all the doubts of the last few hours were just panic at what was really going on—she'd fallen in love with this guy and was afraid of giving in to that feeling, of making herself vulnerable again.

"You don't know if you can believe me."

She shook her head, tears blurring her vision. Holy cow, she wanted to believe.

"What does your heart tell you?"

"To believe. But I don't trust my heart, Rafe. It's led me astray before. It got me locked up for six long years. How do I know this is real, this feeling that I—I want to always be with you?"

He grabbed her hand, sending little shocks up her arm. She didn't pull away.

"Listen," he said. "Both of us have learned from bitter experience not to let our guard down. But now I know there's one voice we can trust, and that's the one in here." He relinquished her hand and gently touched her chest, over her heart. Goose pimples radiated from the spot. "It's that voice that saved me just now, that brought me back from the brink. In the militia, I turned off all emotion, and in the Legion I was taught to act without passion, warned that it is a danger. Today I discovered it can be powerful in a good way. What does *your* voice tell you?"

It told her to give herself to him completely. She chewed her lip. Was she ready to take that risk?

"Holly, I'm in love with you—and I never thought I'd say that about anyone and mean it. I certainly didn't think it could happen this quickly. But I trust this, more than I've ever trusted anything. I never want to be without you—you're the most incredible woman I've met. You're brave and you're smart and you make me feel human—and believe me, that's the biggest compliment I could give anyone." He dropped contact. "I understand if you don't feel the same. I'd deserve that."

She sought out his hand and squeezed it, wanting to acknowledge the depth of what he was sharing, even if she couldn't reciprocate.

Or…could she? What would that be like? She felt like a beached whale being crushed by its own weight.

"You know, Holly, I'm not the only one who has been sending mixed messages. Perhaps the only reason you went all sugar and honey on me was to trick me into helping you survive."

She sat up straight. "No! Well, to start with…yes. But then…"

His lips curled into a grin.

"You're teasing me! At a moment like this?" She couldn't help smiling back. His jab was strangely comforting, a reminder of the bond they'd formed, of the chemistry that zapped between them.

"Then what?" he prompted, pinning her under his gaze.

She swallowed. *Out with it, Ryan.* "Then I realized there was an honorable man beneath the facade." She looked at their linked hands, hers small and freckled, his brawny and brown. "A strong man who understood me like no one ever had. A man I felt I could give everything to, who would keep it all safe and keep *me* safe. I didn't know if it was real or not. And then at Gabriel's compound, with the gun, I thought—"

He dislodged their hands. With one finger, he drew a line from the base of her throat to her chin, tipping it up toward him. She shivered.

"It *was* real, Holly. It *is* real. I don't know if normal people get this feeling all the time, but I certainly don't. I know we have something powerful here. Something that transcends all the pain of the past. Something that can make us both stronger and better. Together." He stroked her cheek with his callused thumb, wiping her tears. "To be honest, I don't know how this is all going to work out. I don't know if I'll still have a place with the Legion, or whether I want one. I don't know if I'll be able to return to Corsica, now they know what I am—what I was. Right now, there's only one thing I know—that I have a home, I have somewhere I belong, and it's right here with Theo and you. If that's all I have left, it is enough. I will never run again. Now, I'm sticking with the people I love, for good."

She covered his hand with hers, where it touched her cheek, and leaned into it. "I'm scared, Rafe. How can I trust this?"

"I don't know, *mon chou.* I desperately want you to, but this is something you must decide alone." He gently disentangled his hand and drew her chin back up. "Before you do, you must know, those things Gabriel said I did, in the militia—they were true, all of them. I've never spoken of it in two decades. You know the worst of me now—more than anyone has ever known. That is the bottom of the black pit. There is nothing more for me to hide."

She held strong to his gaze, sensing Theo's eyes trained on her, too. What must he make of all this? "So don't hide. Not from me."

"I promise you, Holly, if you give yourself to me, I will give back everything I am. I will never do anything to make you regret it. I will work at being a father and at being all you need me to be—whatever that is. I've failed before, with my wife, with Theo." He drew his son closer. "I won't let that happen again. These things I feel... I will not bury them. I will let them come, and that scares me like nothing has ever scared me, and I will need you to help me work through them, to be the strong woman I know you to be. I can't promise it will be easy, but will you try to be with me?"

Holy cow. This was it—time to front up or walk away. She filled her lungs. "I won't just try. That wouldn't be fair on any of us. I will trust you. I will give myself to you—and to Theo. God knows you've earned it."

He smiled, all the way from his mouth to his eyes, leaned in and covered her lips with a salty, lingering kiss. Her heart flipped.

"*Papa, est-ce que cette femme est ton amante?*"

Chuckling deep into his chest, Rafe pulled back.

"What did Theo say?"

He ruffled the boy's hair. "He asked if you were my 'lover.' I didn't know he knew this word."

"Oh." Her cheeks flamed. "That might have been something I said. At the time I was trying very hard not to die."

"*Je crois que je suis tombé amoureux d'elle. C'est OK avec toi?*"

Rafe's gravelly French flip-flopped through her belly. She'd have to learn the language, if she was to become part of this family. *Family.* The thought made her want to dissolve into a puddle of sugar syrup. Holly Ryan, playing happy families? How could that be possible? And how could it feel so right?

"*Oui, Papa.*" Theo peeked out at her shyly.

She looked at Rafe, expectantly.

"I said, 'I think I am in love with her. Is that okay?'" *Mamma mia*, he was handsome when he was happy—brown eyes all sparkly, dimples, white teeth against bronzed skin. She could sit back and look at him forever. Hell, maybe she would.

She winked at Theo, guessing from his *"oui"* she had official permission to snuggle in close to his father, as he was doing on the other side. The boy smiled, bowing his head. Rafe circled her waist and squeezed. "Thank you for helping to save my family."

"I was saving myself, remember?"

"Yes, you did that. And then you went back in, with me."

"You think I did that for you and Theo? Pah. I did it for myself."

"How so?"

She rested her head on his shoulder. What a relief to give in. "Because I couldn't walk away from you. Because I'd choose to be with you no matter how many guns were pointed at my head and no matter how many voices in my head begged otherwise. How dumb is that?"

"Not dumb at all. Very wise, in fact."

A familiar noise thumped through the air. She flinched. "A helicopter."

Rafe squinted out to sea. She followed his gaze to a black bug silhouetted against the cloud cover. "Friendly," he declared, standing slowly, dusting a mist of sand from his clothes.

She stood, too, followed by Theo. "Your 'one guy'? You were expecting him?"

"My guy and the Royal Cambodian Air Force, I'm guessing. They're heading for the wreckage. They'll fan out from there to check the nearest land."

"What happened to not wanting to bring in the authorities?"

"I didn't want to, until you and Theo were safe. It was my lieutenant's idea. He figured the Cambodian government would come under intense international pressure after your friend's message went viral. We have contacts in the air force there, and thanks to your intel on Gabriel's location, this morning he delivered them the last pieces of the puzzle. For them, it was a simple, heroic solution."

He smiled, uninhibited, as if his demons had fled. "It's over, Holly."

"Not if I can help it."

He laughed and spoke a few words to Theo, who jumped up, shouting and waving at the approaching chopper.

In minutes, it hovered down onto the beach, spraying up a fog of sand. A figure jumped out—a big guy in a tight blue T-shirt, khaki shorts and mirrored aviators—followed by a woman in a blue jumpsuit. His buzz cut was like Rafe's but light brown. Rafe's "one guy"—tall and cut like an Olympic sprinter. Jesus, they bred them sexy in the Foreign Legion.

As he neared, he touched two fingers to his temple in a casual salute. "Capitaine."

Rafe lifted his chin. "Lieutenant."

"Really?" said Holly, looking between them. "That's all you've got for each other, after all this?"

The new guy smiled, so reluctantly it looked like someone had stuck a hook in his mouth and was tugging it. "That's about it." His accent sounded French. "I'm Flynn."

"Holly." She shook his outstretched hand, noting that Rafe slid an arm around her waist. If he was claiming her, she was all for it. She caught a quick movement of Flynn's head, as if he was taking a reading of the situation. The way Rafe told it, this kind of thing didn't happen often.

"What took you so long?" said Rafe.

"Capitaine, I had to fly halfway around the world and arrange a joint military operation between two navies and one air force. So, *oui*, it took a while."

Flynn bent and spoke to Theo in quiet French. She caught a word that sounded like "courageous." The boy nodded, his face turning claret, and murmured something. Flynn pulled him in for a quick hug, ruffling his hair. Holly caught a smile on the kid's face. Her eyes stung—that kindness thing getting to her again. Perhaps he would be okay, long-term, if he was surrounded by people like this and his Corsican family. And her. Wow. So much for being a hermit.

"What's the status of the captured women?" said Rafe.

"These guys are all over it." Flynn nodded at the chopper, raising his voice above the whine of the blades. The woman in the jumpsuit was standing back, arms crossed. "A few shots fired, but no casualties among the captives. They're being evacced to a Malaysian frigate. I figured they had everything under control, so I commandeered a crew. We'd had a report of a chopper going down. Thought that might be your style."

Rafe shrugged.

"We didn't find the militia leader."

"He's resting in peace." Rafe nodded out to sea.

The woman shouted, gesturing at the chopper. Her words were lost in the wind, but the inference was clear.

Flynn looked over his shoulder. "You can give me the debrief on board. You all good to go?"

"*Oui,*" Holly said.

Rafe slipped his hand into Holly's as they trudged down the sand to the chopper. Flynn walked ahead, his arm slung around Theo. She exhaled like a release valve, letting every muscle relax for what seemed like the first time in nearly a week. Well, not *every* muscle. Her stomach knotted but in a very good way. She leaned against Rafe and rested her cheek on his shoulder. It was as though she'd been let out of a cage, body and soul. Oh yes, she was ready to believe in him. She was ready to love him.

EPILOGUE

Rafe knocked softly on the bunk room door, leaning against the cramped frigate corridor. Holly's quiet voice answered. Jesus, just the sound of that could tear him apart.

Theo was asleep on one of the four lower bunks, entwined in a gray military-issue blanket. When he slept, he always looked like his baby self again—innocence restored. That sight was worth any reprimand from the *commandant*. Holly lay on a bunk across the narrow aisle, wearing desert-camo trousers and a snug khaki T-shirt, and smiling up at him, as calm as a lake on a summer day and just as inviting. That sight was something else altogether.

"Did I wake you?"

She shook her head and shuffled over on the narrow bed. He eased into the space, propped himself up on his elbow and kissed her thoroughly. She responded, sighing with contentment and desire. Ah, *paradis*. He nudged up her top and drifted his palm across her stomach. She shuddered. His hand hit a dressing and she flinched.

"The medicos got to you, then?"

"Yeah, though they pretty much gave up in the end. It was that or make me into a mummy. No great harm done, but I'm stiffening up by the minute."

"Ha. So am I." He planted a kiss on the sweet skin of her belly, careful to avoid a large, darkening bruise. She smelled of plain soap and fresh laundry. He'd take that over the most expensive Parisian perfume, any day. "I am truly sorry for putting you through all this. Though I'm not sorry I kidnapped you from that yacht. Somehow it turned from the worst thing I've done in decades, to the best."

"I'm not sorry, either. I was just thinking that, actually, it was a rescue mission. I was destined for an empty, lonely life—I was even looking forward to it. I didn't realize it was such a cop-out."

"I was, too." His mind and body were exploding with new sensations. He'd had a smile plastered to his face ever since the helicopter had lifted, with everyone he cared about safely onboard. Flynn had been looking sideways at him all day. "When we beached on that atoll, and I realized you believed I had tried to kill you, I felt like I was dying inside. Like I'd lost you just after I'd found you, just when I thought maybe my life could be different. And I feared that this feeling that was growing inside me—this good feeling—would shrivel up and leave me as empty as before."

"I'm sorry I put you through that. I guess I was overwhelmed—I wasn't thinking straight." She cricked her neck. "What time is it?"

"Nearly midnight. I've had a lot of logistics to take care of. How is Theo?"

"He's okay. He's been muttering in his sleep, but it doesn't sound like nightmares."

"Thank you for looking after him." He'd never have left his son's side if Holly hadn't been there, logistics be damned. It felt right to leave Theo with her. A lot of things felt right, for the first time in his life. And Theo seemed taken with her—even protective, perhaps picking up on Rafe's instinct. Rafe looked at his son, bumping his head on the bunk above. "The only thing I've ever wanted is to protect him from the dark side of human nature. How will he ever comprehend what he's seen? How will this not mess him up?"

Holly laid her palm on his cheek and urged him to meet her azure gaze. "Because he's loved. Because he has a wonderful, strong father who knows what it's like to experience the worst of human nature and come out a good man. He's already started to heal—you've given him that, by restoring his faith in the world. Give him time and love, and I guess the rest will come. You'll figure it out."

"You see? This is why I need you with us."

Us. She liked that word, almost as much as *family.* "How did the phone call go with your *commandant*?"

"Good and bad. He's understandably furious I went into such a volatile, personal situation alone, but he said he couldn't be unhappy with the result—twenty-two women saved today, and more rescues to come as they dismember Gabriel's network and track down the remaining Lost Boys."

He settled on the bed next to her, nuzzling her neck. After he'd washed off the salt and grime, and shaved, the sensation of brushing against her soft, smooth skin was electric.

"It appears Gabriel has been hiding behind a large network of tourism operations," he continued, "which explains his mobility and his ability to disappear. His company owns Suaka and Penipuan, for starters. The French military are happy to take some of the credit for busting it all up, especially with the Americans suddenly so interested in the slavery problem, thanks to the media coverage. They're claiming this was an official top-secret Legion mission, from the start."

"What about what Gabriel did—telling them about your past?"

"My *commandant* says he has no choice but to overlook the allegations. I was a minor, and they cannot verify the evidence. The lieutenant-colonel wants my head, but the *commandant* will try to talk him down to perhaps just a hand, or a few fingers."

She laughed, and slid her hand along his jaw. "It's nice to see you joking. Sexy, even."

"I never joke." He caught her fingers and sucked the tips into his mouth. "Discipline is of utmost importance in my regiment."

"What will happen to the women now?"

"It's still being discussed. Some will be able to go home. There are calls for the others to be offered asylum in America and Australia—their rescue made good television, so all the big networks are talking about it. Amina's death made the story even more poignant. No one's making a connection with Laura Hyland, of course. No promises yet, but they're in a far better position than they were yesterday. And they're very happy— there's quite a party happening on the mess deck."

"Glad to hear it. So, what Gabriel said, about Amina's story being dismissed as a hoax—it wasn't true?"

"He attempted to put that story around, through his contacts, but Amina's lobby group is influential. They refuted it. Your friend did not die for nothing, *ma chérie*. She will be remembered as a symbol of her cause."

"What will w—? What will you do, now?"

He pushed himself up and studied her. Was she having second thoughts? "What will *we* do, you mean?"

She nodded, her cheeks turning the color of sunset. "It's going to take me a while to get used to that word."

"I have called Theo's grandmother." He inhaled. Another difficult conversation. "I had warned her not to tell anyone about Theo's disappearance, to say he'd gone on holiday with me. I had no idea how hard that would be for her. She is relieved. I am thankful she doesn't blame me."

"Of course she doesn't."

"She read the report Gabriel had left for her—about my past. It didn't have the effect he'd intended. She apologized to me, for not having understood why I was the way I am—the way I was. She told me…" He swallowed, his eyes burning. "She told me I am a son to her, always, and she will always believe in me."

He reached into his pocket. "I asked the air force to recover these." He pulled the amulets out and rolled them in his hands.

"What will you do with that one?" She nodded at the largest stone—Gabriel's.

"Keep it, I guess. A reminder that I come from somewhere, that I had a brother who was once an innocent child, that we were both loved. They've found records of our village among Gabriel's papers, which were stashed on a Lost Boys boat intercepted this afternoon. I may go there, try to find out if my sister is still alive—once I'm satisfied Theo is okay."

He leaned over her and pushed Simone's—Holly's—amulet over her head, releasing a clean, fresh scent from her hair. He kissed the stone. Like him, it had found its home.

"I have spoken to my *commandant* about getting a discharge. An honorable one, I hope. I will have to fulfil my next assignment, but I've done more than my time."

"What? You're giving up the Legion?"

He nodded. "It's okay." He'd always feared the day he might have to retire, feared the nothingness that waited on the other side. Now, all he felt was a sense of calm. "I have a chance to make things right with Theo, to be the father I should have been all along. The Legion was always an escape for me, a place of last resort. I don't need to escape anymore. I don't want to turn my back on life, on my son, on a chance to be...happy." He cleared his throat. "I've realized I no longer need the rules of the Legion to be a good man."

"But you still want to go back to Corsica, to be with your wife's family?"

He grabbed her hand, running his fingers over the calluses from her months of sailing. That roughness paired with the softness of the skin beneath mirrored the woman as a whole— tough as steel, but vulnerable, too.

"I would like *us* to, yes. Maybe we could reopen my wife's water sports school. I know it might not be easy for you. I have told Theo's grandmother about you—about how you helped to rescue Theo. She might struggle, but she will make a great effort to accept you as her own, as she has with me. She is a very good woman, and these are welcoming people." His words caught.

He had a lot of people to prove himself to. "It is important for Theo to be with his family." He touched her cheek. "And I want to be with the people I love."

Her mouth upturned, her chin dimpling. "Oh, Rafe, France won't let me in—I have a criminal record. I don't even have a passport."

"I made a phone call about that today, to the office of a certain American senator who would rather have you settled happily in France than unhappily in his country. It will not be a problem. He will use his contacts. He will not jeopardize his new image as an American hero and presidential front-runner."

Holly closed her eyes and puffed out a breath.

"It's over, Holly."

She shook her head and smiled. "You keep saying that. But, no, it's not over. It's just begun." She ran a finger down his forehead. "You look like you've been relieved of a heavy load."

"I feel calmer than ever in my life. I know where I'm from, I've accepted my past and I'm looking at my *très belle* future."

She wound a hand around his neck, pulling him in for a leisurely kiss. When she finally relinquished him, she inhaled and exhaled heavily. There was a lot for her to process.

"So will you take a risk on me?" he said.

Her eyes shone. "Trusting you could be about the least risky thing I've done. Strays and mongrels belong together, right?" She giggled, and her face contorted with a fleeting pain. "Don't make me laugh—everything hurts."

"You made yourself laugh—I had nothing to do with it. Ah, *princesse*, I wish I could kiss your injuries better."

She grinned, and the sight heated his body, lighting up his brain and calming his soul. He wanted to see that smile every day for the rest of his life.

"You should at least try. And you should definitely do it in French."

★ ★ ★ ★ ★

ACKNOWLEDGMENTS

Being a writer mostly means sitting at a keyboard and typing one letter after another until the story is done. "Done," in the case of *Deception Island*, meant almost half a million finished letters—written, critiqued, rewritten, deleted, revised, edited, edited and edited again, proofread and, finally, printed.

The process isn't nearly as lonely as that might sound. I would not be fortunate enough to be writing an acknowledgments page for my debut novel if it weren't for the encouragement, advice and support of dozens of friends, fellow writers and industry professionals:

My editor Allison Carroll and agent Nalini Akolekar, who believed in me and this story from the first chapter, and their colleagues at HQN Books and Spencerhill Associates.

My critique partners, beta readers and writing cheerleaders, who keep me positive, accountable and sane: Christine Sheehy, Cassandra Gaisford, C. A. Speakman, Gina Hagedorn, Mia Kay, Kari Lemor, Carol Opalinski and M. A. Grant.

The talented writers who've so generously given up their time to mentor me: Donna Alward, Valerie Parv and Daphne Clair. And the editors whose perceptive advice has been instrumental in helping me grow as a writer, especially Laurie Johnson.

The many people who've given me technical advice on this story, including Brad McEvoy, J. M. Bray, Deb Harkness, Lynette Eyb, Pippa McKelvie, Matt Otway and Mark Dunn. Any errors are my responsibility alone.

The writing associations and groups that have kept me encouraged and inspired, and given me invaluable opportunities to learn and develop: Romance Writers of New Zealand, The

Ink Spot, the Dragonflies, Flash Forward, the Harlequin Community, Romance Writers of Australia, and Romance Writers of America and its Kiss of Death chapter.

And my beautiful husband and sons. Love you guys to infinity.